THE EASTIE THREAT

Book 5: The Western Lands and All That Really Matters

ANDREW EINSPRUCH

Cover design by Maria Spada of Maria Spada Book Cover Design.

Editing by Vanessa Lanaway of Red Dot Scribble.

Proofreading by Abigail Nathan of Bothersome Words.

Layout by Andrew Einspruch of Wild Pure Heart.

ISBN: 978-0-9806272-8-2

DEDICATION

To Billie and Tamsin

Everything of greatest value that I've learned, I've learned from you.

TWO-BIT PIRATE

Queen Eloise Hydra Gumball III stood in the Queen's Chamber wearing starched, white frillier-than-she'd-like undergarments. Her left hand (the one with the cast for her twice-broken wrist) rested on the small, wooden box tied to her hip that contained the Star of Whatever—a grapefruit-sized, emerald-colored stone that was the most powerful and least-understood magical object in all the realms. The seventeen-year-old queen covered her right eye with her right hand to obscure its blurred vision, while trying to ignore the constant buzzing in her right ear. She frowned at her reflection.

Her handmaid, Odmilla de Platypus, held up a selection of eye patches with her otter-like feet. The monotreme stood on her two back legs as Protocol demanded and balanced herself with her beaver-shaped tail. "What do you think?"

"I think I don't want to wear an eye patch."

"Why not, Your Highness?"

"Because it makes me look like a two-bit pirate."

Odmilla hunched a little and took a step like she had a wooden leg. "Aaaaaar, me hearty."

Eloise raised an eyebrow at the platypus. "Why, Odmilla. Was that a witticism?"

"Aaaaaaar, t'were, me pirate queen."

"How uncharacteristic. Don't let Lady Seneschal hear you. She'll have you polishing silver for a month to teach you—"

"I know, I know. 'Never be impertinent to the queen.'" Odmilla perfectly imitated Lady Seneschal's excruciatingly proper tone—which was a feat, given the platypus's rubbery snout.

Eloise laughed. "Aaaaaar, she's a scurvy one, that wench."

"Who's a 'scurvy one?'" The voice at the door cut through the jocularity like a breath of wind from a crypt. It also sounded exactly like Odmilla's imitation, if frostier.

"Ah, uh... Blessings of the day, Lady Seneschal," said Eloise.

"Blessings of the day, Queen Eloise," said Lady Seneschal Älphonsinä Füüürchtbarkeit Póöòmáäädéëë, who'd run the castle and household since Eloise's grandmother's time. "You're not dressed yet. Good."

"Why good?"

"Because I've asked Eldridge the Apothecary to attend to you this morning."

"Why?"

"You can't go around covering one eye and digging a finger in your ear all the time and expect that those of us charged with caring for you won't take steps to try to help." She turned to speak to someone outside the door. "She'll see you now."

"What? Wait! I don't have time for that." Eloise had no desire to have herself examined, given the origins of those two particular problems. She scrambled for a plausible excuse. "I've had part of the realm overrun by Eastern Lands soldiers. Now is not the time."

Lady Seneschal crossed her arms. "Your Highness, there is little difference to the fate of the realm between now and a few minutes from now. Eldridge has made the journey here from across the castle, and we both know that's an effort."

"Fine." Eloise tied her dressing gown closed. "Send him in, please."

As far as Eloise was concerned, Eldridge the Apothecary had always been at Court, and he had always been gnarled, slow, kind, firm, deliberate, and more effective than any other healer who had ever graced the castle. She liked him, even if he'd forced her to swallow more vile-tasting concoctions than she cared to remember.

She heard the *thock* of his cane before he rounded the corner and limped into the room. As always, he wore an apron and a herbman's grey tunic, both stained with splashes and spills from decades of preparing tinctures, poultices, decoctions, unguents, and ointments. His wispy gray hair flew in all directions, and his white, catkin-like eyebrows perched above clouding blue eyes. He was followed by his assistant and daughter, Bërÿl, a woman who would have been about as old as Eloise's mother, and about as thin as she'd been on her deathbed, but was far from sickly. Her gray herbwoman's tunic and apron were immaculate, her mouse-brown hair was pulled into a skin-stretching braid, and her blue eyes flicked left and right, assessing everything she saw. Bërÿl carried Eldridge's healing satchel, and was careful to match her father's halting gait, keeping two steps behind.

The old man made his way toward Eloise, and when he reached the proper Protocol distance, creaked into a bow, as Bërÿl curtsied. "Blessings of the day, Your Highness," said the herbman.

"Blessings of the day to you both. Thank you for coming to see me."

"Always a pleasure, and much better circumstances than last time."

"True. I'm not lying on the floor, mind numb, and bleeding from the nose."

"Actually, the last time I saw you was when you were lying on your bed, mind numb, and bleeding from a crossbow bolt protruding from your arm."

"Of course," said Eloise. "Sorry, I forgot that one."

"With your permission, we'd like to examine you. Lady Seneschal said you were having some concerns with your eye and your ear."

"A little, yes."

"May we approach, and would you please sit?"

"Of course." Eloise moved to the chair in front of her vanity.

"Bërÿl, can you be my eyes and ears again, while I ask some questions?"

"Yes, Father." She stepped toward Eloise. "Your Highness, I'm now going to touch your face and head. Is that OK?"

"Yes." Eloise leaned her face upward so the herbwoman could see it easily.

"Lady Seneschal said you're experiencing blurriness in your right eye, correct?" As Eldridge asked this, Bërÿl spread Eloise's right eye open and peered at it closely through a glass she'd taken from her pocket. She went back and forth between the two eyes, carefully looking at each.

"Yes, sir."

"No need to 'sir' me, anymore. You're the queen. I'm just an apothecary. How long has the eye been troubling you?"

"Five days."

"Is there a dimming of the vision or just blurring? And is it constant, or does it come and go?"

"Just blurring. And it is constant."

"I see." Eldridge leaned forward, both hands propped on the cane for support. "And the sound in your ear? How long has that been an issue?"

"Also five days."

Bërÿl let go of Eloise's eyelids and moved to gaze into her right ear.

"Can you describe it?"

"What do you mean describe it? It's a sound."

"Is it more of a buzzing or a whooshing? A low hum or a high chime? Constant or intermittent?"

"Buzzing. A high-pitched sound, but not a chime. More like a juvenile bee swarm than a struck bell. And constant."

"Thank you, Queen Eloise. Did either or both of these concerns come on quickly or slowly?"

"Quickly, I guess."

"And can you tell me what precipitated this sudden change?"

Eloise saw that he was staring not at her face, but at the space above her head. She wasn't quite sure what to say. Certainly not the truth. She couldn't very well tell him, "Well, I used a dangerous magical object (which I don't really know how to use, and which was once part of casting the worst spell ever experienced in all the realms) in concert with a second magical object (which people thought was just an ornament) and in conjunction with the spark of something in the first magical object (which I experience on a mental plane as a naked mole-rat named 'Sparky'), and I somehow (not sure exactly how and I don't think I could make it happen again) managed to amplify the second object's unknown innate magical ability to help me experience omniscient perception to find out who had my mother killed (a three-eyed snake from the Eastern Lands), what was going on with my first advisor (he was being blackmailed into betraying her by the same three-eyed snake), and what was going on in Flachberg (a pending invasion from the East)."

No, the truth wouldn't do.

Instead, Eloise shrugged and said, "I'm not sure."

"I see, I see," said Eldridge.

Bërÿl finished looking into Eloise's eyes and ears, took her pulse, palpated her chest a few times, then straightened and walked to stand behind her father. "Nothing seems out of place or damaged. There are a few burst blood vessels in her eye, but overall, she seems fine."

"Thank you, Bërÿl," said Eldridge. "Queen Eloise, I know Protocol would look askance at it, but would you mind terribly if I sat down next to you? My ability to stand isn't what it once was."

"Certainly. Odmilla, could you please organize a chair for the apothecary?"

"I'll get it," said Lady Seneschal. She stepped out of the Queen's Chamber into the Salle de la Famille and came back with a chair from the breakfast table. She set it across from Eloise and returned to her post by the door.

"Thank you, Lady Seneschal. Now, everyone, I'm going to need a few moments alone with Her Highness. Bërÿl, could you please lead the others outside and close the door?"

"Of course, Father."

"No need for that," said Lady Seneschal. "I need to hear what is said to the queen so I can arrange for treatment."

Eldridge slowly swiveled in his chair and looked in her general direction. "Älphonsinä, my dear, scoot along, please. It's not like I present a threat to Her Highness."

"Fine," snapped Lady Seneschal. "We will be outside."

2

WHAT KIND OF HONEST?

As soon as he heard the door click shut, Eldridge the Apothecary leaned in toward Eloise and touched her on the knee. "Young lady, how long have we known each other?"

His familiarity surprised her. She was getting used to everyone being so deferential. He certainly hadn't used anything as informal as "young lady" to refer to her for a long while.

"All my life," answered Eloise.

"Seventeen years, eight months, twelve days, and about four and a quarter hours. Seventeen minutes less for your sister, Johanna. But maybe we could say it was longer, if you count feeling you kick inside your mother's womb. I was the one who saw you into this world. Mine was the first face you ever glimpsed, even before your mother's. Not that you would remember, of course."

"You delivered us? I didn't know that."

"That I did. Your mother insisted it be me and not one of the Brague midwives. You had black hair already, and I swear I could see some of the curl in it even back then."

ANDREW EINSPRUCH

"It's not black now."

"No, and from the little I can see, you've cut it rather severely. If I'm not mistaken, your curls are just starting to come back. Perhaps one day you'll tell me the story of how it turned white. Now, do you remember that time when you and Princess Johanna had been forbidden to have cookies before a Court party, but the two of you snuck into the kitchens, hijacked an entire tray, and ate them all?"

"Ugh, I do. I haven't been able to eat a coconut macaroon since. We came running to you to help us with our stomach aches. You gave us slippery elm."

"Did your mother punish you?"

"No, come to think of it. She didn't."

"And why do you think that is?"

"Because..." Eloise hesitated. "Because she never found out?"

"Correct. So you see my point."

"Your point? No, I'm sorry. I don't quite."

"My point is that we've known each other a long time, and that I can keep a secret. Which means that we can be honest with each other."

"Honest."

"Yes, Your Highness. Honest."

"What kind of honest?"

"Honest, as in I could tell you that my liver, gallbladder, and pancreas are all packing it in, not to mention my eyes, and no amount of care will change the outcome that I will face in the next half year at the most."

"Oh. Oh, no. Surely not."

"Unfortunately, it's true. I will, with any luck, be standing with Çalaht in a timeframe that I, too, consider much too soon." The herbman sighed. "But given the anticipated progression of my symptoms, it also won't be soon enough."

"I don't... I can't..."

"Trust me, if I can, you can." He gave her knee one more small squeeze and let go. "Bërÿl will serve you well if you will have her. She has a talent that is welcomed in the backroom of the dispensary, even if her manner is less suited to the front counter. But in a crunch, she's a brick. You can depend on her."

"I'll keep that in mind."

"Now it's your turn," said Eldridge.

"My turn? For what?"

"For honesty. If you'll pardon an old man's directness, please, let's cut the guff. Tell me, what kind of magic caused these maladies?"

"Um..."

"Otherwise, there's no way I can help you."

"Right. I see," said Eloise. "Magic, you think."

Despite his cataracts, the apothecary's eyes bore into hers. "Magic, I know."

"You know."

"I know."

"Hmmm." Eloise stood, walked to a side table, and poured herself a mug of water. "Can I offer you a drink?"

"Yes, thank you."

She took a sip, more as a delay than anything else. How was she supposed to avoid the old man's question? She could just refuse to answer. She was a queen, after all. But her eye really was bothering her, and the ear buzzing was sending her spare. Eloise wrung out a few more moments by fiddling with a mug and pouring water for him. How much could she safely reveal? She handed Eldridge his water, sat back down, and mulled a bit longer.

The apothecary sipped his drink and said nothing.

Eloise let the silence hang.

Another delaying sip.

Oh, what the heck, she thought. With a sigh, Eloise whispered, "Yes. It was magic."

"That I already know. It's the nature of the magic we need to discuss."

"Two objects. One was the Orb of Alleged Omniscience."

"That's one of the items in the royal regalia. The one you..." He trailed off.

"Yes, the one I dropped and damaged at my Crown Plonking Ceremony. The one that's now shaped less like an orb and more like a snow globe."

"Apologies for mentioning it."

"No, no. We're being honest here. It was not my finest moment, and everyone probably thinks I'm a rubbish queen because my first official act was to treat one of the most valuable objects in the realm like I was a hockey sacking changer trying to haul in a fumble. Then there was the subsequent faceplant and the fact I managed to refracture my wrist. It's pretty clear that my Crown Plonking did not set a tone of ease, success, and competence for my reign."

"Bërÿl said it made quite an impression."

"Yes, it did. Just not a good one."

"And the other object?"

"The second object was the Star of Whatever."

"The Star of Whatever? Really?" Eldridge carefully set down his water. "How is that possible? I thought it was just a myth, like the Chimes of

Chimera or the Prancing Profiteroles of Prophecy. Just made-up stories to entertain children."

Eloise shifted in her seat so she could move aside part of her robe. She revealed the dark box at her hip and tapped it with a knuckle. "I came to it while I was away trying to bring Johanna home. I got it from Melveeta the Elusive herself."

"Wait. Wait. Melveeta the Elusive has been dead for more than two centuries. She died during Gwendolyn the Irritable's reign."

"No, she disappeared during Queen Gwendolyn's reign. And she's certainly dead now, but it's a more recent event than you might expect." Eloise launched into a quick sketch of her time away—how she went after Johanna and rescued her from their uncle; how both of them got tossed into the Purple Haze, but neither died like everyone else; how they followed an inner tug and found the broken body of Melveeta the Elusive, who was literally rooted by the hand into the Star of Whatever and was integral to the spell that created the deadly Purple Haze (which she had cast). She zipped past how Melveeta had tried to enslave the twins as part of her enchantment but failed because Eloise had broken free and ended the spell. "Moments before Melveeta withered and perished, she gave the Star of Whatever unto me—those were her words, not mine." Eloise tapped the box again. "Here it is."

"I see," said Eldridge. "That's quite a tale."

"All true."

"I don't doubt it. And you keep it with you all the time? Isn't it dangerous?"

"Yes, and yes."

"Then why keep it?"

"Who would you rather I gave it to? Where do you think it would be safe to store such a thing to keep it away from the next would-be Melveeta? I'm open to suggestions."

"I see your point." Eldridge was polite enough not to mention that Eloise had already confessed to having used it, to her own detriment. He rubbed his chin, his expression distant. "So, what did you do to cause the eye and the ear problems?"

"It's another long story."

"Is there a short version?"

"Sure. I needed to know what was going on. First Advisor Ligurian appeared untrustworthy. I had no independent sources of information. There was all this unspecific noise coming from Flachberg. And I was desperate to know what happened to my mother. Jerome and I found something in the Bibliotheca de Records and Regrets that made reference to the Orb of Alleged Omniscience being a possibly actual magical object. I worked out that it was, and then drew on the Star of Whatever to help me amplify the Orb's ability."

"And?"

Eloise stood. "And now my world is a mess. My mother was done in by a murderous three-eyed snake from the Eastern Lands court, probably at the direction of their queen. The snake has disappeared into thin air and there's nothing I can do about it. He also blackmailed my first advisor into betrayal. The canton of Flachberg has been overrun by the Eastie queen's forces because she thinks I'm weak." She was practically shouting now. "I still have no idea how to consciously control the Star of Whatever, and I wouldn't dare try using it again because it scares the tar out of me. The same goes for the Orb of Alleged Omniscience, which isn't as alleged as everyone seems to think, and now I'm nearly half blind and the buzzing in my ear makes me effectively half deaf, and it is all due to a combination of my neediness and—dare I say it?—my hubris, because I thought I could harness magic to do what needed to be done without knowing what I was dealing with." She gulped another breath and continued. "There's no one who can help me learn about it because, as far as I can tell, strong magic doesn't exist anymore except in this one glowing, green stone, and there's barely anyone I trust to even know it exists, much less turn it over to them to experiment with. So, I probably won't reach my eighteenth birthday because someone's going to knock me off like they did my mother and I'll be Queen Eloise the Holy-Flipping-Crud-Did-She-Screw-Everything-Up-Or-What! There you go, Master Eldridge. There's your honesty."

Eldridge nodded, not looking at her directly. "Had a bit on your mind, have you?"

"It would appear so."

"Would you care to sit back down?"

"Sure." Eloise flounced back into her chair and found she was shaking. She clasped her hands together, leaned forward, and clamped them between her legs. "Sorry," she whispered. "I didn't mean to yell, and certainly not at you. That was rude."

The apothecary waved the comment off. "You may be queen, but you remain a person. It can be hard to know who you can talk to, or what you can talk to them about. With me, you can say anything and know it won't leave the room. Also, I'll never be offended. Those days are gone."

"Thank you."

"May I make a suggestion, Your Highness?"

"You have a way to make the blurriness go away and the ringing stop?"

He gave a grim shake of the head. "No, no. I have no idea what to do about those problems."

"That's not what I want to hear."

"Maladies due to magic are a thing unto themselves. My usual tools—herbs, poultices, compresses and other treatments—can provide some relief for symptoms. But such treatments don't touch the root cause, because their origin is of a whole other nature. I'm going to have to do some research, but I fear the knowledge of how to address those kinds of problems has faded with the strong magic itself. You'll have to give me some time, and you'll have to give me permission to involve Bërÿl, as I'll need her to be my eyes."

"You trust her, you said."

"Yes, I do. And that's not because she's my daughter, but because she's proven herself trustworthy."

"Then share what you need to, but I ask you not to share more."

"Of course."

Eloise topped up her water, then did the same for Eldridge. "Would you like me to call for brunchberry breakfast muffins?"

"No, thank you."

Eloise was peckish, but figured food could wait. She drank down her mug and poured another. "You said you had a suggestion?"

"I do."

"I'd like to hear it."

"It's simple: lists."

"Lists?"

"Yes. Make lists, then do one thing at a time. From my experience, it's the only way to get to 'done.'"

"I've never been a list maker. That's more Johanna's approach."

"By the way, congratulations to your sister on her ascension to the Half Kingdom throne. I'm pleased for her."

"I am, too. She was much more deliberate about attaining a crown than I was. I'm sure she'll be a good queen."

"Yes, I suspect she will be."

"She's asked that people start calling the realm the Northern Lands once again. On her behalf, I'd appreciate it if you did so, and let people know."

"How very interesting. I think she'll find that more than two centuries of calling it the Half Kingdom will be a hard habit to break. Is it true that the Purple Haze no longer festers across half the realm?"

"Not exactly. The purple fog is still there, and as far as I know, it is as thick as ever. But its killing malignancy is gone."

"Because you broke the spell."

"Yes. What remains is a residual effect."

"Then your sister assumes her throne at a most interesting time. I'm sorry I won't be here to see how she goes."

"Please, don't do that. It's making me sad."

"Sorry. There's my directness again. Now, like I said, lists."

"Like to-do lists?"

"Yes. Lists declutter the mind. Getting things onto a scroll or page of hemp parchment means you don't have to keep them in your head. Lists free up mental space for more useful thoughts than, 'Tell the new Chef not to overcook the asparagus' or 'Remember to find a new first advisor.'"

"The new Chef really is brutal on his asparagus. And I do need a new first advisor."

The old man nodded. "I know who I'd choose."

"Oh? May I ask who? You?"

Eldridge laughed, a surprising, rich, deep sound. "No, no, no. You don't want me. My lens on the world is too specific—I see everything as something that needs healing or that might help with healing. And my time here is too limited. You need someone who will be here years, not weeks."

"Again, please don't say that."

"Facing unpleasant truths is one of the queen's most-needed skills. Many a ruler has come undone by paying attention to what they hoped was true rather than what was actually true. Your grandmother, One, may she stand with Çalaht, was like that, especially when it came to the thing that was most important to her and hurt her the most—her marriage to One's Grand Mistake."

"I've heard. But, of course, I never met her. Was her reign really as bad as they say?"

"No. It was worse. Truly abysmal. You will have to work hard to do as bad a job of being queen as she did. I can't tell you what a relief it was when Two, your mother, ascended to the throne."

Eloise lifted a shoulder. "Well, that's something. I assume no one's sighing with relief that I'm here now."

"The late queen's shoes are large ones to fill. But from what I can gather, people are willing to give you the benefit of the doubt, despite your picking a chipmunk as your first champion and the unfortunate event at your Crown Plonking ceremony. You are young, and it has not been that many weeks into your reign. I haven't heard anyone call you 'Three' yet, but I've also not heard much that's disparaging. You'll always get some, but it's not what it could be."

"So, it could be worse."

"Yes."

"That will have to do. Who are you suggesting be named first advisor?"

"Care to guess?"

"Well, not Lorch Lacksneck. He's suited to being my champion, but isn't the advisor type. And not Jerome Abernatheen de Chipmunk, who's doing much better now that he's Assistant Court Seer to the Court Seer. He advises but doesn't have the experience or connections. His mother, Seer Maybelle de Chipmunk, is a possibility, but I don't think the political side of things suits her. Hmmm..."

Eloise thought about the different people at Court. Lady Seneschal. Various servants and handmaids. Head Scribe. Master Overbolt, her former tutor. Then she hit on it, and in retrospect, it should have been obvious. Eloise liked her, respected her, and found her easy to talk to. "You're thinking of the Other Places Advocate, Bërnädïce-Ändrëä Thëjëts."

"Yes, I am. Bënnïë-Änn is smart, capable, highly knowledgeable about matters of the other three-and-a-half realms, and pleasant to be around. I wouldn't suggest bringing anyone into that role who you couldn't stand to share lunch with at least once a week."

"Former First Advisor Ligurian was definitely not a let's-have-lunch kind of person."

"I can imagine."

"It's a good suggestion. Thank you. So, what do I do about this and this?" Eloise asked, pointing to her eye and ear. "Is there really nothing you can think to do?"

"Not really. Or at least, not yet. But take heart. The mind is a wonderfully malleable and adaptable thing. You might find that your brain adjusts and it becomes less noticeable. And like I said, I'll see what I can find."

"And in the meantime?"

"In the meantime, my queen, grin and bear it."

3

MOVING A WALL

Edremit Amphissis stood on a twenty-length-high scaffolding overlooking the construction job he was running and grumped out a half-satisfied *humph*. "Keep it moving, people. Keep it moving," he yelled.

It was an industrial undertaking the likes of which had not been seen in centuries. Hundreds of workers wearing olive-drab tunics and breeks tore down a section of the Adequate Wall of the Realms and, stone by stone, reassembled it in a new location in the exact same configuration, down to the order of the centuries-worn steps. It was dangerous, exacting, backbreaking work that each of them (like Amphissis himself) undertook with pride and tenacity. Their goal: move the captured canton of Flachberg from behind the wall in the Western Lands and All That Really Matters back into its natural home, the place of their forebears, and the realm with the greatest cultural alignment—the Eastern Lands.

The work was swift, audacious, and broke pretty much every norm that existed between the two realms. Amphissis was kept just a little warmer in the late winter chill by the knowledge that somewhere, 2,437 strong lengths away, that fobbing, flap-mouth, fustilarian Westie child-queen, Eloise III, was mewling in impotent rage and seething jealousy.

He certainly prayed to Çalaht that was the case. Those scuzzy Gumball queens had had it coming for a long, long time.

Amphissis turned from the wall construction and stared at Flachberg proper. The conquered townspeople had accepted their new situation. More or less. Those who hadn't been pleased at the sudden arrival of Eastie soldiers were either dead, in chains, or expelled. Everyone else had enough mutual heritage with the Eastern Lands that it was no big deal for them to swear a loyalty oath to the Eastie queen, Her Majesty, Queen Aglandau Gaeta Cerignola Ponentine.

Ah, Queen Aggie, thought Amphissis. *Light of the realm.*

The foreman didn't mind admitting he had a bit of a crush on the old gal, even though he'd never met her in person and only once saw her across an amphitheater at a performance by legendary singer Lyndia Thrind (her finale of "Three Bags of Groats for my Sweetheart" had given him shivers). He reckoned Queen Aglandau was a solid, guiding hand and a force for good in the realms. Plus, by all accounts, she was still a looker, which didn't hurt.

His pulse raced when he thought of how soon the queen would be coming to the newly annexed Flachberg. They would celebrate righting the centuries-old wrong that had seen the canton handed to whichever craven, clay-brained clotpole had been sitting on the Westie throne at the time. (Was it Gwendolyn the Irritable? Amphissis could never remember which dissembling, dizzy-eyed dewberry Gumball was which. Nor did he really want to.)

But a royal visit from Queen Aggie herself? That was gonna be something.

And it would happen just as soon as the changes to the Adequate Wall were done.

Edremit Amphissis could hardly wait.

Who knew? Maybe Queen Aglandau would take a fancy to him.

ANDREW EINSPRUCH

Probably not. She was three decades older.

And queen. There was that.

But he could think of worse things.

"Keep it moving, people. Keep it moving," he yelled again. "Her Royal Highness will be here before we know it. Let's get this done. "

❧ 4 ❧

FLOPPING

"**I**'d flopping *love to*," said Bënnïë-Änn Thëjëts that afternoon when Eloise asked if she'd be interested in taking on the role of first advisor. They were in the Queen's Study, where it seemed like Thëjëts took up at least half the space. She was easily three times the size of most women, and two heads taller. Her taste in scarves and robes caused even the most narcissistic of peacocks to say, "Come on, that's a bit much." Her mass of long, frizzed hair was tortured into a shade of blue that gave robin eggs a run for their coin, her eyes were perpetually bloodshot from her propensity for hyperbolic emotion, and she was prone to gesturing with a manic earnestness that caused harm to nearby objects. "I was wondering what you were going to do. I heard that old Leccino Ligurian had been tossed in the flopping clink."

"He's under house arrest, not in a dungeon," said Eloise. "Not yet, anyway."

"Why flopping not?"

"I need him to spill his guts, not have his guts spilled."

"And is Ligurian talking?"

"He's talking, but not saying much." Eloise put on a whiney voice. "'I was blackmailed.' 'They have my mother.' 'I didn't know anything about Flachberg.' Blah, blah, blah."

"I detect a lapse of empathy, Your Highness. Perhaps he was truly afraid for his mother."

"I'm sure he was. But then maybe he should have, I don't know, done something other than betray me and the realm. He could have talked to me so we could have come up with a plan or figured out diplomatic measures to exert or threats that could be made in response. There must have been other options besides leaving me ignorant to matters."

"I suppose you're right." Bënnïë-Änn stroked her chin. "When would you like me to start as your first advisor?"

"Today. Now," said Eloise. "Well, not *now* now, but now. I suggest you talk to Ligurian's scribes. They can fill you in on the way things have been done in the past. Try to figure out everything he was doing, like my daily briefings and how he used the royal boxes."

"Ah, the royal boxes. How he flopping loved those flopping boxes."

"You know about them?"

"Sure. I know all about that kind of flopping first-advisory stuff."

"You do?"

"Yes. I haven't always been the Other Places Advocate. A long, long time ago, in what may well have been a previous life, I was an apprentice to a clerk who worked for One's first advisor."

"My grandmother's first advisor? Who was that?"

"Martha Genädige de Pelecanidae."

"That's not a name I know."

"You wouldn't necessarily think of a pelican as being good at all that Court intrigue and diplomacy stuff," said Bënnïë-Änn. "But she was a flopping sharp old bird. I flopping learned a strong weight of stuff from her. So, yes, I haven't done it for a while, but I used to know my way around that office pretty well. I suspect I'll be OK."

"Good. Very good."

"Would you like to set some priorities?"

Eloise thought about it. "I guess the obvious. Flachberg—what's going on and what I'm going to do about it. And the Eastern Lands more generally."

"Anything else?"

"Maybe you can figure out a system that keeps me in the loop with things that are not obviously relevant, but which might be later on."

"Like an early warning system?"

"Something like that, yes. I can't afford any more Flachbergs, and I need to know if there are more of them out there lurking."

"I'll see what I can come up with."

KEEP LOOKING

The next morning, Jerome joined Eloise in the Salle de la Famille. They'd gotten in the habit of breaking fast together when he was her champion, and the habit stuck after his role change.

The new Chef had prepared a perfectly reasonable meal of avocado and tofu toast, a sweet potato breakfast bowl, a slow-cooked almond butter and banana oatmeal, plain toast with a selection of jams, and an entirely passable haggleberry tea.

Jerome dug in with his usual gusto, but Eloise just poked at her food.

Eventually, the chipmunk asked, "What's the matter?"

"What do you mean?"

"You seem distracted."

"What makes you say that?"

"Well, for one, you put brunchberry jam on your toast, set it down, got a faraway look in your eye, stuck your index finger in your right ear, came back, put brunchberry jam on your toast, went off to the La La Realms again, squinted with your right eye closed, blinked back to the present, and put more brunchberry jam on the same piece of toast. You now have Brunchberry Jam Mountain staring you in the face, and you don't seem to have noticed. Nor have you eaten anything. So, again, what's the matter?"

Eloise took two more pieces of toast and scraped off the brunchberry mound in precise amounts so that all three slices had exactly the same amount of jam smeared carefully to the same distance from the edges. "There's a lot going on."

The chipmunk nibbled his crust, waiting. When Eloise didn't add anything, he prompted, "Go ahead, Your Highness."

"Don't you 'Your Highness' me. Not this morning. I'm not in the mood. Not from you, anyway."

"Ooh. Touchy."

"Really, Jer, it's not what I need."

Jerome put down his crust. "Then what do you need?"

"I don't know. But that wasn't it."

"Noted."

Eloise sighed. "I don't know how my mother did it."

"Did what?"

"Did the queen thing. She always seemed so collected, so together. I mean, she had her moments, I guess, but I never saw her screaming at anyone who didn't truly deserve it, and even then, she was more likely to lower her voice than raise it. And maybe it is the ignorance of having been a child, but I never got the sense that she ever did anything wrong at all. Or that she had any doubts. She was queen, she was decisive, her decisions were respected and carried out, and that was more or less it. No one took her land or sent in soldiers. No one sent inappropriate envoys, and she didn't put up with food from the kitchens that was only just good enough. She didn't have to deal with one eye gone wonky and an ear buzzing like an annoyed beehive."

"Keep going," said Jerome.

"This." Eloise tapped the box with the Star of Whatever. "This thing is eating away at me."

"Uh... In a Melveeta-the-Elusive-stuck-for-two-centuries kind of way?"

"No. Well, I don't think so. I don't feel controlled by it the way she was, if that's what you mean. But I have to admit, there's definitely an allure. All that strong magic that's bound up in it is amazing, and I've only glimpsed the barest fraction of it. Despite this..." Eloise held up the cast on her left wrist. "And my dislocated shoulder. And this and this..." She pointed to her eye and ear. "Despite all that, I feel like I need to know as much about it as I can. I mean, I'm certain the Star of Whatever saved my life at least three times—going over Mortimer Falls, falling down the Whacking Great Hole, and then getting out of the Whacking Great Hole. Plus, Melveeta gave it unto me."

"Wait. I don't think I've heard you say that before," said Jerome. "What do you mean, she 'gave it unto you?'"

"I haven't told you about that?"

Jerome flicked his tail. "No."

"Don't get shirty with me. I thought it was all out there. So, when Melveeta was dying, and I mean, right at the end, she said, 'I give the Star of Whatever unto thee.' And I could feel it. It was like her words were laden with ceremony. In that moment, she and I were connected, and I could feel her let go of all affinity and connection she had to the Star of Whatever. But at the same time, I felt myself become more entangled with it. I remember so clearly the shiver that ran down my back. From then on, for good or for bad, the magical stone was mine. Not long after, Melveeta spasmed and breathed her last."

"Huh," said Jerome. "Interesting."

"So that's why I can't just stop trying to find out more. And it's one of the reasons I keep the Star of Whatever with me at all times. Well, that and the fact that it's, you know, exceptionally dangerous, and I don't want it to accidentally disappear when I'm not looking."

"Right," said Jerome. "OK, well, that's helpful. I get the context a bit more. But do you really think we'll find anything written about the Star? I don't think it was exactly a household name. Surely, even back then, it would have been a rumor more than anything else."

Eloise poked a finger in her ear, trying to clear the buzz. "I'm not sure, Jer. Eldridge the Apothecary had heard of it, although he compared it to the Chimes of Chimera and the Prancing Profiteroles of Prophecy. Even if people think they're made-up stories, they have to come from somewhere."

"Well, I've been in the Bilbiotheca de Records and Regrets digging through the archives of Queen Gwendolyn's reign, and so far, it's been a big zilch-arino. I've been in there so much that Head Scribe must think I'm trying to be a scholar."

"Naw, he just likes the fact that we bring him baked goods."

"That does seem to help. Every now and then, the old raccoon looks up from his basket of pfeffernusse or raisin cookies or almond biscotti and asks if there's anything he can do for me. I just say, 'No, no, I'm fine.' Do you think we should bring him in on this? I mean, he's Head Scribe. Maybe he can help."

"Maybe. If we really don't find anything, maybe then. But I still think that the fewer people who know about the Star of Whatever, the better."

Jerome frowned. "Is that realistic? You know what gossip is like here at Court. There won't be a single person within a hundred strong lengths who won't know about it. I mean, you wear it on your hip."

"They'll know about the box. They'll know I keep it with me. But I don't think they'll know what it is."

"I guess. But back to the question at hand. What are the chances of there being a document describing it? You seem to think we'll find something from Melveeta herself. Why?"

Eloise covered her right eye so she could focus on him better. "Here's my thinking. One thing was clear from the little time I spent with her, and from the story she told: Melveeta had an analytical mind."

"Oh?"

"It was clear from the way she went about solving the problem of the Star of Whatever. Chance played a part in its discovery, as well as her coming to realize that it had magical qualities."

"You said there was a juggler who used magic to keep an unnatural number of balls in the air, and that somehow he lost the ability."

"Yes, it was at least nine," said Eloise. "And Melveeta worked out that when the Star of Whatever was near him, he lost that ability. Once it was clear that there was a magical effect, her curiosity took over, and eventually, she was pushed harder by Queen Gwendolyn. Melveeta talked about how she conducted experiments to try to figure out how the Star worked. And she succeeded. More than anyone else we know of, she learned how to harness it. Surely, someone who approached a complex problem with that kind of deliberate determination would have kept notes of her progress to refer to."

"There's logic to that."

"So, maybe those notes survived."

"It's possible."

"It has to be. Otherwise, what am I supposed to do? Conduct a lot of experiments with strong magic on my own?"

"If you do, please give me some warning so I can be elsewhere when it happens."

"Exactly. That sounds like a recipe for all kinds of disaster." Eloise frowned. "At least Melveeta had some context for doing that kind of work. But it has been two centuries since strong magic was in the world. That context is long gone, and with it, all the knowledge that might have supported it."

"True." Jerome picked up a new slice of toast and gestured with it. "Then there are just two things to do."

"What are they?"

"One, I keep looking."

"No."

"No?"

"No," said Eloise. "One, *we* keep looking."

"Fine. One, we keep looking."

"What's two?"

"Two, is have your breakfast. Your brunchberry jam toast is going to get soggy."

❦ 6 ❧

FLINGING FIELD

Eloise started the next day with an exercise run around the Culpability Courtyard, accompanied by Lorch Lacksneck— former soldier, former guard, and current champion—who didn't seem to break a sweat, remaining exactly two strides ahead of her no matter how fast or slow she went. He'd saved her from an assassin's attack in that very spot far too recently to let her circle the courtyard's columns on her own. He didn't seem to be suffering any major lingering effects, despite having taken one of the assassin's crossbow bolts in the derrière, his stride as smooth as ever, although she thought she may have caught him wincing more than once.

After two dozen loops of the courtyard at an increasingly fast pace, Eloise slowed and began her stretching. "Lorch, do you think we could duck over to the Flinging Field? I know it's wintry, but I haven't been there since..." She wafted a hand at the simple band that served as a crown when she was doing anything sweaty.

"Yes, Queen Eloise. I'll organize a patrol to come with us."

"Must we? Can't we just go on our own? I don't fancy throwing with an audience."

"I'll have them turn their backs. They should be watching the perimeter as it is."

"If you insist."

"I do."

"Fine."

It was less than a quarter hour before they were at the Flinging Field, an open paddock designed for practicing anything that involved objects whizzing through the air—knives, arrows, hatchets, cannonballs, and the thing that Eloise liked the most, the hammer. Lorch dispatched a couple of guards to ask two razordisc throwers and a trio of javelin hurlers to clear the field for her. Eloise felt bad about interrupting them, but they didn't seem fussed, and she knew she had to file their inconvenience into the One of Those Things That Happen When You're Queen bucket. She jogged to the far end of the field, where there was a rack of practice hammers. Their metal was pitted and grazed from long use, and their ropes showed hints of fraying. They were not nearly as neatly kept as her personal one, but they were fine for training.

She stretched a few more times, then said, "Lorch, you'll join in the hammer throwing?"

He was very good at it. She remembered he'd placed second at the last Court Tourney. "If you'd like, Queen Eloise, it will be my pleasure."

"Perhaps you'd like to go first, then."

"Yes, Queen Eloise."

That tournament couldn't have been more than two-and-a-half years' previous, but it seemed an entirely different lifetime. Eloise had competed against the men in the hammer throw for the second tourney in a row, and come in ninth to Lorch's second. *Not bad for a teen*, Eloise thought.

Then she was struck by a sudden realization. She probably shouldn't have competed at all. It was hardly fair for her to participate, even against the men, given she had a weak magic for throwing.

Lorch picked up a hammer, a hefty 7 1/2-weight one, and moved toward the throwing circle.

"Ready, Queen Eloise," said Lorch, breaking her line of thought. He took his position in the throwing circle, hefted his hammer, arcing it with his wind-up swings. Then he spun into his turns, his feet dancing with the complicated heel-and-toe movement.

Where most throwers only spun four, maybe five times, Lorch took a sixth full turn, and let the hammer loose with a staggering toss. It flew slightly wide of the center line, but zoomed past the "70 Lengths" sign, falling just short of 75 lengths.

"Splendid throw, Lorch," said Eloise.

"Thank you, Your Highness."

Eloise picked a hammer from the practice rack. Normally she threw a 7 1/4-weight one—heavy for women—but she hadn't tossed a hammer since she'd broken her wrist and dislocated her shoulder. The shoulder still had hints of discomfort, and the cast would make throwing awkward. Maybe she shouldn't put stress on her body this way. But she was here, and she wanted to, so she picked a lighter 6-weight one and walked toward the circle.

Eloise settled into her starting position at the edge of the throwing circle with her back to the release area and her feet shoulder-width apart. She lightly swung the ball on its handle with her cast hand, across her front, to the right, and up. Next, she grasped the handle and looped it in three low-to-high arcs over her head, letting the ball gain speed and momentum. When the sphere came to the front again, she spun her body into the turns. Through the four full revolutions, she felt the weight straining on her shoulder and wrist, the ache letting her know that her healing wasn't complete. On the fifth and last turn, Eloise let the hammer fly. Propelled along by her weak magic, it arced across the field, passing the "60 Lengths" sign and landing halfway to 65, precisely in the middle of the field.

Sixty-two-ish lengths was far from her best throw, but it was acceptable, and nothing in her body had popped out of place or cracked. Good.

"Another impressive throw, Your Highness," said Lorch. "It used to always astound me that you could do that." He shook his head slowly. "I know you much better than I used to. I have seen your, um... ability in action. Seeing you toss the hammer with a once-dislocated shoulder and a fractured wrist still in its cast is less surprising than it once might have been. But it's still astounding."

"Thank you," said Eloise. Then she stopped in her tracks.

"Your Highness?" said Lorch.

"I just realized something."

"Yes?"

Eloise felt her cheeks go pink. "I shouldn't have competed in the Court Tourneys."

"No? Why not?"

"Because of..." She gestured toward the hammer she'd just thrown. "Because of what I can do. All those years, I had an unfair advantage. It was unjust. Inequitable."

"Perhaps." Lorch lifted a shoulder. "But you were young. And you may not have fully understood your own capabilities back then. Maybe this doubt is a sign that you've grown wiser."

Eloise let out a sigh. "Çalaht knows I could use a bit more wisdom. I'll have to hold another tourney to make up for it."

"That might be nice."

She pointed at the rack of hammers. "A couple more throws?"

"If you're up for it."

"I think I am. Your turn, Champion Lacksneck. And thanks."

❦ 7 ❦
BRIEFING

Later that morning, Eloise arrived at the Queen's Study and found newly minted First Advisor Bënnïë-Änn Thëjëts waiting, ready for her first briefing. She looked excited, almost jittery, like she'd had way too much green tea.

Like her predecessor, Thëjëts carried an armload of scrolls and stood next to a sturdy, four-wheeled wooden trolley that held not two (like Ligurian used), but four formidable wooden boxes, each decorated with the Gumball crest—a round seal featuring a weasel on a bushel of onions and a one-eyed otter holding a fire poker. These were the royal boxes, which contained all the scrolls and sheets of hemp parchment that First Advisor felt needed Eloise's attention.

"Blessings of the day," said Eloise. "I'm a little surprised to see you here already."

"Blessings of the day, Queen Eloise. Blessings of the flopping day. I didn't get much flopping sleep last night, but I'm ready for our first briefing."

"Very good."

Yep, thought Eloise. *Too much green tea.*

She peeked in a sack that had been left by the door and saw it was wood and kindling for the fire. Turning a key, Eloise swung open the heavy oak door on silent, well-oiled hinges, grabbed the sack, stepped into the room, and waved for First Advisor to follow. The space, which Eloise was finally beginning to think of as somewhat her own, and not her mother's, was roughly 20 lengths long and 15 lengths wide. Three of its walls were dominated by large windows that would have flooded light into the room were it not a dull winter day. Every surface, from shelves to tables, was stacked with scrolls, sheets of hemp parchment, and bound volumes that, as far as Eloise could tell, took up much more room than the words inside warranted, which meant her mother had kept them for reasons perhaps decorative, or sentimental. Dominating the middle of the room was a huge, surprisingly detailed map of the four-and-a-half realms with a large stretch of purple felt covering the section of the Half Kingdom that was shrouded by the Purple Haze, an oversized representation of Castle de Brague, and numerous other not-to-scale landmarks like the Whacking Great Hole and the Adequate Wall of the Realms.

As Bënnïë-Änn maneuvered the trolley into the room, Eloise moved past the comfortable chair near the fireplace and knelt at the hearth. She used twigs and wood from the sack to lay a fire, then flint and striker to spark kindling into a nascent flame—a skill she'd picked up on her months-long journey trying to bring her sister back home. Eloise coaxed the little flame with kindling and puffs of breath until it was clearly committed to burning. She then eased into the comfy chair, ready for whatever Thëjëts had for her.

Thëjëts looked around and said, "I don't suppose there's a chair I could use."

Interesting. Ligurian had never, not once, sat in her presence, maintaining a strict adherence to that particular point of Protocol.

"Um, sure," said Eloise. She looked around and saw that the only other chair in the room was the desk chair and it didn't look nearly sturdy enough for a woman of Thëjëts' size. "RoyLee!"

The wombat popped his head into the room and bowed. "Yes, Your Highnessness?"

"Could you please have a chair brought for First Advisor Thëjëts?"

"Right away." RoyLee sprinted away shouting, "A chair for the queen! A chair for the queen!"

"It won't be long," said Eloise.

"It's fine."

"Perhaps we can get started?"

"Of course." Bënnïë-Änn rapped one of the royal boxes. "Let's get to it. Let me start by saying that the systems left in place by former First Advisor Ligurian are a flopping disaster."

"A disaster? He always seemed so on top of things."

"I'm sure that's the impression he wanted you to have. But his office resembles a rummage sale organized by inebriated pack rats on their way home from a Hoarders Anonymous meeting. And his scribes are no better. Their work ethic is nonexistent, their pride in their work is fully absent, and their quillmanship is terrible."

"How can that be?"

"I don't know for sure, but I have my suspicions."

At that moment, RoyLee reappeared with two guards carrying the sturdiest chair Eloise had ever seen. They bowed, positioned the chair at a distance from Eloise that Protocol would deem acceptable in a semi-formal setting, and without saying a word, bowed their way out of the room.

"May I?" asked Bënnïë-Änn.

"That's what it's there for. Please, sit."

First Advisor Thëjëts eased her massive frame into the seat. The wood creaked a little, but held. She sighed. "Thank flopping Çalaht. I thought my flopping feet were going to go on strike and run off on their own."

Eloise paused, letting her settle. "So, your suspicions? About Ligurian?"

"Former First Advisor Ligurian was very much into looking out for Former First Advisor Ligurian. He wanted to be the center of everything. Every scroll, missive, letter, and transaction landed on his desk, and nothing left it without his approval. He wasn't so much a royal filter as a royal blockage. Or perhaps he was just a royal pain in the *tuchus*."

"I get it, I get it. I don't want to believe it, but I get it." Eloise shook her head. "Ligurian served my mother so well. On her deathbed, she specifically recommended that I keep him as first advisor."

"I can understand that."

"You can?"

"Of course," said Thëjëts. "I served your mother as well. Ligurian was different back then. There was a sharpness, a cunning, and a propensity for insight. That's why the late queen made him First Advisor ahead of any number of good candidates—myself included, if I may say so."

"I can't say I saw much propensity for insight in his dealings with me."

"Something changed around the time that the late queen went to stand with Çalaht."

"We know what happened. The three-eyed snake from the Eastern Lands who was their lead trade negotiator blackmailed him into complicity."

"No. Well, yes, of course. But there was something else going on."

"What?"

"I think his heart wasn't in his job anymore."

"That's a polite way of saying he didn't want to work for a 'flibbertigibbet' like me."

"Flibbertigibbet?"

"That's what I am, according to the gossip heralds."

Bënnië-Änn snorted. It was surprisingly horse-like. "The gossip heralds. The *gossip heralds*. Sweet flopping, flopping, ten-times flopping Çalaht, why would you give them the energy of your attention? Allow me to let you in on a little secret." The huge woman leaned forward. "According to the gossip heralds, I am a member of a lost tribe of giantesses who hire out their services to scare children into good behavior."

Eloise looked at her, deadpan. "Presumably that's not true."

Thëjëts gawped at her ruler for a full ten seconds, then broke into a deep guffaw. "Good one. No, it's not true."

"Good to know." Eloise rapped a knuckle on her cast. "So, what's being done about it all?"

"About Ligurian's disaster of an office? About Flachberg? About the traitors who were in our midst?"

"Any of them. Or all of them."

"Well, for the state of the First Advisor's Office, I'll start with the scribes and see who needs to be kept, who has potential but isn't there yet, and who needs to be shown the castle door. I'll tap into his network of spies, both within the castles and without—"

"Ligurian had spies *in* the castle?"

"Of course. How else was he supposed to know what was going on? It's not like the late queen shared all her thoughts with him. And nor did you. So, yes, spies. I'll also look at his information processing set-up. I'll track the path each scroll takes from the moment it comes into the castle to the moment it hits my desk, and then subsequently..." She reached over and tapped the nearest royal box. "Eventually, if it is important enough, it will make it in here and we'll discuss it. Ligurian would have had a system, even if it was obscure and warped to suit his own needs. It'll take me a little while, but I'll get there. In the meantime, if you need anything in particular, you'll need to let me know."

"I'll do that. For example, Flachberg. What's going on there?"

"Ah, yes. That was on my list of topics for today." She stood and went to the farthest box. "Things are a bit grim, from our point of view."

"Grim how?"

"It would appear that the Easties have moved the Adequate Wall of the Realms."

"What? What do you mean they moved the Adequate Wall?"

"As in, they took one part of the wall, picked it up, and put it somewhere else."

Eloise wrinkled her nose. "That doesn't make sense. How do you move something like the Adequate Wall?"

"Apparently stone by stone, using a lot of people."

"You're kidding. That's... that's... that's just weird. Why would someone do that?"

"They moved it so that... Here, let me show you." Thëjëts walked to the map table and cleared it of scrolls so all four-and-a-half realms could be seen, along with the beautifully carved wooden sections that denoted the Adequate Wall of the Realms. She leaned over and oriented herself, then traced along the wall. A small grunt indicated she'd found what she was looking for. Bënnïë-Änn placed one hand at a particular spot in the wall and, with an unexpected fierceness, broke the wooden model, tearing off a precise section. She then rearranged the pieces so they were in a different location. "Come, Your Highness. Have a look."

Eloise went to the map table, leaned in and studied the section of the wall that Thëjëts had moved. "Right. Flachberg is now on the Eastern Lands side of the Adequate Wall of the Realms."

"That's where, according to my sources, and I quote them, 'it has always belonged,' end quote."

"Oh."

"Oh, indeed."

Eloise felt her stomach drop. She'd known there'd been activity in Flachberg that originated from the Eastern Lands, that there had been soldiers and guards involved in the skirmish. She'd known that land had been lost, that some of the Flachbergers had received the invaders warmly. She'd learned all that from a Fourth Assistant Junior Trainee Wall Guard named Kÿÿÿlïïïëëë Plööönqüüüëëër, who'd escaped with her life after the canton had fallen.

Intellectually, she'd known all of this for a while.

But looking at the silly map table with its broken, repositioned section of the Adequate Wall somehow made it more real. "I have to figure out what to do," said Eloise.

"Oh, that's easy," said First Advisor.

"Really? What? What should I do?"

"You amass an army, go down there, beat the flopping crud out of them, and take the land back."

"Oh. You think so?"

"Queen Eloise, if I may speak frankly, it's Easties we're talking about. More specifically, it's Queen Aggie that we're talking about. You can try to take other approaches, but I can promise you that ultimately, it's going to come down to rounding up muscle, making sure they have discipline, going down there, and clunking a few people."

"That's not what I want," said Eloise.

"Of course it isn't. But think about it."

"Think about what? That's really not how I want to operate in the world."

"I understand that. But let's be real. Whether you like it or not, and whether you want to call it this or not, the simple fact is that a state of war now exists between your two queendoms."

"That's not how I see it."

"You must. Queen Eloise, your realm has suffered an armed incursion." First Advisor gestured toward the map table. "If the Easties have taken a chunk of your land—and they have—do you think that their reaction is now going to be, 'Oh, good, that'll do?' No. Their reaction will be, 'Oh, good. What can we take next?'" Bënnïë-Änn took a step back from the map table. "My role as your first advisor is to advise. That's what I've done. If you take matters in a different direction, then I will advise to the best of my ability on the course you choose. But I have to feel like I can give fair, free, and frank advice."

"Thank you for that. I never got the feeling that I was getting anything resembling fair, free, or frank from Ligurian."

"No?"

"It was more careful, calculated, and, in retrospect, conniving."

"Not what you want. Or need." First Advisor paused, like she was trying to figure out how to say something. "May I ask a question, Your Highness?"

"Sure. Ask away."

"Why have you not yet met with your Privy Council?"

"I have a Privy Council?"

Thëjëts nodded.

Eloise wrinkled her brow. "I guess I must. Obviously, my mother had one. I couldn't tell you much about it, but I do recall her mentioning it every now and again. Usually with a tone of annoyance or frustration."

"Didn't Former First Advisor Ligurian ever suggest you discuss matters with your Privy Council?"

"No. Not once."

"See, that's what I'm talking about. That, right there, is both his ambition and his weakness. He wanted to be the central figure in your reign. He wanted everything to go through him." Thëjëts leaned forward. "Queen Eloise, you simply cannot take advice from one single person. Not me. Not anyone. You need a breadth of opinions, including differing ones, and especially ones you might disagree with. I can assure you that there were ample times when I said things to your mother that she didn't like, didn't agree with, or really didn't want to hear. But that's the job. It was my job as Other Places Advocate, and now it's my job as First Advisor."

"Isn't that confusing?"

"Maybe it is at times. But know this: it makes you stronger. It makes you think harder about your decisions. Weak queens are afraid of their advisors, or prefer advisors more prone to saying 'yes' than saying something honest or useful."

"And strong queens?"

"The greatest queens have always surrounded themselves with the top minds that they can find, whatever that looks like, and whether those people agree with her or not. Those top minds are likely to give you top input, which makes it more likely that your considerations and decisions will be informed." First Advisor shook her head. "Surely, our beloved late queen, your mother, went through all of this with you?"

Eloise felt pink rising in her cheeks. "No, not like you are talking about. I think that was still to come. She probably figured Johanna and I were too young, or she planned it for later, but later never came."

First Advisor Thëjëts humphed. "Pity. Well, now you're queen."

"Yes, I am."

"And I can see that it isn't just Ligurian's office that needs some shoring up."

"I'm going to choose not to take offense at that."

"Good. It was meant in the spirit of improvement."

"So, let's start improving. Can you please organize for me to meet with the Privy Council?"

"Technically, no. In practice, yes."

"I don't understand."

Bënnïë-Änn's eyes lost focus for a moment as she gathered her thoughts. "Being a councilor is considered a lifetime appointment. However, Protocol states that when, uh, when there is uh…"

"Please just be direct with me," said Eloise. "I know we don't know each other well, but my mother died. There's no point in skirting around that."

"Yes, Your Highness. With the demise of the queen, Protocol states that the Privy Council is automatically dissolved. That's because all appointments from the monarch automatically lapse. So, technically, you don't have a Privy Council at the moment. In practice, everyone assumes that you will reappoint them, which every queen has done for flopping yonks. I can prepare a statement for you to sign that does that, if you'd like."

"Sure. Please, do." Eloise hesitated. "But how about I meet everyone before I actually sign it?"

First Advisor raised an eyebrow. "As you wish."

❦ 8 ❦
US, NOT US, AND EVEN THE SAVAGES

Eloise sat on the Listening Throne in the Receiving Room wearing the I Won't Be Here All That Long Today So Keep It Quick cape, which, as it turned out, was not the correct choice. There'd been a string of representations to her that had stretched over two hours—all things that had piled up in the time between Ligurian being removed from his post and Bënnïë-Änn Thëjëts taking over. Fortunately, it had all been pretty routine—no land disputes, twisty pronouncements of guilt or innocence, or unreasonable pursuit of favorable trade terms relating to turnips. Instead, most of the time had been devoted to interviewing a dozen finalists for the role of Auxiliary Court Poet.

"Why am I doing this?" Eloise asked First Advisor after the first half-dozen candidates had warbled their poetry (largely sycophantic, obscure, or both) at her.

"Because matters of Court culture are shaped to meet the queen's taste," said Thëjëts. "And only the queen can make such decisions."

So Eloise endured the verbal onslaught, which, mercifully, ended with a young dandy wearing a tunic and breeks who had a self-conscious, deliberately-shabby-because-it-reeks-of-haunted-artist look, and who had a way of speaking that made everything sound like a title. Having finished his poem, he struck a statuesque pose, looking out into the middle distance, as if Truth, Beauty, and the Meaning of Life all fell within his gaze.

"Thank you for applying for the Auxiliary Court Poet role, Master..." Eloise stifled a yawn as she scanned the scroll on her lap for his name. "Master Syllablesworth. Is that a pseudonym?"

"Not At All, Your Highness," declaimed the fop. "I Was Named Imascrawling Syllablesworth at Birth."

"So it's nominative determinism that has you stand here today."

"I Beg Your Pardon?"

Eloise waved a hand. "Never mind. What do you call that poem?"

"That Was Called 'Let Me Liken My Sweetheart's Spleen to an Exploding Cigar: A Koan of Suppurating Love.'"

"Uh, I see," said Eloise. "I, uh, I don't recall much in the way of spleens in the poem."

"It Was Done With Metaphor and Allusion." Syllablesworth said this with a completely straight face.

"I see. Well..." Eloise searched for something nice to say. "I'm particularly impressed with the way you rhymed 'orange' with 'door hinge.' Rhyming 'orange' at all is a feat worth noting."

"Thhhhhank You, Queen Eloise," spluttered the poet. "I'm Glad That Resonated With You. Rhyming 'Orange' is One of the Great Poetic Challenges of Our Time."

"I'm sure it is."

Eloise cleared her throat, and First Advisor Thëjëts stepped forward. "Well, thank you for coming in today," said Bënnïë-Änn. "Someone will get back to you."

Syllablesworth launched into a bow that Jerome would have mocked for a month, had he seen it. "Thhhhhank You, Oh, Great Queen

Eloise. I Hope I Can Compose Many a Poem Worthy of Your Wondrousness."

"That would be nice," said Eloise as the young man reverse-pranced his way out of the room.

Eloise allowed herself a sigh, tugged the cape so it sat more comfortably around her, and whispered to First Advisor, "Any of the candidates strike you as worthy of the role?"

"I would never presume to advise Her Majesty on matters of art or self-expression."

"So you didn't like them either."

"As I said, I would never presume to advise Her Majesty on matters of art or self-expression."

"I thought not. We'll have to find someone else for the Auxiliary Court Poet role," said Eloise. "What's next?"

"I believe I'm next," came a voice from the back of the Receiving Room.

It was a mare's voice, deep and self-assured, and she strode forward with an elegant, regal gait. Eloise recognized the unusual coloring of her coat—face, neck and forelegs were raven black except for the white, circular blaze in the middle of her forehead, which sported the smear of ochre that her fellow equines of the Us always wore. Beyond her withers was hair of purest white. The line that demarcated black from white was so distinct, it was like a cartographer had drawn it. Her only adornment was a woven white pouch worn around her neck.

"I'm a little surprised to see you, Naranbaatar Enkhtuya," said Eloise. "Welcome back to Court."

The last two times the mare had stood there, things hadn't exactly gone well. The first time, Eloise had declined the mare's ambassadorial credentials because the horse had refused to represent all the Central Ranges, wanting only to stand for the Us. The second time, Enkhtuya had brought an inebriated mezcal larva as a second envoy to represent everyone that the Us call the 'Not Us' (equines not in their society) and the 'savages' (everyone else). That, too, had been a short, unsuccessful meeting.

"Thank you, Queen Eloise. I've returned from the Central Ranges, and bring you greetings from His Alacrity Khan Nergüi Unbenannt Nime-tuseta and the Us, who send you wishes for sweet grasses and lush fields."

"That's very kind. Please extend my regards next time you communicate with him."

"I'll do that." There was a short pause, then she cleared her throat and said, "I've held discussions with the khan. He has changed his position on representation from the Central Ranges. I told him you rejected our position that I would represent the Us and only the Us, stating you found that unacceptable."

"I did."

"I also told him of my difficulties doing what he next commanded, finding a representative for the Not Us and the savages. I freely admit that the drunk worm was a sub-optimal choice."

"Agreed."

"So..." She hesitated, like she was preparing to say something unpleasant. "With the blessing and guidance of my khan, I've been delegated to represent not just the Us, as remains our preference, but also the Not Us and savages of the realm of Central Ranges."

"I see," said Eloise. "To be honest, I'm surprised. Surprised, but pleased. Do you have your credentials?"

"My documents are in my pouch. You may have them retrieved, if you wish."

First Advisor stepped to the mare, opened a flap on the pouch hanging around her neck, and ferreted out a hemp scroll parchment. She stepped back, and the mare (unlike last time) gave Eloise an elegant bow, then said the words dictated by Protocol. "I am Naranbaatar

Enkhtuya. I offer my credentials as the representative of His Alacrity Khan Nergüi Unbenannt Nimetuseta and the Us, as well as..." Once again, she paused, like it was an effort to speak. "As well as the Not Us and savages of the Central Ranges."

"Welcome to Court, Envoy Enkhtuya," said Eloise. She was going to have to speak to the mare about using the term "savages," but at least the scope of her representation was more to Eloise's liking.

"Thank you. I also have a small gift of our esteem for you. It is the pouch inside my pouch."

First Advisor Thëjëts reached inside again, and this time she pulled out a small, white linen bag decorated with a riot of swirls and glyphs in ochre and blue. Eloise recognized the markings immediately as the same symbols she'd seen inside a tent in the Central Ranges belonging to the one human who was tolerated to live among the equines of the Us. "From the dream wife?" asked Eloise.

"Yes," said the mare. "It is a gift of the vision herb mix she shared with you when you were among the Us. She told me to tell you that she didn't intend for you to use the herbs for questing, because they have not been properly prepared and you are not skilled enough to guide yourself. Instead, they are a reminder of your time with her, and perhaps of the learnings you experienced in the presence of her and the khan."

"That's lovely. Please extend my regards to both your khan and the dream wife."

"I will, when I make my report."

"And I hope we can foster close ties between our realms."

"I'm sure the khan would approve of that, but I can check with him if you'd like."

"No, no. Let's assume that one."

"Yes, Your Highness."

9

PRIVY COUNCIL

The Privy Council met in the Privy Chambers. As girls, Eloise and Johanna thought the name childishly amusing, until they learned it derived from the meaning of "privy" as "private," rather "privy" as "chamber of convenience." Even as she and First Advisor Thëjëts walked toward the room, Eloise hurrying to match the larger woman's long strides, she couldn't help but feel a little silly, heading for a meeting in the privy. "Is there anything I should know going into this?"

"Hmmm..." said First Advisor. "Well, some of them have been on the Council a long, long time. They're a bit set in their ways. They served your grandmother before they served your mother. So there's a lot of experience there, even if some of it is a bit dated."

"OK."

"The older ones like to be respected. It tends to work best with them if you show some degree of deference."

"Deference? I'm queen. Shouldn't they be deferential to me?"

"You'd think that would be the case, wouldn't you? But look at it from their point of view. With respect, they see you as a child with little experience, thrust onto the throne before you were ready."

"I don't know about the child bit, but the latter is fair enough. Anything else?"

"You have to learn to listen to what they say, but for some of them, you also have to listen beyond what they say."

"What do you mean?"

"Well, say one of them says they want to take a question on notice. That means they either don't know the answer—fair enough—or don't wish to let on to what they do or don't know. That's what I always did. Either way, odds are they'll have no intention of actually getting back to you with a response."

"I see. What if I actually do want a response?"

"Ask again at the next meeting. Eventually, you'll get something that resembles an answer."

"Are all of them that cagey?"

"None of them all the time. All of them some of the time." Thëjëts paused a moment, considering. "Everyone except Seer Maybelle."

"Seer Maybelle de Chipmunk is on the Privy Council? That's good news."

"Given that she's a seer, there's ambiguity built into what she perceives. As such, my experience is that she always tries to give it as straight as she can."

"I see. Well, at least there will be one friendly face in there."

They reached a door marked with a crescent moon. "After you," said First Advisor.

The Privy Chamber was a windowless stone room dominated by a massive oak table with a small throne at one end and chairs that were almost as big spaced evenly around it. As Eloise stepped into the room, a handful of conversations broke off and the not-quite-a-dozen people rose to their feet.

"G'mid-morning to you all," said Eloise.

"G'mid-morning," they echoed.

There was an awkward moment, but at Bënnïë-Änn's nod, she walked to the throne and sat. "Please, be at rest."

Eloise glanced around and realized there were only two people she had more than a passing acquaintance with in this intimidating body. She knew Seer Maybelle the best, since she was Jerome's mother. And there was the Venerable Prelate Herself, a tapir who carried the weight of the Çalahtist faith on her shoulders. Eloise hadn't seen the prelate since the unfortunate incident at Festering Resentment when, during a blessing of a brunchberry paddock, Eloise's attempt to encourage the field using magic had backfired spectacularly. The Venerable Prelate Herself had been pinned as the source of the "miraculous" and overwhelming explosion of sunflowers, and Eloise hadn't done anything to dissuade that assumption.

She realized they were all waiting for her to speak. "Thank you for meeting me this morning." Her high-pitched voice betrayed her nerves. "Apologies that it has taken me so long to gather this group. Thank you for your service to my mother, and for some of you, to my grandmother. I hope we can have a productive and fruitful relationship."

They looked at her, silent, like they were waiting for her to deliver a punchline.

"Perhaps you could all just say a few words about who you are and how you've served the crown. Seer Maybelle, could you start?"

The chipmunk stood in her seat. "Yes, Queen Eloise. As you know, I am Seer Maybelle de Chipmunk. As Court Seer, I provide visions, divinations, prognostications, and various connections to the Unseen."

The Venerable Prelate Herself went next. "You know me well, Your Highness. I shall not waste everyone's time with an introduction. "I'll just say, may Çalaht's blessings be with you." The prelate sat, apparently done.

Both humble and a little aggressive. "Right," said Eloise. "Thank you. Who's next?"

A walrus wearing a sharp, pressed, and immaculate outfit dominated by a ruffled collar, a navy tunic, epaulets, and a dazzling array of medals raised a flipper. He was the largest, oldest walrus Eloise had ever seen, with a body that must have weighed two strong weights, impressive white whiskers, and tusks a full length long. His voice rumbled forth like a rockslide. "I am Brigadier General Gideon Horsewhale de Odobenus and I am in charge of your military forces in all their various and sundry forms."

"Oh, good. I'll have some questions for you. But let's continue."

Next was a thin, pale man with a neatly trimmed beard that showed hints of gray. He wore a dark navy tunic that had the thinnest vertical stripes Eloise had ever seen, each spaced less than a finger's width apart. "I'm Cyrus Snorklepipe Borborygmus, Exchequer of the Realm." His voice was a wheezed whisper, like a sibilant puff of reluctant air from a bellow squeezed by an indifferent apparition.

"Oh good. You're in charge of the coffers," said Eloise. "I'll have some questions for you, as well."

"Yes, ma'am."

Across from the Exchequer, a twitchy young man with a wrinkled lavender robe, an unflattering bowl haircut, and fluttering hands half-stood, sat, started to rise again, then settled back onto his chair and jigged his leg.

Bënnïë-Änn Thëjëts waved for him to stand.

"I'm... " He swallowed. "I'm Niville Numptorius." He giggled nervously. "People call me 'Numpty.'"

Thëjëts cut across him. "Not so much anymore. We're leaving that name behind now, aren't we, Niville?"

"Yes, ma'am. Sorry." He bowed to First Advisor and turned back to Eloise. "I've been First Advisor Thëjëts's understudy as Other Places Advocate. She's suggested that I ask to fill that role temporarily until you appoint someone permanent."

Somewhere in the room, there was a snicker.

"First Advisor, is that your recommendation?" asked Eloise.

"It is."

"Master Niville," said Eloise. "As someone who would be in the Other Places Advocate role, tell me about the succession issues that recently faced the Half Kingdom."

Niville got a far-off look, and his hands twitched by his sides. "King Doncaster passed without leaving an heir. Your mother's passing freed up your father, the dowager king, to un-renounce his renouncement of the Half Kingdom throne. He wasn't interested in it, but your sister was, so the dowager king took on the crown, shoring up succession, and then immediately abdicated, handing the crown to Princess, now Queen, Johanna. "

"Tell me something about the Eastern Lands queen that I wouldn't necessarily know, whether or not it is helpful diplomatically."

"Diplomatically, it's probably not germane," said Niville. "But in the last half year, Queen Aglandau has changed her mode of dress."

"How so?"

"She eschews the robes and gowns that she's worn for her entire adult life. In their place, she wears a fancy version of the breeks and tunic worn by olive growers."

"Is there a reason why?"

"No, nothing obvious."

Eloise turned to Bënnïë-Änn. "First Advisor? Any insight?"

"Not particularly, Your Highness. If I had to guess, I'd wager it was political. Everything Queen Aglandau does tends to be political."

"Maybe she just wants to be more comfortable," suggested Eloise.

"It's Easties we're talking about, Your Highness. Comfort is not high on their list of priorities. But if there's really something going on with the change of attire, I assume we'll find out soon enough."

Eloise nodded. "Right. Well, then, Master Numptorius, welcome to an interim spot on the Privy Council."

"Pardon?" he coughed. Niville's face clouded with confusion, not sure he'd heard right.

"Sit down, Numpty," barked the walrus. "She said 'yes.'"

"Oh. I see." The newly anointed Interim Other Places Advocate crumpled into his seat in relief.

Eloise moved on to the others in the room. A tiny, fiery older woman with white hair, wrinkles like a malnourished Shar Pei, and midnight-black robes creaked to her feet. "I am Riri Badenius Gintsshprik, Supreme Magistrate."

"Pleased to meet you."

The magistrate humphed and waved a hand at the next person along, a stick insect who Eloise almost didn't see. Although he was a good 30 weak lengths long, he was extremely narrow, no more than a few weak lengths wide at most, and his legs were even thinner. Plus, his brown color blended almost perfectly with the table he stood on. The stick insect propped himself up on his back legs and bowed. "Rölf de Phobaeticus, Your Highness. Speaker for the Land and That Which Grows On It. From the trees and bushes to the land itself, I give voice to their needs and desires."

Last was a slightly paunchy man roughly her father's age who was dressed in the most outlandish foppery Eloise had ever seen—ribbons, ruffles, powdered wig, false beauty spot, and a tunic and breeks that could have fed an orphanage for half a year. He dabbed his nose with a handkerchief as he stood. "Court Nominee Xertz Oxter Yarborough," he sniveled. "The kind members of your Court have placed their confidence in me to represent the various lords and ladies."

"Very good. Thank you for your service here." Eloise nodded toward Bënnïë-Änn. "First Advisor, is there an agenda?"

"The meeting was gathered at your request. May I suggest you either ask questions or state your concerns so everyone knows what you're thinking?"

"Questions and concerns. OK." Eloise looked down at her hands, which were clasped in her lap. "Flachberg. Anyone have any thoughts?"

"I visited there once," said Xertz Yarborough. He idly tugged at a ribbon dangling from a cuff. "It was at best a pit stop on the way to a better place. I couldn't wait to get out of the canton."

"You're saying it has no value?" said Eloise.

"No, Queen Eloise, I didn't say that." The way Yarborough said her name with undisguised insolence irked her. "I'm saying it isn't exactly a rose in the bouquet that is the Western Lands and All That Really Matters."

"Not everywhere can be Brague."

"I suppose that's true. It just doesn't strike me as a particularly meaningful loss."

"It doesn't? You're suggesting we're better off without it?"

"I'm suggesting that the cost of getting it back may outweigh the benefit of its return."

Eloise could hardly believe that. "Does anyone agree with the Court Nominee?"

The brigadier general raised a flipper. "I do."

The exchequer raised a hand. "I concur. It would be difficult to reconcile the strain on your royal purse against the recovered revenue in terms of tithes and other receipts."

"Anyone else?"

The Venerable Prelate Herself's prehensile snout twitched, and she raised a foreleg. "I worry for the souls of those who might be lost in such efforts."

"Right. Anyone on the other side? Anyone think we should reclaim that which was taken?"

Niville Numptorius moved his hand as little as possible while still raising it. Hardly a resounding endorsement.

No one else moved in support of the idea.

"I see," said Eloise. "Hypothetically, if I *did* want to take action on this matter, what are my options?"

The Privy councilors all looked at each other. Finally, Brigadier General de Odobenus spoke. "That isn't the kind of question we've faced recently. I'll take the matter on notice, with your permission."

"I see. Right. Let me come at this from a different angle. Brigadier General, what is the state of readiness of my soldiers and guards?"

"Readiness? Why, it is excellent. We're drilled and ready to perform when called upon."

"Good. I'd like to inspect them this afternoon."

"This afternoon?" The walrus's whiskers flattened back against his face. "That's a bit soon."

"Tomorrow?"

"Tomorrow works, Your Highness. Name a time, and they'll be ready for you on the Drill Paddock."

"Tomorrow afternoon, then," said Eloise.

"I'm sure you'll be happy with what you see."

10

THE GANG

"Welcome, welcome, welcome," said Hector de Pferd, Eloise's former Equine Designate (he'd lost the role when Eloise became queen, as Equine Designates were associated with princesses, but he did remain the leader of the ceremonial Horse Guard). Hector was a Friesian who, from the top of his ebony mane to the tips of his onyx tail, embodied every possible cliché of beauty. Even in the dim candlelight of the Queen's Stables, his lustrous midnight coat glistened with a reflected sheen, like a thousand cherubs had spent half a day brushing it to perfection. "Welcome to my little corner of Castle de Brague."

Eloise stepped through the horse-sized door into the stable and looked around. The walls were decorated with lavish landscapes depicting haystacks and lounging mares. The floor was covered in clean straw, and two mangers flanked a table and four padded armchairs. "This looks very cozy."

"I call it my 'horse cave,'" said Hector. "It's where I go when I need some alone time."

A gentle snort came from the other side of the stable.

"Oh, hello, Nameless One," said Eloise. "Hector said you'd be here. I'm glad you could make it."

The Nameless One was one of the Guard Horses (not to be confused with the Horse Guard), and was normally partnered with Lorch Lacks-neck, Eloise's champion. The bay horse had a dark brown body and black mane, and gave Hector a run for his coin in the perfectly-muscled department. As a Guard Horse, he kept a vow of silence, but after bowing, he gave a head toss and a foot stomp to show he was glad to see her.

"Yo, yo, yo!" called Jerome. "Hey, Hectorino. Hey, Nameless One-orino." The chipmunk wrinkled his nose. "That doesn't have much of a ring, does it? How am I supposed to come up with a nickname for someone named the 'Nameless One?'"

The Nameless One lifted one shoulder in disinterest.

"I mean, I could go for something more ironic, something that's not a play on your name, like Tiny or Sport or Champ or the Bay One. Or I could use a nonsense non sequitur, like Bertie the Bouffant Bottler."

The bay horse flicked his tail.

"'Bertie the Bouffant Bottler?' What does that even mean, Jer?" said Eloise.

"I'm just saying—"

"Don't. Just don't."

"Don't what?" It was Lorch, ducking through the doorway. He carried himself like the guard he had been and the champion he was, but this was muted by the fact that he was carrying a tray of baked goods in each hand.

"Nothing," said Eloise. "It's just Jerome being Jerome."

"How could Jerome not be being Jerome?" asked RoyLee Pottagecottage, who also carried a tray. The young wombat had left his home with the Wombanditos (the fiercest gang with bad eyesight in all the realms) to come back to Brague, where he now served as a Senior

Page-In-Training (although Eloise was thinking of asking Lady Seneschal to promote him to Junior Assistant Page, as he was an attentive and energetic servant). "'Jerome be being Jerome' no be making sense."

"It's just a figure of speech, RoyLee," said Eloise. She pointed to the trays. "What do you have there?"

"Crullers!" said RoyLee. "They still be being warm."

"I had to stop RoyLee from snitching a few on the way here," said Lorch.

"You be stopping me?" protested the wombat. "I be stopping you!"

"It's true. The temptation was great."

"You talked the new Chef into making crullers?" said Eloise. "That's nice." Her tone made it clear she thought it was anything but. Ever since Chef's son had taken over as the new Chef, the food at Castle de Brague had gone from amazing to merely adequate.

RoyLee beamed. "That no be what happened at all. We be making them, Guard Champion Lorch Lacksneck and me. Or, he be making them and I be helping."

Eloise looked at Lorch. "Really? You bake? I had no idea."

"My late grandmother, may she stand with Çalaht, made the best crullers in the realm. I might have picked up a thing or two."

"I can't wait to try one."

"Great that you could all make it," said Hector. "Just pop those on the table."

"Wow! Look at that spread!" said Eloise. "It's like a comfort food extravaganza."

"That's what I was going for," said Hector. "I have three different kinds of hay for those who like that kind of thing."

"And crullers," said RoyLee. The wombat set down his tray then leaned over, snagged a pawful of hay, and shoved it in his mouth. "Nice. Oaten hay. Very nice. What be the other kinds?"

"Lucerne and barley."

"Excellent. Most excellent."

"For Master Abernatheen de Chipmunk, a selection of walnuts, pecans, almonds, and cashews, plus dried apricots, raisins, pawpaw, and mango, as well as fresh apple quarters."

"And crullers," added RoyLee, munching.

Hector gestured at the table. "For our queen and her champion, and really, anyone who wants any, I've also organized this falafel made from peas and green edamame with a cucumber and mint dip, cauliflower mini-pies with kale pesto, artichoke and spinach cups, and popcorn tofu with a sriracha-spiced dipping sauce."

"And crullers," said RoyLee.

"And crullers," agreed Hector.

"This looks incredible," said Eloise. "And how nice of the new Chef to help you out with all this."

The Nameless One snorted.

"The new Chef didn't help out?"

"We arranged the food through a local catering business called Shove This In Your Gob, which has quite the reputation. From what I can see, it's well-deserved."

"Oh. Well, I won't tell Chef if you don't."

Lorch put his cruller tray down and scanned the room. "You've had this swept for bugs?"

"I did it myself, and then the Nameless One did a second pass. There's no one listening. It's as private as it gets here at Court."

"Good work."

They stood there a moment, looking at it all. Then Eloise asked, "Is it someone's birthday or something? What's the occasion?"

"It was Lorch's idea," said Hector. "Him and the Nameless One."

"Oh?"

"You've been through so much since we've been back, Queen Eloise," said Lorch. "We felt you needed a chance to be private. To be away from the gaze and judgement of Court. To have an hour or two break from worry, and to refresh."

"Oh, just say it, Lorchorino," said Jerome. "El, you need some downtime. Some friend time. The realm will still be waiting after you've snorked down a few cauliflower mini-pies and some popcorn tofu."

Eloise stood quietly for a moment, then did something she hadn't done in way too long—she relaxed out of the rigid "I'm queen" posture she held every public moment of the day. With a relieved smile, she put a hand on Hector's shoulder. "Thank you. Thank you, everyone. I can't tell you how right you are."

"Come on, folks," said Hector. "Dig in."

Jerome hopped onto the table first. "Grab a plate and take a seat. Bless this food. It's time to eat."

The next twenty minutes were dominated by the sounds of snacking and satisfied sighs. Conversation was limited to "Could you please pass..."

Once the initial eating fervor was over, everyone settled into their spot with a plate or a manger and continued picking at their food. Eloise suppressed a belch and said, "I've missed you guys. I know I've seen most of you almost every day, but I've missed *this*, just the gang being together. It's lovely that we can do it without being pummeled by horrible weather, and it's nice to let one's hair down."

"You no be letting your hair down, Princess Queen Eloise. Your hair no be long enough for that."

"Again, RoyLee, it's an expression. Don't wombats say that?"

"No. Not at all. What's it be meaning?"

"It means that you stop being all formal and you loosen up and maybe do things you don't normally do."

"I get it. Wombats be saying, 'Dig a new burrow.' Like you be letting go of what you usually be doing and go be living in a new hole in the ground."

"I can see that," said Eloise. "Hector, do horses have a saying like that?"

"Horses say, 'Catch a breeze in your tail.' Like, you're running wild across a paddock or standing on top of a mountain."

"I like that. Jerome? What about chipmunks?"

"Chipmunks would say something like, 'Eat your stored filberts.'"

"What?"

"Yeah. Instead of being all serious and industrious and storing away your nuts for winter, you're letting go and eating them instead."

"Why filberts?"

"Who knows? Probably because it sounds funny," said Jerome. "'Filbert' is much funnier than 'almond' or 'walnut.' I bet you could put 'filbert' anywhere and it would make whatever you said funnier."

"Catch a breeze in your filbert," chortled Hector.

RoyLee started laughing. "Be digging a new filbert."

"Let your filbert down," said Eloise, flipping what little hair she had.

"'I now pronounce you husband and filbert,'" giggled Jerome. "Or, 'Help! The filbert's on fire!' Really, it works with anything."

"By the power vested in me, I crown you Queen Filbert," joked Lorch.

"No, no, no. There was a Queen Filbert," said Eloise. "That one's not funny."

"*Au contraire*," said Jerome. "That makes it funnier. What was her full name?"

"Queen Filbert Eustachian Whetstone Gumball, known as Queen Filbert the Gibbous."

Everyone laughed.

"You made that up," said Jerome.

"I swear, I didn't."

"Then why was she Queen Filbert the Gibbous?"

"How am I supposed to know? I just read it in a scroll somewhere. Maybe people thought she was as big as the moon. Or maybe she suffered moon sickness in the head, and it was a sly way of saying she was a lunatic."

"Maybe it was supposed to be Queen Filbert the Gibbon, but a scribe somewhere wrote it down wrong."

"That's happened," said Eloise. "~~Queen Brendoid the Flattened~~, for example. Her name is always written with the letters struck through."

Jerome threw up his paws. "Surely that one's fake."

"She was Queen Filbert's granddaughter. Her reign lasted exactly seventeen hours."

"Be that true?" RoyLee stopped half way through a mouthful of barley hay and stared at Eloise. "Don't be telling me that's true. What be happening to her?"

"Seventeen hours after her Crown Plonking ceremony a barrel of molasses that was supposed to sweeten the pudding at her reception fell off its cart, rolled down the hall, hit an unlucky flagstone, took an even less lucky bounce, and whacked her from behind. Her forehead hit the ground, and one of the sapphires from the Gumballic Heraldic Crown came loose and lodged itself deep in her noggin. That was it."

Silence filled the room as they all imagined ~~Queen Brendoid~~ lying on the floor with a protruding jewel and molasses puddling around her.

"That no be a pretty picture," said RoyLee. "That be most ouchy. And sticky."

"Indeed."

Quiet fell over them once again as everyone picked at their food. It was the comfortable quiet of people who knew each other and didn't feel the need to fill each second with chatter.

"Guys," Eloise finally said. "I need this. I need my gang. Can we please do this again? Maybe make it a regular thing?"

"I think you need to decree it," said Jerome with mock seriousness.

"Fine, then." Eloise stood and raised her right hand. "I hereby decree that there shall be regular meetings of The Gang, replete with comfort food and camaraderie."

"The queen has spoken," said Hector. "So shall it be."

11

TAKE IT ON NOTICE

fter lunch the next day, Eloise walked with Jerome and Lorch along a tree-lined trail toward the Drill Paddock. "Any suggestions what I should do when I get there?"

"That probably depends on what they have planned, Your Highness," said Lorch. "When I was a guard, no one in the royal family ever inspected us. Superior officers did, of course, but that's different."

"What did the officers do?"

"They walked from guard to guard, making sure our uniforms were tidy and our weapons were clean. That kind of thing."

"That sounds simple enough," said Eloise. "What sort of questions did they ask you?"

"Questions? They never asked questions, except, perhaps, 'Why are you so worthless?' or 'Does your mother know that you're embarrassing your family and your dead ancestors by looking like that?' That kind of thing."

"Did they really do that?" asked Jerome.

"Yes. Denigration, especially of new recruits, is a well-honed, time-honored practice."

"It doesn't sound very nice. Or very good for one's self-esteem," said Eloise.

"I don't think self-esteem building was a primary goal in that part of soldiering. They're more interested in unquestioning obedience."

"I don't think I can say things like that to the soldiers. I don't have it in me."

"I'm sure you could if you had to," said Lorch. "But I doubt it's necessary to do that here. Leave the haranguing to the professionals."

"I think I will."

They rounded a corner and emerged from the trees, revealing the Drill Paddock before them. It was a large, perfectly flat field with thick grass, immaculately maintained by a dozen groundskeeping sheep. One of them noticed Eloise, swallowed, and said, "G'arvo, Queen Eloise." Then, with an unspoken command, the groundskeeper led her team off the field.

Lorch pointed to a structure along the edge of the paddock. "Look at that. They've constructed a viewing stand. That wasn't here the last time I was at the field."

"That's considerate," said Eloise. "It'll help me see everything."

Brigadier General de Odobenus came toward them, his square flippers angled out as he heaved his massive body forward. De Odobenus wore a dress uniform and a whistle around his neck, and he saluted smartly when he reached them. "G'arvo, Queen Eloise. You're in for a treat."

"Oh?"

"Indeed. Please step up on the stand and take a seat. We'll start as soon as you're in place."

"Right. OK."

The stand had three chairs set up. One, an overstuffed armchair, was the most throne-ish, and it was placed at the front, so Eloise took that one. Jerome and Lorch took the two chairs behind.

De Odobenus followed them up onto the stand, which creaked under his weight. He positioned himself to Eloise's left and watched as she settled in her seat. "Ready?" he asked.

"Ready."

"Please cover your ears for a moment."

Eloise glanced at Lorch, who gave her a small, one-shoulder shrug in response. She put her palms to her head and nodded at the walrus.

De Odobenus' chest and neck twitched, flipping his whistle up and into his mouth. He blew a long, piercing screech that echoed across the paddock, followed by four shorter blasts, like he was setting a rhythm. Somewhere out of sight, drums took up the beats, hammering out a matching pattern. Next came what sounded like the screams of a thousand pig banshees wailing in unison at the death of a hundred thousand cherubs.

Eloise shrank her head into her shoulders and clamped her palms harder against her ears. "What. Is. That?"

The brigadier general either didn't hear her or chose to ignore her. His rear flippers thumped the viewing stand in time with the drumbeat. Moments later, hundreds of soldiers in full dress uniforms marched in from every direction in precise, controlled squads, followed by rank after rank of drums and cymbals, and finally, the source of the agonized wails—dozens of soldiers each playing a bombard, a double-reeded assassin of an instrument with all the musical warmth of a cudgel. Through her hands, Eloise couldn't help but notice that the song they played was an eardrum-pulverizing version of "Uptown Galliard," a song popular from her parents' time.

It was a weird choice.

But the marching that followed was not. For a full quarter hour, soldiers from a range of species and sizes formed geometric patterns that flowed and interleaved with each other from one end of the paddock to the other. Each carried some sort of weapon, mostly pikes, swords, staves, and maces, which were whirled around with well-drilled, artistic flair. Wave upon wave of movement dazzled with its precision. Parading in and out of their positions, wheeling in circles and crisscrossing their lines, groups forming and reforming. It was a spectacular display. "Call Me Possibly" gave way to "The Second-To-Last Countdown," which blended right into "Wonderfloor" as the soldiers high-stepped, glide-stepped, lateral-marched, and backward-marched their hearts out.

Finally, with a final *crash-boom-blat*, the soldiers froze in place, their positions on the field having spelled out "Queen Eloise Gumball Hydra III."

As the echoes faded away, Brigadier General de Odobenus turned to her. "There you go, Queen Eloise. Your soldiers. What do you think?"

"Except for the bombard assault, that was thrilling," said Eloise, choosing not to mention the incorrect ordering of her names. "A truly impressive show of discipline and dedication."

The walrus puffed out his chest. "I promise you, you won't find this sort of professionalism in any of the other realms."

"I'm sure I won't. Um, do they need to stand at attention like that? Can you give them their ease?"

"Of course, Your Highness. Cover your ears again."

Eloise did, and de Odobenus blew another long blast on his whistle, then yelled, "Parade rest!" As one, they shifted so their legs were more comfortably apart. Swords were sheathed, and pikes, maces, and staves were allowed to touch the ground.

"Would it be OK if I walked among the troops?"

"Of course. Inspect away. You won't find a button or hair out of place."

Eloise turned to Lorch and Jerome. "Join me?"

At their nods, she stepped down from the viewing stand and wandered into the mass of soldiers, de Odobenus flopping and waddling to keep up with them. She approached the nearest uniform, the drum major, a stout man whose conductor's mace was almost as tall as he was. He snapped back to attention as the group approached and called out, "Ten-hut!" Everyone behind him did the same.

Eloise figured it must be like the way Protocol insisted everyone stand when she entered a room. "Thank you for a fine performance, Major," she said to him.

"Sir! Thank you, ma'am! Sir!" He practically shouted his response in her face. "Sir! I'm not actually a major, ma'am. Sir! I'm just the drum major, ma'am. Sir!"

"Right. Sorry for my mistake. I'll just inspect the troops, shall I?"

"Sir! Yes, ma'am! Sir!"

"Thank you." She strolled into the lines of soldiers all standing at attention. The brigadier general was right. Every hair was in place and every button polished to a mirrored shine. She looked at Lorch. "Were you like this?"

"No, Queen Eloise. I was in the guards. We marched, but not like this. And there was much less emphasis on the presentation side of things."

She strode briskly through row after row of soldiers. Now and then, she'd say something innocuous like, "Looking sharp," or "Excellent marching." None of them caught her eye, and anyone who responded kept it to, "Sir! Thank you, ma'am! Sir!"

Something niggled at her. Something didn't fit. She continued her inspection, walking from soldier to soldier, looking at each of them and trying to give words to the thought that stalked her. She kept her pace fairly slow, so it was not hard for the walrus to keep up. His species really weren't built for distance travel over land.

"All these soldiers. All these swords. All these pikes and spears. All the uniforms and the discipline," Eloise said to de Odobenus. "This is so incredibly impressive."

ANDREW EINSPRUCH

"Thank you, Your Highness."

"And yet..."

The brigadier general's eyebrows shot up. "Is there a concern?" He drew out the word like it was anathema to even say it.

"I'm sure there isn't. I'm sure they make quite a fighting force." Eloise stopped. That was it. The army actually *didn't* strike her as much in the way of being ready to fight. Not the way Lorch was, for example. Eloise turned to de Odobenus. "Let me ask you something, Brigadier General. How soon could we go to war?"

De Odobenus laughed, a down-in-the-guts, send-jiggles-through-your-blubber guffaw. "War?" His chortle echoed across the paddock.

Eloise stared at him, her expression blank, and waited for him to respond.

He saw her face. "Oh. You're serious." The walrus seemed genuinely surprised. "I wouldn't necessarily call going to war our area of expertise."

"Is that not what soldiers are for?"

He shrugged, and the movement sent waves through his trembling bulk. "In theory, absolutely."

"And in practice?"

"In practice, going to war was not something your late mother valued."

"No?" Eloise raised one eyebrow. "What did she value, Brigadier General?"

"She valued *not* going to war. A lot of her efforts went in that direction. She valued the absence of war, along with, if I may be so bold, precision marching and polished spectacle."

"Really?"

"Really." It seemed like it was taking de Odobenus all he had not to humph at her. "Let me ask a question, Your Highness. When did the realm last go to war?"

That gave Eloise pause. "I'm not sure."

"Let's narrow it down. Was it during your mother's reign?"

"No. Or at least, not that I've heard of."

"What about during your grandmother's time on the throne?"

"I don't think so."

"Correct. Things got close—very close, in fact—but didn't cross the line between skirmishes and all-out war."

"I didn't know that."

"Not many do," said de Odobenus. "It was generally kept quiet. If you read your history scrolls, you'll find that it was your great-grandmother, Elspeth Esplanade Gumball, who last sent soldiers into an all-out war. That war was against The South. They fought to a stalemate. Not a spectacular result, but it was better than losing."

"So let me ask this," said Eloise. "How long would it take your soldiers to achieve an acceptable level of readiness for conflict?"

The old walrus's whiskers drooped, a clear tell. "There are a lot of factors that go into answering a question like that. I'm afraid I'm going to have to take that one on notice."

Eloise looked at him. He was trying to fob her off.

She smiled and said, "Thank you. Please take all the time you need. Just have an answer for me by tomorrow arvo when the Privy Council next meets."

"Uh..." The walrus tried to hide his reluctance. "I'm not sure—"

"I'd like you to help me get across the numbers."

The walrus waddled slightly away from her. "I'm not sure what you mean."

Eloise stepped forward, closing the gap. "The numbers. Like, how many soldiers are there? How many weapons are there, and what type? How many people are actually trained for combat? How many spies do we have and where are they deployed? That kind of thing."

"I don't know if there's enough time—"

She reached out and gave his front flipper a small squeeze. "I have every confidence that there is. And thank you for such a splendid display of parade marching. It really was superb."

✣ 12 ✣

COULD THEY WIN A WAR?

Eloise, Lorch, and Jerome left the Drill Paddock and headed back to the castle. The further from the field Eloise got, the more agitated she grew. "Can you two come with me?" she said, then headed for the Queen's Study.

She waved them through the door and flounced down in her armchair. "This is a disaster. A true disaster."

Both Lorch and Jerome remained standing. "How so?" said Jerome.

"Did you see those soldiers?"

"Yeah. They looked great. All regimented and straight."

"Regimented, straight, and useless. What if something were to happen —say the queendom gets invaded or something?"

"The queendom's already been... Oh," said Jerome. He coughed. "That's your point."

"Yeah, it is. It's exactly my point." Eloise stood and paced. "By Çalaht's curled nose hairs, I feel like stress eating."

Jerome headed for the door. "I'll call RoyLee."

"No. Don't. I'm not really hungry. It's just something to do." She circled the map table in the middle of her study. As she passed her desk, she picked up her mother's letter opener, the one with the handle carved like a woman's hand holding an envelope. She brushed the pad of her thumb across its blade, testing its sharpness—it was about as sharp as her finger, although the point felt like it might be able to do some damage in a pinch. "Here's the question."

"Yes, Queen Eloise?" said Lorch.

"How could my mother do this? How?"

Neither Lorch nor Jerome said anything.

"Really. I mean it. How?"

"She valued peace?" suggested Jerome.

"Of course she did. So do I. Peace is great. Peace is awesome. Peace involves a lot less slashing, impaling, and killing. I'm a big fan of not slashing, impaling, or killing."

"So..."

"You were both there just now. You saw what I saw. The only way those soldiers would win a war is if we could somehow fancy-dress the other side to death."

"Harsh," said the chipmunk.

"Harsh, but true," said Eloise. "We'll see what Brigadier General de Odobenus comes up with in terms of the questions I asked—if he comes up with anything at all—but I'm not holding my breath that he'll come back with anything resembling the capability of an elite fighting force."

Jerome nodded. "What I saw today did not make me think 'resounding victory.' More, 'Oooh. Shiny.'"

Eloise poked the dull letter opener into her palm. "How much control do I have in this situation?"

"In theory or in practice?" asked Lorch.

"You sound like the Brigadier General. Give me both."

"In theory, I'd say a lot. Is it not up to you who leads the soldiers? As queen, aren't you at the top of the hierarchy?"

"I guess so."

"Know so. They serve you and your realm."

"Right. In theory," said Eloise. "And in practice?"

"In practice... May I speak frankly?"

"Always, Champion Lacksneck."

"In practice, they don't know you. They haven't seen many inspiring results from your choices. They haven't had to do anything for you, so their opinions will be influenced by what little they've seen and by what they've heard."

"You mean from the gossip heralds?"

"From them, but also from their family and their neighbors. The usual people who influence them. But most important is their chain of command, up to and including Brigadier General de Odobenus. Soldiers—and guards are like this, too—are trained to follow orders, and to do so without thinking about it too much. People like de Odobenus have a huge amount of influence on how they act, which in turn affects how they think. They serve the queen, yes, but through the instrument of her commanders. If there are hearts and minds you need to win, they will be those at the top as much as those at the bottom."

"And if those at the top aren't amenable?"

"Then it will be difficult. Tell me, what did you see on display this afternoon?"

"Not a lot of mystery there," said Jerome. "It was a bunch of people marching around."

"Then you missed the point," said Lorch. "What you saw were people taking pride in what they do. What you saw was the precise execution of a designated task, people working well as a large team and experiencing a sense of belonging. What you saw was tradition, in the moves they made, the weapons they carried, and the uniforms they wore. A massive effort went into that 'bunch of people marching around,' and it would be a mistake to dismiss it."

"Fair point," said Eloise. "But could they win a war?"

"I don't know the state of their weapons or whether they've been disciplined in anything other than marching. The real problem is the one you've already identified. The question you just asked hasn't been tested for so long that there's no way to know the answer."

"So we're sunk."

"Don't say that, El," said Jerome. "There's a massive distance between pretty soldiers on a parade ground and 'we're sunk.' It might just be a matter of redirecting their focus."

"What am I supposed to do, chuck out the old walrus?"

"It would be your right to do so," said Lorch.

"I can't do that. He's been in charge for yonks."

"True. Certainly, as long as we've been alive."

"Maybe you don't need to get rid of the brigadier general," said Jerome.

Eloise set the letter opener on her desk. "What do you mean?"

"Get them to do more of the things you want them to do."

"Less marching," said Eloise.

"More slashing and impaling," added Jerome.

"Ugh, but yeah, I guess."

"How could they be taught what they need to know?" Jerome's whiskers twitched. "Does anyone even know how to do all that anymore?"

"There must be someone," said Eloise. "What about you, Lorch?"

"Me?" Her champion looked like she'd just suggested he dance through the streets of Brague in his mother's undies. "Why me?"

"You said that as a guard, you've been on six campaigns—you and the Nameless One together. I specifically remember you saying you've been to Inner Splutter, the arid hills of Tooth Dunes, and the sandy drylands of Cactus Bends."

"True. But not for the purposes of war. I was a guard, not a soldier. We undertook peacekeeping tasks at the most, and usually did nothing more exciting than collecting the queen's tithe. We spent most of our time observing and chatting with the locals."

"Why? What good is that?

"It helped keep your mother's peace."

"Yes, but again, at what cost?

"I don't know how to answer that, Queen Eloise. It was what we were asked to do, and so it was what we did."

"Sorry. I don't mean to snap," said Eloise. "We need to crank up our ability to engage militarily. We need to scrape the rust off of the cogs of war, and we need to do it pretty quickly, before Queen Aggie decides to nibble at another chunk of our realm. Which returns me to my question: who? Who can help me turn our parading soldiers into fighting soldiers?"

There was a long silence.

"Actually, I know someone who might be able to help you," said Lorch.

"Me, too," said Jerome.

"You go ahead."

"No, you spoke first. Be my guest."

"That's OK."

"No, really. We're probably thinking of the same person."

"I doubt it."

"Guys," snapped Eloise. "Lorch, then you, Jerome."

"Yes, Your Highness." Lorch rubbed a hand over his short-cropped hair. "The problem, as I see it, is one of experience. How long has it been since the Western Lands and All That Really Matters waged war, or had to defend itself from one?"

"Not in the two-plus decades of my mother's reign," said Eloise. "And not in the three-plus decades of my grandmother's. So easily well over half a century."

"Right. So we need someone who was a soldier more than half a century ago, with experience both in training for war and waging it. There was someone in my village of Lower Glenth, an old reptile neighbor named Tiberius de Sphenodon."

"Just because they're old doesn't make them reptiles," scolded Jerome. "Many older people remain current in their thinking and mannerisms—"

"No, he *is* a reptile," said Lorch. "Tiberius de Sphenodon is a tuatara."

Jerome's whiskers drooped. "Oh. Sorry. My mistake. I thought you were being figurative."

"No. Literal. Saying it figuratively would have been offensive to both reptiles and people."

"I didn't mean offense."

"None taken."

"Why him?" asked Eloise. "Why Tiberius de Sphenodon?"

"First, he's more than a century old. Maybe closer to one hundred and twenty. I'm not sure, to be honest."

"That's quite something," said Eloise. "I haven't met that many tuataras, but I've heard they can live much older than that. Will he be senile? That can be a problem."

"When I was last home he was still sharp as a tack, and that was just over a year ago. As a kid, I used to get him to tell me stories from his soldiering days. He had lots of them. They all involved thrilling missions and lots of fighting. Maybe he was exaggerating for the sake of a good story, but I remember once, on my eighth birthday, he let me touch his medals. He was wounded, too. Took a crossbow bolt to the front right foot, which left it weirdly severed in half, split down the middle. As a boy, I found that endlessly fascinating."

"He has personal experience in war, then."

"Yes."

"Did he lead the troops or just fight?"

"I'm a little fuzzy there. I know he didn't rise all that high," said Lorch. "It's not like he was a colonel or a general of anything. Sergeant, maybe? I'd have to ask. But the stories seemed to have him leading others into skirmishes and battles, so he must have some experience in command."

"Your tuatara neighbor sounds like a possibility. Maybe we can arrange for him to come here and we can see if there's something there for us to explore."

"I'll send a messenger today," said Lorch.

"Good." Eloise looked at Jerome. "So, who did you have in mind?"

"No one as exciting as a decorated centenarian war vet who liked entertaining the local kids with battle tales."

"C'mon, Jer."

"Sylvia Cloisterfeld."

"My mother's champion?"

"Exactly."

"Huh. Interesting."

"She knows how to fight. She did a great job protecting your mother. She's still fairly young and capable, although if we're using Tiberius de Sphenodon as our baseline, she's barely hatched. Plus, being an ex-champion, she doesn't have a lot going on at the moment."

"Worth a conversation, for sure. I'll get someone to figure out where she is."

"Oh, I can handle that," said Jerome.

"Oh?"

"Yeah. She'll be at the Velvet Cask pretty much every evening."

"Sylvia Cloisterfeld's turned into a drunkard? How very sad."

"No. Not a drunk. A singer. She's started doing performances there."

Eloise gawped at him. "My mother's former, lethally trained, could-kill-you-with-a-ripe-banana champion wants to be a lounge act?"

"Apparently."

"How odd."

"I've seen her. She's pretty good."

"Since when have you had time to go listen to a lounge singer?"

Jerome's tail flicked. "Since I'm no longer champion. El Lorcho here being the one to follow you around has freed up a lot of time. I spend much of it in the Bibliotheca de Records and Regrets, but Head Scribe doesn't let me sleep in there, so I've ducked into the Velvet Cask once or twice in the evening. Sylvia happened to be on stage."

"I had no idea."

"You should come one night. You could talk to her after her set. Ask her if she's willing to help."

Eloise wasn't sure she wanted to listen to her mother's champion smashing her way through a bunch of musical numbers, but she had to admit, Jerome's suggestion made sense. "Probably best if we meet her on her own turf. I don't know if she'll want to step back into service to the crown. She did it for so very long."

"It's worth a try," said Lorch.

Jerome nodded. "I'll set it up."

13

BURBLED DISGRUNTLEMENT

Lady Seneschal Älphonsinä Füüürchtbarkeit Póöòmáäàdéëè sat in her favorite café, On Golden Scone, with the most glorious haggleberry tea she'd ever tasted, nibbled the smallest, cutest little lemon curd tart she'd ever seen, which was so good it would make a host of cherubim dance the gavotte, and brooded. She missed her weekly meetings with Picholine Manzanilla, the Eastern Lands ambassador. Well, probably the former Eastern Lands ambassador now, given that she'd disappeared after an attempt on Queen Eloise's life and a military incursion into the far reaches of the realm. But she still felt sad about no longer seeing her. The woman had become the closest thing she'd had to a new friend in decades.

She sipped her tea and felt a disgruntlement burble in her guts.

The thin, older woman wore her customary black robe buttoned from collar to ankles, and ate in such a careful way that no crumb dared fall on her lap. She imagined the conversation she would have had with Manzanilla. "Hi Älphïë," the ambassador would say as she arrived and sat, her thick Eastie accent loading her words with an abundance of superfluous syllables. "How are you?" (That would have sounded like "Hay-ow are-uh yee-ooh?")

"Fine, Picho. Just splendid," she'd have answered, even if things weren't fine or splendid.

Which, lately, they weren't.

"Allow me to order," Manzanilla would drawl.

"No, no. It's my turn," Póöòmáäàdéëè would reply. "Positively not."

They'd banter back and forth until, inevitably, Manzanilla would tire of the haggling, say, "I insist," and then wave over the serving wench and have her bring them far too many of the café's very rich, very expensive, very small nibbles. If the ambassador was in a particularly sparkly mood, she'd spring for the overwhelming grandeur that was the café's Ultimate Delicacies Selection, an indulgence that, until she'd met the Eastie, Lady Seneschal had only ever allowed herself when she sat on her own celebrating her birthday.

Lady Seneschal sighed. The Ultimate Delicacies Selection was a divine perfection. But now, just seeing it on the menu made her melancholy for her friend.

She took another sip and bit off a corner of the lemon curd tart.

Sip.

Nibble.

Maybe this mood was simply a sign that she was feeling her years. She'd moved up from Lead Lady-In-Waiting to Lady Seneschal midway through the tortured reign of the first Queen Eloise Hydra Gumball. She'd never referred to that particular queen as One (like the gossip heralds had), but she'd definitely referred to that dead loss of a king as One's Grand Mistake, along with everyone else. She found her feet in the role as the two of them made each other as miserable as they could, as publicly as they possibly could. Thank Çalaht, One's Grand Mistake finally did everyone the kindness of carking it. Póöòmáäàdéëè wasn't sure if it was irony or sheer perfidy of fate that One did the same within two sundowns of the king shuffling off.

Then Two had taken over, and the second Queen Eloise had kept Lady Seneschal in the role instead of opting for someone more the new queen's age. Lady Seneschal stayed in the role for the twenty-plus years of Two's reign. The late queen was fair, tough, and had, above all, valued the order Póöòmáäädéëè had exerted over the castle's running. The two of them had never been chummy, but that had been fine. Lady Seneschal enjoyed the fact that she was appreciated, as well as the status afforded by her position.

Sip.

Nibble.

And now she was on her third Queen Eloise, and somehow, the job just wasn't what it used to be. If she'd been one to think in terms of enjoyment, she would have said it wasn't fun anymore. But she didn't think in those terms. She thought in terms of duty, loyalty, and a devotion to doing one's best.

Still, the repetition of the job was getting tedious. Any challenge she faced was one she'd met dozens of times before in one form or another. It should have been interesting to help the household adjust to a new queen. But it wasn't. Having a new queen just made everything harder.

She didn't need harder at this stage of her life.

Sip. Nibble. Nibble. Sip.

And now, her one and only real friend had disappeared with no warning and just a slip of a note, devoid of explanation and emotion. The absence left her unexpectedly bereft, made worse by the lack of goodbye. Would a farewell in person have been so hard? If she were honest with herself, she couldn't help feeling a bit miffed at the whole thing. Childish, maybe, but there it was.

Póöòmáäädéëè allowed herself a frown as she thought about something that her Picho had once said. "You know they don't appreciate you. The lady seneschal in my queen's household is treated almost like a queen herself."

That had really stuck with her.

None of the Queen Eloises had treated her like a queen. One had barely seen her. Two wasn't bad. But this third one? She'd known Eloise Hydra Gumball III since she and her twin had emerged squawking into the world. Póöòmáäàdéëë had gotten along with the younger one, Johanna, well enough—distant but respectful. But she'd never warmed to Eloise. It probably wasn't the child's fault.

But now that child was queen, and the relationship between the two of them hadn't exactly improved.

If she were honest with herself, she really just didn't like the new Queen Eloise.

And Póöòmáäàdéëë suspected the feeling was mutual.

The child was really nowhere close to being ready to sit on the throne. I mean, she'd picked that fool of a chipmunk as her champion! Thank goodness she'd swapped him out for a better model. And not that she paid much mind to the gossip heralds, but she didn't think the way they were calling her "the Flibbertyqueen" was that far off the mark.

Maybe it would have been different if the girls had swapped roles and Johanna had been the one to put on the Gumballic Heraldic Crown, while Eloise wandered off to rule the Half Kingdom.

No point in wishing for that. Wishes got you nowhere.

Except, sometimes they helped you clarify what you did and didn't want in your life.

Sip.

Brood.

Nibble.

Brood.

Sip.

She knew what Picho would have said. "Älphïë, do you really need the *tsuris*?"

Lady Seneschal would have maintained her strict policy of never saying anything against the crown. "It's no trouble. Really."

And then she would have gone home and the word "tsuris" would have rattled around in her head for days, and she would have seen trouble everywhere she looked.

Póöòmáäàdéëè picked up the last corner of the lemon curd tart and then set it down. She couldn't taste the thing, and the cheery little pastry was too stark a contrast to her mood.

"Thanks for meeting me, Picho," she'd have said. "So lovely to spend time with you."

The ambassador would have waved that off, saying, "The pleasure is always mine. See you next week?"

Except she wouldn't see her next week. Or ever. Manzanilla was gone.

Lady Seneschal carefully slid the ambassador's final note from inside her sleeve and read it for the thousandth time. "Remember to make sure you're treated like the queen you are, my Älphïë. Don't let the child queen get you down. And allow yourself to taste the sweetness of life now and then. Yours, Picho."

Póöòmáäàdéëè wondered if she even knew how to taste sweetness anymore.

"You need a change, Älphïë," the ambassador would probably have said if she were there drinking tea and eating tarts.

And she would likely have been right.

Lady Seneschal knew she had to accept that things had changed. Plus, she still felt she needed to help the child queen find her way, if for no other reason than the late Queen Eloise had asked her to, as she lay on her deathbed, and Póöòmáäàdéëè had readily agreed.

She just wished that she actually liked the child. That would make going on so much easier.

Sip.

Brood.

Nibble.

Brood.

Sip.

14

CORNUCOPIAS AND CISTERNS

As he was the exchequer, Eloise might have expected Cyrus Snorklepipe Borborygmus's office in the Counting House to be an opulent tribute to the wealth of the Western Lands and All That Really Matters, a reflection of the queen's support from her people and a sign of the financial robustness of the realm.

Nope.

Borborygmus's domain was a dank basement cavern crammed full of ledgers, scrolls, quills, and ink pots that relied on a band of mice and rats to keep the mold and dust at bay. The only natural light snuck in through a series of round windows set along the roofline, each no bigger than a cantaloupe, which gave Eloise the feeling of being imprisoned belowdecks on a ship. And since they faced west, there wasn't much illumination outside them at this time of morning. The paucity of sunlight meant the exchequer and his assistants relied on soy vanilla and orange-scented candles for light, the smell of which blended with the threatening mildew to give the room the feeling of a catacomb converted to a day spa. Borborygmus worked at a desk the size of a banquet table (which Eloise guessed it might once have been), and it was situated so that when he sat, his back was directly opposite the doorway. Having to look over her shoulder anytime there was a noise at the door would have made her jumpy, she thought.

What Eloise didn't see was anything that looked like coins. Apparently, that was all stored elsewhere. Or, at least, she hoped it was, otherwise she and the realm were in big trouble. She cleared her throat to get his attention, and when he didn't turn around, she said, "Blessings of the day to you, Exchequer Borborygmus."

He stood slowly and turned to face her, not so slow as to be offensive, but slow enough that Protocol might have had something to say about it. "Blessings of the day to you, Queen Eloise." He wore the same navy tunic with the thin vertical stripes, and his beard showed signs of having been trimmed in the last day or two. The acoustics of the basement were such that his whispery voice carried well across the space. "To what do I owe this unexpected honor?"

"I was hoping to have a chat. I haven't been in here since Johanna and I were playing Fiend and Foe, and I was the fiend trying to find her. It took me a whole afternoon to discover her in here."

Borborygmus smiled. "Actually, I remember that. Princess Johanna appeared in that very spot holding a bound volume, and in the most polite way, said she was foe at the moment, and asked if she could sit in a corner and read while you looked for her."

"She had something to read?"

"I think she suspected you would be fiend for quite a while. Please, come in, Your Highness."

Eloise stepped into the room. "Johanna was always a tough foe. Or maybe I was just terrible at being fiend."

"Do you remember how it was that you finally found her?"

"One of the serving wenches took pity on me. She'd spotted her in here when she brought you your afternoon tea. After that, I always insisted we limit the hiding places to a smaller portion of the castle."

"A sensible adjustment to the rules."

"I thought so, but I suspect it might have affected my sister's reading time."

Eloise was surprised at how comfortable the exchequer felt in his domains. He hadn't seemed like the kind for small talk, yet here he was remembering an afternoon more than a decade gone. "Exchequer Borborygmus, can I get you to give me your sense of the realm's finances?"

"Does First Advisor not cover this with you?"

"She does, and before her, he did, although I think former First Advisor Ligurian tried to drown me in ledgers as a way to obscure rather than enlighten. First Advisor Thëjëts seeks to bring clarity, but she is still new in the role. I thought it might be useful to get your perspective directly from you, here at the center of it all."

"I see."

"So, if I may ask, how stand the realm's coffers?"

The exchequer looked around the room like he was trying to figure out the answer to the question. It was like there were vaults on the other side of the walls and he was picturing their contents.

Perhaps that's exactly what he was doing. It was the Counting House, after all, and coin that had been counted had to go somewhere.

"How shall I put this? I wouldn't call the coffers bare, Your Highness. But we're not exactly dealing with an overflowing cornucopia of abundance."

"Are we closer to the bare end of that scale or the cornucopia?"

"I suppose that depends on how large your cornucopia is."

"Let's say a need-to-run-the-realm size."

"Then about in the middle."

"Is that good or bad?"

The exchequer's lips curved into a wry smile. "That depends. Are you a cornucopia half-empty kind of person, or a cornucopia half-full kind of person?"

"Which are you?"

"Queen Eloise, I am Exchequer of the Realm. It is practically my job to be a cornucopia half-empty kind of person. I am constantly concerned that the cornucopia does not hold enough, and that that which flows out drains faster than that which flows in."

"I see." Eloise strode around the room, taking it in and trying to determine what it was she was trying to figure out, as well as how freely she could speak. Borborygmus watched her, hands clasped behind his back, and waited. She stopped at a stack of bound ledgers and ran her finger along their spines. Without turning back to him, she asked, "What if the cornucopia needed to be larger? Not just need-to-run-the-realm sized, but need-to-run-the-realm-and-get-back-stolen-territory sized?"

"At that point, we're talking about a very different kind of cornucopia."

"Are we? Are we, really?"

"Absolutely."

"How so?"

"With your permission," said Borborygmus, then without waiting for her to give it, he moved to a side table, slid a chair from it and dragged it so that it was next to his. He took a handkerchief from a robe pocket and, with more vigor than seemed warranted, wiped it down. Then he gestured to his own chair and said, "Would you like to sit?"

"This is going to take that long?"

"You strike me as the kind of queen who wants a real answer, not a convenient one. Your mother was the same. Your grandmother was most decidedly not, which, come to think of it, might explain why your mother was."

Eloise sat, surprised at how comfortable the chair was. Still, Exchequer Borborygmus spent much of his day parked in it, so having it be comfortable was sensible, she supposed. "Ready."

"If I may change the analogy, I'd encourage you to think of the realm's finances as more like a flowing liquid than solid like a coin."

Eloise shook her head. "I don't follow."

"As I alluded to before, the coffers and vaults of the realm are not static places. The realm's coin, and in particular, the queen's tithe, is a stream, flowing in, but also flowing out. The vaults..." He gestured to the walls. "They are akin to storage ponds or cisterns. They fill and they empty. Sometimes they hold a lot, and sometimes they don't."

"That makes sense."

"How fast that stream flows depends on how effective our collectors are at gathering the queen's tithe, and that depends on things that are not always under our control, like is there a drought or flood that's damaged crops? But it also depends on what we're spending coin on. Your household, for example, is a very, very expensive undertaking. All these people under your roof require food, healing, shelter, and coin so that they can take care of their families. Every single thing you do as queen dips into those ponds and cisterns in one way or another. Your trip to Festering Resentment, for example, where you and the Venerable Prelate Herself blessed a brunchberry paddock. That required dipping a ladle into the cistern and pouring out some of the water. Or more, ladling it up and distributing it. Metaphorically speaking. The analogy starts to strain after a while."

"It's OK. I'm with you."

"So, if you want to undertake an activity like, say, trying to take back stolen lands, you're not just dipping into a cistern with a ladle, you're going in there with buckets. Big buckets."

"I get that. But can't you adjust the stream of water flowing in so that it matches?"

The exchequer smiled, and he raised his arms like he was offering a hosannah to Çalaht. "There's hope yet."

Eloise felt her cheeks go pink. "Please, don't mock."

"I'm not. I'm being serious. My predecessor told me how long it took to get the basic ideas across to your grandmother. I'm not sure she ever had much interest in that part of the realm. The fact you've come here this morning and are engaged in sensible conversation fills me with hope. Your late mother, may she stand with Çalaht, was practical and sensible in many ways, but she tended not to pay much attention to what went on here in the Counting House. It's not like she never spoke to me, but she was always very hands-off. So long as I didn't complain much and she could do what she wanted to do, then she let matters of the Counting House stay in the Counting House. And fair enough. She had other things to think about. But so do you, and yet here you are."

Mollified, Eloise returned to her question. "So, why can't we adjust the flow of the stream so that it matches the change of situation?"

"At some level, you can. And at some point in your reign, you will. But any time you do, it affects people's lives. At a fundamental level, all things equal, more for you means less for them."

"But you've already said that things are not always equal. Droughts and floods and the like."

Exchequer Borborygmus stroked his beard for a few moments. "Let me ask you a question. Why would anyone pay the queen's tithe? Why do the people allow us to demand coin or goods from them, and why would they hand them over? Why don't they tell our collectors to get lost or to do something anatomically unlikely?"

Eloise lifted a shoulder. "Inertia? Because they always have?" she said. "Or because they have to. There's the threat that we'll send soldiers in if they don't."

"That's part of it, for sure. People are used to paying the queen's tithe, so they don't always stop to think about it when the collectors show up. And we've certainly sent out our share of guards to support the collectors. But that's not the important part."

"What's the important part?"

"It's a question of value."

"What do you mean, value?"

"Whether they think about it consciously or not, every time the collector shows up, they do a kind of internal calculation. They weigh whatever perceived value they're getting from the queendom against the pile of coin or corn or cloth that they're handing over. If the scale more or less balances in their head, then they're more or less happy to hand it over. But if the crown's side of the scale is too heavy, then—again, consciously or unconsciously—they grumble."

"So the people have to feel like they receive value for their tithe. I guess that makes sense."

"So the next question is, what value does the queendom provide? What sits on the other side of that scale, balancing those bushels of corn?"

Eloise stood, feeling the need to move. The exchequer stood when she did and watched her pace across the room. "I'm not sure," she said. "It's not like we're trading barley for corn. Or that we give corn back."

"Not strictly true. If a village was starving due, say, to a fire having wiped out their grain stores, you might send some of your corn their way."

"But that's not what you're talking about, is it?"

"No, it's not."

Eloise paced some more.

"Think in terms of abstractions, Your Highness."

"Ah, I see." Eloise stopped. "You mean things like justice and order?"

"What else?"

"Safety, although I don't know how safe the people of Flachberg think I kept them."

"It's true that the abstractions don't always hold up in reality," said the exchequer. "To add to the list, there are also things like having a sense of belonging, and the provision of a kind of order."

"So you're telling me that raising the queen's tithe to fund a military undertaking is a bad idea."

Borborygmus flicked his hand. "With respect, I'm saying no such thing."

"Then what are you saying?"

"Your Highness, please. Take a moment. Think about what we've discussed, then tell me what I'm saying. What did I say was the important thing?"

Eloise sat back down. "Value."

The exchequer remained standing, arms crossed, waiting.

The words came slowly. "What you're saying is that if the people paying the queen's tithe think they're getting value from the increase, then they'll be more willing to continue paying, enforcement guards or not."

"Keep going."

"That value might be in the form of good feeling about the queendom, or in righteous retribution. Or in reinstating a correct order to the working of the realms. That kind of thing."

"Yes, that kind of thing. Or it could be in perceiving their queen to be acting on their behalf. People tend to care about you if you care about them."

"Did my mother do that? Did my grandmother?"

"Your grandmother? No. One was so wrapped up in herself, her pain, and her unhappiness that people definitely did not get the sense she cared about them. Two—apologies, your late mother—had a coldness to her that no doubt you are familiar with. But people got the sense that she was fair and maintained order, and that was close enough to be pretty effective."

"And me?"

"It's early days. I think people are inclined to give you the benefit of the doubt if they haven't spent too much time listening to the gossip heralds.

Eloise stood, sensing she was done. "Speak plainly, Exchequer of the Realm Borborygmus. Do I have a full enough cornucopia to take back Flachberg?"

"No."

"Do you think I could raise the queen's tithe to cover the difference?"

"Maybe."

"Do I have other options?"

"Always. There are always other options. You just have to figure out what they are."

"Got it. Thank you."

15

A FAVOR FROM MOPEY

At the exact moment that Eloise was discussing cornucopias with Exchequer Borborygmus, a full realm away, her sister Johanna was in a commandeered side room in Castle Blotch at Stained Rock, the seat of the Half Kingdom (which she was trying to rebrand under its previous name, the Northern Lands) having a very similar, if less circuitous, discussion with her father. She stared at a scroll of numbers, trying to make them work. "This is a disaster," she said. "Endless, boundless, calamitous disaster."

Her father, the dowager king, Chafed Motley Gumball née de Chëëëk-fliïint, looked up from his own copy of the scroll and frowned. "What do you even do with this kind of thing?"

Johanna leaned back in her chair. "Exactly. Maybe curl up in a corner and cry."

"You could go sit in the streets with a sign that says, 'Alms for the poor.' Maybe you'll get enough charity to balance the budget."

"How did Uncle Doncaster run this place?"

"Not well, apparently."

"You think we could sell the furniture?" asked Johanna.

"Have you seen the furniture?"

"Point taken."

Chafed slid the scroll away with a single finger, like it was contaminated, or covered in pond slime. He drew a deep breath and slowly sighed. "You know what you need to do, right?"

"No, I absolutely and most certainly don't. I have no freaking idea what I should do."

"Think about it."

Johanna dipped her quill in an inkpot and started doodling a vine in the margins around the hateful numbers. Chafed watched her draw leaves, stems, and tendrils around embarrassingly low intakes and staggering outflows, giving her time to let ideas sift in her head. By the time she'd decorated the whole scroll, she was ready to speak.

"I need to go back to basics, and look at all income and expenses to see what's coming in, what's not coming in, and why, as well as what we're spending money on and if it's worth it."

Chafed nodded. "And?"

"And I need to let go of assumptions and try to look behind the information that the exchequer and his scribes put together." Johanna pointed at the scroll. "Are things really that bad? Are they worse? And what can we do about it? Because what that thing says is that this realm has long been limping along on the back of its wart cream exports and not much else."

"Sounds like a plan." Chafed stood, ready to leave.

"I need to ask you something, please. Do you mind sitting a minute longer?"

"Sounds ominous," he said, lowering himself back into his chair. "Go ahead."

Johanna drew a couple more leaves, then put down the quill and clasped her hands in her lap. "Father, I need a favor."

"What favor?"

"I need you to help me."

"I *am* helping."

"Yes, and it's been great. But I need more than that."

"Sweetie, I—"

Johanna put up a hand to stop him, not realizing it was a gesture Chafed had seen a million times from his late wife. He flinched.

"What?" said Johanna.

"It's OK," he said. "Go ahead."

"I'm asking you if you'll be my first advisor."

Chafed furrowed his brow and shook his head. "I don't think that's a very good idea."

"Look, I know it's not common for a former king to take on that kind of role. In fact, I don't know if it's ever happened. But let's face it, you're wafting around the place aimless and mopey."

"Mopey. Really?"

"You're still mourning Mother. And I get it. I'm grieving for her as well. But you have this little rain cloud above your head following you around the castle. It's sad."

"I am sad."

"I know. And that's completely OK. But I also get the sense you need a role. Something to do. When Mother died, it couldn't help but upset the order of things for you. You've lost your place in the world."

"This isn't news."

"I know. But look at it this way. Being my first advisor, even if it is an interim role, will divert your attention to more productive matters than how terrible you feel. You can still spend your days mopey, but at least it will be a useful mopey."

"What about the old first advisor?"

"Sufferous Clench? What can I say? He's kind. He's as old as Çalaht's bunions. But the truth is that Clench, as Uncle Doncaster's first advisor, was effectively sidelined long ago by Doncaster's jester, Turpy. When Turpy... How should I say it?"

"Was removed from the situation?" suggested Chafed.

"That sounds much better than 'Ended up a cloud of bone dust at the bottom of the Whacking Great Hole,' which is what Eloise said happened."

"I... I don't know that I got that part of the story. That sounds horrid. I heard about her broken wrist and dislocated shoulder. I wasn't told the bone dust bit. That's... That's horrible."

"You didn't know?"

"No. I didn't."

"It was a pretty dramatic part of the story." Johanna paused. "My apologies, Father. I thought you knew. I guess Eloise was trying to spare you in your time of distress after Mother's passing."

"That would be like her."

"Yes. Do you need a moment? Do you want me to spell out everything she told me?"

Chafed frowned. "Maybe later. I get the gist. Let's stay on topic."

"OK. Anyway, where I was headed was that with Turpy removed from the situation and First Advisor Clench ineffectual, there's a gap. I'd be grateful if you could fill it."

"You're saying..."

"Be my first advisor. At least for a while."

Chafed sighed. "I don't know if I can."

IOO

"Why not?"

"Because."

"That's not an answer, is it?"

"No, it's not." He took his scroll of numbers and absently began folding it. Johanna knew that exactly one of two things would emerge: a swan or a lotus flower. Those seemed to be the only parchment-folding tricks he knew. She'd seen him do this often enough that she could decode him better than he could himself. If he produced a swan, the answer would be "no." So she hoped for the lotus blossom, which would signify something between a weak "maybe" and a fairly resolved "yes."

He dropped the result on the table.

Lotus blossom.

Johanna smiled with relief. "Thank you, Father."

"I haven't said anything yet."

"No need. Again, thank you. I suggest that you set up shop in here. It's close to the Throne Rome, and turfing out First Advisor Clench right away just seems cruel. We can let him occupy his current office for a while longer while he gets used to the idea of retirement."

"But..."

"I'll find a herald and put out a formal statement. I think it will be good for you. And good for me. And, if I may say so, good for the Northern Lands, too."

"I—"

Johanna stood, kissed her father on his cheek, and left the room before he could talk either of them out of it.

Chafed looked around his new office and muttered, "What just happened?" Then he picked up Johanna's copy of the realm's accounts and started making notes.

❧ 16 ❧

BEHIND FIPPLEDIP

"Lady Seneschal, I'm hoping you can help me with something," said Eloise, having tracked her down to a hallway near the kitchens.

"Your Highness, as I've said before, if you need something from me, you need to send a page to fetch me. Your time is more valuable than anyone's here at Court. I beg of you, please act like it."

Eloise sighed. "I have to admit, I haven't gotten used to ordering people around yet. It still goes against the grain to send someone on an errand that I can so easily do myself."

"And yet..."

"And yet, I know you are right."

"Don't think of it as ordering people around," said Lady Seneschal. "Think of it as asking for help from someone whose job it is to provide exactly that."

"I'll try to do better. Shall I go back to the Receiving Room and send a page?"

"In principle, yes. In practice, no. You're here. I'm here. Let's not waste any more time. What is it that you need?"

"I need a room to hold meetings. Can you assign me one?"

"A room to hold meetings? What's wrong with the Receiving Room? That's where the late queen and her late mother before her held their meetings. Sometimes they met in the Salle de la Famille for small, private gatherings. Your grandmother had meetings in the Queen's Study, although your mother didn't care for that, preferring it to be a sanctum sanctorum."

"I think I need something more private than the Receiving Room, but more public than the table in the Salle de la Famille. Something a little larger than my study, if possible. A table and chairs. Maybe a side table or two. Storage for scrolls. No need for a desk, I don't think. The tables will do. And blue, if you have it. I'd like a blue room."

"Why blue?"

"It's a nice color."

"Right."

"No windows. Also, it needs a lockable door with a new lock."

"No windows? Won't that be gloomy, especially if you're going to be in there a fair bit?"

"I thought there would be better privacy if there are no windows. Proximity to the Queen's Study would be good, if that can be arranged. I don't know of any rooms near it that fit the bill, but you might think of something I haven't."

"Noted." Lady Seneschal unscrolled the bit of hemp parchment she always kept with her, found a quill, and jotted some notes. "Why a new lock?"

"To give us a fresh start. And to minimize the likelihood that someone from who knows where got a copy of the key who knows how."

"Fine. Anything else?"

"Four sets of keys. One for me, one for Jerome, one for Lorch, and one for you, assuming you want one."

"If you feel you can trust me with it."

This struck Eloise as odd. She couldn't tell if Lady Seneschal was being deliberately snippy, or if this was some sort of test. "You have a copy of every other key needed in the castle, right?"

"Of course."

"Then please add this to your collection."

"Most kind, Your Highness. Thank you for your confidence."

Again, it wasn't clear if that was sarcasm, but Eloise let it slide.

"You don't want a set for First Advisor?"

"That's a very good question." Eloise hadn't thought of First Advisor Thëjëts when she'd been devising her Planning Room. It made sense to include her, and there was no obvious reason not to. "Make a set for her as well, but please give them to me to pass on."

"Consider it done, Your Highness."

It did not take Póòòmáäàdéëè long to find a reasonable possibility. That afternoon, RoyLee delivered a message to the Queen's Study. "The Lady Seneschal be requesting that you be meeting her in the Salon des Champions."

"Really? There?" said Eloise. "How interesting." She grabbed a robe and made her way through the chilly halls

The Salon des Champions, which Eloise and Jerome had always called the Mush Room because of the *champignon* pun they had cackled over when they were more than a decade younger, was a gallery of grouped paintings, each depicting a champion, next to the royal they served. There were hundreds of them—generations worth—reaching back to Agnes Delion Frostbite Gumball, the first Gumball monarch, and Townshend Bellicose Shinglehefter, the first champion. The only paintings missing so far were the ones of her and Jerome, and her and

Lorch. Eloise wondered who was in charge of making that happen. Lady Seneschal, maybe? Perhaps she'd bring it up.

Perhaps not. It wasn't like Eloise wanted to spend hour after hour sitting for a couple of portraits. She couldn't think of anything worse.

Eloise found Lady Seneschal in front of the paired portraits of Sylvia Cloisterfeld and her mother. She approached her from behind and chirped, "G'mid-arvo, Lady Seneschal."

Póöòmáäàdéëè spun around, startled. Her eyes were wet and red, and she shot Eloise a hateful look.

"Apologies," said Eloise, surprised by the fierceness of her expression. "I'm sorry I interrupted. Are you OK?"

"I'm fine," she snapped.

"I'll leave you alone and come back later."

Lady Seneschal's face slackened to neutral and drained of emotion. She dug a handkerchief from her sleeve, dabbed each eye exactly once, then spoke with her usual cold composure. "Not at all."

The moment passed, but it had been there. Eloise had seen it. *What was that all about?* "I don't want to intrude."

"There's no intrusion," said Póöòmáäàdéëè, as if the last fifteen seconds hadn't happened. "Thank you for coming. I believe I have a room for you. Please follow me."

Lady Seneschal led them to the very far end of the hall to a pair of portraits Eloise didn't recognize. She leaned forward and read the gallery label for the top one, which depicted a pinch-nosed queen with mouse-brown hair tortured into ringlet curls that, surely, were never in fashion and which would have been a complete pain to create. "Queen Aubrey the Parasitic. So that's what she looked like. I didn't know. And this is... Fortescue Fippledip, her champion, seen in the late evening. You know, I think I've walked past here a thousand times and never actually taken a moment to look at these two paintings."

"They're not that good," said Lady Seneschal. "You've likely saved yourself any number of minutes that were better spent in some other, more productive way, like washing socks or having teeth pulled."

That sounded like something Jerome might have said, and it was unexpected, coming from Lady Seneschal. "I see."

"As it stands, you'll be seeing plenty of them if you're happy with my proposed room." Póöòmáäàdéëè took five keys from her pocket and handed four to Eloise.

"The door is behind Queen Audrey and Fippledip?"

Lady Seneschal pointed at a dark spot in Fortescue Fippledip's right ear. "The key goes there."

Fippledip's painting had a hole in it, camouflaged by the dark shading of his ear. The key fit perfectly. When Eloise turned it, there was a definite *chunk-clunk!* as tumblers fell into place and the section of the wall behind the paintings swung inward on silent hinges.

Eloise walked into the darkness behind it.

The room had a just-been-cleaned smell, as if it had been musty for years, but had been given a scrub that morning. Lady Seneschal came in behind Eloise with a lit candle and walked along the walls lighting a dozen scented oil lamps. The room was a third bigger than the Queen's Study, but because it was more or less empty, it felt enormous. The walls were unfinished stone, deliberately left rough because no one was ever supposed to see them. The requested tables and chairs were arranged in a rectangle. The only decorations were three strange, dark tapestries that depicted cane toads dressed as crofters. They deserved whatever obscurity they had in this room.

"It was a storage room," said Póöòmáäàdéëè. "Apologies that it is not blue. I had it emptied and tidied. There wasn't time to have the tapestries removed, but that will happen shortly."

"That's OK. Leave them for now, please. They're weird, but oddly compelling. And don't worry about the color. The blue preference was just that—a preference." Eloise wandered around the room, touching the chairs, the tables, the walls. "What was in here before?"

"It was an odd collection of things one might call 'art' if one was being generous, but all of which deserved to be banished in here."

Eloise gestured at the cane toad tapestries. "Any of it better than this?"

"No. Definitely not."

"OK." Eloise found the exact center of the room, covered her blurry eye, then turned a full circle, getting a feel for the space. "I like it. Thank you for suggesting it, and for getting it ready for me."

"A pleasure as always, Your Highness," said Póöòmáäàdéëè. Again, Eloise couldn't tell if something was wrong. "Will you be needing anything else, Your Highness?"

"This should do for now."

17

SOMETHING FROM THE FAMILY CRYPT

Eldridge the Apothecary's daughter, Bërÿl, sat with Eloise in the Queen's Chambers and examined the cast on her wrist. "I bet you're ready to have this off, Your Highness."

"It's driving me spare," said Eloise. "I'm going to spend a week scratching at all the places I haven't been able to reach."

"I can imagine. It won't take all that long to get it off. I just need to be careful not to hurt you as I do it. So I'll go slower than you might expect."

"That's fine."

Bërÿl spread a towel across Eloise's lap to protect her clothes, then removed a tool from her father's healing satchel. It was a half circle with teeth like a saw, fixed to a handle, like part of a pair of scissors. "Ready?"

"More than ready."

The assistant apothecary gripped the handle, placed the blade edge against the cast, and began rocking it. The teeth bit into the hard surface, making a groove that went a little deeper with each half-circle movement. Plaster dust dribbled onto the towel as Bërÿl moved the device along Eloise's arm, creating a divot, then a channel.

"If it's not too distracting, may I ask after your father?"

"He told you he is ill, yes?"

"Yes, he did."

"It's worse. He's finding it harder and harder to get out of bed." She tapped Eloise's cast. "For routine matters like removing this, he's asked me to take over and not involve him."

"It will be sad to lose him."

Bërÿl hesitated. "I will be devastated. Absolutely gutted. You've met him. How could I not be? But at least I've had time to come to peace with the inevitable. As has he."

Eloise reached out with her left hand and gave the apprenticed apothecary's arm a gentle squeeze. "I'm sorry, Bërÿl. I really am."

Bërÿl sniffed and blinked back tears. "So am I. Thank you, Your Highness." As she cut through the plaster cast, she returned to business. "Your hand and wrist will be changed, but that's to be expected. They'll be weaker. There might be residual soreness or pain. I'll show you some stretches to improve flexibility and exercises to increase strength. I'll need you to do them several times a day. Can you do that?"

"Yes."

Eloise let the healer work in silence for a few moments, then asked, "Did your father happen to tell you about the other concerns I have?"

"Your eye and ear?"

"So he did."

"In detail."

"And?"

"And he has yet to find anything to help you. He's been going through his personal library of healer's notes and documents, but his ability to extend his research to the Bibliotheca de Records and Regrets is limited."

"I see. I'm sorry."

"He's asked me to take over his research, but to be honest, I don't feel I can leave him alone for long. I will have to redouble my efforts after..." She trailed off. "Just, after."

"I understand. Do what you can, but obviously your priority has to be your father. Do you need me to find someone to help tend him?"

"He is beloved. The healers organized themselves to take it in turns to see to him. It is a sign of his decline that he deigns to let them."

"I'm glad to hear he is well cared for. And again, if you need anything..."

"I'll let you know."

Bërÿl finished cutting through the hard plaster, revealing the length of cotton wadding beneath. She put down the saw, found a pair of bandage shears in her bag, and began scissoring through the padding layer.

"I'd like to formally ask if you would be willing to step into your father's role when the time comes."

The apprentice glanced up at Eloise, then returned to snipping. "Are you sure, Your Highness? There are many talented healers in the realm."

"Are you saying you don't want the role?"

Bërÿl paused and looked Eloise in the eyes. "Oh, I want it. I've been training for it my whole life." She returned to the last few weak lengths of plaster. "But I don't want to presume. And I don't want you to make a decision because you feel sorry for me or for my father."

"Feel sorry for you? I like you. I trust you. And, more importantly, your father trusts you, and I trust him."

The apprentice gripped the split cast and spread it so Eloise could remove her hand. She took off the padding and bandage beneath it, revealing the healed wrist and arm.

"My skin," said Eloise. "It looks like something we'd find down in the family crypt. And these lumps weren't there before. Not that I remember, anyway."

"That's where the bones have grown back together. Something like that is unsurprising." Bërÿl retrieved a bowl of warm water, some soap, and another towel from Eloise's vanity, and washed away the flakes of dead skin. She dried the arm and then gently manipulated the hand to test the movement. "How does it feel?"

"Bloody brilliant to get that thing off. The wrist feels fine so far."

"Good. Let me clean up the mess, then I'll show you the exercises."

The apprentice gathered the discarded cast and bandages, neatly folded the towel on Eloise's lap so the loose plaster dust didn't spill, and put her tools back in the satchel.

Eloise held her wrist in front of her face and turned her arm to examine it from all directions. "Bërÿl the Apothecary," she said. "It has a ring to it, doesn't it?"

"If you say so, Your Highness." But Bërÿl was smiling. "Thank you, ma'am."

18

LIKE A WEDDING

Lady Seneschal Póöòmáäàdéëè rapped on the door to the Queen's Study. "Queen Eloise, may I have a few minutes?"

"Of course, please come in." Eloise covered the parchment she was working on. "I could use a break."

Póöòmáäàdéëè eased through the door dressed in her usual black and holding the scroll she always carried as a kind of To Do List, a place for her to make notes, and sometimes a tool for rapping wayward staff on the noggin. "G'late arvo, Your Highness."

"G'late arvo to you as well. Would you like to have a seat?"

"Thank you."

Eloise moved to her armchair and invited Lady Seneschal to take the chair near to the left, positioned so it was closer to Eloise's buzz-free ear and her clear eye. "What's on your mind?"

"Your formal coronation, Your Highness."

Eloise slumped a little. "Ugh."

Lady Seneschal's face soured. "I beg your pardon?"

"Sorry, there's a lot going on. I really don't want to think about it yet. That's all."

Lady Seneschal pursed her lips. "Well, that's that then. Thank you for your time."

"Really?" Eloise felt a blossom of hope.

"Of course not. The event is rushing toward us, even though we don't have a firm date yet. There are people to invite. Entertainments to organize. A ceremony to coordinate. Lots and lots to get right, so the day is smooth, impressive, and memorable for the right reasons, not the wrong ones."

Eloise assumed this was a reference to her disastrous Crown Plonking ceremony, but let it slide. "How much time do I have?"

"Protocol spells it out, but there's wriggle room. Do you have a sense of when you'd like to do it?"

"Later rather than sooner?"

"That's fine. I can put together a list of proposed dates for you to approve."

"How about you pick a date that suits and just let me know."

"Fine." Lady Seneschal's scowl made it clear it wasn't, but she held her tongue. "Let's turn our attention to the guest list. Normally what you'd expect is that—"

Eloise put up a hand. "Please, Lady Seneschal. Just invite whoever you think should be invited. I trust you."

"Do you now." She unrolled the scroll and checked a note. "So, no input on the guest list. Shall we discuss the color scheme? How many feasts and balls you'd like to host? The number of—"

"I really am happy to leave it in your capable hands."

"And that's supposed to be enough?" sniped Póòòmáäàdéëè. "Or flattering? Or an adequate delegation of responsibility?"

"All I did was ask you to do what you would normally do anyway—competently put together something spectacular. Like I said, I trust you on it." Eloise watched the muscles in Póöòmáäàdéëè's jaw clench. "What's the matter? You're unhappy with that."

"Unhappy. Is that what you see? Not frustration? Not irritation? Not overwhelm?"

"Lady Seneschal, I ask that you remember to whom you're speaking."

"And now you play the queen card? Unbelievable. Really astounding."

Eloise felt heat rising in her face. Lady Seneschal was right. She'd only pulled that manner because she felt threatened. "My apologies."

"No, no. You have every right to do that. I just didn't think you were the type. I have known imperious queens. I had thought you unlikely to fall into that category."

Eloise stood, forcing Lady Seneschal to do the same. "Have you come here to argue? Is that why you're in my study?"

"I am in your study to discuss a vital matter and I don't think it is getting the degree of attention it deserves."

"My coronation? That's a vital matter? Not the attack on Flachberg or the fact that coffers are stretched? Have you spoken with the Exchequer of the Realm about financing the coronation?"

"I shall not concede the point. I believe you are shirking a duty."

"So now I'm a shirker?"

"Please, Your Highness. Stop. This is not how I intended this conversation to go."

"Well, it's gone that way."

They stared at each other for several very long moments.

Eloise broke the impasse by sitting. "Please, Lady Seneschal, have a seat. Let's start over." Her tone came nowhere close to matching the politeness of the words.

Póöòmáäàdéëè sat, unscrolled her parchment, checked something, and then let go one end so it could roll in on itself. "May I speak freely?"

"Please do."

"Queen Eloise, a coronation is similar to a wedding."

"You're not asking me to wear a veil, are you?"

"Please, don't be so literal. Tell me, what do you think makes for a good wedding?"

"I wouldn't know. Nice outfits? Good food? That sort of thing?"

"I've planned weddings. I also planned your mother's formal coronation. So I have some experience with this. A successful coronation, like a successful wedding, has little to do with what's worn or eaten."

"I'm listening."

"The difference between a good wedding and a not-so good-one lies in not following the usual path."

"What usually happens?"

"Usually, wedding planning follows the Golden Rule of Weddings, which stipulates that the person with the gold—that is, the person whose coin is being spent—makes the rules."

"That seems fair."

"Fair rarely comes into it," said Lady Seneschal. "The Golden Rule of Weddings more often than not leads to tears."

"What works better, then?"

"What works best is this: the happy couple has the wedding *they* want to have. They don't try to meet someone else's expectations. They don't fulfill someone else's vision of a wedding. They think, 'This is who we are. This is what we want.' And if the person with the coin is smart, they'll help them achieve that, whether it is a devotional house wedding with a thousand guests and a string quartet at the reception or sitting on a mountain top naked and drumming at the clouds for thirty minutes before opening up a couple of picnic hampers."

"OK."

"Because what you *don't* want is for the happy couple to be saying days, months, or years later, 'I wish we'd...' You don't want to look back with regret."

Eloise leaned back in her chair. "And how does this apply to me?"

"Isn't it obvious? You need to have the coronation that you want to have." Lady Seneschal crossed her arms in front of her and tapped the scroll against her bicep, a gesture Eloise had seen countless times. It was a tell that Lady Seneschal was trying to make sure she was being heard. "Sure, there are things that Protocol insists on, but even in that context, there's a lot of scope to make it personal and have it reflect who you are and the kind of queen you want to be. How fancy is the food? How many people are invited? Do you do something for people who aren't invited or who can't come? What do you wear? What do you say? What should the decorations involve?"

"That's a lot to think about."

"It is. And while you can (and will) delegate some of it to me and my staff, it is up to you to choose the tone, the direction, and the feeling you want to convey."

"I see."

"So you understand, you can't just say to me, 'Go handle it.' I could, but it would be wrong of me to do so. I'd no sooner plan a wedding without making sure to first understand the wants of the happy couple."

"Right." Eloise gently rapped her left knuckles on her right wrist. "OK, yes."

"Yes, what, Your Highness?"

"Yes, I'll participate. Yes, I'll figure out what kind of coronation I'd like. Yes, I'll provide input."

"Good. Excellent."

"Can you do something for me?"

"Certainly."

"Come up with a list of things you need me to decide and think about. Then have First Advisor book you in a few slots so we can go through it."

"I'll do that. I'll have a list for you first thing in the morning."

"I can hardly wait."

Lady Seneschal's cheek twitched, but she held back what she felt like saying, which was, "I can hardly wait for you to hide from your responsibility again." Instead, she offered a simple, "Thank you, Your Highness" and left Eloise alone.

She hadn't gotten exactly what she'd come for. Far from it. But the child had taken a step in the right direction. Thank merciful Çalaht.

That would have to do. For now.

BARN BURNER

T he Velvet Cask was as upmarket a public inn as Eloise had ever seen. On her travels, she had eaten and slept in inns that embraced the word "dump" as a guiding principle and then built out a whole philosophy around it, as expressed in decor.

Not the Velvet Cask. From the moment she, Lorch, and Jerome stepped through the door, Eloise realized that not every drinking establishment made you want to scrub your skin with pumice for a week. The whole place, from the black-painted ceiling to the purple velvet-clad walls to the polished ironwood floors, felt clean and inviting. Sofas with low tables filled the room, arranged in an arc facing a well-lit stage, and they were filled with patrons wearing their finest robes and sipping beverages served in bulbous mugs with little decorative umbrellas. Eloise wanted to take off the cloak she wore to obscure her identity and nestle into one of the comfy couches.

A panda wearing a bow tie and the black and white tunic and breeks of a maître d' approached them. "Welcome to the Velvet Cask. How may I—Oh. Your Highness. I... Uh... We didn't realize..." The panda bowed, then bowed again, lower, unsure how much bowing Protocol would demand in the setting.

"The reservation is in my name," said Jerome. "Under Abernatheen de Chipmunk. We're trying to not attract attention, which I'm sure you understand. So, a little less bowing would be OK. Her Highness is merely trying to avail herself of the ambience and umbrella beverages offered by your fine establishment, and to listen to a little music."

"I see."

"I asked for a spot in the back."

"That sofa is hardly fit for a queen. You must let me——"

"No, no. That will be fine," said Eloise. "And if you could keep my presence here quiet, I'd be most grateful."

The panda swallowed, nodded, started to bow again, stopped himself, then waved them forward. "Yes, Your Highness. Everyone, please follow me."

Their sofa was an overstuffed three-seater in a purple velvet that matched the walls. They sat, and the panda handed each of them a page of hemp parchment. "This is the beverage list. A serving wench will be with you shortly, but if you need anything at all during the evening, please let me know."

"Thank you. You're most kind. Remember, mum's the word, yes?"

The panda reflexively bowed again. "Of course," and left them.

Eloise looked over the drinks menu. "Ugh."

"What?" said Jerome.

"The drink names don't exactly say, 'That's yummy.' 'Bilge Blaster.' 'Snort This Through Your Ear.' 'Jester's Belch.' 'Unpalatable Acts With Unlikely Consequences.' How's their haggleberry tea?"

"It's fine. They prefer it if you drink something with a stupid name because they make more coin from it, but I usually just get tea as well. It's not the best I ever had—they steep it for a couple of minutes too long and their water is a few degrees too hot, which bruises the leaves. But it's palatable."

A waitress took their orders, and as their tea and scotch finger cookies arrived, a second panda hopped onto the stage, garnering surprisingly robust applause. The panda wore a purple velvet sequined tunic and breeks with a matching sequin bow tie, make-up that rouged his cheek fur like an out-of-work jester, and a blonde toupee that would have embarrassed a fright wig. "Ladies and gentlemen, welcome to the Velvet Cask Cabaret," he cooed. "I'm Martin de Ursidae, your host for the evening."

"I love you, Marty!" yelled a woman in the crowd.

"Me, too," yelled a man across the room.

"Be chill, everyone. There's plenty of Marty to go around."

The audience chuckled, but it seemed fake.

Eloise wrinkled her nose and nudged Jerome. "What's the gig? It seems forced."

"The schtick is a kind of an in-joke. Everyone pretends to love Marty. Marty pretends to not want to leave the stage, but eventually he introduces the first act and they get on with it."

"There's more than one act? How long are we going to be here?"

"There are half a dozen acts through the night, but Sylvia is on third. She's working her way up the line-up, but doesn't really have much traction yet. If you want, we can leave after we talk to her."

"She knows we're here, right?"

"Uh..." Jerome's face hair flattened, a sure sign he was about to deliver a whopper. "Let's put it this way—"

"You didn't tee up a conversation?"

"I thought it would be a nice surprise for her."

"Jer, having the queen show up at your singing gig unannounced is no one's idea of a good time, even if she could kill me with the stub of a burned-out candle for doing so." Eloise stood and waved at the maître d', but his back was turned.

Lorch stood. "I'll get you a quill and parchment so you can write her a note."

"Good idea. Thanks."

As Lorch left, Martin de Ursidae said, "Our first act is new to our stage, a quartet of siblings who've been polishing their act since they were pups in the sand box. It's the Juggling Jerboas!"

Four jerboas came through the curtain at the back and positioned themselves in a line on the stage. The rodents looked like miniature kangaroos, with long back legs, short little forelegs, long tails, and a hopping gait. Each juggled three small, bright green balls, first with their forearms, then with their feet while lying on their backs. At a yell from one of them, still on their backs, they started passing the balls between them—an astounding display of agility, timing, and skill. "That's amazing," whispered Eloise, joining the applause.

"Keep watching," said Jerome.

At another yell, Marty the MC wheeled a hoop to the middle of the stage, and lit it with a candle. The jerboas began tossing the balls through the flaming ring, and one by one, the balls caught fire. Marty blew out the stage candles, and all Eloise could see were the fiery spheres flying back and forth between the rodents, crisscrossing, barely missing each other. At a final yell, they flung the balls in an arc toward a table at the front, where they cascaded into a beer mug and hissed out, plunging the stage into total darkness.

The crowd broke into thunderous clapping and whistling as Marty panda-danced around the stage, relighting the candles. The rodents clasped hands and bowed in unison. The "I love you, Marty" woman yelled, "I love you, Juggling Jerboas!" and blew them kisses. They bowed again and exited, leaving Marty to launch back into his patter.

"That really was something," said Eloise.

Jerome nodded. "Thought you might like it."

"Bad news," said Lorch as he returned with the quill, ink, and parchment. "There are gossip heralds here tonight, and you've been spotted."

"Really? Çalaht on a bungled blueberry brioche, I hate them," said Eloise. "Should we leave?"

"No point. You'd just draw attention to your having been here, and you'd miss the chance to talk to Sylvia."

"It's like a queen isn't allowed to slip out of the castle every once in a while."

"Don't worry about it, El. Just focus on having a nice time."

"I guess." She took the quill and ink, scratched out a quick note asking Sylvia if they could speak after her performance, and gave it to Lorch, who took it to the maître d' to pass on.

Marty the MC wheeled on the second act: a cart carrying a pair of thick-bodied black adders, each roughly two dozen weak lengths long. On the cart with them were thirty-six wine glasses of different sizes, all filled to different levels.

"Ladies and gentlemen!" said Marty. "I present you the glasstastic musical stylings of the Sound Vipers!"

The snakes raised their heads and bowed. Then, in perfect unison, they lowered their chins toward the water, dipping in just enough to wet the area underneath their heads. Lifting back out, they began swaying in a clockwise circle above each glass, lowering themselves carefully until they were rubbing around the rims of the glasses, setting off ringing vibrations.

"Johanna and I used to do this with our forefingers at feast day celebrations," whispered Eloise. "It drove our mother spare, although Father usually joined in."

"I bet you didn't do it like these two snakes," said Jerome. "Listen."

He was right. The snakes began moving from glass to glass, setting off different pitches, sometimes in harmony, and sometimes with deliberate dissonance, but without pattern or rhythm. Then one of them counted off, "A-one, a-two, a-three, a-four, and a..." And, fast as lightning, the adders swept from glass to glass, setting off ringing chords and notes, and hissing out lyrics.

"What's that song?" asked Eloise.

"A classic," said Jerome. "'(Because You're Mine) I Slither the Line.'"

"Right."

This was followed by "Stand By Your Serpent," "Bye Bye Glove," "Viva Las Vermin," and a very sweet love song, "You Can Kiss My Asp."

When they were done, the crowd cheered, and the snakes bowed as Marty rolled the cart back through the curtain.

"I liked them," said Lorch, who'd come back to the table during the set. "You should get them to play at your coronation."

Eloise looked at him. "My coronation? What made you think about that?"

"You're only crown-plonked at the moment," said Jerome. "Surely someone's planning out the full coronation ceremony?"

"Lady Seneschal raised that issue just this afternoon. She gave me a lecture on weddings."

"What do weddings have to do with anything?"

"Something about golden rules and happy couples."

"Whatever. It's good that you're not putting it off too long. I'm sure Protocol has rules for when it has to happen."

"It does. Lady Seneschal is all over them."

"Good."

The panda lumbered back onstage and shushed the murmuring crowd. "Let's welcome back a woman who's fast becoming a regular attraction here at the Velvet Cask. She used to slice through enemies of the queen. Now she slices open our hearts with music. Ladies and gentlemen, once a champion at Court, now a champion of our stage, Sylvia Cloisterfeld!"

A trio of musicians came onto the stage carrying their instruments—a lute, a sackbut, and a viol. It struck Eloise as an odd combination, but there wasn't much time to wonder about that, as they immediately struck up their first notes. Cloisterfeld burst through the curtain, and Eloise barely recognized her. Gone were the gauntlets, chain mail, and champion's sword, along with the sash embroidered with the Gumball coat of arms. Sylvia Cloisterfeld looked fabulous in a simple slinky, sleeveless black shift that showed off her muscled arms to full effect.

And her voice! Cloisterfeld entered while belting out a barn-burner version of "Cry Me a Reasonably Large Creek," moved straight into "Inadequate Romance," which blended seamlessly into "I Wanna Morris Dance With Somebody." When she finally stopped after "Hatched This Way," the room burst into a raucous standing ovation that lasted a full five minutes.

She answered their cries of "More! More!" by holding up a hand and asking for quiet. "Thank you," she said. "If you know this one, feel free to join in." The trombone-like sackbut began a slow, grinding solo, with a melody that tickled with familiarity. The lute took over, winding in, out, and around the sackbut, and finally, the viol player took up her bow and joined in. It was sultry, somber, plaintive. Then Sylvia Cloisterfeld began the first verse, and the crowd sang with her.

"There's a lady who knows all that glitters is groats..."

"Oh," whispered Eloise. "This. 'Three Bags of Groats For My Sweetheart.'"

"Yep," said Jerome. "But listen to how she does it."

"I'm going to have this in my head for a week. Worse, you're going to have it in yours, and you're going to keep putting it back in mine."

"Probably. Now, shhh."

Jerome was right. Eloise had heard the famous diva Lydia Thrind sing it, as well as Jaminity Delgado Blister, who wrote it, and Gouache

Snotearrow McCcoonnch, her uncle Doncaster's second jester, who came alive when it came out of his mouth. She'd sung it in public herself, once in a Çalahtist devotional house when she was off her skull under the influence of prattleweed, and once to a throng of horses in tribute to the hospitality and friendship provided by the khan of the Central Ranges and the Us.

So, yeah, she had more than a passing familiarity with the song.

But Cloisterfeld brought something different to it. An impish quality. A delivery that was curious about the lyric, but avoided sliding into mockery, like the singer sort of wanted to take the story seriously, but knew not to. When she got to the end where the singer convinces his sweetheart to trade the three bags of groats for true love's first kiss, the listener couldn't exactly be sure who in the song struck the better end of that bargain. Perhaps both. Perhaps neither.

Either way, Sylvia Cloisterfeld sang the heck out of it, so much so that for just a little while, Eloise was able to ignore the buzzing in her ear and the blurriness of her eye. What a relief.

Once again, the crowd went wild, and the three of them couldn't help but join in. Cloisterfeld smiled, genuinely pleased, and then her mother's champion did something Eloise had never even hinted at—the always stoic, ever-watching, ready-to-spring-into-lethal-action warrior teared up. Then, with a curtsy, she and the accompanists retreated through the curtain.

"Well, who knew?" said Eloise.

Jerome nodded. "I know, right?"

Silently, the maître d' appeared. "Mistress Cloisterfeld invites you to speak in her dressing room, if that would suit. It will be quieter and more private than out here."

"Certainly."

❧ 20 ❧

LEGITIMATE REASONS

The panda led Eloise, Jerome, and Lorch along a side wall and through a curtained doorway, down a dark hall, and into a lighted space behind the stage. A series of closed doors led to dressing rooms, and each had a piece of hemp parchment tacked to it with the name of one of the acts. "Here you go," said the maître d', and he gently knocked on the door with Sylvia's name. "Mistress Cloisterfeld, your admirers are here."

"Send them in, send them in."

The panda opened the door and let them pass into the tiny dressing room. With them all in there and the door closed, there was an uncomfortable togetherness.

Cloisterfeld now wore a dressing gown pulled over her shift, and she bowed (not curtsied) to Eloise, a military-grade bow that reflected the exact dictates of Protocol. Standing straight again, the blonde-haired woman towered a full head taller than her. "Your Highness. What a surprise. You honor me with your attendance."

"You really were incredible," said Eloise. "Really wonderful. I particularly liked what you did with 'Three Bags of Groats for My Sweetheart.'"

"Thank you, Your Highness. That's very generous of you to say so."

"No, I mean it. Really, really good."

"You're too kind. Of course, I've known the song for years, but I was inspired when I heard the Northo jester sing it for the late queen when the late Half Kingdom king visited."

"Northern Lands," said Eloise.

"I beg your pardon?"

"Queen Johanna is trying to reinstate the use of 'the Northern Lands' instead of 'the Half Kingdom.' So, I'm trying to help her with that."

"I see. Well, then, I heard the *Northern Lands* jester sing it when the *Northern Lands* king visited. Anyway, his performance piqued something inside me, and, after everything that's happened in the months since then, well, here we are."

"Yes, here we are. All I can say is that you really do deserve a bigger audience."

"Well, if I've learned anything, it's that the only way to have the chance of pleasing a large audience is by pleasing a lot of smaller audiences along the way. Step by step by step. That's what I'm doing."

"I must say, I'm impressed."

They stood there, an awkward silence building, as Eloise wasn't sure how to broach the subject.

Cloisterfeld helped. "Is there something else?"

"Yes, actually. There is. I'm not sure how to phrase it."

"How about directly? It was your mother's way, and it served her."

"True." Eloise didn't add that she was now seeing things that were her mother's way that might not have been as awesome as she had thought. "OK, direct. Champion Cloisterfeld, I'd like to ask you if you could train our soldiers in the ways of fighting."

"I see. Yes, well, that was certainly direct." Sylvia pulled her dressing gown tighter around herself. "With respect, Queen Eloise, thank you for the offer, but no thank you."

"No? Really?" Eloise felt herself sink. "May I ask why not?"

"I've given my service, Your Highness. Not necessarily to you, but to your mother and to the queendom. Decades of service. Year after year, my first and last waking thoughts were about the queen's safety, the king's safety, too, for that matter, and your and your sister's safety, along with the potential vulnerabilities posed by Court and the castle itself. I trained and sweated every day to remain in top condition and was ready to deploy a variety of weapons. I tracked political winds to be aware of threats and ensured protective measures shielded the late queen and those around her."

"That makes you perfect for this role."

"No, it doesn't."

"Again, why not?"

Eloise could see red creeping up Cloisterfeld's neck and into her cheeks, but it wasn't clear if it was out of anger or some other agitation. Embarrassment, perhaps?

"Because of how your mother died."

"That wasn't your fault. Someone slipped raw haggleberries into her pie."

"There you're wrong. Not about the haggleberries, but it was absolutely my fault. Her safety was my responsibility. Her death stains my psyche and hangs like the Purple Haze above my reputation and my remaining days. I will never, ever escape what happened under my watch."

"I—"

"Please, let me finish. If I go back to the castle and take up the role, all I will ever be is that champion who let her queen die. Out there..." She pointed through the wall toward the stage. "Out there, I can forget my failures for a few minutes. I can be someone other than what I am when I am not on that stage. Your Highness, I understand that you may need help. But I'm really not your woman. I can't be."

"Please, Champion Cloisterfeld—"

"You shouldn't call me that."

"I disagree. You were champion, and despite what you just said, you served my mother with honor and devotion. So I will refer to you as such." Eloise gestured, palms up. "You're right. My mother died. We all have to live with that. And maybe, just maybe, there was a system in place or some level of protection that failed. Maybe. But you know as well as anyone that sheer will alone is not enough to keep someone alive. You can take responsibility for her death, but only as far as your role reached, and only within the limits of human capability. But you did not cause my mother to die, nor did you spur on the hateful actors who killed her. You did your best for her. You can 'what if' yourself to the grave, but it won't bring the queen back."

"It is generous of you to say that, but words are a thin salve."

"Champion Cloisterfeld, the queendom needs you. *I* need you. For that matter, the memory of my mother needs you."

"I don't know that you can say that."

"But it's true. We are under threat. You've heard what happened in Flachberg?"

"Of course."

"That aggression can't remain unanswered. But we are under-prepared. I'm trying to change that, but I need people to help me. I need *you* to help me. I won't ask you to honor some sense of duty. You have filled that ledger and written on the back of it. But I am asking you to help me in my time of need. To help the queendom in its time of danger."

The tiny space felt crowded and overheated. Eloise hadn't thought the conversation would be so intense, but the more she spoke, the more the need for Cloisterfeld's help solidified.

The former champion shook her head slowly. She didn't speak, but Eloise got the sense that her argument wasn't carrying.

"Look, Champion Cloisterfeld. You don't have to think of this as a forever thing. It can be temporary. A few months, perhaps. I can't say how long, but it can be a temporary engagement, not a permanent one."

"I know what Court is like. I know the demands of a queen. Court does not easily let go of that which gets in its clutches."

"I can put it in writing. Or maybe we can come to some sort of accord that would benefit you as well."

"With respect, Queen Eloise—and also with respect, I can't tell you how it tears my heart to address you with that title—I don't think there's anything you have to offer that could tempt me. I don't need coin. I don't need status. I no longer crave a role at Court. It is a relief to be away." She motioned again to the stage. "This is what I want. This is where I want to be. Not teaching the uncoordinated and the unready how to wield a sword."

"Audience," blurted Jerome.

"What?" said Eloise.

"I said audience."

"We're having an audience. This is an audience."

"Not this kind." He pointed in the same direction as Sylvia had. "That kind."

"What about it?"

"We can deliver one," said the chipmunk. "A big one."

Eloise looked at him and suddenly understood.

"Champion Cloisterfeld, he's right. I can guarantee you an audience. A big one. The biggest one."

"How big?"

"Help me out, and it can be as big as you want. Thousands big. Once-in-a-generation big."

The woman's eyebrows narrowed. Interest and wariness warred on her face. "What do you mean?"

"I mean, I can have you perform at my formal coronation. And at the reception. And at a special Queen's Gala Performance, if you want. You name it, and I'll make sure it happens."

"Really? You'd do that? You think I'm good enough?"

"I know you're good enough. It would be a delight for you to be part of the celebrations."

Cloisterfeld crossed her arms across her chest, tilted her head a little, and got a far-off look on her face. Then she smiled and bowed a soldier's bow. A champion's bow. "Queen Eloise, I'd be honored. Thank you."

Eloise felt relief flooding her. She wanted to hug the woman, but didn't know her that well.

She hugged her anyway.

"Thank you. Sorry for the hug, but thank you. We'll work out the details, but I'll make sure you're happy."

"I'm sure you will."

"Welcome back to Court. I'm grateful."

Cloisterfeld flinched a little. "It's not the Court part I'm looking forward to. But it is part of the package. I understand."

"Well, this is wonderful. Thank you again. We'll leave you be."

"Queen Eloise, I'm glad you enjoyed the performance. And thank you for the opportunity to sing for you again."

"Not a problem." Eloise turned to leave, but hesitated, and then turned back. "Actually, there's one other thing."

The champion looked wary. "Oh?"

Eloise clasped her hands in front of her and looked down at them. "I'd like, if you're willing, to have fighting lessons as well."

"Whatever for, Your Highness?"

"I feel like I need to know."

"You had Weapons and Stratagems classes growing up. Surely that's enough tutelage."

"It's been years. And it always struck me as fake fighting. Not real. Like no one was allowed to pose a genuine threat to a young princess."

"Probably true. I wasn't part of the classes, so I can't say."

"Also, I can't ask soldiers to do something that I'm not willing to do myself."

"A noble sentiment, Your Highness," said Cloisterfeld. "But a foolish one, if I may say so."

"Why?"

"You need to think in terms of specialization. You, as queen, need to specialize in leadership, strategy, and motivation, and let other people specialize in spilling blood."

"I understand what you're saying. But consider it from my point of view. I've had crossbow bolts shot at me, toxins in my correspondence, and a jester who shoved me into a hole so deep I should never have been able to escape it. And that was not long after he pushed me backwards into a campfire. I've been face slapped by a king who was much bigger than me, and thrown into a deadly magical fog by someone three times my size. And that's just listing things off the top of my head. Trust me, I have legitimate reasons to want to learn how to defend myself. I would be grateful if you could teach me at least some of your craft."

"Right. I didn't know all that," said Sylvia. "That's... That's a lot. Quite a lot."

"Yes. It is."

The former champion looked Eloise up and down, then stood and extended her hand. "Would tomorrow work for you?"

Eloise took the offered hand and shook it. It was like shaking hands with a granite statue. "How about tomorrow morning?"

Cloisterfeld smiled. "Yes, Your Highness. I'll be there first thing."

21

BREAKFAST SOUP

"**B**lessings of the day, Queen Eloise," said Jerome as he walked into the Salle de la Famille the next morning. "How goes it?"

"It goes," said Eloise as she flipped through a stack of correspondence that First Advisor Thëjëts had given her the day before. Eloise hadn't been able to face it, and now she was running out of time if she was going to get through it before her morning briefing. "Did you know that I get marriage proposals several times a week?"

"No. I didn't know that."

"Well, I do."

"Good practice."

Eloise glanced up from the letter she was reading. "Pardon?"

"I said, 'Good practice.'"

She stared at him, silent.

"You said, 'I do.' And I was saying that saying, 'I do' is good practice for when it comes time to get married."

She blinked at him.

"It was a joke, El."

"Right. Got it. Ha ha." She went back to her letter. "Sit. Breakfast just arrived. I'll have mine in a minute. Start if you want. I'll be with you in a sec."

"OK. Thanks."

"Just don't eat the soup."

"No soup. Got it." Jerome jumped up on the table and considered the pile of pastries. Then he paused. "Did you say 'soup?' It's first thing in the morning. Why is there soup?"

"It's breakfast soup, apparently."

"Breakfast soup?" said Jerome. "What is breakfast soup?

"I have no idea. From the look of it, it involves boysenberries and not a lot else."

"Is it hot? Warm? Cold?"

"Dunno. I only glanced at it. Just don't eat it. There's something wrong with it."

"Noted." Jerome went back to the pastries, debating whether to go for a sweet roll, a croissant, a muffin, or some tea cake. Or maybe a bit of each.

There was a clatter in the hall, and the door to the Salle de la Famille slammed, accompanied by frenetic wombat claws skittering on stone. It was RoyLee looking frantic. "Princess Queen Eloise! Princess Queen Eloise! Stop!"

"What's the matter?"

"Stop!" RoyLee ran toward the table, tripped, and tumbled toward Eloise. He righted himself and kept running. "Don't be eating the soup! No soup!"

"It's OK, RoyLee. It's OK. I'm not eating the soup."

"Thanks be to Çalaht you're OK. I thought you be a goner."

"A goner?" said Jerome. "What's going on with the soup?"

"Chef be taken ill. He be coming down with a powerful strong stomach ache."

Jerome wrinkled his nose. "That's no good."

"And he be making the breakfast soup!" RoyLee's hair stood up on his back and he gasped for air. "Be you having the breakfast soup? Do I be needing to get you the healer or the apothecary?"

"No RoyLee,: said Eloise. "Thank you, but no thank you. I didn't have any of the breakfast soup."

The wombat slumped against the wall, trying to regain his breath. "That be so good to hear." *Wheeze!* "I be powerful worried."

"But, you can see I'm OK, right. And so is Jerome."

"Wombats don't be seeing so very much."

"Of course. You were part of the Wombanditos, the fiercest gang with bad eyesight in all the realms."

"Heeyahhhh!" gasped RoyLee.

"Heeyahhh!" echoed Eloise. "Thank you for rushing here to warn me. I appreciate it."

"You're welcome, Princess Queen Eloise. I'll be getting one of the serving wenches to come take the breakfast soup away."

"No hurry."

RoyLee left and Eloise again turned her attention to her paperwork. After a minute or so, she realized Jerome wasn't making breakfast noises, so she glanced at him.

He was staring at her.

"What?"

"How did you know?" asked Jerome.

"How did I know what?"

"How did you know about the breakfast soup?"

"What are you talking about?"

"You said, 'Don't eat the soup.' How did you know to say that?"

"I don't know. It looked wrong. Who cares?"

Jerome leaned forward. "What do you mean, it looked 'wrong?' It's soup. In a tureen. How can soup look wrong?"

"I really don't know, Jer. It was a breakfast soup. I got a sense of 'wrong' from it. I'm not sure how complicated this is."

The chipmunk pointed at her. "That. That right there. It just seems odd. You said to me 'don't have it,' and then moments later, RoyLee's slamming through the door yammering about not having any. To the casual observer, that comes across as unusual."

Eloise slid the pile of documents away, folded her arms, and leaned back in her chair. "I'm listening."

A serving wench appeared in the doorway, a woman in her late teens wearing a scullery maid's uniform. "Pardon me, Your Highness, but may I clear the soup? I can bring you something else, if you'd like."

"Hold on, please. Can you leave it for just a little while longer?" said Jerome. "Maybe come back in twenty minutes?"

"Of course, Assistant Seer to the Court Seer Abernatheen de Chipmunk."

When the door was closed again, Eloise said, "You're making a canyon out of a crack."

"Humor me, El. I'm your Assistant Seer to the Court Seer. That has to be worth a few minutes."

"Go ahead. What do you want me to do?"

"Can you recount the steps that got you here this morning?"

"Sure. I was born in—"

"Please, Queen Eloise."

"Oooh, all formal. OK." Eloise sighed and idly began stretching her wrist the way Bëryl had shown her. "I got up, got dressed, grabbed that stack of things to read from my bedside table. I'd taken them to bed to read before I fell asleep, but sleep didn't take long to come, as I was reading something about sheep flock unionization and whether they were going to join with an alpaca flock collective action effort. I came out of the Queen's Chamber into the Salle de la Famille. Breakfast was already laid out. I glanced at it, but wasn't ready to eat, so I sat down and went back to my reading. I read through several scrolls—three maybe—and then you came in. When you went over to the food, I warned you."

"Again, why? Think about it."

"It wasn't a conscious thing. I just did it."

"Huh. Let me ask it differently. When did you first get a sense of wrongness?"

Eloise switched to stretching her other wrist. She'd gotten into the habit of doing both wrists, just to keep things balanced. "Let me think." She closed her eyes and replayed the sequence in her head, starting with when she stepped from the Queen's Chamber into the Salle de la Famille. Walking to her chair. Putting down her reading. Sitting down. Glancing at the food, then back to her reading. By then, she already had the sense that the soup was off somehow. "When I looked at breakfast just after I sat."

"Hmmm..." Jerome's tail twitched as he thought. "Can we try something?" He walked to the tray and slid away all the dishes and other food, leaving the soup tureen on its own. "Go ahead. Look at it again. Do you still get the sense of wrong?"

"Yes." The strength of the feeling surprised Eloise. "Yes, I do."

"Can you tell how?"

"I'm not sure. Give me a sec." She closed her eyes again. How *had* she perceived it? She sniffed. Not that. She hadn't tasted it, so that wasn't it. Soup didn't have a sound, unless it was being slurped, so that probably wasn't it, but she listened anyway. Nothing. She opened her eyes and looked. There was the sense of it. How odd. She closed her eyes a third time and opened them again. Still there. She saw Jerome scrutinizing her, but she ignored him. She used a palm to cover her blurry eye and looked with the clear one. Nothing particularly jumped out at her. She swapped hands and looked with her blurry eye.

Eloise gasped.

"El? El, what's wrong?"

"I can see it." She turned to Jerome, eye still covered. "I see the danger."

"What does it look like?"

She looked again. "It's like a feeling fused with a color."

"That doesn't make sense."

"That's the only way I can think to describe it. My skin crawls and my stomach clenches, and it's inextricably imbued with red. If I had to name it, it would be something like 'danger red,' but that's a very blunt way to describe it."

"You must have gotten just enough of that when you glanced at the soup for it to register in your mind, but not enough for it to have taken your full attention." Jerome's tail twitched even more. "What happens if you look at the sweet roll?"

"Happy blue."

"The tea?"

Eloise covered her left eye and looked at it. "The teapot is happy blue, but the blue is really faint, like the happy part isn't all that strong. The tea itself is disappointed brown."

"Really? Why?"

"I think because it's now too cold and won't be all that nice to drink."

"What if it was fresh-brewed the way you prefer it?"

Eloise lifted one shoulder and let it drop. "I'd only be guessing. I'd have to see."

"Let's get some," said Jerome.

Eloise looked at the door. "RoyLee! Are you there?"

The wombat popped into the doorway. "Yes?"

"Could I please get a fresh pot of tea?" asked Eloise.

RoyLee sprinted away calling, as always, "Tea for the queen! Tea for the queen!"

"I have so many questions," said Jerome. "Like, how long have you had this? If it's new, what caused it? What else can you detect? Can you command this gift at will, or do certain conditions have to be in place?"

"This 'gift?' You're getting way ahead of yourself. I kept you from getting a tummy ache from some wonky soup. It's not like I've been revealed to possess some great power of weak magic."

Jerome looked at her.

"What?"

"Magic. This is something new. I mean, you've never talked about it before."

"Alright, so it's new."

"What else is new?"

Eloise put her hands to her temples and massaged them. "Jerome, I have a strong weight's worth of stuff I need to do. Just say it. Please."

Jerome walked over to her and put his paw on her arm. "I don't mean to be obscure. Two last questions. You say that the blur and ear ring are with you all the time, right?"

"Yes."

"And the blur and ring started when you used the Star of Whatever to amplify the Orb of Alleged Omniscience to work out what happened with your mother and what's going on in Flachberg."

"Yes."

"So it seems pretty straightforward logic to say that using magic the way you did has affected you."

"This isn't news. These..." She gestured to her eye and ear. "These problems are clearly the result of what I did."

"Yes. But what I'm suggesting is that it might not just be a blur and a ring. I'm saying that you've been altered some way, in some *magical* way, that's not obvious, that is lasting, and that helped you know that the soup was dangerous."

"Your saying my magical malady might not just be a malady."

"I'm thinking of it more as a result."

"Rather than an injury."

Jerome nodded. "This has affected you, but we don't know how, exactly. But something has changed in your brain."

"That's a bit dramatic, don't you think?"

"Seems like a cold fact to me. The blurriness in your eye and the buzzing in your ear are manifestations of something that happened. Manifestations that you don't really understand. That you *can't* really understand, perhaps."

Eloise's throat suddenly went dry, and she was glad she was sitting. "This is big."

"I think it might well be." Jerome squeezed her arm then let it go. "It's like you mucked with so much magic that you got stained by it somehow."

"Stained. I don't like how that sounds."

"Stains aren't necessarily bad," said Jerome. "But they're sometimes hard to remove."

"And a stain is a bit of whatever caused the stain, that sticks around," said Eloise. "So a magical stain would be like small, residual splotch of magic stuck to me. A little connection with the spark of something in the Star of Whatever that's not coming out. That's always with me now."

"It's an analogy, but it seems like a sound one." Jerome smoothed down his whiskers. "Weird."

"I know. Weird."

Jerome's tail twitched one more time. "There is an obvious question. I'm not sure I wanna ask it, though."

"What's the obvious question?"

"Just how dangerous is that magical stain?"

22

MASTER CLOISTERFELD

"So, where do we start?"

Eloise stood in an echo-filled training hall on rush-covered floor mats dressed in her usual exercise breeks and tunic. Sylvia Cloisterfeld stood opposite her, not in sequins like last night but in tunic and breeks, reminiscent of the champion's outfit from her time serving her mother.

"With those." Sylvia pointed to a set of staves resting horizontally in a wall-mounted rack, each a uniform length-and-a-half long, but with different thicknesses and each made of different wood. Next to these was a second rack that held a series of wooden practice swords of differing sizes and shapes, both one-handed and two-handed. "And this." She took a wooden knife from a pocket and extended it on her open palm.

Eloise took it.

"You just lost all of your fingers and half your thumb."

"Sorry?"

"The way you handled the knife. You grabbed the blade. Right now, your enemy is either beating you to a pulp, stabbing you with your own knife, or laughing at the fact that you're having to pick your fingers up off the ground."

This irked Eloise. "It isn't a real blade."

"How do you know that?"

"I'm looking at it. I can see that it isn't a real blade. It's made of wood."

"That's a dangerous assumption."

"There's no assumption there at all. It's wood. I can see it's wood. There's no edge on the blade. It's as blunt as my elbow."

"Looks can deceive, Your Highness." A twinge of sarcasm coated her words. "How do you know it isn't a clever, vicious simulacrum of a false knife? Or maybe a real knife that somehow has weak magic that camouflages its true nature?"

"Right."

"Exactly. Hand the knife back to me. No, handle-first and holding the blade so that your fingers are safe. Offering someone a knife, even in training, is an exercise in trust and vulnerability. In this hall, we treat the practice weapons as if they were sharpened to lethality. It's a good habit to get into because, in the right hands, they *are* lethal. In fact, anything, in the right hands, can be lethal. Part of your training will be to recognize those possibilities in the things around you."

"Why?"

"To consider how you could use them against someone."

"Oh. OK."

"And to consider how they could be used against *you*, and what you could do about it."

"I see. That's a mindset I'm going to find strange."

Cloisterfeld raised two open palms. "All of this is optional. If you don't want me—"

"No, no, no. I want to. It's just going to take some adjusting, that's all."

"Rest assured, Your Highness, you have no idea how much adjusting there will be." She clasped her hands behind her back. "Do you have any questions before we get down to it?"

Eloise looked down at the wooden blade in her hand, which she still held in a way that would have cost her fingers. She adjusted her grip to hold it by the handle. "Could I get an overview, perhaps?"

"An overview?"

"What you think you can teach me."

"What I think I can teach you?" Her mother's champion laughed. "With enough time and dedication, I could teach you to be me, a champion. But I don't think that's what you're looking for. So I'm narrowing the scope. There will be three major areas: fitness, tools, and what you've called mindset."

"That seems reasonable."

"For fitness, I know you've had injuries, but I've seen you running—at least, I did while your mother was still alive—so I know that part of your fitness is at least adequate. But it is too specific. You need different kinds of fitness. So we'll improve your strength and stamina. For tools, we'll go into weaponry and weapons improvisation. Then there's mindset, which we've more or less covered."

"Right. OK, let's get to it."

"I need something from you, first."

"Oh. Right. We haven't discussed remuneration. I—"

"No, Your Highness. What I need is a commitment."

"I'm here. I'm committed."

"We haven't come close to testing that. Here's the thing." Cloisterfeld pointed at the door. "Out there, you are queen. In here, I need to be queen. I need you to do what I say and follow my instructions without hesitation or question. I know what I'm doing. You don't. For me to teach you, you have to accept that."

"Right." Eloise wasn't sure she liked where this was going.

"I can't be pussyfooting around here. If I have to worry about offending you or crossing you or having you take offense, I won't be able to be effective in the way that you need me to be. Is this acceptable?"

Eloise swallowed. Swallowed again. She felt herself baulking at giving herself over fully to someone else's dictates. "How often will we train?"

"Daily. It can replace whatever exercise you're otherwise doing, at least for now. But, seven days a week, first thing in the morning, at the time of your choosing."

"OK."

"Without exception."

"Right."

Silvia paused. It looked like she was waiting for something.

"Yes?" asked Eloise.

"I need you to be explicit. Do I have your commitment?"

Eloise took a deep breath, set aside her hesitations, and said, "Yes. You have my commitment."

"Good. When we are training, I ask that you refer to me as 'master' or 'Master Cloisterfeld.'" Again, she paused, waiting.

"I... I..." Eloise was surprised by the resistance she felt at this. She'd had teachers before, but always—and she meant *always*—they were, at their core, deferential to her and her sister. Clearly, deference was off the menu here. Eloise would have to wear it, or give up on her idea of gaining some of the champion's skill.

Hold it. Not always. There was one who showed no deference at all. One who had demanded complete obedience and subservience to every whim.

Baroness Sÿlvia Nûûûttëëërlïïïng Stúüübenhocker née de Gumball.

She was the royally appointed Thorning Master who'd trained Eloise and Johanna for their Thorning Ceremony, and she'd been merciless and pitiless to the moment of her death, right before the ceremony took place.

Eloise had hated her.

Hated.

Hated the way she'd imposed silence. Hated the menial tasks she'd doled out to them. Hated the way she'd made Eloise feel inadequate. Hated her subject matter—teaching the twins to pierce their skin with the different thorns used in the ceremony, and how to deal with the varying discomforts they caused.

Eloise suppressed a shiver and the rising rage that came with those memories. She fought to keep her face neutral as she remembered the indignities of that training, the way it had broken something between her and Johanna, and the isolation and misery she'd felt.

But then, she'd been successful at the task. In front of Court, she'd pierced herself, had an epiphany of love, and been named Future Ruler and Heir of the Western Lands and All That Really Matters.

And now she was the ruler.

She'd survived everything the Thorning Master had thrown at her, and she'd succeeded.

If she could do it once, she could do it again. Plus, there was no way Sylvia Cloisterfeld could possibly be as bad.

Eloise cleared her throat. "Yes, Master Cloisterfeld."

"Good, Student Gumball."

Eloise's cheek twitched at the moniker, but she held her tongue.

"Next," said Cloisterfeld, "I have a recommendation."

"What's that?"

The champion said nothing, waiting.

Eloise got the hint. "What's that, Master Cloisterfeld?"

Sylvia nodded. "I suggest you invite your champion to join us. He should know what it is that you're learning. Also, with respect, there might be a thing or two that I could teach him as well."

"I'd be happy to have Lorch train with us. He'd be hanging outside the door anyway, so we may as well bring him in. I'll ask him."

"Same rules. He has to commit. And in here, he has to submit to me fully."

"I can't speak for him, but my guess is that will work out fine."

"Good, any last questions before we start in earnest?"

Eloise shook her head. "No, Master Cloisterfeld."

"Good. Let's start by seeing how many push-ups you can do."

Eloise hated push-ups. Hated them almost as much as she hated chin-ups, but she kept that opinion to herself. She lowered herself to the rush-covered floor and formed a plank.

Her mother's champion did the same, saying, "I won't ask you to do anything that I myself am not willing to do."

"Yes, Master Cloisterfeld." Eloise began heaving herself upward, then lowering herself down, counting out the repetitions. "One. Two. Three."

Cloisterfeld easily matched her push-up for push-up, while Eloise strained to make it to ten. Her wrist and shoulder were making their previous damage known, and she worried that it was too soon after two wrist fractures to do this kind of exercise.

One thing was certain: this was going to hurt.

She hoped it would be worth it.

❧ 23 ❧

HEADLONG HELDA

Lady Seneschal Póöòmáäàdéëè had a secret vice—she loved listening to the gossip heralds. It embarrassed her to admit it, even to herself, but she just couldn't help it.

Póöòmáäàdéëè knew that what most of them said was undiluted rubbish, and that the volume of lies they spouted invariably smothered the smidgen of truth that any given story might hold. But more often than she cared to count, she found herself standing at the edge of Herald Plaza (like she was at that very moment) where the gossip heralds plied their trade. "G'mid-morning, Mertyl," she said to the ribbon monger whose stall she'd reached. "How's the ribbon business today?"

"All tied up with a bow," said Mertyl, as she always did.

Mertyl, it turned out, shared Lady Seneschal's love of the gossip heralds, and her ribbon stand provided the second-best vantage point in Herald Plaza to hear them. She didn't mind if Póöòmáäàdéëè pretended to buy ribbons so she could hear the gossip heralds, since pretending to buy turned into actual buying often enough. Besides, Mertyl much preferred Lady Seneschal to hover near her stand instead of over by the kohlrabi stall run by her nemesis, who had, arguably, the best vantage point for hearing the news.

"Not that I care, but who's up today?" asked Lady Seneschal, feigning disinterest and disdain—another part of their ritual. They both knew they each hung onto absolutely every shouted word, that neither of them could tear herself away from the combination of juicy titillation and outrageousness.

"Headlong Helda."

"I see." Póöòmáäàdéëë shook her head. "She's not very good."

"No, not at all. Terrible. The worst."

In fact, they both knew that Helda de Anatidae was the best of them all. Helda was a graylag goose—large, gray-feathered, irritable, and brash—and she was known as Headlong Helda because there wasn't a story that she wouldn't rush headlong into without a thought for propriety, personal safety, or the feelings of others. She'd find out what's what, figure out if there was anything in it worth braying out to the world, then rush to the Herald Plaza and let fly—sometimes literally, if she thought a few lengths of height might help her get her story out. Beyond that, Headlong Helda could honk incredibly loudly, which made it easy for everyone to hear what she was saying. Inevitably, her listeners showered her with coins, making it possible for her to gossip another day.

But the best (or worst) of all were Headlong Helda's commenters—those listeners, both devoted and casual, who stood nearby giving their opinions about what the heralds were saying. Commenters, as a rule, were noisy, strident, ignorant, lived for disagreements, inclined toward fury, besotted with conspiracy, and felt that not paying any mind to the words that actually came out of a herald's mouth did not disqualify them from spewing out their own form of vitriol, craziness, or random, unrelated nincompoopery. Because of their arch nature, commenters were confined by edict to a roped-off section that was at least a dozen lengths away from the herald they followed, in an area called the comments section.

Since Headlong Helda was the most famous herald there was, her comments section was bigger, noisier, more strident, more ignorant, more besotted, crazier, louder, and more bug-eyed than anyone else's. A mere glance at them was enough to make it clear why the first rule of heralds is "Don't listen to the comments section."

It was a rule Lady Seneschal followed strictly. Doing so required staunch discipline to avoid being distracted by the comment section. It was a tall order.

Her friend Picholine Manzanilla hadn't needed that kind of discipline. Like Mertyl, the East ambassador had shared her love of gossip heralds. Her dear Picho, however, had the means to do so privately. While she was in Brague, she'd subscribed to half a dozen gossip heralds who each came to her house on different days of the week and privately declaimed their dubious scandals and marginal intrigues. That meant Manzanilla didn't have to rub elbows with anyone else to stay up to date with the alleged goings-on, and she completely avoided the comments sections. It was an extravagance that Póöòmáäàdéëè had experienced only once, when she visited the ambassador's home, and one she would have dearly loved for herself. But Lady Seneschal couldn't have afforded even one private gossip herald subscription, much less six. And if she had, there would have been logistical issues—the likes of Headlong Helda were barely tolerated within the castle walls.

Lady Seneschal pointed to two of Mertyl's wares. "I'll have a spool of the navy and a spool of the maroon, please."

"Excellent choices, Lady Seneschal," said the ribbon monger. "I'll have them wrapped."

"Thank you."

Póöòmáäàdéëè drifted back into her thoughts as Mertyl used a hair-thin sheet of hemp parchment to bundle the spools together.

The thing was, every now and then, Lady Seneschal heard something that had enough of a nugget of truth in it to actually be useful. It didn't happen often, but it definitely happened. Like the time decades ago when she'd used the scandalous words of three different gossip heralds to piece together the fact that Eloise II had settled on Chafed Motley de Chëëëkflïïïnt as the leading candidate to win her favor to king and husband—a shocking, thoughtful, and completely unexpected occurrence. That bit of foreknowledge had let Póöòmáäàdéëè arrange things behind the scenes to the queen's best advantage, even without the late queen knowing exactly what was going on. Lady Seneschal was happy to have rendered that particular service.

There was another time when a gossip herald intimated (well, he'd shouted it, actually) that one of the late queen's Privy councilors was concealing a prattleweed problem. She'd been able to give Queen Eloise II a heads up, which let her do something about it before it evolved into a full-blown Court scandal. The late queen's Midsummer gift had been particularly generous that year.

Lady Seneschal sighed. She really did miss Two.

So even though it was gossip, and usually scurrilous at that, Lady Seneschal kept up with it, and justified this to herself as fulfilling a kind of civic duty. That logic wouldn't withstand scrutiny, so she was careful not to interrogate it very far.

Mertyl pointed upwards, interrupting Lady Seneschal's wandering thoughts. "There she is."

Póöòmáäàdéëè turned to see a goose flying down into the middle of Herald Plaza, wings wide, neck long, face determined and proud. Her feathers shone with a gloss that bespoke hours in an avian salon. She wore a snug, gold choker covering the lower half of her neck, made like chain mail to be fully flexible. The claws at the end of her webbed feet were painted in matching gold. As she landed on a raised platform, people applauded and gathered around, filling the space between her and her comments section. "G'mid-arvo to you all," she honked. "Who'd like to hear all the news that's fit to bleat?"

The crowd chuckled, and a few encouraging coins were tossed onto her stage.

"Well, thank you, darlings." Helda stretched out her wings, then folded them in. She tilted her head and scanned the crowd with one eye. "Let's see. What might be interesting? Oh, I know. There's a certain duck..."

And she was off. Her words did not go after their subjects directly— even the gossip heralds had to be careful about what they said. Helda didn't directly name names, but instead used obvious nicknames and euphemisms that gave her the veneer of deniability. And she couched as much as she could as opinion rather than fact, because opinion couldn't get her hauled before a magistrate and prosecuted for an Improper Utterance or Attack. "I think Jane Smith is an idiot" wasn't actionable the way saying "Jane Smith beats her husband" without evidence might be. Headlong Helda's great skill as a gossip herald was walking the tightrope of rumor, innuendo, and allegations of scandalous behavior without falling into the abyss of libel, defamation, and slander.

But there was no question that the result of what she said was slanderous enough, even if one had to read between the lines.

And that, of course, was the point.

"There's a certain duck known for his vocal cords who has been seen getting overly familiar with considerable volumes of liquid consolation," Helda honked. "He's engaging in a pathetic *cri de coeur* because his wife started laying her eggs in someone else's nest."

"That one's easy enough to figure out," said Mertyl. "Old Tom de Mallard."

"The folk singer?" said Lady Seneschal.

"The same."

"I didn't know he hit the bottle."

"It's new. And he's not consuming bottles. Casks."

"Poor fellow."

"I've seen him perform a few times recently. He's stopped singing love ballads and switched to songs that are basically, 'My baby done left me.'"

They returned their attention to Helda, "The censer hugger is probably hoping that the Venerable Prelate Herself doesn't find out about the alleged financial indiscretion or she'll be defrocked before you can say, 'Çalaht doesn't like it when you steal from the devotional house.'"

"I wouldn't want to get on the prelate's bad side," said Mertyl. "Did you catch who she was talking about?"

"I'm guessing 'censer hugger' refers to one of the bishops."

"Makes sense. They seem prone to temptation. But stealing from the devotional house? And the Venerable Prelate Herself? That's just asking for it."

Headlong Helda's honking got their attention again. "A certain flibbertyqueen was seen two nights ago at the Velvet Cask, a local entertainment establishment frequented by the hoi polloi and elite of the elite. As the hoi-est polloi-est in all the realm, her attempt at incognito attendance fell as flat as a jaded jester's jape. Was she there to hear the dulcet sounds of the rising star chanteuse-in-residence? Or was she there to coax the swordsmith out of retirement to replace the replacement for her first champion disaster? At this rate, it'll be my turn as champion sometime next month. Dis-as-ter."

"Do you reckon that's true?" asked Mertyl. "Was the queen sneaking around Brague listening to music in clubs?"

"Helda's a gossip herald," said Lady Seneschal. "You can't rely on anything she says. If Her Majesty left the castle, I'd have known about it."

"Fair enough," said Mertyl.

But the corner's of Lady Seneschal Älphonsinä Füüürchtbarkeit Póòòmáäàdéëè's mouth drooped, and she no longer heard what the goose was saying. Had Queen Eloise slipped from the castle without letting her know? Even after the chaos of having gone missing the morning after she'd been crown plonked?

Her mother would never have done that, because she wouldn't have wanted Court thrown into a tizzy. Two would have let Lady Seneschal know not to worry, would have said something if she was going to leave her usual half dozen rooms in the castle—the Receiving Room, the Throne Hall, the Salle de la Famille, the Queen's Chamber, the Culpability Courtyard, the Hall of Bald Opulence, the Bibliotheca de Records and Regrets. If she was headed anywhere else, even within the castle walls, she'd have sent a page to inform Lady Seneschal so adjustments could be made, as needed. Two had trusted her.

But this one? She wouldn't put it past her to pull a stunt like heading out unannounced to a honky tonk or whatever the Velvet Cask was.

And what that meant was the pipsqueak queen didn't trust her with small matters like her whereabouts.

Unacceptable. Simply unacceptable.

✣ 24 ✣

TOTALLY BLINKING LOVELY

"Queen Eloise," said Lorch from his station just outside the door of the Salle de la Famille. "RoyLee has brought a messenger."

"Send them in." Eloise welcomed the opportunity for a break from the migraine-inducing Privy Council documents that she'd been reviewing, none of which seemed very useful or made much sense.

The wombat led in a capybara dressed in a Northern Lands messenger's purple road tunic and dark purple breeks. It wasn't Master Zïïïm-mëëërmäään, who'd previously delivered Johanna's letters, as he was now the realm's ambassador to her court and stationed full-time in Brague. The new messenger was a much smaller capybara, and she lacked Zïïïmmÿÿÿ's verve. "I bring you a note from Queen Johanna Umgotteswillen Gumball, the upstanding, righteous, and rightful crown-plonked queen of the Northern Lands," the messenger squeaked as she held out a wax-sealed envelope.

Eloise let RoyLee bring it to her and wondered how she was announced at the other end. Somehow, she doubted "upstanding, righteous, and rightful crown-plonked queen" was part of it. She waved the letter and said, "Thank you for this. May I ask your name?"

"Jïïimééénëëëz. But everyone calls me Jïïimmÿÿÿ."

"Thank you, Mistress Jïïimmÿÿÿ. Tell me, that little announcement that came with the letter."

"Yes?"

"Are you trained to say that?"

"Not specifically. They allow us some degree of latitude in what we say, so long as it is complimentary to the subject."

"I see. If I send a note back with you, will you do the same at the other end?"

"Yes, Your Highness. I will. It's part of the gig. A fun part, if I may say so."

"What would you say?"

The messenger's cheek hair stood up, presumably the capybara equivalent of blushing. "I don't rightly know."

"That's OK. I don't—"

"I'd think about it all the way back, trying to capture the essence of the communication."

"Really, it's—"

Jïïimmÿÿÿ's expression became pensive. "The choice of words is important. 'Up-' words work really well. Upstanding, like I said. Or uprightness. Uplifting. That kind of thing. But not all of them. I wouldn't use uppity, uproarious, upchucking, or upholstery."

"I—"

"Probably I'd say something like, 'I bring you a note from Queen Eloise Hydra Gumball III, the diligent, up-reaching, perspicacious, deserved and proper crown-plonked queen of the Western Lands and All That Really Matters.' That's just off the top of my head."

"That..." Eloise hesitated. "That was rather lovely."

The capybara's cheek hair bristled again. "Th-thank you."

"Do you require a place to stay or something to eat? You must be tired after such a long journey."

The messenger stammered with deepening embarrassment. "I, uh, no, Your Highness. I'll be staying with Ambassador Zïïïmmÿÿÿ. I understand the ambassador's residence has a very good browsing garden. That will do the likes of me."

"Very good. Thank you for this." Eloise waved the letter. "I'm sure I'll have a reply for you tomorrow morning at the latest. Please see me before you leave."

"Yes, Your Highness."

As soon as she was alone again, Eloise broke the wax seal and opened the letter.

۞

DEAR EL,

I never quite know how to start these letters to you. For so many years, we knew each other's every thought and mood, and shared every moment. Then we grew apart, which was awful, looking back at it. Last year, we breached that gap. Now, once again, we're apart.

It's weird. I keep thinking that you should already know things, so I shouldn't need to write them. But there's no way you could know them, because you're not here and we haven't communicated. I assume there are things you know that I don't know that you know, thanks to whatever spies and informants are still in place here at Castle Blotch. Certainly there's a small flow of information trickling back here from Castle de Brague from sources that remain embedded in and around your court. People, I might add, who I would never in a bazillion years have guessed were acting as informants.

(We might want to revisit the whole spying thing. Don't we know each other well enough to just go directly? It's something to think about. If we could dismantle some of the clandestine information network, it might spare the

budget some of the bribes and off-book payments to keep that kind of thing propped up. Çalaht knows I could handle cutting down on those expenses a bit. The finances of the Northern Lands are an unmitigated schemozzle. Consider yourself lucky to be queen of a solvent realm.)

So, how are things with you? I know from a few little birdies (and I mean that literally in this case) that Bënnïë-Änn Thëjëts is now First Advisor Bënnïë-Änn Thëjëts. Good choice. I always thought she was good value. Or should I say, flopping good value?

I have similar news. I've managed to convince Father to be my First Advisor, at least for a while.

⚜

"WHAT?" SAID ELOISE. "WHAT. THE. ACTUAL—?" SHE SMACKED down the letter with a *slap!* then stood so suddenly that her chair tipped over backwards. "Unbelievable," she growled. "Un-be-Çalaht-benightedly-liev-able."

She kicked the prone chair.

Kicked it again.

Paced the room.

Gulped breaths.

She tried to pour herself a mug of water, but her hands shook so much she sloshed a small tsunami onto the tablecloth.

Resumed pacing.

Tried to fight off the swelling emotions.

Hyperventilated.

Straightened herself.

Deliberately slowed her breathing.

Deliberately slowed her pacing.

Try again with the water.

Eloise picked up the pitcher.

Managed to fill the mug without incident.

Tried to drink.

Spilled water all down her front.

Last straw.

Eloise felt rage mix with jealousy, frustration with confusion.

How?

Why?

She snatched the mug from the table and hurled it at the stone wall. She put everything she had into it, throwing it with all her strength, all her emotions, and every hint of her weak magic.

The mug should have shattered. With that much force and feeling behind it, it should have been rendered a cloud of powder, pulverized shards, and memory.

It didn't.

Instead, the mug embedded itself into the solid stone. It was like the rock wall opened up, caught the mug in an embrace, and closed over as much of it as it could hold.

Eloise barely registered the small miracle, being too caught up in her head.

Our father.

Johanna's First Advisor.

It wasn't enough that Johanna had coaxed their father to return to the Half Kingdom, but she'd convinced him to take on an official role? When he left, he could barely string two sentences together without crumbling into a grief-stricken heap.

Plus, he'd absolutely refused to hang around so she could get his advice. In their last one-on-one conversation the day before he left Brague with Johanna, she'd specifically said to him, "You can support me. I want you to support me. I need you to support me." And he'd replied, "I don't think I can," and "You don't need me hanging around in the background making you second-guess things, or making you wonder what your mother would do or decide."

Now he was Johanna's first advisor?

A sudden loneliness washed over Eloise, as strong as the rage and jealousy she'd just been feeling. She was now motherless, sisterless, and fatherless. She was struggling here on her own. Flat-out struggling to get from one end of the day to the other without the carriage of her reign veering off a cliff and smashing itself on a sea of boulders.

Here she was, overwhelmed and head under water, while somewhere across the Adequate Wall of the Realms, Johanna and her father were swanning around Castle Blotch together, whispering secrets, trading confidences, and making plans.

Well, how nice for them. How totally blinking lovely. Eloise would just make do with her mountain of a First Advisor, her geriatric, ossified Privy Council, and her ranks of soldiers who had more in common with circus ponies than elite fighters. It's not like she needed advice or anything. It's not like her realm had anything serious going on, like, say, an invading force taking one of her cantons without so much as a "by your leave." It might have been nice to have her father contribute the odd bit of sage wisdom based on his years at Court, any insights he might have gained talking to Eastie ambassadors, traders, or, heck, even Eastern Lands minor nobility. Or maybe he knew something about magical objects and could have helped her figure out what to do with the Star of Whatever.

But no. Johanna was getting all that. Johanna was getting the attention, support, advice, and fatherly love.

Eloise was just a sibling-less orphan, alone in a cruel world that saddled her with responsibilities beyond what she knew how to handle. But that was OK. She could take it. She could do it on her own. Why not?

She felt like wadding up the letter and shredding it into a thousand little pieces. Or maybe lighting it on fire and getting a decent little flame going in the Salle de la Famille hearth. She could dunk it in the mug of water, if she could find another mug, and keep her hand steady enough to fill it.

But she didn't do any of those things.

Instead, she went back to the table and forced herself to read the rest of it.

I KNOW WHAT YOU'RE WONDERING—HOW DID I GET OUR SAD, LEADEN, *grief-stricken father to take on a role like First Advisor to the Northern Lands throne, which takes a mind capable of analysis and attention to detail?*

I asked him.

Mind you, I did it in a way that didn't give him much opportunity to say "no."

I figured he needed something to give him a bit of meaning, and I sure needed the help coming to grips with the queendom.

Still, I can't help but feel like you've been left on your own somewhat.

"YA THINK?" MUTTERED ELOISE.

BUT AT LEAST YOU HAVE A FUNCTIONING REALM WITH A COURT THAT'S *inclined to like you, and people who are actually inclined to pay the queen's tithe.*

And you have a competent First Advisor well-suited to the role (I'm not sure I ever cared much for Ligurian). Father is willing, and probably capable, but he's... How to put this... He's rusty. He's having to exercise mental muscles he hasn't used for a while. Mother either wouldn't let him, or didn't need him to.

Let's see... What else to tell you...

Oh! The Purple Haze.

You know that we're starting to explore it. I can confirm that while it still hangs there like a lavender curtain, people are going into it regularly, trying to figure out if the land within it is redeemable at all.

Of course, the first thing people found when they went in was what you and I found—all those skeletal remains, those thousands upon thousands of deaths by fogging that had piled up over the decades.

It is as horrid now as it was then.

And it was so, so wrong for our forebears on the throne to use the Purple Haze that way. I can't see Çalaht condoning that kind of cruelty. Sure, maybe they didn't know it was cruel, since no one could come out of there and tell them. But fogging people like that was a great wrongness. It seems like something we need to atone for, even if we weren't the ones to have done it.

THAT WAS SOMETHING THAT ELOISE COULD AGREE WITH. THE Purple Haze had been a nightmare, and the way fogging had been used as part of the justice system struck her as unspeakably evil, even if it was (allegedly) done in ignorance. Eloise allowed herself a sigh and the consoling thought that if she never did anything else with her life, at least she'd been able to break the evil spell that was the Purple Haze.

That was something, at least.

To foster healing, I've done a couple of things. First, I've disbanded the Foggers Guild and made sure that all foggers have access to training so they can pursue other livelihoods.

✦

Clever, not to just take away their work and leave them hanging. Still, Eloise wondered how hard it would be for them to shed a history of being a fogger.

Fortunately, not her problem.

✦

I've asked that all remains be brought out of the Purple Haze, identified, if possible (mostly they won't be, since the bulk of it is nigh-on dust), and properly buried. That way, people who need to say goodbye can, and it might provide some closure for those who need it. It might also be a distracting enough project that it gains me some time while I figure out what to do about the realm's disastrous finances.

(Can I interest you in a few dozen strong weights of the finest Northern Lands wart cream?)

I hear Father calling for me, so I'll go now. Let me know how you're doing.

Love,

J

PS. Gouache Snotearrow McCcoonnch asked me to say hello for him. I've relieved him of his role as a jester, since he was so terrible at it and he didn't enjoy doing it. Instead, I've given him the title of Personal Assistant and had someone make him a sash, which he never seems to take off. He's useful in surprisingly strange ways, like if I need something unusual or need to find someone, he seems to always know where to get the thing or find the person. It's uncanny. Give him a task that involves deductive reasoning or a string of actions with consequences, and he's no more effective than a lump of putty. But ask him if he knows where one can find a pair of left-handed scissors or a stick of taupe-colored sealing wax, and he's your man.

Plus, he's completely devoted to me, which is sweet. I've had to promise him that if I ever get married, he can be my maid of honor. So, I'm warning you now that if for some reason the peal of wedding bells comes into my future—Çalaht knows I hope that's not any time soon—you'll need to make allowance for Gouache (because, obviously, you should be maid of honor). —J

ELOISE SET THE LETTER DOWN, ULTIMATELY GLAD SHE HADN'T destroyed it. Johanna really seemed to be settling into the role of queen. It made Eloise feel like she'd been pfaffing around, wasting her time for weeks and months. She recognized that she felt something similar every time one of her twin's letters arrived, which meant it was Eloise's problem, not her sister's.

Burying the dead was a good idea. Exploring the remains of the land beneath the Purple Haze was also a good idea. So was getting their father to be First Advisor. So was the thing with the Foggers Guild. "Lots of good ideas there, Jo. Good for you."

She almost meant it.

25

BUZZING, DUSTY
DISRUPTION

T he next day, Eloise found Jerome waiting for her outside the door of the Queen's Study. "G'mid-morning to you. You weren't at breakfast."

"G'mid-morning, Your Highness. No, I wasn't. I have something I want to discuss, and I've been trying to figure out how to say it."

"Sounds ominous." Eloise unlocked the door and waved for him to follow her in. "RoyLee will be here shortly with morning tea. Will you have some?"

"Maybe. We'll see how we go. And I'm not talking about anything ominous. More something we need to puzzle out."

Eloise walked through the room and performed a small ritual of orienting herself. First, she straightened a painting of her parents that Lady Seneschal had suggested she might like to hang as a reminder of them, though it was far from the world's best portrait. She then touched the teapot on a tray with a tea set that included a half-full cup of tea and three ginger snaps, one of which had been nibbled—remnants of her mother, They had been there the first time Eloise had come into the room, and she couldn't bring herself to have them cleaned away. She picked up a scroll from her desk, squinted at the writing, then covered her right eye so she could read it more easily. She set it down with a grunt, picked up her mother's letter opener, and leaned against the edge of the map table. Idly, she poked the letter opener at the spot on the map that represented Flachberg.

Poke.

Poke. Poke-poke. Poke.

"I'm ready," Eloise said. "Let me have it."

Poke. Poke. Poke.

Jerome straightened his tail, clasped his front paws behind his back, stood upright, and spoke to her from the floor. "So, as you know, since we got back from our journey I've spent most of my time in the Bibliotheca de Records and Regrets, researching. You've been there a lot, too, but mainly, it's been me."

"Yes. And?" *Poke.*

"So we haven't actually found anything useful yet. Not really."

Poke. Poke-poke. "No, not really."

"Not at all," said Jerome.

"OK, that's fair. Other than finding Melveeta's note that described acquiring what she later called the Star of Whatever, we haven't turned up anything about the Star itself, nothing to help us figure out how it works."

"That's right." Jerome hesitated, then said, "I think we need to take matters into our own hands."

"Meaning?" *Poke. Poke-poke-poke.*

"Meaning we do what you said Melveeta the Elusive did. She experimented. She figured it out on her own. We're smart enough. We should be able to do the same."

"Sure, and risk getting fried, damaged, killed, or permanently sucked into a spell in the process." Eloise stopped stabbing at Flachberg and unconsciously dug her pinky into her right ear to try and mute the buzzing. "Don't get me wrong. I want to know how the Star works. More—I *need* to know how it works, for the safety of Court and the realm. Maybe even the world. Look at what the Purple Haze did. Ruined half a realm."

"But you ended that spell. You have some credentials in the handling-the-unexpected department."

"My ending that spell was an accident, Jer. A fluke. Look at every other time I've tried to use the Star of Whatever. A dislocation. A fracture. A ruined brunchberry paddock. A messed-up eye. A messed-up ear. This thing is taking its toll."

"And yet..."

"And yet what?"

"And yet, I think you have to try something."

"Why?"

"Why? Exactly because of what you said, Queen Eloise. Because it's taking its toll. The less you understand it, the greater the danger there is to you and to the realm."

"You didn't meet Melveeta the Elusive, Assistant Seer to the Court Seer Abernatheen de Chipmunk. You didn't see what being trapped in a spell for more than two centuries will do to you." Eloise started poking at Flachberg again with the letter opener. "It." *Poke.* "Was." *Poke.* "Awful." *Poke. Poke-poke. Poke-poke-poke.*

Jerome scampered up a chair and jumped onto the map table. "El. Stop."

"Fine." She set down the letter opener.

"You don't start by casting a spell like the one that created the Purple Haze. You start small. Tiny. Minute. You try to limit the scope of what you're doing so you can gain incremental understanding."

"Like what?"

"Like working out how you knew the breakfast soup was wrong. Or... I don't know. Let me ask, did Melveeta mention how she figured out how the Star worked? Like, something must have provided the first clue. Did she say?"

"I don't think so. But there was a lot going on."

"Think about it, El." He looked around the Queen's Study. "How about you go sit down in the armchair, give it some focus, and see what you can remember."

"Fine. But I'm really not in the mood." She stabbed Flachberg one last time, set the letter opener on the desk as she went past, and flounced down into her comfy chair.

"Lean back, close your eyes, breathe slowly, and let it come back to you."

She did what Jerome said, letting herself relax into the memories of her experience in the Purple Haze. As she did so, Eloise realized she'd been avoiding thinking about it. Her memories of the time she and Johanna spent in the dense fog felt both very far away and like it had just happened yesterday. It had only been a matter of months—a short enough time that she couldn't yet pull her hair into a pony tail (a term equines found offensive) after she'd hacked it off in a fit of uncontrolled disgust, having been soaked by Melveeta's blood. Some of the events she could recall with incredible clarity, like slamming into Gouache and tumbling down into the mist. Others were only just there, like almost dying and being rescued by Hector de Pferd and the Nameless One.

Plus, there had been a strange time effect inside the Purple Haze. It had felt to Eloise and Johanna that they'd wandered around the dusty, dayless, nightless wasteland for weeks, when outside the magical fog, it had been a matter of mere days.

But none of that was what Jerome was looking for. Eloise narrowed her focus to memories of meeting Gwendolyn the Irritable's champion,

Melveeta the Elusive, and what the old woman had said in the few hours of contact they'd had with her before she'd tried to subsume Eloise and Johanna into the spell, and, when that failed, died.

What exactly had Melveeta talked about?

Eloise remembered she'd told them the story of Gwendolyn the Irritable, Queen of the Western Lands and All That Really Matters and Eloise's forebear by more than two centuries, and how Gwendolyn had gotten in the family way by King Brüüütus of the Northern Lands during their parlay. But then Brüüütus had jilted her, which Gwendolyn hadn't taken well, and she'd mustered her forces for an attack on the Northern realm. Gwendolyn had commanded Melveeta to learn to use the Star of Whatever. What had she said? Eloise fought to recall Melveeta's exact words. Slowly, they came. She'd quoted her queen as saying, "I believe you have not been trying hard enough, Champion Melveeta Gumball. I think it can be channeled to greater use. I need what it can do—but more, bigger. You will apply yourself, Mel. You will learn to extend the range of the Star of Whatever, to focus its knack for magical dampening as a weapon. And you will do that now. I will have the Northern Lands."

She thought about that. "Magical dampening." Eloise had always thought of the Star of Whatever as a way to enhance and reinforce a magical object. That's what she had done with the Orb of Alleged Omniscience. But Melveeta had come at it from the other side. She had twigged that something was going on with the Star by its ability to disrupt magic. After all, that's what the Purple Haze had done—it was the buzzing, dusty disruption to the magic and life force of half a realm.

No, not just half a realm. The Purple Haze corresponded to the weakening of magic everywhere. It had dampened most of the magic out of the entire world, like it had sucked it up and swallowed it.

And all of it, Eloise continued to suspect, was inside the Star of Whatever.

She thought about the Purple Haze again—a buzzing, dusty disruption of magic.

Eloise gasped and opened her eyes. "Wait, I just thought of something. Two things, actually."

Jerome leaned forward. "Go ahead."

"First, when Johanna and I were going through the Purple Haze, there were two things that were annoying. One was the mist that occluded almost all visibility. We were wandering around with very limited sight. But the other was a buzz. There was an annoying, incessant, mind-numbing buzz that pervaded the thing. It stopped when we were close to Melveeta—like when we were more or less close enough to touch her. But outside a circle just a few lengths in diameter, the buzz was constant and annoying. Remind you of anything?"

"Your ear?"

Eloise nodded. "My ear. It seemed like the buzz in the Purple Haze was a manifestation of active magic, a noise associated with an existing, functioning spell that was working then and there."

"Why didn't anyone else talk about the buzz?"

"Maybe they did. I vaguely remember a light buzzing when I was standing on Fogging Hill. It was ignorable, but it was there. But you didn't say anything about it."

Jerome shook his head. "I can't say I remember a buzzing."

"Maybe it is as simple as no one lived long enough to comment on it. Or perhaps Johanna and I could hear the buzz because the spell didn't work on the two of us. It killed everyone else, but because we were of Melveeta's blood, the can't-use-magic-against-blood rule shielded us, which actually gave us the chance to hear the spell. We both heard it. It drove us spare."

Jerome's tail oscillated slowly as he thought it through. "So the theory we're talking about is that the buzz in your ear is not damage caused by using the Orb of Alleged Omniscience and the Star of Whatever together. Instead, it's an active artifact of magic still somehow in play?"

"Something like that—magic still going on in my head somehow."

"That's a scary thought."

"Yes. It is."

The two of them let the idea sink in.

Eloise covered her right eye, then switched to her left, and then back. "If that theory is true, and we don't know that it is, it would mean that mean that my eye blur—"

"Would likely be the same," finished Jerome. "A remnant, active magic."

"And maybe that's how I could tell—"

"That the breakfast soup was off. You had—"

"Some sort of magic-tinged perception or something."

Jerome let out an excited chitter, then covered his mouth. "Sorry. But this is... This is..."

"Petrifying?"

"I was going to go with 'fascinating,' but 'petrifying' will do."

Again, they fell to silence. Then Jerome said, "So, what was the other thing?"

"What other thing?"

"You said you just realized two things."

"Oh, right. That." Eloise mimed tossing balls in the air. "Nostrum Kruscheltante."

"What is a nostrum kruscheltante?"

"*Who is* Nostrum Kruscheltante." Eloise stood up again and resumed pacing around the map table. She was tempted to resume stabbing

Flachberg, too, but didn't. "Nostrum Kruscheltante was Gwendolyn the Irritable's jester. Melveeta said the first time she noticed that the Star of Whatever affected people was when Gwendolyn called Melveeta in to see him. When she entered the room, the jester fumbled his clubs. It was the first time that had ever happened to him. As soon as she was out of the room, he was back to his usual skill, so Gwendolyn called her back in, and he promptly dropped everything again. I remember her talking about how this piqued her and Gwendolyn's curiosity. They ran a little test and eventually worked out that if she left the Star of Whatever in the hall, Kruscheltante could cascade eight rings perfectly. I remember her saying, 'Having the Star within ten lengths when I could see him, or five lengths on the other side of a stone wall, was enough to render him a bumbling klutz.'"

"Wow."

"I know."

"We should try to recreate her experiment." Jerome mimicked juggling with his forepaws and tail. "Do we have a juggler at Court?"

"Stoofy, the jester, used to juggle," said Eloise. "A little. Badly."

"No good."

"I know you don't like him—"

"No, it's not that. I mean, you're right, he creeps me out. But we need someone who uses weak magic to help their juggling. That's not Stoofy Trebuchet McNniister."

"No, it isn't. Not by a long shot."

"Leave it with me, El. Let me see what I can come up with."

26

TIBERIUS DE SPHENODON

Eloise sat on the Listening Throne in the Receiving Room wearing a new cape that Seamstress Linttrap had just completed. It was deep burgundy red, soft and smooth to the touch, and featured delicate lace along the cuffs and hems, and knot-work embroidery. Eloise had fallen for it immediately, liking the rich color and the way it highlighted her dark eyes, and immediately dubbed it the You Have Five Minutes Cape, figuring it was best to be clear about its use.

She was glad she was wearing it, as she wasn't sure how much more she could listen to from the master of the Traveling Piepersons' Guild. "What's your concern again?" she asked.

"Your Majesty, there have been numerous reports of members of our guild, in the process of moving themselves from one fair to another, being accosted by alleged customers. These alleged customers—Simons—are members of a protest group. They pose as potential customers and demand to taste our wares. When the accosted member of our Piepersons' Guild asks them for payment, they are told in no uncertain terms that such an exchange of value will not be forthcoming. When pressed, the Simon says, 'Indeed I have not any,' then runs away cackling."

"I see..." said Eloise, although she didn't.

"As if that's some sort of proper commercial interaction," harrumphed the guild master. "This orchestrated, systematic attack strikes at the very heart—"

"What about signage?" interrupted Eloise.

The guild master paused. "I beg your pardon, Your Highness?"

"Why not put up a sign? 'No freebies. That means you, Master Simon.' Something like that? That would do the trick, wouldn't it?"

"But this breach of the fundamental principles involved warrants extreme—"

"Go for outcomes, Guild Master Pieperson." Eloise stood and everyone in the room fell silent. "Do me a favor."

"Yes, Your Highness?"

"Try some signs. See how you go. You can report back to me, if you'd like."

"But, Your Highness, I—"

Eloise turned to First Advisor. "What's next?"

Bënnïë-Änn Thëjëts checked her agenda scroll. "Champion Lacksneck is next, Queen Eloise."

"Very good."

First Advisor waved to Harold Hairauld the herald, who immediately declared, "Chammmmmpion Lacksneck, accommmmmpanied by Tiber-rrrrrrrrius de Sphenodon, Master Serrrrrrrrgeant of Herrrrrrrr Majesty's Forrrrrrrrces, Rrrrrrrretired."

Lorch Lacksneck strode to the dais with calm purpose. He was followed by an elderly yet spry tuatara, who moved with surprising grace on just his hind legs, holding the rest of his body upright, exactly as Protocol demanded. He wore an immaculate, perfectly pressed, long-out-of-date dress uniform of greenish brown and grey that matched the colors of his scales. His antiquated jacket was cut to accommodate the spiny crest along his back, and sported shiny brass buttons and an impressive row of medals. His black tricorn hat had a single royally bestowed pin with the Gumball crest on it—not the one with a weasel on a bushel of onions and a one-eyed otter holding a fire poker, but an older variant, where the bushel held shallots and the otter still had two eyes. He made no effort to hide his front right foot, which had been cleaved in half, split between two claws.

"Queen Eloise, I present to you Master Sergeant (Retired) Tiberius de Sphenodon," said Lorch with a deep bow.

Eloise nodded to the tuatara. "Thank you for coming to Brague, Master Sergeant. I appreciate it."

"It is my pleasure, Your Highness," said de Sphenodon. "It has been a few reigns since I had the honor of appearing before the Gumballic throne." He spoke with a rural-tinged accent that Eloise found charming. His voice sounded elderly, but far from feeble, and the formality of his speech harked back to an era long past.

"Oh? You've been here before," said Eloise. "I didn't know that. Who received you here?"

"It was Queen Amelianna Zahnschmerzen Caltrop Gumball who invited me to appear before her Court."

"Really? My great-great-grandmother?"

"It was toward the very end of her reign, but yes."

"Amazing." Eloise leaned forward. "What was she like?"

"The late queen was an imposing figure. You knew where you stood with her, whether you wanted to or not. And she was very proper," said the tuatara. "Exceedingly proper. Follow-Protocol-to-the-smallest-comma proper." Then one side of his mouth crooked into a smile. "The late queen, may she stand with Çalaht, was also prone to puns."

"Puns?"

"Specifically, bad puns. Total groaners. She was proud to say she was 'punstoppable.' She always called it a form of 'punishment.'"

"I had no idea."

"But on the whole, she was a brick. A granite block. Solid as a crypt and just as dependable. I was..." The tuatara appeared to blink back tears. "I was fond of her."

"That's lovely," said Eloise. "Perhaps I'll get to speak with you more about her later. Did Champion Lacksneck tell you what I was hoping you could help us with?"

"He said you have concerns about the battle readiness of your troops."

"Yes, but I don't think I want to talk about it in the Receiving Room. Let me wrap up here, then you, Champion Lacksneck, Assistant Seer to the Court Seer Abernatheen de Chipmunk, First Advisor, and I can meet more privately."

"I'm at your service, ma'am," said de Sphenodon. "But if you have confidence in me at all, then perhaps we can start with an inspection of the troops so I can get a sense of what we're up against, and then we can discuss options."

"We just had a parade inspection, but I'm sure that Brigadier General Gideon Horsewhale de Odobenus would be happy to organize another one. He seems very proud of them."

"With respect, Your Highness, what I have in mind would go in a slightly different direction."

"Oh? Tell me more."

"I suggest a small surprise."

27

SIR, MASTER SERGEANT, SIR!

Ten minutes later, Eloise, Lorch, and Tiberius de Sphenodon were marching toward a number of large, high-roofed buildings on the edge of the castle compound.

Eloise tugged at Lorch's sleeve and murmured, "Are we allowed to do this?"

Lorch gave a head wagging yes-no-yes. "You are queen. By definition, you're allowed to do this."

"It seems wrong just to front up to the soldiers in their barracks unannounced."

De Sphenodon's hearing had clearly not faded with age. "The element of surprise, Queen Eloise," said the tuatara. "A good soldier is aware. Vigilant. Observant. Ready for the unexpected." His words had the feeling of having been said ten thousand times, not from rote repetition, but because they were words to live by. "We're going to see how much awareness, vigilance, observance, and readiness are displayed under a surprise attack—in this instance, in the form of an impromptu visit from their queen."

They arrived to stand in front of seven identical entrances leading into the same number of buildings. "Which one?" asked Eloise.

De Sphenodon's tongue flicked out, testing the air, then he lifted one shoulder. "In my day, it wouldn't have mattered. I doubt it does now."

"Then the middle one."

Lorch walked to the center barracks door, pressed down the latch, and bowed Eloise and the retired sergeant major through the opening door.

Eloise had expected to find soldiers of varying species doing soldierly things—polishing shoes, repairing uniforms, studying maps, considering strategies and tactics, or maybe comparing the relative merits of different weapons.

She did not expect to find a couple hundred people lounging around, mostly in their undies, in a prattleweed fug with their focus on playing cards, rolling dice, sleeping with pillows over their faces, and bickering about who should or shouldn't eat the last chocolate éclair.

Eloise, de Sphenodon, and Lorch wandered into the middle of the open-plan room without anyone so much as twitching a whisker or glancing up from whatever they were doing. "Are we suddenly invisible?" asked Eloise.

"Not that I'm aware of," said Lorch.

Suddenly, an ear-fracturing whistle cracked through the air. It was Tiberius de Sphenodon with two claws curled in his mouth. "Ten-hut! Queen present!" He bellowed it so loud, Eloise was pretty sure Queen Onomatopoeia in The South could have heard it.

A shocked, two-and-a-half second silence that felt like three years followed, as the soldiers parsed what had been yelled. Then, reflexively, they jumped up in whatever state of undies-ness they were in and snapped to attention. Another silence followed, broken only by the sound of dice clattering to a halt and cards fluttering to the ground.

Tiberius de Sphenodon strode through their ranks like their commanding officer, which he most certainly wasn't. After looking several dozen of them over, he snapped, "Which one of you sorry sacks of Çalaht-forsaken sap suckers is in charge?"

There was another long pause, then a voice from the far side of the room said, "I am."

"What was that?"

The person cleared their throat. "I said, 'I am.'"

The tuatara clasped his forefeet behind his back and walked over to where the person stood, his face stonily neutral. He reached the man— a stubby, wine cask of a man wearing pugilist drawers, and, to Eloise's discomfort, nothing else. De Sphenodon waved him down so he could speak eye to eye. Using a surprisingly friendly tone, he asked, "What's your name, soldier?"

"Garderobe. Plantar Garderobe."

"And how long have you served in Her Majesty's armed forces?"

"Fifteen years."

"Did you undergo basic training?"

"Yep. Sure did."

De Sphenodon lowered his voice. "Did you miss any days? Skip any of the lessons?"

"Nope. Did the whole thing."

"Was the learning hard? Did you need a tutor or anything?"

"Naw, I did OK," said Garderobe. "Graduated fifth in my class."

"Good. Very good." The tuatara pointed to a patch on the shoulder of his uniform. "Do you happen to remember what this insignia means?"

"Sure. Those are a master sergeant's stripes."

De Sphenodon dropped all pretense of friendliness and yelled right in Garderobe's face. "Then why have you not addressed me appropriately?"

Garderobe jerked back. "What?"

"I! Said! Then! Why! Have! You! Not! Addressed! Me! Appropriately!?"

The soldier snapped upright, straight as a rake handle. Eloise could see long-dormant soldierly habits kick in.

"I didn't hear that."

"Sir! Master Sergeant, sir!" Garderobe yelled at the top of his lungs.

"Do you happen to recognize the young lady who came into the room with me?"

"Sir! That's the queen, sir!"

"Good, good, good." De Sphenodon's voice had ratcheted back to normal. "And how do you address the queen when she walks into a room?"

"Sir, Master Sergeant, sir! I don't address the queen when she walks into a room! I shout, 'Queen is present!' to alert my fellow soldiers, then stand at attention and remain quiet, sir!"

"And if she asks you a question?"

"Sir, Master Sergeant, sir! I answer the question without making eye contact, sir!"

"Good to see the queen's coin has not been wasted on getting the soldier hammered into you. Do you recognize the other chap who's wandered into your barracks with me?"

"Sir! That would be the queen's champion, sir! I'm sorry, sir, but I don't recall his name, sir!"

"That's Champion Lorch Lacksneck of Lower Glenth."

"Sir! Thank you for informing me, sir!"

"What is your rank?"

"Sir! Staff sergeant, sir!"

"Staff Sergeant Plantar Garderobe, I'm going to walk out the door with the queen and her champion. We're going to wait exactly 90 seconds, then we're going to come back in. I'm looking forward to seeing the kind of reception we get."

"Sir! Thank you for the second chance, sir!"

Tiberius de Sphenodon turned around without another word and strode out the door. Lorch and Eloise followed him out, closing the door behind them.

As soon as the door clicked shut, there was a rain of muttered oaths and the scramble of bodies from inside the barracks.

The tuatara chuckled. "I thought that went pretty well."

"You did?" said Eloise.

"Of course. What I just did was completely unfair. We stormed into their midst with no warning, interrupting a pattern of lax behavior that must go back a decade or more, then berated their leader for being the way his superiors have allowed him to be. But listen to them in there, rushing to get themselves together in an unreasonably short amount of time. That means the basics have been inculcated into them. That's a good sign. It tells us there's something there to work with. "

"I'm glad to hear it."

De Sphenodon tapped a foot, ticking off the mental minute and a half he'd given them. Finally, he said, "That should do us. Champion Lacksneck, would you do me the kindness of getting the door again?"

Lorch opened the door and de Sphenodon led them back inside.

"Queen is present!" barked Staff Sergeant Plantar Garderobe from across the room, and 200 fully dressed soldiers snapped to attention.

"Not bad, not bad," said the tuatara as the three of them walked through the ranks to the middle of the room. He stopped in front of Plantar Garderobe. "At ease."

"Parade rest!" yelled the staff sergeant.

The soldiers assumed a more comfortable position, with hands or forepaws clasped behind their backs and legs wider apart (those species who could, anyway).

"The queen would like to say a few words," said de Sphenodon, then nodded at Eloise.

Eloise hadn't wanted to say anything, but didn't want to contradict the tuatara. "Thank you, Master Sergeant de Sphenodon. I would, yes." She cleared her throat. "I wanted to say thank you so very much for your service to the crown and the realm. On behalf of myself, my court, and everyone in the great realm of the Western Lands and All That Really Matters, I express my heartfelt gratitude for your dedication, your commitment to our values, and..." She was running out of platitudes, but kept going. "And your willingness to embrace change. For change is coming. It's always coming, but it is most definitely coming now. For all of us. So thank you again, for what you've done, for what you're doing, and for what you will do."

She wasn't sure if that was inspiring or just plain stupid. Possibly both.

A silence lingered as it became clear she had nothing else to say.

"To the queen!" shouted Garderobe.

"To the queen!" echoed everyone.

"To the queen!" repeated the staff sergeant.

"To the queen!"

To Eloise's surprise, it seemed heartfelt. "Thank you, everyone. I hope to see you again soon."

At a nod from the tuatara, she strode out of the building, followed by the other two.

Once the door latch clicked behind them, Eloise asked, "What do you think?"

The tuatara shook his head. "I think you have a lot of work ahead of you. But you're not starting at zero, so that's something. Plus, they seemed warm enough toward you. A personal connection is good. It makes people try harder. You're going to need that. A lot of it."

🎋 28 🎋

(RETIRED) NO MORE

Eloise, Lorch, and de Sphenodon returned to what Eloise now thought of as the Fippledip Room. They were joined by Jerome, First Advisor Thëjëts, and Sylvia Cloisterfeld. The latter two hadn't received much prior notice. Eloise had asked Lady Seneschal to organize refreshments, and when they arrived, they found Läääcy de Aardvark setting out dishes to go with a light lunch that was already laid out. She'd also brightened the room with more oil lamps and several vases of fresh flowers.

"Thank you, Läääcy," said Eloise. "Everyone, help yourself and let's get started."

When they were settled into their seats with cups of haggleberry tea and salad sandwiches dressed with a spicy peanut sauce, Eloise kicked off the meeting. "Thank you for being here. Let me start by saying that I don't think of this as a secret meeting, but I would still prefer we keep what we discuss here to ourselves, recognizing that there are sensitivities involved. That's why we're here and not in one of the more public rooms. Agreed?"

Everyone nodded assent.

"For those who haven't met him yet, this is Master Sergeant (Retired) Tiberius de Sphenodon. He brings a much-needed practical, military perspective."

More nods.

Eloise continued. "I'm hoping that all of you in this group will provide me with a kind of shadow privy council, one that can give me a different kind of input to what I get from the other body."

"What kind of input?" asked Cloisterfeld.

"I'd like you to help me focus on preparedness."

"What kind of preparedness, Queen Eloise?" asked First Advisor.

"Military preparedness. As much as it pains me to say so, we need to be better equipped for conflict. Our troops are woefully unprepared for anything that takes place off the parade ground."

"With respect," said First Advisor, "I still think this is a matter for your Privy Council."

"I'll raise it with them this afternoon, but there's a problem with that."

"Yes?"

"I don't have confidence in my current military leaders to change the situation. For that matter, I don't think any of them would know what to do if it came to all-out conflict with the Eastern Lands. Look how easy it was for Flachberg to fall. Look how little resistance the Eastie forces met. When I asked for an inspection of troops, I got a parade."

"I believe that Brigadier General de Odobenus was merely trying to show you the best and brightest of your soldiers. Again, I think this is a matter for the Privy Council."

"With respect, First Advisor, I think the brigadier general was showing me what he had, whether it was best or bright or not. The brigadier general never saw conflict. He's spent his entire career meeting the expectations of queens who ruled in times of peace, however that peace was maintained. I don't mean to be unkind, but he's like the equipment held by the soldiers I saw at inspection—dull and disused."

First Advisor Thëjëts eyed her thoughtfully. "What do you propose to do about it?"

"Sharpen the weapons, First Advisor," said Eloise. "And more importantly, sharpen the people holding them."

"How do you propose to do that?"

"By asking people with the requisite experience to help. You know Champion Cloisterfeld. She's agreed to help me with training the soldiers to be more soldierly—weapons instruction, hand-to-hand tactics, and the like."

"I see." First Advisor tapped the handle of her teacup, thinking.

"But more than that," Eloise continued, "we need to reframe our fighting forces into something that's actually ready to do that—fight. I'm hoping Master Sergeant de Sphenodon will take the lead there. He's actually been to war, so he—"

"I beg your pardon?" said Sylvia Cloisterfeld. "With respect, sir, how old are you? We haven't been at war for decades and decades."

De Sphenodon lifted a shoulder and tilted his head. "My people are less fixated on calendars and years than most species. I can tell you I was born, and I first served, in the reign of Queen Amelianna Zahnschmerzen Caltrop Gumball."

Cloisterfeld let out a whistle. "Wow. That would make you 135, at least."

"So I'm told."

Cloisterfeld stood from her chair and bowed to him. "Master Sergeant (Retired) Tiberius de Sphenodon. It is an honor to meet you. I hope that you will accept me as your student, as I would be grateful to learn from you."

It was an unexpected gesture of acceptance and respect. Eloise was grateful to her mother's champion and found herself blinking back tears.

"It would be my pleasure, Champion (Retired) Cloisterfeld."

Suddenly, Lorch stood and bowed as well. "Master Sergeant (Retired) Tiberius de Sphenodon. It is an honor to have known you since I was a boy. I hope that you will accept me as your student, as I would be grateful to learn from you once again."

"Ah, Lorchy. You're no longer the wee scamp you used to be." The tuatara chuckled, then straightened. "It will be my pleasure to take you on as well, Champion Lacksneck."

Eloise let the moment's emotion hang, in part to see if Jerome would join them.

He didn't. Apparently, he didn't feel the need.

The two champions and the master sergeant sat down, and Eloise went on. "As I was saying, my hope is that the master sergeant will take a more active role in developing the military's capabilities in strategy, and to put them on a more disciplined footing. If what we've seen up to now is anything to go by, we have a lot of ground to cover."

"Do we need to consider anything else?" asked First Advisor.

"Yes. Time. Somehow, I need to win us enough time to get the various changes in place. The events at Flachberg came more or less out of the blue. Who knows what Queen Aggie has in mind next. Or when she'll do it."

"How much time do we need?"

"Master Sergeant?"

"Normally, I'd say months," said the tuatara. "I'm afraid we'll be lucky to have weeks."

"Then we'd best get to it. Please let me or any of the others know what you need. The same goes for you, Master, sorry, Champion Cloisterfeld. I need you both to be properly resourced, whatever that looks like. That's all I have. Anyone else want to say anything?"

"Just that it'll be nice to be '(Retired)' no more," said de Sphenodon.

"Welcome back to active duty," said First Advisor. "To both of you."

BLEEDING BEFORE YOU
WERE BORN

Eloise and First Advisor Thëjëts made it to the Privy just as the horological cuckoo called the top of the appointed hour. The other members of the Council were all already seated and the temperature of the discussion was hot, although Eloise couldn't tell the topic. "G'mid-arvo everyone," she said, going to her seat at the head of the table.

The room fell silent and everyone stood as she took her place.

"Please be at rest. Good to see everyone again."

Everyone sat, save the brigadier general.

Eloise ignored him for the moment. "First Advisor, if you'd do me the kindness of passing out the agenda scrolls."

"Certainly," said Thëjëts. "I—"

"Your Highness," interrupted Gideon de Odobenus. "I beg leave to speak."

"Of course, Brigadier General. What's on your mind?"

"What's on my mind?" The old walrus's blubbery jowls undulated in suppressed outrage. "What's on my mind is the uncalled-for assault on my barracks this morning. That's what's on my mind."

"Uncalled-for assault? That's your characterization?" It had been. Deliberately. But no point giving ground right away.

"Permission to speak freely, Your Highness."

Eloise had known something like this would be coming. Best to get it over with. She used her most mollifying tone. "Please, speak as freely as you'd like."

"I refer to your unplanned visit to Barracks Six Alpha this morning, and the rough manner with which your... I don't know what you'd call him... Your accomplice treated my soldiers, with no regard to chain of command and not so much as a by your leave from me or any of my subordinates."

"I was there," said Eloise. "That doesn't count for anything?"

"Of course it does." De Odobenus spat the words. "You are queen. It counts for everything. But that's not my point."

Eloise kept her cool. "What's your point, then?"

"My point is that an ambush was perpetrated in such a way as to show my soldiers up in the worst possible light."

"Worst possible light? Really?" Eloise stood, and everyone around the table followed suit. "Champion Lacksneck!" she called.

Lorch opened the door and poked his head into the room. "Yes, Queen Eloise?"

"Could you please ask the master sergeant to come in?"

"Yes, Queen Eloise."

Moments later, the tuatara strode through the doorway, still wearing his antiquated uniform with all its decorations. It was hard to believe that Eloise had only met him that morning. He seemed so much of a fixture in her thinking already.

Unasked, de Sphenodon moved to the front of the room and positioned himself to Eloise's right.

"May I introduce Master Sergeant (Retired) Tiberius de Sphenodon, who is unretired as of today and who's taken on the role of Special At Large Advisor to the Queen." Eloise hadn't actually granted him that title, but it sounded good.

"Special At Large Advisor for what?"

"Whatever I want, Brigadier General. But if you really want to know, I've asked him for some pointers on military preparedness."

The walrus snorted. "Military preparedness? You brought in a low-ranked unknown to advise you on military preparedness?" The brigadier general aimed his heft at the tuatara. "Indulge me, sir. What exactly do you know about military preparedness?"

"I have been in combat in the name of the queen. Does that count?"

"Combat? There hasn't been combat in forever. What combat did you see?"

The tuatara's face was neutral. "Most recently, I fought in the Battle of Sloth Hill. Before that—"

"Impossible," blustered de Odobenus. "The Battle of Sloth Hill was over a century ago. But more to the point, it was a massacre. No one survived."

Tiberius de Sphenodon held up his damaged forefoot. "No one was unscathed. But it's inaccurate to say no one survived. There were a few of us who did, which is the reason you know how that one went."

"Queen Eloise, this imposter presumes to come into my barracks and start barking orders—"

"Imposter? You call me an imposter?"

"You heard me. This imposter—"

"Stand down, sir," snapped the tuatara. He stepped over to the walrus, his manner imposing despite being a tenth the size. "I was bleeding on the battlefield before you were born, you whelp."

"Listen, you fossil. Assuming you're who you say you are, there's one thing that's universally true—nobody wins when it comes to war."

"To the contrary. War is many things. It is madness. It is tragic. It is a drain on the realm. But war is never one-sided. It always produces both winners and losers, and in all sorts of ways. Weapons-makers, for example, do just fine. So do coffin-makers, flag-sewers, armor smiths, and the hangers-on who provide distraction and personal comforts. Not to mention those who vanquish the others. To say nobody wins shows naiveté and ignorance."

"How dare you!"

Tiberius de Sphenodon leaned forward and jabbed the air with his injured claw hand. "Let me tell you this, you soft, unfit insult to the uniform you wear. I've seen more death and glory, more gore and grace, more honor and bravery in a week than you would have seen in your entire pampered life."

The walrus whirled toward Eloise, only just missing the tuatara with his rear flipper. "Your Highness, I must protest this in the strongest possible terms. What has been done is unacceptable. I cannot tolerate such interference."

Eloise hadn't meant for it to come to this. But here it was. She felt a sudden clarity. "OK, then," she replied.

"If there are concerns that the crown has, then... I beg your pardon?"

"I said, 'OK then.'"

That stopped de Odobenus, whose eyes narrowed, wary. "Um, good." His voice inflected it more as a question.

Eloise folded her hands across her lap and rested her elbow on the box containing the Star of Whatever. "I accept what you said. That you can't tolerate it. And believe me, I don't want you to suffer. If you find the situation intolerable, then I hereby free you from it."

"I don't think..." The walrus's whiskers drooped as his bluster drained away. "Your Highness, there's no need to—"

"No, Brigadier General. I insist. I don't want you to have to do anything that you can't tolerate. As such, allow me to say thank you for your service, and I wish you luck in your retirement."

A stunned silence filled the room. Eloise let it linger, then softened her voice. "Brigadier General de Odobenus, you have served the crown well for many, many years. My mother always spoke highly of you. The decorations on your uniform testify to a lifetime of distinguished contribution to the Western Lands and All That Really Matters. But the military needs to evolve if we're to be ready for the threats—the very real threats—we're facing."

"Please, Your Highness. Don't—"

"There need not be any loss of face, Brigadier General. We don't have to announce anything right away. I'm not stripping you of your pension or anything. And it would be my pleasure to throw a big send-off for you with so much pomp and circumstance that it will make your tusks ache. You'll go out in a fashion that is completely well-deserved and a testament to your rank and position, both within the military and at Court. Plus, you'll need time to bring your successor up to speed on matters of import. So, let's say we'll have the whole thing done and dusted by the end of the month. I trust you find this acceptable?"

"Queen Eloise, I don't know what to say."

"I believe 'thank you' is traditional."

"That's not what I meant."

"I know that."

"This hasty—"

"Hasty? Hasty? Let me ask, Brigadier General (Now Retired) de Odobenus, what would you have me do? It's been weeks since Flachberg was invaded and we've barely sent a peep in response. Do you know why not?"

"Because we weren't ready to do so, Your Highness."

"Exactly. We weren't ready. That's my point." Eloise stabbed an index finger into the table. "That is my exact, complete, and entire point. We weren't ready. We're still not ready. But you know who's ready? Queen Aggie and the Easties. They're ready, whether anyone else likes it or not. They proved that in Flachberg. My fear is they'll prove it again. Again and again." She was shouting now. "I will not be the Gumball queen who loses the Western Lands and All That Really Matters to an olive-sucker. I just *won't*." She slammed her fist into the table for emphasis and immediately regretted stressing her healed fracture.

Lorch and First Advisor both winced. De Odobenus looked distressed. The others maintained forced, blank expressions. An even more shocked silence gripped the room.

Eloise forced herself to take several long breaths to regain her composure, and rubbed her sore wrist.

"My apologies for such language," she said. "My mother always said name-calling is unbecoming. As with most things—although, as I'm coming to learn, not all—she was right. I'll try not to embarrass myself like that in the future."

More silence.

"My point is that trouble is at our doorstep, and we can't pretend it isn't. So, with respect, a change or two is in order. Brigadier General (Retired) de Odobenus."

"Yes, Your Highness."

"Thank you for your service to the military, to the crown, and to this Privy Council. Your presence will be missed." It was unclear if she meant that as a promise or a mollification, but either way, it was clear the walrus was through. "If you wish to provide advice on your successor, I would be happy to hear it, but try to bear in mind which qualities are needed in these times."

"Thank you, ma'am. I will."

Eloise stood and looked around the table as everyone once again stood in her presence. She gripped the sides of her robe to conceal her shaking hands. "Does anyone have anything pressing to say? No? Good. I'm abandoning the rest of the agenda for today. We're adjourned."

❦ 30 ❦

COLD

Eloise swooped out of the Privy and headed to the Queen's Study so she could be alone and recover. She unlocked the door, locked it again from the inside, flounced down into the comfy chair, and tried, more or less successfully, not to cry.

Fifteen minutes later, there was a quiet knock at the door. "Queen Eloise?" It was Bënnïë-Änn Thëjëts.

Eloise wiped her eyes and sighed. "First Advisor," she said without getting up. "What can I do for you?"

"I brought you some haggleberry tea."

"Oh. Thank you." A pleasant surprise. She couldn't imagine former First Advisor Ligurian ever coming to her with a mollifying tea tray. "Just a tick. Let me get the door." Eloise unlocked it and let her in.

"Thought you could do with a little something." First Advisor set the tray down on the table next to the comfy chair. "May I pour for you?"

"Yes, thank you."

Thëjëts pointed to a plate covered by a napkin. "And the new Chef had just pulled those from the oven. They're date macaroons."

"Are they any good?"

"I did have one. As with everything the new Chef makes, they're perfectly adequate."

"That will have to do. Sit, please. Join me."

"Thank you, I will. I'd flopping kill for a cuppa."

They sipped and nibbled without saying anything until Eloise felt like she could face what had just happened.

"So, advise me, First Advisor. How bad was I?"

"How bad were you? That is not a question that is becoming of a queen, and I refuse to address it."

Eloise arched an eyebrow at her. "What kind of question would you deign to address?"

"Is what I did effective? Was my decision useful? What will be the consequences of what I just did? That kind of thing."

"I see. So, advise me, First Advisor. Is what I did effective?"

"It will certainly have an effect. You've sent a message to the military that change is afoot. It remains to be seen if they dig in and resist you or if they embrace your changes."

"Was I wrong to handle the brigadier general the way I did? I got angry. That's not a good look."

"What you did was flopping cold, no question about that."

"Was it? It just seemed necessary. And sort of sad."

First Advisor reached for a fifth date macaroon and gestured with it. "Welcome to being queen—doing a lot of things that are necessary, many of which are sort of sad. You want my honest opinion?"

"Always."

"Brigadier General Gideon Horsewhale de Odobenus is exactly what he appears to be and what you identified. He's the product of his era, suited to a queen who needed ceremony more than swords. He's perfect for that, and ill-suited to what's facing you. So far, so good. The thing is, he has always been popular among the soldiers and, more importantly, among his fellow officers, and he's very unlikely to take well to being dismissed so summarily by, if you'll pardon the expression, nothing more than a flopping wet-eared pipsqueak whose tuchus has barely started warming the throne."

"That's what he said when I left?"

"That's what he said before you got there, according to Seer Maybelle when I spoke to her afterwards, although the 'flopping' was my addition and 'tuchus' is a variant."

"Is it certain he'll turn against me?"

"You haven't made a friend, but it will help that you offered him a face-saving way out. He'll enjoy being celebrated. He's always had an ego ripe for stroking. Put Lady Seneschal onto the task of farewelling him. Maybe give him a meaningless title that makes it sound like he'll still have input. I liked your Special At Large Advisor to the Queen. Something like that, but grander, should unruffle some of his feathers."

"I could name him Ex Officio Supreme General (Retired), or something like that. Something with a lot of words."

Thëjëts smirked. "It'll sound like a promotion. If it comes with a bump to his retirement stipend and a stipulation that it's dependent on his cooperation in the transition, I think he'll go for it."

"You'll take care of it?"

"As you wish. Now, next matter. You have a vacancy on the Privy Council. What do you intend to do with it?"

"I haven't thought that far ahead. I've only just stormed out of there. And it wasn't like I was planning on removing the brigadier general from his role beforehand."

"What about de Sphenodon?"

"I don't think so," said Eloise. "I really do need him in an advisory role. Something really hands-on. Plus, I don't know him that well yet. I think he's what the military needs, but I don't think it makes sense to plonk him into the Privy Council. Perhaps you can recommend some candidates, even if we have to reach down into the ranks a little to elevate someone with a more martial orientation."

"I'll put together some names. I'll need a day or two."

"Thank you."

They returned to tea sipping. Eloise had a second macaroon. First Advisor had a seventh.

"Queen Eloise, I need to ask you something. Do you really intend to lead the queendom into war?"

"Isn't that what you advised me to do in your first briefing with me?"

"I guess. And my advice, more or less, still holds, but it was premature of me to suggest. I wasn't across everything as I am now. It's as you say —we're just not up to taking the fight to Queen Aggie, and I'm not sure we're up to it if she brings the fight to us again, either. But focusing on getting ready, and being better, that's all we can do at the moment. That, and hope, like you said, for more time. By the way, 'olive sucker' is not—"

"I know, I know. I shouldn't—"

"No, hear me out. That's not a bad angle. There's value in denigrating your enemies. You might want to keep that one in your pocket."

"Not what I expected you to say, but OK."

"Queen Eloise, there's a lot of rebuilding and reshaping ahead of you. You can't lead your realm into war by yourself. You'll need to amass resources and gather allies, those who believe in what you're doing. That's far from certain. Difficult days lie ahead. I hope you're up for them."

"I hope so, too."

31

PEACOCK ROOM

Johanna's uncle, the late King Doncaster Worsted Halva de Chëëëkflïïïnt, had always received subjects in Castle Blotch's most opulent space, the Throne Room. Johanna wasn't so sure about it.

"This strikes me as overkill," she said to her father as they considered the space. "Why wave your wealth as monarch in everyone's face? I mean, unless you were trying to overawe those who came before you. Or maybe compensate for something of one's person that was smaller than one felt it should be."

"Now, now, no need for that."

A day later, Johanna gestured around a different room. "What do you think?"

"Hmmm... I always hated this room, growing up," said Chafed. "You've improved it."

It had been called the Peacock Room, due to the tens of thousands of peacock feathers that had been painted on the walls, floor, and roof in a vertigo-inducing excess. Added to this had been a forest of peacock sculptures, packed in so densely that it was practically impossible to enter the room. These ranged in quality from the most exquisite works of art down to clay smudges produced at the hands of toddlers. The Peacock Room looked like a strange, abandoned art installation by someone so lacking in taste they must have been chased out of town by people wielding pitchforks.

It was so bad there had been a sign on the door that read, "Warning: It's Bad In Here. We Suggest You Go Elsewhere."

Johanna had had the sculptures catalogued, and then carefully packed away. She'd had the floor, roof, and three of the four walls painted over in a simple peacock blue, and chose a modest throne from a storeroom and had it installed on a low dais. She left the one wall behind the throne covered in the painted feathers as an accent, a reminder of what had once been there, and as a possible distraction to those who would come before her.

"Think this will work as a Receiving Room kind of place?" she asked.

"The access is good for people who need to come here. There's a side door you can use for your entrances and exits, which is key to the theatrics of it all. The size is better for actually getting work done. So, yes, it should be OK. I like that it emphasizes practicality over ostentation. Definitely an improvement over the Throne Room."

"Good. I'll start receiving people here. Are there any requests to come before the crown, or should we just toss open the doors and see who saunters up?"

"Actually, there has been a request."

Johanna arched an eyebrow. "Really? Someone wants to talk to the Half Kingdom's semi-accidental queen?"

"Don't call yourself that. It doesn't help your image if people hear that you think of yourself that way."

"Yes, Father. One must not speak the truth in such matters."

"Queen Johanna, if you want me to be your first advisor, I have to be able to give things to you straight."

"Of course, First Advisor Gumball née de Chëëëkflïïïnt. Who wants to see me?"

"The Eastern Lands ambassador and trade envoy wish to present their credentials."

"Well, good. I guess that means they're taking this queen thing seriously."

"Did someone sprinkle some cynicism on your breakfast porridge?" said Chafed. "You're as legitimate a ruler as they come. Crown-plonked and everything. Our little machination of me taking the crown, then abdicating it so you could take it, seems to have provided much-needed clarity."

"Thank you, First Advisor Father, for keeping me on track. Let's forge ahead and receive our brethren from the east."

"I'll arrange it for tomorrow."

"It can be the first reception in the Peacock Room."

The next morning after breakfast, Johanna met her father behind the side door to the Peacock Room.

"How do I look?" Johanna's handmaid, Nesther de Duck, who'd served her since her Thorning Ceremony, had plaited Johanna's hair into a Southie braid and pinned it with hair combs painted to look like a series of ladybugs. That Nesther managed this using her bill and webbed feet was a small miracle, but it was a daily small miracle that also included taming Johanna's unruly curls, one of the things she shared with Eloise, along with the inexplicably white hair that remained a souvenir from their time in the Purple Haze.

"Like a queen." Chafed looked around to double-check they were alone, then leaned down and gave her a peck on the forehead. "Knock 'em dead out there."

"Not literally, of course."

"No, sometimes you really do need to knock 'em dead."

Johanna looked at her father to make sure he wasn't being serious.

He winked.

"Right. Got it. Let me ask a question. How come they don't do the capes thing here? It seemed like Mother always used them to good effect. You knew when she had on the Cape of Dashed Hope that you weren't likely to get what you wanted, and that it might be better to come back another day."

"We can institute that if you'd like."

"I think I'd like to. Can you ask the seamstress to sew me a few? We can name them as we get them."

"Yes, Your Majesty."

"In the meantime, this one..." Johanna lifted the hem of the cape she wore, fanning it out to either side. It was a heavy cape in a blue that complimented, but didn't match, the walls of the Peacock Room. "This one can be the Equanimity Cape."

"What does it symbolize?" asked Chafed.

"I don't know." She looked at it a moment, then let the sides fall back down. "Let's say that it means I start the receiving session in a reasonably good mood and it would behoove everyone to help me remain that way."

"Noted. Ready?"

Johanna took a breath. "Ready."

"After you." He held open the side door and Johanna stepped through. As the few people in the room fell to silence and stood, she stepped up onto the dais and faced them. "Thank you for coming today. Please be at rest." She sat, so they could as well. "First Advisor, what's first on the agenda?"

"The representatives from the Eastern Lands, Your Majesty."

"Proceed, please."

Chafed turned to the room and raised his voice. "Grëëëgööörÿÿÿ? Are you there?"

A bullfrog in Northern Lands herald livery hopped into view through a crack in the door. "Yes, First Advisor." His voice was a basso perfection that echoed through the room, amplified by the bellows of his frog throat.

"You may announce our first petitioners."

"Yes, First Advisor." The door opened fully, and the bullfrog said, "Presenting the Ambassador Designate Manzanilla and Lead Trade Negotiator de Coluber from the Eastern Lands."

A tall, thin woman and a blue snake moved toward the dais. Johanna recognized them at once, as they'd arrived at Castle de Brague to take roles in her sister's court. She'd never seen them from closer than across a room, though, and had never spoken directly to them. Johanna vaguely remembered something about them in one of Eloise's letters, but she hadn't gone into detail, saying she'd cover it when they met next, or when she had more time to write.

The woman wore a breezy, unseasonably cool robe dyed the expected olive-green of her realm. Her hair was braided and curled up on her head, and her minimal make-up emphasized the deep black of her eyes and set off her olive-green eye shadow. Her mouth was smiling, but even from across the room, Johanna could see it didn't fully reach her eyes.

Then there was the snake. He was a mesmerizing python in a bright, almost glowing blue on top that blended to a pure white underneath. But Johanna barely noticed his scales. She was drawn immediately to his face.

He had three eyes.

Two were on the sides of his head and worked together as one would expect. The third was on top, in the middle, and seemed to gaze independently of the other two. When he blinked it, Johanna could see that the lid had been colored with the same olive-green as Manzanilla's forehead dot.

How very strange, thought Johanna. *And how very interesting.*

They stopped in front of the dais, and the woman handed Chafed the scrolls that held their credentials. Then to Johanna, she said, "I am Picholine Manzanilla. I will be the Eastern Lands ambassador to your queendom if you'll do me the honor of accepting my credentials on behalf of Her Imperialness, Queen Aglandau Gaeta Cerignola Ponentine. Queen Aglandau sends her greetings from the Eastern Lands, along with her felicitations for your reign and boundless wishes for your good health. She desires that her queendom and yours work in harmony, friendship, and with enduring cooperation."

"Thank you," said Johanna. "The Northern Lands welcomes you."

"This is Bosana de Coluber," said Manzanilla. "Our lead trade negotiator."

"Your Majesty," said the snake, without the lisping usually found in his species. "Long may you sit on your throne, and long may the trade between our realms flow like the River Thurmond."

"Thank you, Lead Trade Negotiator de Coluber." Johanna looked at them both. "Weren't you both representing the Eastern Lands at my sister's court in the Western Lands and All That Really Matters?"

Manzanilla nodded. "Yes, Your Majesty. We were, indeed, at your sister's court. Then Queen Aglandau withdrew us from our service there, and instead asked us to be her mouth, eyes, and ears here in your fair realm. We serve at her pleasure, of course."

"Of course. Yes. Well. I see. Good, then, I guess."

This line of enquiry was interrupted by an Eastern Lands page, who came through the doorway wearing a kalamata-olive-brown tunic and carrying a jar on a pillow. Manzanilla took it and handed it to Chafed, who glanced at it and handed it on to Johanna. "Queen Aglandau asked us to give you this gift. The jar contains olives from her personal grove, and she sends it with affection and hopes for a personal meeting one day."

Johanna looked at the olives, impressed. "These are splendid. Simply magnificent. Don't tell me. Do they come from the Enlightenment Tree?"

Now Manzanilla smiled for real. "Well spotted, Your Majesty."

"Amazing. Simply amazing. They say the tree is supposed to be over 6,000 years old. Is that true?"

"We know for sure it is at least 2,000 years old, but yes, Your Majesty, as far as we know, 6,000 years is the real truth."

"It's astounding to think that the Divine One herself sat beneath the tree that these olives came from and attained her enlightenment." Johanna found herself tearing up. "I shall treasure these always. Thank you so very much."

"I shall convey your words to Queen Aglandau."

"Yes, please do." Johanna hesitated, then said, "I'd like to know more. Can I invite you to dine with me this evening?"

The snake and the ambassador glanced at each other, then Manzanilla nodded. "We'd love to."

"It won't be formal, so don't dress up too much."

"Yes, Your Majesty," said the snake, and his strange third eye closed with a languid but definite wink.

32

FROM OUR REALM TO YOURS

That evening, Johanna, Chafed, Manzanilla, and de Coluber met in one of the smaller dining rooms suited to quiet conversation. At first, the conversation was awkward—a lot of "How are you enjoying the season?" and "How was your journey?" and "Did you encounter any marauding bands of bandicoots?" and "It really is sad how bandicoots are still so unfairly maligned." Nothing but trivialities exchanged over appetizers of stuffed mushrooms, chickpea pesto, and cucumber spring rolls.

And then the conversation turned to growing things, and suddenly the talk flowed. It started with a simple question from Johanna: "Is there a type of olive cultivar that is beloved in the Eastern Lands that would grow here in the Northern Lands?"

"Let's start with the 'beloved' part of your question," said the ambassador. "Different varieties are beloved for different purposes. Do you want a table olive? An olive to press for oil? Will the tree be in a place where it needs to be beautiful to the eye? Do you prefer a green olive, a brown olive, or a black one?"

"I see. It's a bit like apples. There are a lot of factors that go into what makes a particular apple appealing, like will it be mostly for baking, are you mostly interested in how the flowers look, or do you want something that you can pluck from a tree and bite?"

"Now, turning to the other part of your question. Are there olive varieties that can thrive in colder climes? Yes, I think there are a couple. The Ascolano is a table olive that is cold-hardy. They can also be used for olive oil."

"What about the Ghjermana?" said the snake. "It's got that lovely black color when ripe."

"Another good choice," agreed the ambassador. "They can resist the cold as well. Your Majesty, would it be of interest for me to procure some cuttings for you to plant here at Castle Blotch?"

"I'd like that. Very much. It would be like having a little of your homeland here at Stained Rock."

"Consider it done," said Manzanilla.

Over a main course of black bean stew with rice based on a Central Ranges recipe, the talk meandered from olives to orchards, to Johanna's love of growing things and her nascent regreening of the castle's gardens, and on to the realm's efforts to explore the devastated land within the Purple Haze, to wondering if that land might somehow be cultivated again. Johanna felt so at ease with Manzanilla and de Coluber that, despite a cautionary raised eyebrow from her father, she quietly shared the struggles her queendom faced in financing some of the ambitious programs she had in mind. "Actually, it's not just the ambitious improvements that are difficult," she said. "Despite my efforts to begin the process of lifting the realm back to a proud, can-do Northern Lands frame of mind, it seems like the people have rusted themselves onto the limitations of their Half Kingdom ways."

"Is it just a matter of coin?" asked the ambassador.

Chafed jumped in. "Not entirely, no. There are other factors."

"Come on, Father. Coin is everything. And the coin is lacking. It's not like that's a huge secret."

"It's supposed to be secret, but I guess it isn't now." He looked uncomfortable with the way the conversation was going.

"We're among friends. I think it's OK."

"Yes, Your Majesty."

Once again, the snake and the woman shared a look, then the python said, "Since we're among friends, perhaps a friendly gesture would not go astray."

"Oh, sorry," said Johanna, not sure what sort of gesture would be appropriate. "I could, uh... I..."

"No, no," laughed Manzanilla. "A gesture from us to you. From our realm to yours."

"Right. Apologies. I misunderstood. Did you have anything particular in mind?"

"In fact, we do," said de Coluber, and he fixed her with that strange third eye of his, locked onto her gaze and stared into her. Johanna got the odd feeling that he was looking far deeper into her than she ought to let him. He was like a mesmerist. "Queen Aglandau knows what it is like to be a new queen, and just as well, what it is like to have ambitions beyond what one's coffers will sustain."

"Yes," said Chafed, still cautious.

"Queen Aglandau wishes to enter into a mutually beneficial arrangement. An alliance, if you will."

"What kind of alliance?"

"We can explore the details, but think in terms of infrastructure support."

"Infrastructure? What kind of infrastructure?"

Manzanilla used her spoon to score a line in the tablecloth. "An obvious first project would be the Queen's Road between Stained Rock and the Adequate Wall of the Realms into the Eastern Lands."

"That would facilitate trade," said the snake.

"Good idea," said Johanna. "There's the other stretch of the road that goes to the Western Lands and All That Really Matters as well. That needs at least as much work."

There was a pause. "I can see how that would be on your list," said the ambassador. "But from our point of view, that's less of a priority."

"I see," said Johanna. "So we'd be filtering potential projects for how, uh, mutually beneficial they might be. That's the idea?"

"Something like that, yes."

"Right."

The discussion was interrupted by the serving wenches clearing the main meal and bringing dessert—charred pineapple with a lemon and ginger granita served with cashew pralines. Johanna hoped the Easties would be at least a little impressed, but while they dug in and ate it all, it seemed somewhat perfunctory.

Chafed put down his dessert spoon and dabbed his mouth with his napkin. "Tell me. With this offer, this alliance, what's in it for you?"

The snake licked his mouth with his split tongue. "What do you mean?"

"It seems very one-sided."

"Can't one queen reach out to another who clearly needs a hand without having her motives questioned?"

"No. Not without strings."

"Father."

"Queen Johanna," said Chafed. "There is an axiom when you're dealing with other people's coin, and that's this: all coin comes attached with opinions. The question is always and only, whose opinions can you tolerate having to listen to?"

Picholine Manzanilla's lips tightened. "Does the dowager king impugn our motives?"

Chafed stood. "Do not bring my late wife into—"

Johanna stood. "Stop. Both of you. Please don't drag down our evening with quibbling."

Chafed looked at the Eastie ambassador, then at the lead trade nego-tiator, and then finally at his daughter. "Apologies, Your Majesty, and to you, Madame Ambassador. I meant no harm. Of course, our friends from the east have only good intentions. I look forward to hearing the details of their kind and generous offer."

"Thank you, First Advisor."

"I apologize as well, Queen Johanna and First Advisor Gumball née de Chëëëkflïïïnt. We came to you with arms open and I was merely surprised that it was not seen as such. Our intentions are simple. We wish to foster cooperation and better relations. We recognize that you have a pressing need for coin to be able to do good works for your realm, which will, admittedly, have flow-on benefits for our realm. We would like to help you meet that need for coin with terms that are fair in your eyes as well as ours. We look forward to going into details at your earliest convenience."

"Very good, Ambassador. Apology accepted. Now, let's enjoy our dessert, and we can set up a time, perhaps tomorrow, to hear the specifics. Consider us interested, and please thank Queen Aglandau for her consideration."

"Very good, Your Majesty," said the ambassador. "I'll convey your response."

The rest of the evening reverted to trivialities, which left Johanna time to consider just how much good she could do for her people with non-empty coffers.

When the ambassador and the lead trade negotiator said their good-byes and were riding away in a carriage, Johanna looked at her father. "What do you think?"

"I think we need to be a bit careful, but I'm also intrigued by the possibilities such an alliance might open up."

"My thoughts exactly. You can set up the meeting?"

"First thing tomorrow, yes."

"Good."

At that same moment, a similar-ish conversation was happening in the carriage as it trundled over cobblestones to the ambassadorial residence.

"Do you think they bought it?" asked Manzanilla.

"Oh, they bought it," said de Coluber. "They bought it all, soup to nuts. Now all we have to do is find a couple of olive tree cuttings to give as a sign that we will uphold our end of a bargain."

"Where are we going to find an Ascolano or Ghjermana in this part of the world? We'll have to get one sent from home."

"No need."

"No? Why not?"

"Any olive cutting will do. It's unlikely to survive in this climate, which means it will never get to a maturity where the species would be discernible."

"Very efficient, Bosana. Very. We'll also need to draw up something that looks like terms of trade. I'll take care of that."

"Be generous with what you offer, but not too generous. We want them to sign on without becoming suspicious."

33

CELESTIAL LOTUS

Eloise's arms burned, and she feared her fingers would blister instead of getting calloused. She was in the mid-seven hundreds on her way to a full thousand practice strikes with the wooden two-handed practice sword. Each strike involved two parts. First, she pushed the wooden pommel up with her left hand while stepping back with her right leg, raising the sword above her head so her hands were positioned above her crown and the blade was angled at precisely 45 degrees. All that while breathing in. Then, while breathing out, she stepped forward so her right leg landed about her body's width in front of her left, slicing the sword along a straight vertical so the blade ended parallel to the floor and she would have cleaved a foe from skull to navel.

Repeat, repeat, repeat to a thousand.

Lorch, next to her, did the same.

This was part of what Cloisterfeld called the Three Pillars—sword work, staff work, empty hand work. Each drew on the others and was informed by them. But of the three, Eloise liked the sword work best, probably due to the formality and ritual of it.

Step back. Step forward and cut. Step back. Step forward and cut.

Now and then, Cloisterfeld remarked on their style or got them to adjust some detail of their technique. "Strike from your core."

Or, "Your power comes from your body, your hips, your center—not your arms."

Or, "Your feet form more of a triangle or inverted T."

"Yes, Master Cloisterfeld," they both said each time she commented.

Other times, her mother's champion talked about purpose. "You're doing this to develop strength in your arms, shoulder, and core."

Or, "You're learning to move your body as one unit—arms, legs, torso, and breath all in one."

Or, "By connecting breath to the movement, your movements can eventually be as fast and as fluid as breathing."

Or, "Create perfection in deliberate practice to instill perfection in combat."

"Yes, Master Cloisterfeld."

But most of the time, Sylvia simply did the thousand cuts alongside Eloise and Lorch, providing a model for them to follow.

A thousand cuts with the sword. A thousand cuts with the staff.

At her sixth lesson, Cloisterfeld said, "You've got the basic movement. Now we're going to expand it to what I call the celestial lotus sequence. You'll use that cut, but we'll vary where we're cutting by moving the body and feet so that in one cycle, we strike in each of the eight directions. In the process, you roughly inscribe the shape of a celestial lotus blossom with its 80 petals."

"So, one strike per ten petals," said Eloise.

"It's not meant to be quite so literal, but, roughly, yes."

Cloisterfeld demonstrated the pattern of movement. She started with a right foot forward step slice to the front, then a hip turn to the back as the sword was raised, followed by a cut with the left foot ahead. Eloise thought of this as north, then south. Next was a ninety-degree turn to the right (west), then another 180 degree hip swivel and a left foot cut (east). A forty-five degree cut to the right (northwest). A turn and left foot cut to the southeast. A quarter turn step and slice to the southwest, and a turn and strike to the northeast, which set up another pass through the compass starting with the north.

Eloise found this pattern particularly appealing. The way it flowed from position to position. The way it nodded to the eight directions like a greeting to the world. The way the sequential movement of the feet eventually drew a circle.

They practiced this for a full quarter hour. For Eloise, it was bliss.

Then they put their weapons back on the rack and Cloisterfeld said, "I'd like to teach you the Balancing Way. Do you know it?"

"I've seen it," said Eloise. "Lorch would practice the moves when we were traveling. Sort of..." She made an imitation of what she'd seen him do. "And the horses of His Alacrity Khan Nergüi's the Us trained using what looked to me like an equine variant."

"That's called Shining Mane style," said Cloisterfeld. "It's a far cousin, but stems from the same origin. What do you practice?"

"I was taught Fist First style," said Lorch.

"That is a good style. I'll be teaching Bright Sun style. Many of the forms will look familiar, but the names are different and the approach to training incorporates more weapons at the advanced levels, if we happen to get that far."

Lorch nodded. "I look forward to it."

"So, we start with steps." For the next quarter hour, Cloisterfeld had Eloise and Lorch make steps in specific ways—the arc step, the nothing step, the washerman's crouch, and the ale house step. They were simple moves, but Cloisterfeld insisted on precise foot positioning, correct balance, and meticulous movement from step to step.

Like the celestial lotus sword work, Eloise loved the Balancing Way.

When the horological cuckoo called the top of the hour, Eloise and Lorch bowed to each other, then to Sylvia, to end the lesson.

"Tomorrow?" asked Eloise.

"Tomorrow and the day after, until you no longer want to."

"Thank you. I look forward to it. May I ask something else?"

"Yes, Your Highness."

"How goes your training with the soldiers?"

"It's early days, but Master Sergeant de Sphenodon and I are starting to see the first signs of progress. Certainly discipline is improving."

"I'd like to see what you're doing, if that's OK."

"Would this afternoon suit?"

"I'll come out after lunch."

"I'll let Master Sergeant know to expect you."

✣ 34 ✣

OBSTACLE COURSE

That afternoon, Eloise made her way to the Drill Paddock with Lorch, Jerome, and First Advisor Thëjëts. They rounded the corner and emerged from the tree-lined trail. Eloise stopped. "Oh. That's different."

Gone was the large, perfectly flat field with thick, immaculately trimmed grass. Gone was the flock of a dozen groundskeeping sheep. In its place was a series of marked-off areas, each devoted to a different purpose, from fitness to weapons training. Hillocks had been sculpted, holes had been dug, and boulders had been brought in and placed in strategic clusters. The whole paddock teemed with grunting, sweating, cursing bodies driven on by hectoring, whistle-blowing drill masters.

"We've only just gotten here," said Jerome, "and I'm already tired just from looking at them."

"I asked for change," said Eloise. "I guess this is what change looks like. Shall we?"

They walked to the closest area, a mud-splattered training course featuring vertical walls, slackline balancing, climbing ropes, high-stepping nets, overhead rings spaced at odd intervals, things to crawl under that looked like they'd hurt if you got too close, things to crawl over that looked like they'd hurt even more, and dozens of other tortures. A mass of soldiers were doing their best to get from one end to the other, where they had a short breather before starting over again. Presiding over them from a raised platform was Tiberius de Sphenodon, who chided, chivvied, cheered, and browbeat, yelling at some, encouraging others, all the while asking for more from all of them.

It was immediately obvious that the course was well beyond most of the soldiers. It was also obvious that they were all trying as hard as they could.

It was something, at least.

The tuatara spotted Eloise, smiled, and saluted. Next to him, Staff Sergeant Plantar Garderobe was making notes on a slate. De Sphenodon said something to him and the staff sergeant's head jerked up. When he saw Eloise, he stiffened, fumbled for his whistle and blew a screeching blast, then yelled, "Queen is present!" Other drill masters picked up the call, blowing their whistles and echoing, "Queen is present."

All over the obstacle course, soldiers dropped to the ground, emerged from tunnels, stood up in the mud, and shouldered or sheathed their weapons. Each snapped into orderly formation. From the first trill of Garderobe's whistle to the furthest grunt at the far end of the field, it took no more than ten seconds for everyone to snap to perfect atten-tion—a distinct change from the lackadaisical performance Eloise had seen in the barracks.

Eloise looked up at Master Sergeant de Sphenodon. "Impressive," she said. "Very impressive."

"Thank you, Your Highness." The tuatara stood at rigid attention like everyone else. "I'm sure the soldiers will appreciate the compliment."

"Apologies for interrupting everyone's hard work. Please, continue. I just wanted to see how it's going."

"Yes, Your Highness." De Sphenodon turned to Garderobe. "Staff Sergeant. You have command."

"Sir! Thank you, Master Sergeant, sir!" Then he blew another air-cracking whistle and bellowed, "Reeee-suuuuume!"

The soldiers went back to their struggles and grunting, although, Eloise noticed, the level of cursing had dropped off.

Tiberius de Sphenodon climbed down from his platform and approached. He saluted, rather than bow, and said, "Your Highness. Welcome. Can I give you all a tour of our little updated facility?"

"That would be wonderful."

"Very good. You've seen the obstacle course. I've kept the design fairly easy to start with, so we have somewhere to go."

"Easy?" said Jerome. "They look like they're dying out there."

"They probably feel like they're dying out there," said the tuatara. "But trust me, three weeks from now, most of them will think it a doddle. I'll have to notch it up from there."

"I should come out here and train," said Lorch. "I'm not sure I'd be up to your easy level."

"You're more than welcome to join us. I'm sure having the queen's champion grinding away with the troops would do wonders for morale."

Eloise looked at the course, then at the master sergeant. "Would it?"

"Absolutely. The soldiers are doing it tough right now. They don't yet know what they're capable of and they're still hurting in places they didn't know they could hurt. So, yes. Something like that would be a real boost."

"Good to know."

"Now, if you'll come with me," said de Sphenodon, "I'll show you where the weapons training is being led by Champion Cloisterfeld."

But Eloise didn't follow him. "Master Sergeant, where is the starting point of the obstacle course?"

"The soldiers line up on the other side of that puddle. Why?"

Eloise turned and jogged toward the beginning of the course.

A shrill whistle screeched again. Plantar Garderobe yelled, "Queen is present!" All around her, soldiers shot back to attention.

"Hello again, Staff Sergeant Garderobe."

"Sir! Queen Eloise, sir!" Again, he didn't meet her eyes.

"Would it be too inconvenient if I had a go?"

"Sir! It would be an honor, Your Highness, sir!"

"Thank you. Please, let everyone back to what they're doing."

"Sir! Yes, ma'am, sir!" Garderobe called "Resume!" for the second time.

The soldiers all relaxed and went back to their training.

"Oi, you lot!" shouted Garderobe at the ones on the obstacle course. "Clear off so Her Highness can have a turn!"

Dozens of soldiers moved to the sides. Eloise saw them commenting to each other, bemused. A few of them even pointed at her surreptitiously.

"Queen Eloise?" said Lorch, who'd caught up.

Near the puddle, there was a line of rope on the ground marking the start and end of the course. Eloise slipped off her cloak. "Lorch, would you please hold this?" Without waiting for his answer, she handed it to him, as well as her simple day crown. Eloise wondered what to do with the box containing the Star of Whatever. She really didn't want to take it off, but the odds of it getting dirty were high. Then again, the thing had been through plenty since she'd had it, including landing in the disgusting muck at the bottom of the Whacking Great Hole. It could handle a bit of dirt. Eloise retied the sash, so it was positioned under her tunic at the back rather than at her side.

The tuatara scuttled up. "Are you sure, Your Highness?"

"No, I'm not sure at all. But I should be willing to at least try." Eloise began stretching her arms, her wrists, neck, and legs.

"Your Highness," said First Advisor. "This is truly not necessary."

"Did you not hear? Morale needs a boost. Perhaps I'll give them something to laugh at, which might lift spirits."

"It's not exactly regal to splash through mud, Queen Eloise."

"I'm sure it's not. But Queen Gwendolyn led her troops into battle from the front. Surely I can give an obstacle course a go."

Lorch handed the queen's cloak and crown to Thëjëts. "Would you be so kind as to hold these?" Then he removed his own cloak. "And this? Please?"

"I don't think this is a good idea."

"Good idea or not, I'm not going to have Queen Eloise doing this by herself."

"Thank you, Lorch." Eloise looked down at her outfit. "These aren't exercise clothes, but at least I'm not wearing a dress. I hope no one is scandalized by seeing their Queen in breeks and a tunic." She waved the tuatara forward. "Anything about the course that we need to know?"

"If you aren't willing to get muddy, you won't finish the course. Getting dirty is part of the gig."

"Noted. Lorch, do you mind if I go first? I'm sure you'll be passing me soon enough."

"As you wish."

"Hold on, hold on." It was Jerome. He took off his Assistant Seer's robe and gave it to Thëjëts. "I can't let the two of you have all the glory."

"You don't have to do this, Jer."

"Neither do you. Now let's get this done."

"Fine. What order should we go in, then?" asked Eloise.

Garderobe interrupted. "Sir! It doesn't matter, Your Highness, sir! You can all start at the same time. We have enough horological cuckoos to time everyone separately. Please, just line up."

"Works for me," said Jerome.

"Positions," said de Sphenodon. "Staff Sergeant, would you like to do the honors?"

"Sir! Yes, Master Sergeant, sir!" Garderobe gave three quick pips on his whistle, then yelled, "On your marks, get set..." Then another long whistle blast to start.

35

FROM DRUNKARD'S CARRIAGE WHEELS TO NIGHT SNEAK'S RINGS

Eloise, Lorch, and Jerome sprinted away from the starting line, heading for the first obstacle—a mesh of rope squares pegged calf-high above the ground. Lorch got ahead of her and did a high-stepping jog through them. Eloise followed, careful to keep her knees up and her feet clearly in the middle of each square. The grass had worn away from where soldier after soldier had been through, and her feet squelched as she went. Half way along, she misjudged a step, caught one of the ropes with her foot, and tripped, landing on the mesh. It held her weight, so she avoided a full, mud-enriched faceplant, but extracting herself was awkward.

"Keep going, Your Highness." It was Jerome, who'd crawled up onto the rope grid and was running along the top of it. "This isn't so bad."

"It's possible you're cheating there, Jer."

"Meh. I'm a chipmunk. What do they expect?"

She watched his tail bob along as he scampered on ahead. That made her even more determined. Eloise gritted her teeth and kept going.

She made it to the end of the high-step grid, and ran to the next obstacle, a set of monkey bars (a name all simians found both reductive and offensive). She wiped her hands on her breeks, jumped up, and grabbed the first overhead rung with both hands, ignoring the lingering soreness from the morning's efforts with the practice weapons. Both her injured shoulder and wrist immediately made themselves known, but they weren't too bad, so she swung her legs to get some movement and grasped the next bar with her left hand. She hung there a few seconds, then heaved her right hand over, even with her left. A bit more of a kick, and she reached for the second one. Waited, then moved her right hand forward.

This was going to take all day.

"Cycle your legs, ma'am."

Eloise looked down at two soldiers watching her, a squat one and a lanky one. It was the squat one who'd spoken. "I beg your pardon?"

"Cycle your legs, ma'am, sort of like you're running on air," said Squat.

Lanky nodded. "Aye, he's right by that. You want to be cycling your legs like you were in a pond and trying not to drown, and rocking your hips for momentum."

"Aye," said Squat. "Focus on the bars in front of you, and try to keep moving. The mistake is stopping, ma'am."

"Right. Thank you. What are your names, please?"

"He's called Squat," said the squat one.

"He's known as Lanky," said the lanky one.

"So, that's deliberately backwards, right?"

"Yes, Your Highness. The nicknames are meant to be ironic."

"Got it. Squat. Lanky. Pleased to meet you. Here I go."

Eloise did what they suggested, moving her hips to get some swing, running on nothing, and instead of going one rung at a time, trying to swing from one to the next.

She made it and waved to the two of them. "Thanks, gents."

"Pleasure, Your Highness," said Lanky.

She ran to the next obstacle—a hangover wall a good two lengths high and angled toward her. She arrived in time to see Lorch scramble over it, followed by Jerome, who was particularly suited to scaling it, being a chipmunk.

Eloise jumped up to grab the top edge, just catching it on her third try. She dangled a while, then tried scrabbling up using her feet against the wall, only to lose her grip and fall into a sandpit at the bottom.

Another try.

Same result.

She stood staring at the thing, and murmured, "What in the name of Çalaht's cantankerous carbuncles am I supposed to do with this?"

"You got to use your heel, ma'am." It was Lanky, who'd come over again to watch, along with Squat and a dozen of their mates.

"My heel? How could I possibly use my heel here?"

"You have to swing it up and hook it." Squat motioned with his hand. "Like so."

"Mind you point your toe, like you was at the ballet," said Lanky. "It helps with the hooking."

"Then you sort of scooch along and get your knee hooked where your foot was."

"Really?" said Eloise.

"Oh, aye," said Squat. "Mind, you have to keep your leg solid, like a wall bracket for a bookshelf. From there, you sort of heave and shove to lift your body over. But's not all about muscle. This one is about mind. You have to really commit."

"I see. Can you show me?"

"Aye, Your Highness."

Both Lanky and Squat had spoken in unison. They then did an "after you," "no, after you" thing, until they decided to do it at the same time. In moments, they were both over and on the other side.

"Like that, ma'am," said Lanky. "Be careful on the far side that you don't hurt yourself on the landing."

"Right." Eloise took a moment to focus, then tried the method they'd just demonstrated. She swung up her left foot, managed to slide it to the knee, and then, red-faced and huffing, she levered her body up and over, and lowered herself on the far side.

The soldiers erupted in cheers. "Good on ya, Your Highness!" said Squat, clapping.

A chant started. "Go, Your Majesty! Go! Go, Your Majesty! Go!" More soldiers joined the crowd of onlookers as she ran to the next obstacle, a rope climb. This one was no problem. She'd been climbing ropes since she was a little girl. It was a fast shimmy up, a tap on the top, back down, and off to the next obstacle, with soldiers running alongside, shouting encouragement.

Next was a rope slung across a large mud puddle. "What am I supposed to do, walk across it like a tightrope? I'd never make it."

"No ma'am," said Squat. "You traverse it however you want."

"Well, there are two main ways," said Lanky. "I prefer to go above the rope and slide along kind of like a caterpillar. But him, he likes to go below and moves along more like a sloth."

"Which is better?"

"Sloth," said Squat.

"Caterpillar," said Lanky.

"Right. I might go sloth, since I'm probably better at hanging than balancing."

"Aye, very good, Your Highness," said Squat. "Remember to hook the rope with your heels, not your calves, and the power is in your legs, not your arms."

"Really? Legs, not arms? Right." Eloise wiped her hands on her breeks. "Well, here goes."

Up she went on the rope, dangling down, holding by the arms. Remembering what Squat had said, she propelled herself forward using her legs.

"Keep your belly tight so your back don't droop, ma'am," said Lanky.

"Aye, sloth needs a tight belly and no droopy back," agreed Squat.

"Thanks, guys."

Five minutes later, straining and sweating, she made it across, to applause and whistles.

Eloise continued to traverse the course, moving from obstacle to obstacle with the crowd growing at each one, the cheering getting louder, all as she grew more and more fatigued, the unfamiliar exercises hammering her endurance and resolve. Each obstacle had a name. At the Witch's Necklace she lost her grip and plunged into a thick soup of mud, which soaked her to the waist. Running through the Drunkard's Carriage Wheels, she stepped on the edge of one and twisted her ankle. The barrels in the Publican's Casks were too high for her to jump, so she had to flop over them. The Roofer's Peril required a balanced walk across a narrow beam, which normally wouldn't have been that hard, except her thighs and calves were trembling by the time she got there, which made it near impossible, and she landed in a creek beneath it three times. That helped wash off some of the mud, but the water was winter cold and she had to keep moving to stay warm. The Hangman's Mistake involved navigating between a series of hanging ropes, each with a noose-like loop at the bottom. If she'd been a chimp, it would have been fine, but the balance and strength needed frustrated her almost to tears. Each station was a small torture in its own way, a torment that she somehow—with advice and pep talks from Lanky and Squat—managed to complete, to swelling yells, clapping, and whistling.

"What are those?" asked Eloise, panting and pointing to the last obstacle.

"Those are the Night Sneak's rings," said Squat. "You move by looping the rings from peg to peg as you hang from them."

"I see. Do me a favor, will you?"

"Yes, Your Highness?"

"Just pop a coffin down below so I can fall into the thing and be done with it. It'll be easier for everyone involved."

"Come on, Your Highness," said Lanky. "You can do this. The Night Sneak's rings are much more about mind than muscle."

"They'd better be, because I left all my muscles somewhere back at the Hangman's Mistake."

"Aye, mind is right. And technique," said Squat. "Jump up and grab a ring with each hand."

There was a bowl of chalk dust near the start, so Eloise dusted her palms, then jumped up and caught a ring with her left hand, dangled for a moment, then reached up and grabbed the next one along with her right hand. "Now what?"

"Swing your hips left to right to get momentum," said Lanky. "When you think you can reach it, hoist yourself along and move the ring to the next peg. Once that's solid, bring over the ring in your other hand to the peg you just left."

"OK, I get the theory."

As Eloise summoned her last reserves of strength and nerve to swing her body left and right, a chant of "Go, Queen El, go!" rose up from the hundreds of soldiers now watching. Lorch and Jerome, who'd finished what seemed like half a day earlier, joined in. Her shoulder and wrist were screaming worse than they had in weeks, and her muscles protested the unfamiliar abuse. She missed her first try looping the next peg, and hung by the one ring for a while. She missed the second attempt as well. On the third, she got the combination of swing and ring movement right and progressed a single peg. *One down,* she thought. *Fifty bazillion to go.*

The forward move was met with hoots and whoops from what by now must have been every soldier training that day.

"You are the queen," she mumbled to herself. "You don't have to freeze your tuchus off and embarrass yourself in front of everyone. You could be sitting in your study with a warm fire, a nice pot of haggleberry tea, and one of the romance scrolls your mother hid in there."

But she couldn't stop now. She'd come too far. Hanging above yet another muddy pool with the cold seeping into her like it wanted to eat her soul, there was no way she'd quit with all those soldiers watching. Judging from the noise, there must have been more than two thousand eyes out there—all on her (although, thinking about it, she'd need to know the arachnid population to get her estimate anywhere close to accurate—a thought that she realized probably meant she was close to delirium).

The chanting simplified to, "Go! Go! Go! Go! Go! Go! Go!"

So she went.

Swing, reach, loop, loop, swing, reach, loop, loop. Fall. Splatter. Wrench right knee. Limp back to the starting point. Hop up using one leg and grab, grab. Swing (ouch!), reach, loop, loop, swing (ouch!), reach, loop, loop. Repeat, repeat, repeat, repeat with arm, shoulder, wrist and knee now screaming with every move.

Sixteen reaches later, she swung down to a platform at the other end, landing badly on the bum knee but managing not to topple over. As hoorays burst out, a different chant took hold. "Run! Run! Run! Run! Run!"

"What?" wheezed Eloise.

"You have to run to the finish."

"Of course." Eloise turned to the finish line, which looked half a realm away, and limp-jogged toward it, wincing with every second step. She stumbled, collapsed, considered staying there for a year or two, but got back up and pushed on.

Suddenly, Squat and Lanky were by her side. "Come on, Queen Eloise! Come on! You can do it!"

Then Lorch and Jerome were with them, doing the same. The four of them matched her step for painful step. Then more soldiers surrounded her, shouting for her to keep going—ten, then twenty, then 100, then all of them, jumping up and down so they could see how she was going, as if their noise could help her make the next step.

Which it did.

Eloise was overwhelmed by the emotion of it all, blinking back tears of embarrassment for having made such a botch of it mixed with tears of gratitude for their enthusiasm and support.

She staggered across the finish line and collapsed in a muddy, sodden heap. The crowd rewarded her with loud, raucous cheers. "Hooray for Queen Eloise!" "Well done, ma'am." "Good on ya!"

Eloise got to her hands and knees, then, with Lorch's hand under her elbow, struggled back to her feet. She waved at the soldiers, saying, "Thank you, everyone."

The still-hooting soldiers parted to let Tiberius de Sphenodon through. He waved for quiet. "You made it, Your Highness."

"Barely."

"Most people don't on their first try. Or their fifth."

"Really?" She looked around at the obstacle course that had almost beaten her. "This thing is a menace."

The tuatara smiled. "If you say so, ma'am."

"I'll be back tomorrow to take another crack at it."

And the soldiers cheered her again.

36

JUGGLING JERBOAS

The next morning, Eloise did her best to ignore a thousand screaming muscles as she struggled through her session with Cloisterfeld and Lorch. She postponed her morning briefing with First Advisor to the afternoon, so she could have a soak in the castle's underground hot spring to ease the pain.

It helped.

A little.

Well, it wasn't the first time she'd been sore down to the marrow. She'd get over it.

Eloise dried off, pulled on her clothes, and headed for the Throne Room, where Jerome had asked her to meet him.

She found him waiting for her outside the doorway. He wasn't alone, as she'd expected. On the Throne Room's side stage, a group of small, furred performers were milling about, chittering.

"Who are they?" she asked.

"You don't recognize them?"

"They look familiar."

Then one of them started tossing balls in the air.

"Oh," Eloise said. "It's that juggling act from the Velvet Cask."

"The Juggling Jerboas."

"Right. Why are they here?"

"Well, I remember you saying that Melveeta's breakthrough with understanding the Star of Whatever came from an interaction with a magic-infused juggler."

"Yes. That's right."

"I figured the Juggling Jerboas act was so good, there was a reasonable chance that some sort of weak magic was involved."

"But you don't know for sure."

"No. That would be too awkward of a conversation. 'Hi. Your juggling is really great. Is it skill or magic?'"

"It could be both."

"True. So, I've invited them here under the pretense of auditioning for the queen's formal coronation. You'll just 'happen' to arrive and stay to check them out."

"You're using my coronation as a lure?"

"You did it with Sylvia Cloisterfeld. Besides, they're great."

"True. But if they are using magic and the Star of Whatever does affect them, they're going to mess up terribly. It won't be a great addition."

"Maybe. I'll deal with it. See the one in front with the red sash?"

"Yes."

"That's Uprightness de Dipodidae, their head of family and leader."

"Uprightness? I don't think I've ever met anyone named that before."

"Apparently it's religious. Juggling is part of their way to connect with the divine, kind of like those sects that dance in circles or balance stacks of stones on their heads. All the jerboas have that kind of name. These five are," Jerome pointed at them using a scroll he was holding, "Uprightness, Rectitude, Probity, Obligation, and Due Diligence."

Eloise wrinkled her nose. "They're not very juggler-ish names."

"No, they sound more like the joke name of a firm of actuaries dreamed up by an improv group."

"Anyway, head on in and get them started. I'll come in once they're going and we'll see if there's an effect."

"See you in a minute." Jerome strode into the Throne Room and Eloise heard him ask the jerboas to take their places and get started.

One of them—was it Obligation?—sat down at a drum kit and started hammering out rhythmic patterns. The others formed a rough square, bowed to their audience of one, and launched into a hoop juggling routine that was completely different to what they had done in the club. They took advantage of the larger space and higher ceiling to include more rings thrown higher and further. Even just peeking through the doorway, Eloise could see they really were spectacular. She'd be happy to have them at her formal coronation.

Two minutes later, she stepped into the room and walked toward the stage.

"Keep going, keep going," said Jerome. The Jerboas didn't miss a beat, trading hoops and cascading the rings in a way she had never seen before.

Eloise came up to the stage, but there was no obvious effect on their performance. She sat down to one side and surreptitiously reached beneath her cloak to crack open the box containing the Star of Whatever. When she had the lid slightly open, one of the jugglers wobbled with a couple of the hoops, but recovered without missing a beat or dropping anything.

Certainly not a conclusive disruption like Melveeta had spoken of.

With a drum flourish, the jerboas tossed the hoops over one of them—Rectitude, maybe?—so they formed a stack over her, hiding her from view. She then sprang up from them, having somehow changed her costume.

Eloise couldn't help but applaud. "Very nice. Very nice."

"Thank you, Your Highness," said Uprightness de Dipodidae. "It is an honor to be here."

"Thank you so much for coming in today," said Eloise. "I very much enjoyed your performance at the Velvet Cask. I'm going to want to see just a bit more, but I need to confer with Assistant Seer to the Court Seer Abernatheen de Chipmunk for a moment. Just a sec." She walked away from the stage and waved for Jerome to follow.

"How did you go?" asked Jerome when they stopped at the threshold.

"With the Star closed in the box, nothing. With the box lid cracked open, maybe a little something, and maybe not. Hard to tell."

"Can you take it all the way out of the box and try again?"

"If you think it's worth it, I guess. I'll need to duck away for some privacy to take it out."

"You do that. I'll get them juggling again."

Eloise ducked into the hall and checked to be sure there was no one coming, then shifted the box so it hung in front of her and opened it all the way. She removed the Star of Whatever, closed the box, slid it back to her hip, then concealed the hand holding the Star in her sleeve and walked back into the Throne Hall. Once again, she approached the stage while the Juggling Jerboas were in mid-performance. This time they were juggling a strange collection of differently weighted, irregularly shaped objects—a slice of bread, a marble, a domino, a small pewter candlestick, and an apple that one of them—Due Diligence, perhaps?—took a bite out of every time it came to his right forepaw, which changed both its shape and weight.

Another impressive effort.

And one not prone to disruption when Eloise came close. Either the Juggling Jerboas didn't use magic to perform their act, or the Star of Whatever didn't affect them. She felt confident that if she connected with spark of something in the Star of Whatever, she could work with Sparky to affect the juggling. But that wasn't the point. Melveeta had discovered the Star's disruptive power in this way. She hadn't been trying to control it or harness it. She just had it with her, and the proximity to the juggler is what made the difference.

"Keep going," she said. "I just need to see what it looks like from your point of view." Eloise stepped onto the stage and walked near the jerboas, careful not to impede their work. The performance proceeded without a hitch. "Looks good, Assistant Seer to the Court Seer. Can we confer again?"

"Of course, Your Highness. Keep juggling. We'll be right back."

At the back of the room, Jerome whispered, "Anything?"

"Nothing, Nothing at all. Not the least wobble."

The chipmunk stroked his whiskers, thinking. "I have an idea. Try it without the Star."

"What do you mean?"

"Leave the Star out of it. Put away or keep it out, but try looking at the jugglers with your wonky eye and listening to them through your buzzy ear."

"What's that supposed to do? I won't be able to see or hear anything."

"Think of it as being like the breakfast soup. Your perception of the problem with the soup wasn't conscious. It just happened, and we suspect your eye and ear were involved. So let's test it. See what you can see and hear without drawing on the Star."

"I don't know..."

"Just try it."

"Fine."

In the interest of time, Eloise left the Star hidden in her sleeve. She sat down at a chair not far from the stage, leaned her elbows on the banquet table, covered her non-blurry eye, and angled her head so the buzzy ear was forward. Then she relaxed into watching and listening to the scene in front of her. She gave it a full seven minutes, long enough for the jugglers to get all the way through their next routine and start another, this one featuring clubs they'd lit on fire.

Jerome sat down next to her. "Well?"

"Uprightness, the lead jerboa, thinks this is the stupidest thing he's ever been asked to do, but they want the coronation gig, so they're playing along."

"You can hear their thinking? That's amazing."

"No, it was more like getting a sense of it, using both my eye and ear together. It's vague, but that's what I'm gathering."

"So you can't read minds."

"Definitely not. Nothing so precise. Or noisy."

"What else?" asked Jerome.

"Rectitude is worried she might be in the family way, and is also worried that she might not be."

"Is she?"

"I don't think so, but I wouldn't bet the castle on it. I feel like I'm making guesses based on a kind of amped-up intuition."

"This is fascinating. Try focusing on just your eye. Is there anything that strikes you as dangerous, the way the soup did?"

"Beyond the flaming clubs? No."

"Can you think of anything else we should try with them?"

"No, I can't."

"OK. I'll let them go, but if you have another half an hour, there's something else I'd like to try."

"Half an hour? That should be OK."

"Back in a sec." Jerome walked toward the stage, applauding. "Fantastic, folks. Really good. Thank you so much for coming in today. We'll be making a decision about the coronation in the next few weeks, and someone will let you know one way or the other. Anyone have any questions?"

The jerboas looked at each other and shook their heads.

"Then, thanks again, and we'll be in touch. I'll get a page to escort you out."

Jerome walked back to Eloise. "Let's go out to the Flinging Field."

"Oh, Jer, don't make me. I can barely move, much less throw something."

"Come on, El. Aren't you curious?"

"Fine. But don't expect much from me, and I'll need to keep it quick. I'm meeting First Advisor this afternoon." Eloise stood, and as they left the Juggling Jerboas to pack up, she slipped the Star of Whatever back in its box. "You want to hop up on my shoulder? It'll be quicker."

✺ 37 ✺

HAMMER THROWS

Ten minutes later, Eloise and Jerome were at the rack of practice hammers at one edge of the practice field, along with Lorch, who'd joined them as soon as he saw they were leaving the castle. "What are we doing?" he asked.

"I'm trying to help Queen Eloise get a better handle on what's going on with her..." Jerome gestured to his eye and ear, not wanting to risk being overheard. "I thought we could experiment a little to see what she might be able to do."

"But why here, Jer?" asked Eloise.

"We know you have a weak magic for throwing. It's a known magical element that you control and are familiar with. If we tweak the odd variable that has to do with throwing, we might learn something."

"Seems reasonable," said Lorch.

"Good. So, let me start by asking some questions." Jerome took a small slate and chalk from a bag he carried and prepared to make notes. "First, when you throw, does it always involve weak magic, or can you throw without it?"

Eloise wrinkled her nose. "I have no idea. I just throw."

"You don't control it at all?"

"No, I can control it, but it isn't so clinical. It's not like a tap that I turn on and off. I don't think, 'Now I'm throwing with weak magic.' 'And now I'm not.'"

"How does it work, then?"

Eloise ran a finger along the rack that held the throwing hammers. "It's more emotional than that. If my emotions are up, or my intention is really focused, then it's more likely to kick in."

Jerome scratched some notes onto the slate. "Can you give me any examples?"

"I've noticed my hammer throws in tourneys are usually farther than they are when I practice. I've always put that down to me needing to concentrate on throwing well and not wanting to embarrass myself in front of others."

"Good, good." Jerome made more notes. "Anything else come to mind?"

Eloise closed her eyes and searched for instances of throwing where weak magic would have been involved. "I can remember throwing grapes at my mother's head to test the no-magic-against-blood rule. That's not a spectacular example. A better one would be when I used it to win Cäääsëëëy Liïïss, the chameleon, his freedom."

"You mean in Inevitable Splat, at the Aloe Vera Jamboree? When you got the balls through the hoops?"

"Yes."

"I hadn't realized. I thought you'd just nailed it."

"No. I drew on it very deliberately."

Eloise thought some more. "Of course, there's the obvious example of when I threw the rope and managed to hoist myself out of the Whacking Great Hole."

"Right. Yes," said Jerome.

"Another would be when I beaned Turpy in the back of the head with an apple. He'd just taken the Star of Whatever from me and called me a 'stupid bitch.' I put everything I had into that throw."

"I remember that. He's lucky he didn't have apple seed shooting through his forehead. Instead, he just went sprawling and landed —*splat!*—in the couscous."

"Yeah. So, that's an example of me throwing with whatever weak magic I have that both of you would have seen."

"Good, good, good. If you threw your hammer without drawing on your weak magic, how far would it go, roughly?"

"Hard to know. Fifty-five lengths, maybe. More or less. It would be hard for me to work out what would be a throw without using weak magic and what would be me just half-assing it."

"And a throw with weak magic?"

"More in the sixty-two and above. Sixty-eight is about my personal best."

"I saw you throw seventy-two once," said Lorch. "It was a practice throw, not in a tourney, but you did it."

"Seventy-two lengths? Did I? I don't remember that, but I believe you. That would have been before I popped out my shoulder and broke my wrist. It wasn't near that far last time I tried—well, you saw that—but I haven't trained much recently."

Jerome made a few more notes. "And how accurate would you be?"

"How accurate?"

"The hammer is about using strength and speed to achieve distance," said Lorch. "The direction is secondary." He pointed to two lines that marked an arc of about forty-five degrees. "So long as it lands in the designated area, it counts."

"But let's say you were trying for both distance and accuracy. What can you do?"

Eloise looked at the chipmunk. "I really don't get where you're going with this. I don't know. Reasonably close to the middle line, I suppose."

"You never try for both distance and accuracy?"

"No, not with the hammer. With the grape-throwing, sure. When I aimed for Turpy's head—absolutely. But not out here."

"OK." Jerome looked over his notes. "Good. Now, pick a hammer and let's try a few throws."

"I told you, I can't. The obstacle course practically killed me yesterday. I've had training this morning, and come tornado or tsunami, I'm going to beat the obstacle course again today. So, no, I'd rather not throw the hammer."

"Except that now's the perfect time, Your Highness."

"How do you reckon that, Assistant Seer to the Court Seer Abernatheen de Chipmunk?"

"Your physical exhaustion means you're going to have to rely on other means to get a good result, so let's see what we can tease out from a few throws. Then you can go have your lunch or whatever it is that you need to do."

Eloise groaned. "Lorch, if I die doing this, can you promise me you'll torment him for the rest of his life?"

"Yes, Queen Eloise. I'll do that."

Without another word, she began her usual stretching routine. Arms. "Ow." Hamstrings. "Ow." Neck. "Ow." Shoulders. "Ow." Hips, calves, wrists, nostrils. "Ow. Ow. Ow. Ow." Then she picked up a hammer from the rack and said, "OK, what do you want?"

"Can you do an ordinary, non-magical throw?"

"I'll try."

"I'll measure the distances, if you'd like," said Lorch. "And retrieve the hammers."

"Thanks. You probably won't need to go very far, the way I'm feeling."

Eloise stepped into the throwing circle, wound up, moved into her spinning, heel-toe hammer throw moves, and let fly. To Eloise, the throw felt better than half-hearted, but well below fully engaged. If it had weak magic in it, it wouldn't have been much.

"Fifty-one lengths, Your Highness," said Lorch.

Jerome flipped over his slate and noted the distance on the back. "Again, please."

"What kind of throw?"

"Same. Just a plain throw."

She did. "Ow."

"Fifty and a half," said Lorch.

Scribble. "Again, please."

"Jer, you said this wouldn't take long."

"I lied. Come on, we're here. Let's keep going."

"Fine. Just flopping fine."

"Your First Advisor's infected you with her linguistic quirk."

"May-flopping-be." Eloise picked the hammer that Lorch had returned.

Throw. "Ow."

Lorch jogged over to it. "Fifty-one."

"Good, good, good," said Jerome, noting the distance. "Now do the opposite. Give me a throw that has your full power behind it. Like you wanted to fling into the Eastern Lands and land it on Queen Aggie's head."

"Right. Queen Aggie. Queen flopping Aggie." She picked up a hammer that was a full weight heavier than the last ones she'd thrown. She spun into the circles thinking about Queen Aglandau, careful to keep her hands and the ball of the hammer in front of her, picturing it clunking Queen Aggie in the head as it whizzed past her. Eloise channeled all the anger, frustration, and sadness she'd been keeping bottled up for weeks. She added in a direct call to her weak magic and even imagined Sparky helping her. Giving it everything she had, Eloise let out a primal yowl and an "Ooooowwwwwwww!" and let fly a massive throw.

"Wow," said Jerome, watching it go.

"Goodness," said Lorch as it sailed over his head. He turned around to see it land. "By holy Çalaht's elongated thumbs, that's ninety-three lengths. I... I've never..." He shook his head, like he was clearing it. "I'll go get it."

"Was that what you were looking for, Jer?" said Eloise.

"Yes, I rather think it was."

"You gonna write that one down?"

Jerome looked at his slate like he'd never seen it before. "Yeah. Right. Sure." He scratched down the distance. "Can you do a few more?"

"Maybe not like that, but yes. I don't know when I'll be able to get back out here, so let's do what you're trying to do."

"Try doing one that involves your buzzy ear and blurry eye."

Eloise wrinkled her brow. "How's that supposed to work?"

"I don't know, El. That's what we're trying to figure out."

"I'll do what I can then." She went back to the lighter hammer and stepped into the circle, but before she started the wind-up, she thought about what Jerome had asked of her. Draw on her ear and eye? How? The hammer throw could hardly be improved by seeing and hearing less.

Still, it was worth a try.

ANDREW EINSPRUCH

To make it easier to isolate herself to the buzz and blur, she took a large tulip-embroidered handkerchief from a pocket and fashioned a blindfold to block off her good eye. She then poked a corner of the hanky into her non-buzzy ear to muffle it. The arrangement kinda worked and was kinda ridiculous.

"Whatever," she mumbled.

Eloise started her wind-up swings, doing her best to track her position through the blur. Worried she might release the hammer at the wrong time and throw wide, she concentrated on making sure she could see where the middle of the throwing range was and on aiming for it.

Release. "Ooowwww!"

Moments later, the hammer thunked into the Flinging Field's turf.

"Huh," said Jerome.

"What?"

"Can you see what it's done?"

"Not really."

"Seventy-eight lengths," called Lorch.

"That's... That's quite good," said Eloise.

"Yes. But what's also impressive is where it landed."

"Where?"

"In the exact middle. Straight down the center. If there was a line marked there, it would have hit it right in the center."

"Huh," said Eloise. "Let me try again."

Another throw. Same focus.

Same result, within half a length's distance.

And again.

And again.

"It's consistent, whatever it is you're doing," said Jerome.

"Let me cover the blurry eye and just use my buzzing ear," said Eloise.

The next throw was different again. Much shorter, and not nearly as straight down the middle, but it landed with an audible *thump!* and Eloise heard Lorch say, "That's insane."

"What's insane?" she asked.

"I beg your pardon?" said Jerome.

"Lorch said, 'That's insane.' What's insane?"

"Um… I didn't hear Lorch say anything." Jerome cupped his paws around his mouth. "Hey, Lorch. Did you just say, 'That's insane' or something similar?"

The champion jogged back to the throwing circle. "I may have mumbled it."

"I heard it like you were standing next to me."

"That's odd. But the reason I said it was that the hammer plowed into the ground almost half a length. I had to yank on it to get it back out."

"Oh. Shall we try that again?"

"Yes," said Jerome. "Absolutely."

She did. Three more throws. By now, Eloise was tiring, so they got shorter and shorter, but each buried itself in the ground an inexplicably long way.

"I have to get back," she said, and the three of them tidied up the hammers.

As they walked back toward the castle, Eloise asked, "So, what does this all mean? Have we learned anything?"

"Yes, we've learned something," said Jerome. "I'm not sure what, exactly, but definitely something. As for what it means, who knows? But I think we're closer to figuring it out than we were before."

🐦 38 🐦

MAYBE TALK TO HER

E loise found it hard to sit as First Advisor Thëjëts ran through the afternoon briefing. She'd asked what she was coming to think of as the Fippledip Council—Lorch, Jerome, Sylvia Cloisterfeld, and Tiberius de Sphenodon—to join them in the Fippledip Room, feeling the need for additional minds on matters at hand.

The briefing had a lot of numbers, which, on the surface, Eloise liked. However, they told a story of limited options.

"Any action that involves the movement of people and equipment, along with everything that supports them, places a burden on the realm's coin coffers," said First Advisor.

"Are you saying I shouldn't do anything?"

"Not at all, Your Highness. I'm saying you need to be aware that the realm's coin is not infinite, so that any choice you make considers both costs and trade-offs."

"Costs I get," said Eloise. "What do you mean by trade-offs?"

"As in, if you commit in one direction, then other choices no longer become available. For example, if you send half your soldiers to Flachberg instead of sending all of your soldiers, the consequences will be different. Say you send them all. That means there won't be soldiers to send elsewhere. And given what it would cost, it would inevitably preclude other things you might like to do for the realm."

"Like what?"

First Advisor puffed her lips a little, looking for an example. "Like, for example, you couldn't provide subsidies to radish farmers of Lower Glenth, should you want to boost radish production in the realm, since there wouldn't be the coin available to do so."

"Can't I just promise the farmers that Court will buy more radishes?"

"Sure. And they may even plant more of them if they trust you or, more likely, if they have a contract that obligates you to buy them. But you're jumping to tactics. I'm talking strategy. Bigger picture."

"Right. Sorry. I see what you're saying. So, what's the right answer?"

"There isn't one."

"Are you saying I shouldn't do anything about Flachberg?"

"Not at all."

"Am I to send all of my soldiers?"

First Advisor looked at Tiberius de Sphenodon and Sylvia Cloisterfeld. "What do you think?"

"Absolutely, you could send all of your soldiers," said the Master Sergeant.

"Right—"

"If you want them all slaughtered in their first encounter with the enemy."

"I see. So, not a good option at this time."

"No, ma'am."

Eloise stopped pacing and looked around at them. "Any suggestions on what, realistically, we should do?"

No one said anything for a very long time.

Finally, Jerome raised his forepaw and spoke up. "Maybe you could try talking to her."

Everyone stared at him.

"To whom?" asked Eloise.

"Queen Aggie."

"What do you mean?"

"Talk. As in, 'Hello, my name is Eloise. I'm queen of the Western Lands and All That Really Matters. How about we talk this thing through.'"

"You want me to parlay with Queen Aggie?"

"Why not?"

Eloise leaned over the table and spoke quietly. "Because my mother hated her, and apparently the feeling was mutual. Because she invaded my realm. Because she took my canton and built a wall around it."

Jerome stood on the table and leaned in closer. "So you'd rather go to war with soldiers who will get slaughtered right away?"

Eloise leaned back and crossed her arms. "No. I wouldn't."

"Then be the bigger person, Your Highness. Offer to parlay."

Eloise turned to Bënnïë-Änn Thëjëts. "What do you think?"

"It's an option. To be honest, it's an option I should have thought of."

"Right." Eloise resumed her pacing. "So, how would it work?"

"You get together. Just the two of you," said First Advisor. "Somewhere neutral, and with your armies at a distance from each other, so you don't have any accidental military encounters. When you meet with her, you both raise issues and try to work things out."

Eloise shook her head. "And that's actually supposed to work? With someone like Queen Aggie?"

"I don't know, Your Highness. It's been a while since anyone has needed to try. The only example I can think of was Gwendolyn the Irritable and King Brüüütus, more than two centuries ago."

"I'm not sure I'd call that an overwhelming success."

"You wouldn't?" said Jerome.

"What, you would?"

The chipmunk listed off points on his claws. "They connected. They fell in love. They were intimate. They had a baby. They were happy."

"And then he blew her off, and she got mad, massed an army and marched on his realm. Plus, she sent her champion to cast a spell, and we ended up with the Purple Haze. All in all, not a good outcome."

"But there was a child. So something came of it."

"Queen Audrey the Parasitic. Also not necessarily a success."

"Wow, you're being very goblet-half-empty here. If you ignore how it all fell apart a while later, it looked like a success, at least for a while. And you can't say that the king's behavior was a consequence of the parley. It was a consequence of him being a horrible person who was terrible with women. Or, if some of the accounts are correct, it was because he was ensorcelled."

"Ugh. Just, ugh. Anyone have any thoughts on this?"

Silence.

"No one?"

More silence.

"Apparently my mother had a parley with Queen Aggie years and years ago. Do you know anything about that, First Advisor?"

"No. It was before my time in service to her."

"Apparently it was a disaster."

"I've also heard that."

"How a disaster, Your Highness?" asked Lorch.

"I don't know. No one seems to know what happened. But they never spoke again. And there's always been an uneasiness between the two realms."

Eloise took her seat at the head of the table. "We don't seem to have any better ideas, so I guess I need to consider this one. First Advisor?"

"Yes, Your Highness?"

"Can you please find out if there are any records that talk about what happened when Queen Aglandau and my mother met? There may be proclamations that came out of the meeting, or some sort of personal record from my mother. Jerome can help with the search, if you like, right, Jer?"

"Certainly."

"Let's see if there's anything that might clue us in on what took place. And then I'll figure out if that's what we should do."

39

A GREAT AND GLORIOUS
UNDERTAKING

First Advisor Chafed Gumball née de Chëëëkflïïïnt poked his head into the heated tent by the side of the road, which had been erected for Queen Johanna's privacy. "Your Majesty?"

"Yes, First Advisor Father?"

"I'm not sure 'First Advisor Father' quite works. It sounds a bit religious, which I'm most definitely not."

"Agreed. But 'First Advisor Dad' is too informal. 'First Advisor Gumball' is odd. So is 'First Advisor Gumball née de Chëëëkflïïïnt.'"

"Maybe just stick to 'First Advisor' for now?"

"Yes. But we'll need to find something that works."

"As you wish. Anyway, they're ready for you."

Johanna stood and smoothed down the front of her robe. "Is there actually anyone here for the ceremony?"

Chafed tried to mask his disappointment. "Let's stipulate that it's as cold as a retiring cleric's attitude out there."

"Noted."

"The road maintenance crew are here, obviously, since that's who you're addressing. There are a couple of news heralds and one of the lower-tier gossip heralds. And there are a handful of villagers—six, maybe?—here for the free food."

"We only got six people here with free food? What kind of spread is it?"

"Finger sandwiches."

"Ugh. In this weather? At this time of the morning? We'll have to do better next time."

"The table's already pretty empty. I suspect if you asked everyone to turn out their pockets, we'd find quite a spread in there."

"Right. I guess that's to be expected. So, less than two dozen people." Johanna sighed. "You know what the actors say, right?"

"Do you actually know any actors?"

"No. This is more of a theoretical understanding. They say, 'We play to the audience that's there.' That strikes me as sound advice. Besides, we have to start somewhere."

"I'm just not used to a royal visit being so widely ignored. My brother really didn't inspire much enthusiasm, did he?"

"Apparently neither have I. Do I look OK?"

"Very regal, sweetie."

"Then let's see if I can make an impression. In a good way, mind you, and not in a falling-down-during-your-Crown-Plonking way."

"I'm glad your sister isn't here to hear that."

"It happened. And it left a big impression on me."

"It left a bigger impression on the royal regalia."

"Ouch! Better that she's not here to hear that. Still, one must be able to learn by example, even if it is a negative example." Johanna took a deep breath, double-checked her crown was firmly on her head, and said, "It's showtime."

"Yes, Your Majesty."

Johanna stepped from the tent onto the verge at the side of a road, and into an icy wind. She put on as warm a smile as she could and made her way toward the minuscule crowd waiting for her.

The road crew clustered together near a cart full of stones and a mound of dirt. The desultory group was covered in dust, despite having almost certainly not done any actual work that day. Someone had apparently told them to have their shovels with them, as each leaned awkwardly on one. They all bowed in her direction, although Protocol would have had ten thousand comments about the way they'd done it.

Nearby, the free food seekers stopped chewing, quickly shoving half-eaten sandwiches into overstuffed pockets. The three heralds stood at a distance. Two of them took out slates and chalk, ready to jot down a few notes. The third one, presumably the gossip herald, looked like she'd imbibed a soporific on her way there. Possibly she had.

Inwardly, Johanna groaned at the poor turnout. Outwardly, she notched up her energy a tad too high and said, "G'mid-morning, every-one. Thank you for joining me today, despite the brisk weather."

There were a few mumbles in response.

"So, who's in charge of our road crew?"

A burro in a workman's cap and tunic stepped forward. He bowed several times to her, but she saw his tail tucked. Nerves, presumably.

"And you are?"

"G'mid-arvo, Your Majesty. I'm Sequaciousness de Asinus, the crew foreperson. Thank you for being here today." The words spilled out in a single blob of concertinaed syllables, then the burro realized he'd gotten the time of day wrong. "Sorry, sorry. I mean, g'mid-morning,

Your Majesty. I'm Sequaciousness de Asinus, the crew foreperson. Thank you for being here today."

"Pleased to meet you, Master de Asinus. How long have you been doing road maintenance?"

"Practically three weeks, Your Majesty."

"Three weeks? And you're already in charge? You must be very talented."

"No, ma'am. I merely have seniority."

Johanna blinked at this a few times, doing her best to suppress her reactions. "I see. Well, good for you." She looked around, but didn't see anyone else she felt compelled to speak with. "Shall we get started?"

"Over here, ma'am." The donkey led her to the far side of the stone cart. A decoratively painted orange crate stood on its own, save for a new shovel, bedecked with a ribbon in Northern Lands wart-cream purple, leaning on it. Not exactly a bunting-covered, flower-strewn dais. "Your stage, ma'am."

"I see. Thank you." Johanna stepped onto it, wobbled, overbalanced, and was very close to toppling when Chafed grabbed her elbow and steadied her. She nodded her appreciation, found a way to stand on the crate that was stable, and cleared her throat. "Everyone ready?"

There were at least three nods in response. Maybe a fourth, although that could have just been someone looking at his sandwich in his pocket.

"Good, then." She slid a scroll out from a pocket, unfurled it, and began her speech. "We're gathered today here at the start of the Greatish Eastern Road, the main road that connects the seat of the queendom here at Stained Rock with our cousins in the Eastern Lands." She looked around, hoping to draw them in. "For decades, nay, centuries, this road has been a vital link between two great and noble realms. Commerce has moved both hither and yon. Friends, families, diplomats, and merchants have walked, ridden, hopped, slithered, and crawled its great and mighty lengths. Today, we come together to launch a new era in the history of the Greatish Eastern Road, one that will lift it back up to a state of usefulness and comfort, free of the potholes, washouts, cracks, and ruts that have plagued it for much too long. Today marks the first day in the renewal of our realm, as we begin the process of renewing its most important of roads."

Johanna paused and turned her attention to the road crew. "To you who will provide your sweat and your muscle to the uplift of this critical thoroughfare, know that you are serving your queendom. I commend you for being part of this great and glorious undertaking."

A couple of the road gang applauded. Sequaciousness de Asinus stamped his feet a few times and brayed.

Johanna waved her thanks. "We'll now have the ceremonial laying of the first stone and the turning of the first shovel of dirt." She extended her arm, and Chafed held her elbow as she stepped down. They walked to the cart with the cobblestones and found one that had been painted Northern Lands purple. It was huge, meant to serve as a reminder of the start of roadworks. "How am I supposed to carry it?" she whispered to her father.

"You want me to help?" said Chafed.

"Could we do it, just the two of us?"

"It's pretty big. And my back's been bothering me."

"We could make it a group activity. Is it too much less regal if they all help?"

"No, Your Majesty. It would be very 'of the people' of you."

Johanna wrinkled her nose at her father and shook her head. Then she fixed a smile on her face and turned to the road gang. "I invite you to participate in this great and momentous moment."

They looked at her. Comprehension did not mar any of their expressions.

She cleared her throat. "Can you help me move the rock?"

"Oh. Got it," they mumbled.

The road gang moved to the cart and, with Johanna helping, hoisted the purple stone and shuffled to the designated spot at the side of the road. As they were about to lower it, there was a shout. "Hold it!"

It was one of the two news heralds.

"What?" said Johanna, straining.

"Let me make a quick sketch. I'll show it when I proclaim the story." Without waiting for an answer, he flipped over his slate and scratched out a quick line drawing of the scene as Johanna and the road gang groaned to hold up the small boulder. After an interminable pause, he nodded and said, "Done. Thanks."

Moments later, the rock was dropped into place. Johanna had expected a couple of cheers. Instead, there were just murmurs of relief.

Chafed handed her the shovel with the bow. Johanna held it in front of her like a precious relic. "And now, we shall have the ceremonial first shovel of dirt." She walked over to the mound, shoved the blade in deep, and hauled up as much dirt as she could. "Behold, the first shovel full." Johanna balanced it over to the road and held it over a pothole, which was large enough to swallow a carriage. She was about to dump it in, when there was another shout of, "Hold it! Hold it!"

It was the other news herald.

"Another sketch?"

"Yes, Your Majesty."

"Fine. Make it quick, please."

The herald frantically scratched marks on his slate, glancing up at her over and over, shading and cross-hatching to make a completely reasonable likeness, and taking way too long about it. "Got it. Thank you, ma'am."

"Very good." Johanna turned the shovel, so the dirt slid into the pothole as dramatically as possible. The act was met with a smattering of applause and several clandestine sandwich munches.

"Thank you everyone. Sequaciousness de Asinus?"

The donkey stepped forward and bowed. "Yes, Your Majesty?"

She held the shovel out to him, then realized he couldn't take it, so handed it to one of the other workers instead. "The road is all yours to repair. Thank you to you and your team for your service to the queendom."

"It's an honor, Queen Johanna."

With that, the road crew hauled the cart of stones toward the road and began what was certainly going to be a months-long process of getting the Greatish Eastern Road to be a little more great.

Johanna and Chafed stood watching the workers.

"Your Eastern Lands coin at work," he said.

"Indeed. Let's hope it does some good."

"And let's hope the price is not too steep."

"I can't imagine this lot gets paid all that much."

"That's not what I meant."

"Oh." Johanna nodded. "I see what you mean. Yes, let's hope not."

40

TWEAKING THE PUDDLE
OF COIN

The very moment Johanna was dumping dirt in a hole, Eloise was holed up in a meeting with her Privy Council. Exchequer of the Realm Cyrus Borborygmus looked even more dour than usual. "The trend of the queendom's coin reserves is distinctly in a non-positive, outflow-wise direction."

"Please speak plainly, Exchequer Realm Borborygmus. Are you saying we're losing money?"

"In the aggregate and over time, the direction is regressive and dispositive."

Eloise was pretty sure he'd used those words incorrectly, but wasn't so confident as to call him on it. She took another tack. "Answer the following with a yes or no. Let's say I wanted to buy a dozen loaves of rye bread every day for a year. Is there enough coin for that?"

"Yes."

"Let's say I want to launch an all-out assault on the Eastern Lands. Is there enough coin for that?"

"Your Highness, factors—"

"Yes or no?"

"Your Highness, that's a 'how much soup can a weasel slurp?' kind of question. The answer could be anything."

"Come on, yes or no?"

Borborygmus pursed his lips. "Well, Your Highness, how long will this campaign take? Are you expecting anyone to return home alive? Will there be minimal support or maximal support? Do you intend to take down the new wall at Flachberg or attack some other way? Do you intend to scorch the earth or find it scorched, or will your soldiers be able to survive on what they find there? Will you conserve ammunition for use over time or throw everything into the initial fight? Will there be scribes, bards, and/or heralds going along to record the proceedings? Is there going to be any—"

"Yes. Or. N—"

"No, Your Highness. You do not have the coin to pursue a successful all-out invasion of the Eastern Lands, unless you draft everyone in the realm to do it with you, and they don't mind dying on your behalf." The Exchequer swallowed. "Apologies, Queen Eloise. I did not mean to interrupt you."

Eloise nodded. "I appreciate the straight answer, at least. Here's what I'd like you to do. I need some lists."

"Lists, Your Highness? What kind of lists?"

"I'd like a list of the two hundred most expensive things the Crown pays for. I'd like a list of the two hundred most valuable sources of revenue. I'd like your two hundred best suggestions for where costs can be reasonably cut, as well as the two hundred most promising ideas for additional inflow. Can you do that for me?"

"Yes, Queen Eloise."

"By tomorrow?"

Borborygmus flinched. "I'll have an initial list for you tomorrow, and a more complete list in three days."

"That will do. Thank you, Exchequer. I look forward to seeing what we might be able to do to tweak the puddle of coin in the coffers."

"Yes, ma'am."

Eloise looked around at the rest of the gathering. First Advisor was scribbling notes. The Venerable Prelate was either praying or dozing (perhaps they were one and the same for her). Brigadier General Gideon Horsewhale de Odobenus' chair was conspicuously empty. She'd have to fill it soon. Niville Numptorius, Interim Other Places Advocate, had presented the latest news from the other realms, but had managed not to say anything of value at all. Lead Magistrate Riri Gintsshprik, Speaker for the Land Rölf de Phobaeticus, and Court Nominee Xertz Yarborough had contributed nothing to the discussion yet. Seer Maybelle was knitting, but had followed every word.

"Anyone have anything else to contribute?" Eloise asked. "I'd be very grateful for anything that passes as a useful input."

No one spoke.

"It has been suggested that I might offer to parlay with Queen Aglandau. What do you think of that idea?"

That got their attention.

"A parlay is a risky strategy," said Niville Numptorius.

Eloise was surprised he was the first to speak. "How so?"

"For one, you're on your own. It's just you and the other monarch. No advisors. No support staff. It's a..." His hands fluttered in that nervous way he had, and his voice pinched upward. "It's a raw experience. Decorum can be tossed out the window. No one has ever been killed, but there've been plenty of fights, and more than one pregnancy."

"Wait, you're saying King Brüüütus and Queen Gwendolyn weren't the only ones to come away with an allegedly blessed event afterward?"

"That's correct."

"Well. I didn't expect that." Eloise drummed her fingers on the table. "I don't think Queen Aggie and I will be getting pregnant. But point taken. What else?"

"Parlays have a history of being last-ditch efforts to avoid war."

"Do they achieve that end?"

"Usually not," said the Interim Other Places Advocate. "War almost always follows, sooner or later. Normally by then, things have deteriorated so much that there's not much chance of talking out the tensions. At best, you'll be buying time. At worst, you'll be tipping your hand unnecessarily."

"OK."

"Next, and I say this with respect, the Eastie queen is several decades your senior. She has more experience than you do in matters of state, in negotiation, in diplomacy, and inter-realm politics. The odds of you being, uh..."

"Outmatched?" suggested Eloise.

"I was going to say, 'played like an out-of-tune, second-hand lute,' but 'outmatched' will do. The odds of that happening are not small."

"Hmmm..." She looked around the table again and lit on Seer Maybelle Abernatheen de Chipmunk. "Oh, well, we have a solution. Seer Maybelle, you could do a prognostication for me. That could help me make a more informed decision."

For some reason, Seer Maybelle looked desperately unhappy. "I'm sorry, Queen Eloise. I cannot offer you a prognostication at this time."

Eloise raised an eyebrow. "Really? Isn't that the Seer's role? Or am I missing something?"

"No, Your Highness. It is the Seer's role." The chipmunk stood on her chair in the exact posture Protocol demanded. "Your Highness, with regret, I must offer my resignation from your Privy Council."

"Whoa, whoa, whoa. That's not what I want."

"If I cannot provide you with a prognostication, then it is only appropriate that I free my space for someone who can serve you better."

"Wait. What's happening? Please don't leave me."

"It appears I must."

Eloise put up her hand. "Hold on a tick. Anyone else have anything that's pressing?" When no one raised any issues, she said, "Seer Maybelle, can I invite you to a cup of haggleberry tea in my study? We can discuss the matter in private, if you don't mind."

"A cup of haggleberry tea would be lovely, Queen Eloise. When would suit you?"

Her tone indicated reluctance, which Eloise found odd. She'd always been comfortable with Seer Maybelle. She'd spent lots of time in her home playing with Jerome when they were young. Maybe this was just one of those things that had changed when the crown had plonked on her head. "Do you have time now?"

"Yes, Your Highness."

✌ 41 ⁊

CLOAKED MYSTERY

A quarter hour later, RoyLee had fetched tea, Eloise was in her comfy chair balancing a cup and saucer, and Seer Maybelle sat opposite, nursing her own cuppa. The chipmunk blew across the rim and sipped, and Eloise noted that despite her penchant for biccies, the chipmunk hadn't served herself a sweet and salty tahini cookie (one of the better baked goods to emerge from new Chef's kitchen).

"Lovely weather we're having," said Eloise. "It won't be that long until the snow drop blossoms will herald the impending spring."

Seer Maybelle smiled weakly at the irrelevant conversation opener. "Apologies, Your Highness. I've been preoccupied."

"May I ask with what?"

"Matters of the Unseen. Not unlike what you asked me at the Privy Council meeting."

"You said you couldn't give me a prognostication at that time." Eloise gestured to indicate her study. "Would now be better?"

"I'm sorry, Queen Eloise, but I can't." Seer Maybelle seemed genuinely distressed.

"You can't or you won't?"

"Oh, I'm your seer, Queen Eloise. I'd absolutely help you if I could, but I can't."

"That doesn't make sense to me."

"Nor does it to me." The chipmunk's whiskers drooped. "I've never run into anything like this before. At all. Ever. And I've been Court Seer for decades, since well before you and your sister were born."

"Could you say what's going on? Is there a, uh, a diminution of your connection to the Unseen?"

Seer Maybelle put her cup on the table and hopped down to the floor. Out of habit, she assumed the upright posture called for by Protocol. "As you would have learned in your Oracles and Insights studies, consulting with the Unseen is always a nebulous undertaking. It's not like reading a scroll or having a conversation. It depends on what the need is and what question is asked. As we've discussed before, highly specific questions can yield maddeningly vague answers, and broad questions sometimes draw forth incredibly precise instructions. Usually a queen's questions fall in between those extremes, and through my encounters with the Unseen, I can generally divine a response that is of use. I've done this for years. Were your mother here, I'm sure she'd testify to the utility I provided."

"No doubt. You wouldn't have been on her Privy Council if you hadn't provided solid counsel."

Seer Maybelle nodded at the truth of it. "So imagine my consternation that I cannot provide similar service to you."

"What's going on? Is it something that can be fixed?"

"I don't know and I don't know." The chipmunk swished her tail, a gesture that, when Jerome did it, Eloise associated with suppressed annoyance. "When I connect to the Unseen in relation to you, it's like you're just not there. No, that's not a good description. It's like you're an absence. Or your presence is occluded. I can sense you, the way one senses a person's presence from their shadow. It is analogous to that."

"I see," said Eloise, even though she didn't. "Has this always been the case?"

"No! Not at all. That is part of what's so strange. It is relatively recent."

"When did the change happen?"

Seer Maybelle got a faraway look and tugged the fur on her chin. It was another gesture Eloise recognized from Jerome, and the similarity made her want to smile. "It is more recent than your journey across the realms to try to retrieve your sister."

"Oh? How can you say that?"

"Because while you were away, I was able to get a sense of you. I could tell if you were in danger or not, and roughly in which direction you could be found."

"You tracked me while I was away?"

"Tracked is too strong of a word. I was able to provide comfort to the late queen by reassuring her that you were OK."

"But... But too often I wasn't. I wouldn't want to say it to anyone else, but I was in danger over and over."

The chipmunk was quiet.

"Seer Maybelle?"

"Your Highness, I was aware of the extent of the danger, even if I didn't know the cause of it."

"What did my mother say?" She could see the seer's cheek hairs bristle. Embarrassment? Eloise gasped. "You didn't tell her!"

Her cheek hairs stood up even straighter. "At first, I did. It was an adventure, and you were on track to come back in a reasonable manner. And then you weren't and the late queen fell ill. So, yes, I must admit to not being entirely forthcoming, to avoid making her days more distressing than they already were."

"You knew she was not going to recover."

The chipmunk looked down. "One did not need to be in touch with the Unseen to come to that conclusion. She fought a heroic fight, but..." Seer Maybelle trailed off. "Anyway, you did not become opaque to me while you were away. It was once you returned, although it's hard for me to say when, as I stopped consulting the Unseen for a while once you returned."

"Why?"

"You were home. It seemed less necessary. Plus, with your mother's passing and Jerome returning to me, there was a lot going on for me emotionally."

It hadn't occurred to Eloise that Jerome's absence might have caused his mother anxiety. She felt stupid for not thinking of it sooner. Did the same apply to Lorch's family? To the families of Hector and the Nameless One? Eloise felt a creeping shame for not having considered the impact of taking the others with her. She wasn't sure what to say, so she let the point slide. "It was kind of you to shield Mother from the truth of what was going on for me. A lot of it might have looked, shall we say, problematic. Or possibly, at least, unbecoming to a queen or crown princess."

Seer Maybelle's mouth quirked. "I've gathered as much."

"Let's think a bit more about when your inability to see me in the Unseen happened. Was it before or after my crown plonking?"

"After. Definitely after."

"OK. Before or after my trip to Festering Resentment?"

"After, I think. No, I'm pretty sure of that—after."

"Before or after that assassin almost killed me?"

"Again, after."

"Are you sure?"

"Definitely."

"How so?"

Seer Maybelle smoothed her whiskers with a paw—another gesture Eloise had seen Jerome do thousands of times. It was one of his "I'm thinking" gestures. "I checked with the Unseen when I heard that something had happened," said the chipmunk. "I saw you there, still perceptible in most of the available futures, which I took to mean that you would be OK." Suddenly, she stopped. "You know what?"

"What?"

"That was the last time I saw you in the Unseen. Sometime after that, you were no longer available to me."

"So, I'm dead now. That's what you're saying."

"Please don't joke like that, Your Highness. But, no, it's not like you're dead. Death, even future death, leaves a particular imprint on the Unseen world going forward. That's how I see the late queen there—a presence that is no more, but which echoes in a way that fades the further from her death I get. But you, Queen Eloise. It's like you've disappeared, or you have been cloaked, somehow. I can see your influence in the Unseen, say, on my son. So I can infer your presence. But it is different. Very different, in a way I can't understand or explain, and which, I'm sad to say, renders me useless as your Court Seer."

"It's OK, Seer Maybelle. We'll work it out, somehow."

The two of them returned to their cups of tea, each lost in thought. Eloise returned to the attack on her life. The *ting! thwup!* of the crossbow bolt hitting her crown still made an appearance in her dreams at least once a week, waking her up in a cold sweat. How could that have been the last time she'd appeared in the seer's connection with the Unseen? What had happened around then? Had the crossbow bolt somehow affected her energetic presence? No, not that. Seer Maybelle had perceived her after the attack.

She'd been attacked. She'd gotten a new crown from the Crown Jeweler. She'd called Jerome to the Queen's Study. Jerome had gone to Lorch. And then she'd...

Oh, thought Eloise. *And then I used the Orb of Alleged Omniscience, amplified by the spark of something in the Star of Whatever. I saw and heard the truth, and afterward, had the blurry eye and buzzy ear.*

"Seer Maybelle?"

"Yes, Your Highness?"

"How much does Jerome tell you about what I've done in the way of exploring the Star of Whatever and the use of weak magic?"

"Jerome has given me a broad, annoyingly vague picture," she said. "He demurs to protect Your Highness's privacy." Clearly there was a deeper discussion that had been had, which she kept to herself.

"Let me tell you about something that happened. Perhaps it will shed light on the change in your ability to see me in the Unseen." Eloise lifted the pot of haggleberry tea and offered Seer Maybelle a refill. "This will take a little time."

Eloise sketched a quick summary of what she thought would be the relevant events. Finding Melveeta the Elusive, broken and a husk of herself after two centuries' enslavement to the Purple Haze spell. Her literal connection to the Star of Whatever. Some of what Eloise knew about the Star, including how it was the amplifying force behind Melveeta's spell that created the Purple Haze, and how it could draw in or affect magic nearby. How Melveeta had given the Star of Whatever "unto" Eloise, which seemed to transfer it to her. How Eloise had been able to tap into its magic a few times, including getting out of the Whacking Great Hole, the sunflower disaster in Festering Resentment, and how she'd drawn on it and the Orb to uncover relevant truths about Flachberg and her mother's death. How that had left her with a magic-affected eye and ear.

During the retelling, Seer Maybelle nibbled her way through an entire tahini cookie, and she was halfway through a second when Eloise finished. The chipmunk dabbed crumbs from her furred chin with a napkin and said, "That's quite a story, Your Highness. I had no idea. Jerome kept all of that from me."

"Sorry about that."

"No, no. As your champion and confidant, that was appropriate."

"Thank you for understanding."

Seer Maybelle pointed a claw at Eloise's waist. "The Star of Whatever is in the box that's always on your hip?"

"Yes."

"Fascinating. Simply fascinating. I have experience with certain objects that display weak magical effects, but I've never encountered anything like what you've described. I have so many questions. What kind of range does it have? How does one control it? What color is it? What color is it when one's eyes are closed? Does it have an aura? Does it make a sound? How does it taste? Is it intrinsically magical or is it magical by spell, command, or having been imbued in some way? How old is it? Does it affect light when light shines on it? Can it burn? Can one—"

"You put me to shame, Seer Maybelle. Me and Jerome, we've asked ourselves a few of those, but your questions show a much broader line of inquiry."

"Mere inexperience. I do wish you might have consulted me about it sooner. May I ask why you didn't?"

"To be honest, I don't think either of us thought of it. My apologies." Eloise sipped her tea. "But there is also a bigger reason."

"May I ask what that is?"

"Danger."

"I don't follow."

"I suspect it is the most dangerous object in all the realms. It scares the Çalaht-blessed stuffing out of me. I fear what would happen if it was lost or stolen. So I keep quiet about it, and I keep it near me at all times. You're now one of the few who even knows of its existence. I didn't even tell my mother before she passed."

"Who else knows?"

"Jerome, of course. Lorch. Hector. The Nameless One. Johanna. Anyone she's told, though I don't know if she has. Turpy knew enough about it for it to have caused his death, but that's no longer a risk. There are handmaids who know I have a box I keep with me, but they don't know what it is, and they know never to touch it. Others would have seen it, but would have had no reason to wonder what it is."

"Again, I'm absolutely captivated. The odds of it affecting my ability to see you in the Unseen seem high. The obvious first thing to do would be to see if your proximity to it makes any difference. You could leave it in another room or—"

Eloise held up a hand. "Hold on, hold on."

"Yes?"

"I think we can skip that. I mean, we can maybe get to it another time. But you've already said it did not cloak me from your scrying while I was away. Correct?"

Seer Maybelle nodded. "That's right."

"I had it with me for at least half the time I was away. So its proximity to me was not a factor, otherwise I would have disappeared as soon as Melveeta gave it unto me."

"No, you're right."

"I think the reason you can no longer perceive me in the Unseen is because using the Star of Whatever with the Orb of Alleged Omniscience has caused me a magical malady. My eye and ear. It has left its mark on me. And that mark is what hides me from you in the Unseen realms."

"You speculate, Your Highness."

Eloise tilted her head to the side and looked at the Court Seer. "Yes, I do. If you come up with a better explanation, feel free to put it forward. I'd love to hear it.

"I shall think about it, but for now, I don't have a better explanation. But you realize what this means, right?"

"It means someday the Star of Whatever will suck away my soul and I'll end up like Melveeta, a dried-up old nothing living a fragment of life."

Seer Maybelle wrinkled her forehead. "What? No. That's not what I meant at all. Is that what you're afraid of?"

"If I'm honest, yes."

"I can't comment on what will happen decades from today. What I meant to say was that you are at a disadvantage when it comes to me providing advice. Without access to you and the Unseen, I can't help guide your decisions. You'll be on your own in that sense."

"I guess you're right."

"But there's another implication, Your Highness."

"That I'm going to shrivel up and—"

"No, no, no. What I'm trying to say is that if I can't see you in the Unseen, then the odds are very good that other seers cannot see you either."

Eloise set down her empty cup and saucer. "By 'other seers,' you mean Queen Aglandau's seers?"

"Exactly. You will be a veiled mystery to them as well. It'll leave them unsure."

"That's a little something, I guess."

"It's more than a little something. It's a distinct advantage. They won't know why they can't see you in their future, even though they know you should be there. It might make them cautious, or cause them to miscalculate. You'll need to be alert to any opportunities that presents to you."

Eloise nodded. "Sage advice, Seer Maybelle. And you didn't even need a connection to the Unseen to provide it."

The chipmunk brightened. "Why, you're right."

"So you'll stay on my Privy Council?"

"It will be my pleasure."

42

DIPLOMATIC POUCH

Two days later, Jerome and First Advisor Thëjëts presented the fruits of their research into the parlay between the late Queen Eloise II and Queen Aglandau.

"It's not much," said Jerome as First Advisor put a bound volume on the map table in the Queen's Study. "Your mother kept a kind of diary."

"That doesn't sound like her. I can't imagine her confiding in a diary."

"Well, it's not 'Dear Diary, Today the gossip heralds were mean to me.'" Jerome pulled on cotton gloves, opened up the bound volume, and slid it toward Eloise. "It's more like terse notes to herself."

"Terse sounds about right." Eloise read the first entry, careful not to touch it. "'Crown Plonked today. I am queen. Çalaht help me.'" She looked up at them. "Actually, this is interesting."

"We thought so, too," said Jerome.

"Head Scribe showed it to us," said First Advisor. "It's a recent addition to the Bibliotheca de Records and Regrets, which is obvious in hindsight."

"Did you find anything about the parlay with Queen Aggie?"

"Yes, but there's not much there." Jerome flipped to a bookmarked spot about a quarter of the way in. "Here."

Eloise read out loud. "'Arrived at the encampment. Soaking rain. Meet tomorrow with Q. Ag when the sun is at quarter sky.' So, they got there OK. Do you have another pair of gloves?" Jerome took a pair from a pouch at his waist and gave them to her. Eloise pulled them on as she read the next line. "'Well, that could have gone better. No agreement or meeting of minds. We depart immediately.' That doesn't sound like a very good result."

"No. And that's all she says," said Jerome. "Anywhere."

Eloise scanned the entries above and below the two she'd read. "Hmmm... Were there any memos or directives? Did they make a joint statement? That happens sometimes. Or did she make any pronouncements or decisions in the days or weeks that followed that had to do with the Eastern Lands?"

"Not that we've found so far," said First Advisor. "It's like the parlay was so insignificant that no one spoke of it ever again."

"Insignificant? Maybe it was profoundly significant, and it smothered them into silence."

"I guess that's also possible. But unless we find some other documentation, we'll remain in the dark."

Eloise looked at Jerome. "You'll keep looking?"

"Yes, of course."

"First Advisor, were you involved in diplomacy at the time? Do you remember anything that might be relevant?"

First Advisor laughed. "I was at the Studium Gymnasium when the late queen's parlay with Queen Aggie happened. My first year."

"And?"

"At the time, most of my brain power was split very unevenly between learning about the history of other realms and a deep exploration of the fermentation qualities of hops, barley, and wheat. If I had any knowledge of what happened at the time, I left it at the bottom of a mug."

"Ah. Right."

Eloise flipped idly, but carefully, through the bound volume. "Can you leave this with me? I'd like to look at it more closely when I have a minute."

"Head Scribe thought that might be the case. He asked me to say, and I quote, 'It's one of my babies. Please treat it as such.' Does that make sense?"

"Yes it does."

Eloise closed the bound volume and took a seat. "I guess we know all that we're going to know, for now, anyway. I've made a decision."

"Yes?" asked First Advisor.

"We see if she'll parlay."

"As you wish, Your Highness. I think it is a reasonable choice."

"How do I send a message to Queen Aggie?"

"It would be best to go through your ambassador there."

"Who's that?"

"Oh, that's right, she hasn't been back to Court since your ascendancy. It's Ernestina de Setonix."

"So she's a quokka?"

"Yes. If I may say so, she's lovely, and rapier-sharp. We knew each other at the Studium Gymnasium. She was two years ahead of me, but we overlapped enough, and had enough in common, to be friendly."

"Was that commonality the exploration of hops, barley, and wheat fermentation?"

First Advisor laughed. "No. Or not usually. Our interests were in the other realms we were studying."

"And how do I get a message to the ambassador so she can put our request to the queen?"

"You send it by diplomatic pouch."

"How does that work?"

"Any marsupial will do, but typically, we engage numbats because they are fast and have very good stamina. Plus, they are fierce when it comes to protecting whatever is in their pouches. We tend to avoid bandicoots, given their history, whether that's fair or not. Ernestina herself came up through the diplomatic ranks, starting as a diplomatic pouch. She'll know what to do when your message arrives, assuming we're clear enough."

"So do I write Queen Aglandau a letter requesting we parlay?"

"Yes. Also, you write to Ambassador de Setonix with your instructions to her—the when, how, and why of your message to the queen, so that when she delivers it, she's not surprised when she gets a response."

"Right. Well, let's grab a quill and some fancy parchment and get writing."

Two hours and fifteen drafts later, Eloise was happy with both the letter to Aglandau and the instructions to de Setonix. A diplomatic pouch had been summoned, the documents entrusted, and the numbat dispatched.

"Now what do we do?" asked Eloise.

"We wait for a response," said Thëjëts. "And we hope it comes soon, so we're not left twisting in the wind waiting for an answer."

"Let's assume a 'no' and continue to plan accordingly. If we get a 'yes,' we can adjust our approach."

43

THE FLIBBERTYQUEEN'S DOING

Lady Seneschal was taking a brief respite in her office. She didn't have time for tea and a nibble, but a few moments to put her sore feet up on the pouffe wouldn't go astray.

It had been a challenging morning, to say the least. A rickety cart pulled by an overawed young colt making his first delivery to Castle de Brague had taken a turn too sharply and spilled turnips all over the courtyard. In the winter rain. The turnips had to be picked up and cleaned so they didn't go to waste, the colt had to be calmed, and the whole mess had wiped out a solid hour of work time for four kitchen wenches.

That was four kitchen wenches lost from an already short staff, as an entire third of them hadn't shown up for morning duties, sending excuses filled with unconvincing complaints of a vague ague. Lady Seneschal strongly suspected the malady was a widespread case of idontwanna-itis. She'd have to make a surprise visit to their quarters and see if there was more giggling than coughing going on.

That is, she'd make the surprise visit if she could convince her sore feet that it was worth the trek in the rain.

There was a time not that long ago when no one would even dream of skiving off from their duties. That they felt like they could possibly get away with it irked her more than she cared to admit.

Lady Seneschal sighed, covered her eyes with her hand, and tried not to hear the chaotic shouts from the understaffed kitchen as the new Chef struggled to produce lunch to an adequate standard, a bar he would clear (Lady Seneschal made sure of that), but with, at best, half a hair's width of margin.

He really was the most stupendously middling cook she'd ever encountered. His efforts bore such spectacularly prosaic fruits, it was like he had a weak magic for the mundane and uninteresting.

And yet, the new queen put up with it. Lady Seneschal would have expected the Flibbertyqueen to give him the sack, but she tolerated his fare with suppressed grimaces and attempts at polite praise. Her mother would have turfed him weeks ago. Now there was a woman who knew how to be queen, a woman who was a pleasure to serve.

Lady Seneschal Älphonsinä Póöòmáäàdéëè made a deal with herself that she could sit there for a count of ten, and then she'd get up and continue the endless list of tasks that demarcated the minutes and hours of her day. She'd make it a slow, lingering ten count. She deserved that much, at least.

A page knocked at her door, disrupting her reverie. She cracked open one eye and spread the fingers over her face just enough to let her glare penetrate. "You interrupt. Can this not wait?"

"A scroll and a sealed message for you, Lady Seneschal. Would you like me to come back?"

She moved her fingers back together, shut her open eye, and used her other hand to wave him over. Póöòmáäàdéëè opened her palm and waited. He gave her the items, which she dropped on her lap, then dismissed him with a backwards flick of the hand.

One. Two. Three. Four. The scroll could wait. Nothing good ever came in the form of a scroll. Fiiive. Scrolls were boring at best, and officious guff at worst. Siiiiiix. A sealed message was something different. Some-times they were good, like a letter from your cousin saying the uncle you hated died in a freak parsnip mishap. But some sealed notes made you wish you'd never opened them, like an invitation to your late uncle's boring, depressing funeral. Seeeeeeeeeven. Yes, the sealed message could wait. Really, it could. Eeeeeeeeeeeight. Niiiiiiiiiiiiiiiiii-iiiiine.

"Oh, blast," she muttered. Lady Seneschal opened her eyes, held up the envelope, and looked at the dark green wax seal. It clearly depicted a cluster of olives. She smiled and flipped it over to confirm who it was from.

Picholine Manzanilla. Her Picho.

What a pleasant surprise. She hadn't heard from her friend since the Flibbertyqueen banished them from Brague. Although, if she was being honest, she couldn't exactly say if it was the pipsqueak's decision or not. There was a version of the story that said the Eastern Lands ambassador and lead trade negotiator had already left by the time that directive was sent. But she couldn't imagine her friend leaving without a proper goodbye, so she was disinclined to give the queen the benefit of the doubt.

Sore feet and tiredness forgotten, she sat up and reached for her letter opener. After carefully breaking the wax seal, she let herself enjoy the scent of the hemp parchment, then retrieved the folded letter within and began reading.

My dearest Älphïë,

I hope this finds you thriving like the beloved olive tree that grows in the court-yard of my ancestral home and that Divine Çalaht rains blessings on your days like olives at a harvest festival.

This is a quick note to let you know I've been thinking of you, and remembering those delicious times we spent together. How I miss On Golden Scone, and how I miss your company. My queen, the beloved, righteous and most honorable Queen Aglandau, has seen fit to have me serve her as ambassador to the Half Kingdom. Or should that be "Half Queendom" now? I'm not sure. I don't think QJ's insistence that one says "Northern Lands" will hold much sway. She is weak. Weaker than her uncle, if you can believe such a thing is possible. But again, you practically raised her so you know of what I speak.

⚜

THIS DIDN'T QUITE SIT WITH LADY SENESCHAL. SHE HAD ALWAYS thought of Princess Johanna as the more stubborn, stronger-willed of the two. Perhaps Manzanilla had seen something that happened once the dandiprat's twin was made queen. Hmmm...

⚜

I WAS HOPING YOU MIGHT HELP ME WITH SOMETHING. THE LADY Seneschal here seems, like you, to be a particularly lovely and competent woman. Like you, she runs a tidy castle and works incredibly hard. I always felt you were under appreciated, but there wasn't much I could do about it except commiserate. In a brief encounter I had with QJ, I happened to mention my appreciation of the work of her Lady Seneschal. QJ asked me what I thought an appropriate mark of recognition might be. Something more than a token acknowledgement. And I thought, I know the perfect person to ask. So, my dear Älphïe, I'm hoping you can help me help QJ. What sort of recognition, be it a thing or an action, would you like to receive from your queen?

⚜

OUCH. JUST OUCH. WHAT KIND OF RECOGNITION WOULD SHE LIKE to receive? How about any? How about a kind word in acknowledgement of a job well done by her and her staff? Beyond a few polite exchanges, it was like the Flibbertyqueen was avoiding her. How was she supposed to do her job if the queen barely spoke to her? Being Lady Seneschal was not a task that one set up, pushed in the right direction, and then forgot.

Çalaht on a piece of burned toast. How she missed the late queen.

For her friend's sake, she'd have to come up with something and write back. A day or two in a pamper spa would be nice. Massage, pedicure, hot spring baths, cucumber slices on your eyes—the works. Lady Seneschal groaned and rubbed one of her feet. To be gifted a couple of days of pampering would be delightful. For that matter, a fruit basket, a pastry box, and some flowers wouldn't go astray.

Lady Seneschal humphed. It was never going to happen. The Flibbertyqueen just didn't think that way.

She was upset now, so put the letter away, leaving it for when she was calmer.

She looked at the scroll in her lap. May as well get it over with. She unscrolled it to find a snippy-toned directive.

TO: LADY SENESCHAL ÄLPHONSINÄ PÓÖÒMÁÄÀDÉËÈ

From: Exchequer of the Realm Cyrus Borborygmus

AT THE REQUEST OF HER HIGHNESS, QUEEN ELOISE HYDRA GUMBALL *III, Sovereign Ruler of the Western Lands and All That Really Matters, in recognition of the evolving circumstances of Court and the realm, and in line with the duties prescribed the* Livre de Protocol, *you are hereby directed to undertake a review of the expenditure of coin that occurs within your budget and sphere of influence in order to find a minimum savings and/or decrease of one coin in ten, pursuant to the details given below.*

IT WENT ON FROM THERE, DOWN TO A SIGNATURE THAT READ "EOTR C. Borborygmus."

Lady Seneschal felt her cheeks flush pink and her jaw clench. Her head lowered into her shoulders like a boxer ready to take a punch. Or, more likely, ready to throw a few.

How dare he. How *dare* he ask her to pinch her coins even tighter. She ran a tidy castle—just like Picho had said. She bargained, blustered, and browbeat her suppliers to stretch the realm's coin like taffy at a village fair.

Borborygmus was a persnickety, officious old codger who knew a lot about numbers, but nothing about people. His bumptious manner had the subtlety of a stepped-on garden rake introducing itself into one's face. But she knew his work, and as her blood pressure spiked, she knew he wouldn't have done this on his own initiative.

"At the request of Her Highness." Lady Seneschal scoffed. Did the jumped-up wee queenling think she had a place to tell her how to do her job? How galling. How absolutely aggravating, and she didn't even have the decency to come tell her herself? Infuriating.

Lady Seneschal scowled and crumpled the sheet of parchment. "Unacceptable. Simply unacceptable," she mumbled. It took everything she had not to smash her teacup and saucer into the stone wall.

Intolerable.

She could hear Manzanilla's voice, like she was sitting next to her. "If something is intolerable, Älphïë, then perhaps it ought not be tolerated."

Perhaps.

Perhaps.

Perhaps.

Perhaps.

Perhaps.

❧ 44 ❧

THE HOUSE THAT MISERY
BUILT

For the tenth day in a row, Eloise found herself sucking wind on the soldier's obstacle course. Lorch and Jerome were way ahead of her, yet again. Squat and Lanky, however, were doing the course with her, providing encouragement and their inevitable, usually useful, advice. Some of the obstacles were now very familiar and getting easy, like the high-step grid and the monkey bars, and some of them, like the hangover wall and the slack rope across the mud puddle, bedeviled her each and every day.

What was hardest, though, was that every other day, some new torture appeared, lengthening the course and adding new misery. Two days before, it had been a series of thick logs propped up like saw horses at chest height that one was supposed to get over—a menace called the Titan's Hurdles. Before that, it had been the Barbarian's Mire, a 20-length mud puddle that had a mesh anchored just a few weak lengths above it. She'd had to drag herself along on her back to get from one end to the other.

"What's this one called?" Eloise stared stupidly at the day's new challenge, an A-shaped structure that reached 30 lengths in the air at the apex and was covered in a rope mesh tied in length-wide squares. At the bottom, a wall of boards spanned from the ground to the mesh. Which started well above head height. The wall section was slicked with some sort of oil, making it almost impossible to get enough purchase to make it to the mesh.

"The House That Misery Built," said Squat

"Charming. Is there a trick?"

"Climb up. Climb over. Climb down. Don't fall off."

"Don't fall off? From something that high? Good, solid, actionable advice, Squat."

"Thank you, Your Highness," said the soldier.

Lanky chucked him in the arm. "She was being facetious, doofus."

"Oh. Sorry. Missed that." Squat stared up, examining the obstacle's structure. "You might need a boost to get up to the mesh part."

"Isn't that cheating?"

"No. Master Sergeant says cooperation is a good thing."

"That seems like a sound perspective."

"Yes, ma'am. I believe it is."

"Squat, give us a boost," said Lanky.

"Sure." The soldier laced his fingers, and Lanky stepped into them with one foot. "On three?"

"On three."

"One, two, three!" Squat heaved Lanky upwards, flinging him past the slippery wall. He grasped onto the mesh and hauled himself up, mostly using his arms, since his feet could do little more than scrabble uselessly.

"Your Highness?" Squat offered his laced fingers for her to follow Lanky up.

"With permission, Your Highness, I'll try to catch you," said Lanky. "Is that OK?"

"Sure. Just don't drop me."

"No, ma'am. I won't do that."

She stepped into Squat's entwined fingers and said, "One, two, three!" The soldier heaved her skywards. She sailed past Lanky, skidding upwards along the mesh. Then gravity caught her, and she bounced along, going downward. Eloise managed to stick an arm through the mesh and hold on. It jarred her shoulder and left her dangling, but she managed not to plummet to the ground.

"You OK, ma'am?" asked Squat.

"Peachy." Eloise found the mesh with her feet and steadied herself. "How are you going to get up here?"

"I got this," said Lanky, who lowered himself to the top of the wall, stuck his legs through the mesh, and hung like the catching half of a trapeze act. "On three?"

"On three," said Squat.

"Hold it. Just a sec. Let me help." Eloise moved down so she was next to Lanky and had one hand free. "Ready. On three."

Squat took a few steps back so he had a short runway. "One, two three!" He sprinted forward, then launched himself at the wall. He hit it flat, arms high like a hockey sacking referee after a point is scored.

Lanky grabbed one arm in each hand and held tight. "Got you."

Squat then used Lanky like an impromptu ladder, pulling himself up hand over hand until Eloise was able to grab him by the collar and help him up the last two lengths.

"Thank you, Your Highness," huffed Squat.

"Pleasure. Let's get over this thing."

"Yes, ma'am," said the two soldiers in unison.

ANDREW EINSPRUCH

The rest of the House That Misery Built was both easier and harder than Eloise expected. The height didn't bother her, but the mesh squares were large enough that it didn't work simply to step from one to the next. She had to shimmy and hoist herself up, Squat and Lanky keeping pace, until she finally reached the A-frame's top and could descend the other side. This was similarly difficult, as she had to make sure she didn't lose her foot and fall through the mesh holes. When she made it to the top of the wall, she lowered herself down it and dropped the last bit. She gave a self-deprecating, "Ta da!" as she landed. Unlike the first time she'd done the course, there were no soldiers gathered to cheer. Having their queen fling herself at the obstacle course was no longer a sight worth noticing. That was good. Or, at least, she hoped it was good.

"Good on ya', ma'am," said Squat, dropping down next to her. "You did it."

"Thanks."

"Incoming," yelled Lanky, and he jumped from the top of the wall, did a somersault in mid-air, and stuck the landing like a gymnast, even throwing his arms out like he was trying to impress a judge.

"Wow. Impressive," said Eloise, still panting.

Lanky smirked and bowed. "Thank you, ma'am."

A voice came from across the Drill Paddock. "Queen Eloise!" Tiberius de Sphenodon hurried toward her.

Squat and Lanky snapped to perfect, rigid attention. "Sir! Master Sergeant, sir!" they yelled in unison.

"Master Sergeant," said Eloise. "Good to see you."

"I see you've conquered the House That Misery Built. Congratulations, Your Highness."

Eloise nodded toward Squat and Lanky. "I had some help, but yes."

"Very good." The tuatara smiled. "I'd like a quiet word, if I may. Would you have time?"

"Is it urgent?"

"Pressing, but not urgent."

"Then do we have time for me to finish the course first? And maybe wash the mud off me?"

"Of course, Your Highness. When would suit you?"

"An hour? In the Fippledip Room?"

"I'll see you there." He looked at the soldiers. "You two will continue taking care of our queen?"

"Sir, Master Sergeant, yes, sir!"

"Good."

❧ 45 ❧

AUTOTOMY

Course finished, muscles complaining, and body bathed, Eloise found the tuatara studying the portrait of Fortescue Fippledip on the Fippledip Room's door. "What do you think, Master Sergeant?"

De Sphenodon slowly shook his head. "This is, perhaps, one of the worst portraits I've ever seen."

"That's the consensus, but why, specifically, would you say that?"

"Let's start by saying that I don't know anything about the subject, so I can't tell you what he should have looked like. But for one, there's a strange attention to particular details like the wrinkles, like that one that goes from mouth to nose. Or the way the artist emphasizes the darkness under his eyes. He may as well be the loser in a boxing match. Or a raccoon. Neither is a good look for one's champion. Second, there's an immature simplicity to the shapes. The head is so perfectly round it looks like it was drawn with a thumbtack and a piece of string, and his scowl is so unsubtle as to be a caricature. Finally, the colors neither flatter nor fairly represent. Look at the overly white eyes, the comically red lips, the unsubtly yellow hair. They may as well have hung a child's finger painting."

"Interesting that you can express it so clearly. I just look at it and think, 'ugh,' and leave it at that."

"'Ugh' certainly covers the detail and nuance it deserves. Anyway, Your Highness has better things to do than listen to me speak ill of a painting done so long ago. I'm sure the artist was doing the best he or she could under the circumstances. Or perhaps they held a grudge, and freezing this likeness in time was a kind of retribution."

"Possibilities that hadn't occurred to me." Eloise took the key from her pocket, unlocked the door, and stepped through. "So, what's on your mind, Master Sergeant de Sphenodon?"

The tuatara followed her in and waited until she was seated. "Permission to speak directly, Your Highness?"

"I hope you'll always be direct. But yes."

"I'd like to discuss our progress with reshaping the troops."

"Go ahead."

"Is it true that you've offered to parlay with Queen Aglandau Ponentine?"

That took Eloise by surprise. She thought the letter had been drafted and sent in secrecy. "How did you hear that?"

"I considered it a likely possibility, given the state of things in your queendom. I put the question to First Advisor and pressed until she confided that an offer to parlay had, indeed, been transmitted to the Eastern Lands castle."

"Then there was no need to ask." Eloise began the wrist stretches that Bërÿl the Assistant Apothecary had recommended what now seemed like years before, but was a matter of weeks at most. The exercises were much more comfortable to do now, and although she still experienced residual ache, she felt like she was at least 85 per cent healed. "Do you have a comment on the matter of parlay?"

"Yes, Your Highness. I hope it goes well."

"Do you? I'm told they normally don't."

"That's my understanding as well, Your Highness." The tuatara reached up and scratched one of the spiny plates at the back of his neck, which Eloise took as him looking for the right words.

"Please, Master Sergeant. Just say what you have to say."

"The good heralding is that the soldiers are making progress. Fitness is improving. Attention spans are lengthening. Former Champion Cloisterfeld's lessons in weaponry are popular and people seem to be learning new fighting skills. Where previously our foes were more likely to die of accidental tetanus if they encountered one of our swords, these days there's an almost 50-50 chance that blood might be spilled, and a promising percentage of that would likely be the enemy's and not our own."

"Right. So, what's the bad heralding?"

"The bad heralding is that our numbers are still low, our skills are months away from going from miserable to barely adequate, and the armory has been depleted of everything that's not ceremonial in nature. I have grave fears about what would happen on the battlefield. Which is why it's my hope that your parlay is successful."

"What do we do if it isn't?"

"You work out what 'Discretion is the better part of valor' looks like in your particular situation."

"I'm not sure I like the direction in which that takes me or the queendom as a whole."

De Sphenodon paused. Once again, he reached up and behind to scratch his scales. "Queen Eloise, are you familiar with the characteristics of a tuatara's tail?"

"Not overly. Only what I've been able to observe of you. If I may say so, you are the first tuatara I've had close contact with."

"My people, like some of our lizard and salamander cousins, can shed part of the tail. This process, which we call 'autotomy,' is normally in response to an attack."

"I knew that about lizards and salamanders, but not tuataras. I imagine for a soldier, it could be very handy on the battlefield."

"Yes, it can be. Some autotomized tails continue to move, which can provide a useful distraction. I, myself, owe my life to it. An enemy stepped on me and held me in place while he sliced down with his sword. Autonomy let me escape what otherwise would have been certain death." His tone was matter of fact, like he was reporting that someone had wanted to give him a birthday cake, which he'd had to decline.

"How interesting. What's autotomy like?"

"It's like losing part of your being. It is profound, but also completely ignorable. It is as significant as you might expect losing a limb would be. But it's also entirely meaningless, as life-changing as humans find discarding a fingernail clipping." The tuatara held up his own tail for emphasis. "To my people, shedding one's tail comes naturally. In the moment, you think nothing of it. If it's imperative or advantageous, then you drop the tail without hesitation. Only later does the thinking about it, the chewing on it, start. Did I really need to do that in those circumstances? What kind of questions will I get from friends and family? How will the tail that grows back be the same, or different? Stronger? Younger? More flexible? That's usually the case, although it can also come back stunted or lesser in some way."

"It sounds complicated. How do you handle it?"

"Some of us just tough it out. Some of us ignore the whole thing, although that's hard since the change is so pronounced. Some of us cope with it through ritual. We have ceremonies that are not unlike funerals to commemorate the loss. They structure our grieving for the autotomized tail, and try to help us apply a psychic balm so that the loss one feels does not turn into lasting emotional damage."

"I'm not sure I understand where this is going."

"My point is that every tuatara instinctively knows when it's time to drop this thing that has value to them, and to do so without regret. We recognize that the action provides an associated value that usually has to do with the extension of one's life or maintaining the well-being and sanctity of the rest of the body. There may be emotion around it, but our culture ensures there's broader perspective."

Eloise stopped stretching her wrists and looked at him. She felt her stomach sink. "You're talking about Flachberg. It's the potentially-left-behind tail in this scenario."

"Yes, Your Highness."

"How narrowly or broadly am I to take this metaphor?"

"I wouldn't presume to tell you that, Queen Eloise. It will depend on the situation." De Sphenodon swished his tail for emphasis. "I'm simply saying that if she accepts your invitation and you do parlay with the Eastern Lands queen, you may find that the advantageous thing to do is to drop the part of your tail that does not serve you at that moment. Remember that it can regrow and come back stronger."

"You said it can also regrow and come back weaker."

"There is that risk."

"Thank you. I'll keep it in mind. But first we have to find out if it's happening at all, and in the meantime, keep improving our readiness."

46

REMEMBRANCE OF FOGGINGS PAST

Queen Johanna stood on top of Fogging Hill, on the exact spot where Turpentine Snotearrow McCcoonnch had ordered his brother Gouache to fling her down the hill into the once-deadly mist. She wore a somber, black dress and an even blacker coat that was cinched tight against the icy late winter wind. Around her was a sea of people wearing black armbands and dark expressions. Johanna had expected maybe a handful of people to come to her Remembrance of Foggings Past ceremony. That there were hundreds of people across dozens of species showed that her memorial idea had hit a nerve.

A herald cleared his throat and announced her. "Her Majesty, Johanna Umgotteswillen Gumball, the rightful crown-plonked queen of the Northern Lands!"

There was a smattering of applause, and about half the crowd bowed or dipped into a curtsy. Johanna stepped forward, and Chafed held her hand as she stepped up on an apple crate so she could be seen. "Thank you all for coming. I'd like to say a few words and make an announcement. Afterwards, I invite you to afternoon tea down in the tent just next to the Purple Haze at the bottom of the hill."

She paused, saw that people were more or less nodding, and figured she had their attention. Johanna took a deep breath to project her words over the wind. "I invited you here today for the Remembrance of Foggings Past as a way to acknowledge a deep wrong that was done for two centuries in the name of justice. Perhaps sometimes justice was served, but too often, those who died in the Purple Haze were inconvenient or subject to whims. You might have heard that I, myself, was fogged. Had my sister not come after me, I'm sure I would have perished or lost my mind. The Purple Haze was a terrible way to die. It didn't have to be like that, yet those who came before us chose to use it to terrify and kill."

There were plenty of nods, and a couple of people said, "Hear, hear."

"That there are so many of you here today is testimony to how pervasive the hurt caused by fogging was. I feel for you. I really do. I know what it feels like to lose a parent, a sibling, a friend. So let us take a few moments to think silently about those who were lost to the Purple Haze. Let us bring to mind those who were forced into it, those who went into it of their own accord, those who perished in it by accident, and those who, two centuries ago, were caught in it when the spell of the Purple Haze first consumed the land, air, and water. They were loved ones. They were friends. They were strangers. But they were people of all species whose lives were cut short. We remember them with hearts open and filled with sorrow. May their souls fly free so they may stand with Çalaht. So may it be."

"So may it be," echoed the crowd.

"And now, let us close our eyes and observe three minutes of silence for those who came to their end here at the bottom of Fogging Hill, as well as wherever the Purple Haze choked out life in misty death."

The crowd hushed, and Johanna joined them. If she'd been smart, she would have brought along a horological cuckoo to time it accurately. Too late now. She'd have to guess. She counted seconds in her head. *One one thousand. Two one thousand. Three one thousand...*

Somewhere around one hundred one thousand, Johanna cracked open her eyes and looked at the crowd. Easily half of them were wiping away tears or snotting up their handkerchiefs. That surprised her. She hadn't expected such emotion. Should she have brought along one of the Çalahtist religious leaders? No, she was right not to involve them. Protocol didn't have much to say about it, and that would have made it more of a religious thing. She wanted this to be more of a healing event. Plus, she was functionally the head of the Çalahtist faith here in the Northern Lands, so that was covered.

Johanna realized her thoughts had strayed. What had she been up to? How long had she not been counting? She closed her eyes again and resumed. *One hundred ten one thousand. One hundred eleven one thousand...*

When she reached 180, Johanna broke the snuffle-filled silence, saying, "For those who've come before us, ancestors all, may you be at peace and stand with Çalaht. So may it be."

"So may it be," echoed the crowd.

"Thank you, everyone." Johanna glanced at her father, who gave her a "go ahead" nod. "I'd like to say a few words about the Purple Haze. For two centuries it loomed over the Northern Lands, a constant, luminous, ominous threat. For over two hundred years, it consumed all that crossed its boundary. That is, until my sister and I entered it. She and I traveled its shrouded hill and dust-caked plains. We found its source, and my sister managed to break the spell that created it. As we can all see, the Purple Haze is still there. But it is changed. It no longer devours, it merely cloaks. One can now go into it and return."

There was a murmuring assent, with a level of apprehension.

"Today, people of all species still avoid the Purple Haze. Why? Habit. People were so afraid of it for so long, and it caused so many people such terrible suffering, that they don't trust that the danger has passed. But that avoidance also avoids something else—reality. Our reality as people who live in and love the Northern Lands is that the Purple Haze hides a mystery. A mystery, and a potential. What is that potential?"

Here, Johanna paused, wondering if anyone would brave an answer.

Silence.

"The potential is that buried in the dust and sadness within the Purple Haze are opportunities for the betterment of the queendom that could be drawn on while still honoring the memory of those who perished within it."

"Are there really opportunities in there?" asked a woman toward the front.

"I'm glad you asked," said Johanna. "Do you know what the answer to your question is?"

The woman shook her head.

"Exactly. Who knows? So, then, what does that mean we need? We need some brave souls... No, 'brave' isn't the right word, since the threat from the Purple Haze has gone. We need some *pioneering* souls. People with the will and desire to go into the Purple Haze and figure out what's in there." Johanna counted off points on her mittened fingers. "What can we do to heal the land still covered by mist? Can tilth be restored to the barren soil? Is the dust that covers everything viable somehow? Is there infrastructure that could be repurposed? Did anything at all survive in there? How are things changing now that the spell is no more? I tell you, that land is *brimming* with adventure. It is a place that is ready for us to come together to explore, to heal, and if it is at all possible, to return it to its living glory ."

She looked from face to face. Clearly, they were at least curious.

"Let's take a diversion for a moment. Do you know what group of people have been most affected by the change in the Purple Haze?" She paused to see if anyone would venture a guess. "No one?" She waved forward three people in purple robes that matched the color of the Purple Haze, as well as matching rucksacks. Discontent bubbled through the crowd, but Johanna waved it off and continued. "It's people like Abigail Bronzer Splintfinger, her apprentice, Öööscar, and Guild Master Frÿÿÿdenburg. They are all members of the Foggers'

Guild. Yes, they were tasked with carrying out the late king's capital justice, which they all regret."

This wasn't strictly true. Some of the Foggers she'd met were totally unrepentant. But that was not a nuance that needed exploring just now, and these three at least felt bad about what they'd done.

"But with the ending of the Purple Haze's spell, their work disappeared. No longer were their particular, specialized skills needed. They were immediately without work."

The crowd wasn't showing much sympathy. Understandable, given that the Fogger's jobs had been to force people to their deaths in the lethal fog. They hadn't exactly been the most popular people in Stained Rock.

"I spoke before of dealing with reality. Well, one reality is that there is no longer any need for foggers. As such, I hereby and forever disband the Foggers' Guild.'

That got a smidge of applause.

"However, they need a role in the realm and the realm has a need—to investigate what lies hidden within the Purple Haze. So while I may have disbanded the Foggers' Guild, in its place rises a new guild, one dedicated to researching the riddles and secrets within this great lavender fog. Ladies and gentlemen, I present to you the first three members of the newly constituted Amalgamated Fellowship of the Queen's Purple Haze Explorers."

Slightly more applause. Good. Johanna hadn't exactly expected wild cheers, given the ill feeling the foggers had previously engendered, but better that there was a tiny round of applause than pitchforks or rotten squash projectiles.

"With the aid of the Amalgamated Fellowship of the Queen's Purple Haze Explorers, we shall do our best to realize the potential of this purple enigma for the betterment of all and in memory of those who perished in it." She waved the three former foggers forward. Former Guild Master Frÿÿÿdenburg, a gruff, paunchy, silver-haired man, sloped forward first. He bowed to Johanna with the air of a person being asked to suck down a bushel of raw lemons. "Master Frÿÿÿdenburg, do you freely accept the role as head of this new organization?"

"Yes, Your Majesty."

"And will you faithfully explore the lands within the Purple Haze to the best of your ability and report back faithfully on your discoveries to Court and Crown?"

"Yes, Your Majesty."

"Then I name you Master Fellow, Head of the Amalgamated Fellowship of the Queen's Purple Haze Explorers."

Frÿÿÿdenburg hefted his rucksack higher on his shoulders and bowed again. "Thank you, Your Majesty."

Next came Abigail Bronzer Splintfinger, who'd spent years and years as an ambitious fogger working her way up the ladder. She'd been on duty the day the Purple Haze was found to be broken, and it had sent her into a financial panic. When the new crown-plonked queen had offered her a role as an explorer, she'd jumped at the chance, as it would help her keep up her payments on her cottage, as well as the arrangement she had with the apothecary to cover her ailing mother's prattleweed needs.

Queen Johanna took her through the whole "Do you freely... yada yada" bit, and the "Will you faithfully explore... hummanuh hummanhuh hummanhuh" part. Splintfinger curtsied where needed, said "yes" where she was supposed to, and happily took the title of Senior Hazeologist in the Amalgamated Fellowship.

Third was the apprentice, Öööscar, who was Master Fellow Frÿÿÿdenburg's nephew. He'd had a crisis of confidence when he'd been ordered to chop off Johanna's head. In the chaos surrounding the death of King Doncaster and the ascension, he'd decided that he didn't need to remove the princess's noggin from the rest of her body, so he handed the sword to a nearby guard, took off his fogger's robe, and simply left. It had been a freeing thing to do, but he was already tainted as a fogger and couldn't find any other work. So when Splintfinger had contacted him about becoming a Purple Haze Explorer, it seemed like as good an option as any. He, too, took his oath of office with a bow and a feeling of relief.

Ceremony done, Johanna spoke again to the crowd. "Join me in wishing our newest guild Çalahtspeed in this, their first foray into the mists." She began clapping, and was gratified when at least two dozen people joined her.

The three purple-clad figures adjusted their rucksacks. Frÿÿÿdenburg looked dour, Splintfinger determined, and Öööscar overwhelmed and apprehensive. With a final bow to their queen, they trudged down Fogging Hill to the spot where so many had perished by their own hands. Noiselessly, they slipped into the curtain of fog, and the applause petered out.

"That's it for our Remembrance of Foggings Past. Thank you everyone for coming and please, enjoy the refreshments."

To Johanna's relief, they did exactly that—approached the border of the Purple Haze where the tables were set up and filled plates with finger food.

Chafed lifted his chin and indicated both the tables of food and, beyond them, the spot where the purple-clad explorers had disappeared into the fog. "Once again, your Eastern Lands coin at work."

"Yes."

"Think they'll find anything useful?"

"Honestly, I doubt it. It was desiccated and dead. A true ruin. But at least we can help those foggers stop being pariahs. That has to be good for the community. Plus, we all have to stop looking over our shoulders at the Purple Haze like it's a monster that might devour us at any second. It's draining."

❧ 47 ❧

IMPUGNED

"Your Highness, I need a word with you, if I may."

Eloise looked up from the intelligence scroll she was reading to see Lady Seneschal glowering at her from the doorway of the Fippledip Room, holding a scroll of her own. She thought, "What is it this time?" but said, "Certainly. Please, come in and sit."

"We need to discuss—"

"I apologize if I'm still doing things wrong. Am I not using the pages enough still? Am I not letting you know where I am regularly enough? Have I not expressed food preferences clearly enough and early enough? I'm sorry if that's the case."

"No. None of those things are why I'm here this time. It's this." She thrust the scroll forward.

Eloise took it, spread it out on the table in front of her and read. She glanced down at the signature, then went back to the top of the page and kept reading. When she finished, she said, "Yes? And?"

Calm indifference. That had not been the reaction that Lady Seneschal had been expecting. Embarrassment, maybe. Or defensiveness. Maybe chagrin or a duplicitous denial. But not this nonchalance.

"This is unacceptable," spluttered Lady Seneschal.

"How so?"

Her calm irked Lady Seneschal, who could feel her anger spiking. "Your Highness, my management of the household has been impugned."

"That's not how I see it. You do a fantastic job."

"Then why is a hatchet being taken to my coin purse? Your Highness may not know it, but I squeeze every coin until it begs for mercy before I spend it on behalf of the realm."

"I'm sure you do," said Eloise. "Still, the Exchequer's request seems a reasonable one. He's asked you to save one coin in ten. He hasn't directed the budget be cut in half or a third. He's asked for ten per cent."

"He hasn't asked for it. *You* have asked for it. He's just the messenger."

"Does that matter?"

"Of course it matters! Never in the decades that I have been of service to the Gumball Crown has anyone even hinted at asking me to spend less coin or account for coin. There has always been a fundamental trust. A trust that has now been fractured."

Eloise set down the exchequer's scroll. "Tell me, Lady Seneschal. Do you know anyone from Flachberg, or know someone who has a friend or relative there?"

That stopped Póöòmáäàdéëè, who thought a moment. "I have a cousin whose former paramour hailed from Flachberg, but I don't see—"

"Surely you've heard of the incursion into the Western Lands and All That Really Matters that happened there."

"There's been mention of it by the gossip heralds, yes."

"Tell me, Lady Seneschal, what do you think my options are?"

"It is no business of mine to think in such directions. I guess, at a high level, you acquiesce or resist."

"Which would you do?"

"I would resist."

Eloise nodded. "That's my inclination as well. But to do so requires coin, and coin is more scarce in the Court coffers than one would hope. That means I have to look at both sides of the coin, so to speak —what's coming in and what's going out."

"That may sound reasonable now, but you won't think so when you have beans for brekky, beans for morning tea, beans for lunch, beans for afternoon tea, beans for dinner, beans for supper, and beans for your midnight snack. And you know who will get the blame for it? I will."

"I don't think—"

"That we can agree on, Your Highness. You don't think."

Eloise flinched at that, but decided to let her say her piece. But Póòòmáäàdéèè wasn't just saying her piece. She was winding up like Eloise had never seen before.

"You seem to assume that the Court and the castle somehow run themselves automagically," snapped Lady Seneschal.

"I—"

"Well, they don't. It's a lot of hard work. A lot of under-appreciated hard toil. A lot of do this, do that, do the other. A lot of jumping to other people's whims while doing one's best to stay out of the way."

"I—"

"Your mother never questioned anything I did. We got along like two kapok seeds in a fluffy pod. Your grandmother was more distant, but we had an understanding."

"I—"

But Lady Seneschal had left anger behind and was well on her way to righteous indignation. "I have been proud to serve the Gumball family. This Court, this castle, your family—they have been my life's work. But this..." She snatched back the scroll and scrunched it in her fist. "This is beyond what I can tolerate."

"Please, don't—"

"If I do not have the authority to do my job as I see fit and for the benefit of the crown, if I no longer have the unquestioning confidence of the monarch, then I have nothing. Nothing. At. All."

"Lady Seneschal, please, just..."

"There really is no pleasing some people. Some people have no loyalty. Some people have no appreciation. Some people have no grace. Some people have no honor or decency or sense of nobility. I cannot work for such people. I will not work for such people." She threw down the mangled scroll and ripped the apron from her front. "I am done working for such people. I'll have someone get my things. Tell my successor I wish her luck. She's going to need it."

"Lady—"

But it was too late.

Älphonsinä Póöòmáäàdéëè turned her back on Eloise and shouldered her way out of the Fippledip Room. She hit the door so hard that both the portrait of Queen Aubrey the Parasitic and the painting of Fortescue Fippledip flew off their hooks and crashed on the flagstone floor. The resulting splintered frames and cracked paint caused irreparable damage (not that anyone would ever actually notice).

Eloise watched as the most trusted and knowledgeable member of her household staff disappeared in an angry bustle of ankle-length dress and robe. She felt blindsided by the outburst and unsure of what she should do. Apologize? Go after her? Give her time to cool down? Send a gift basket? Ask someone to speak to her? But who? Maybe First Advisor, but that wasn't her role.

Eloise felt in the pit of her stomach that nothing she could say or do would bring Lady Seneschal back. And after that kind of invective, she wasn't sure if she could trust her anymore.

"That's not how I expected today to go," Eloise muttered to the empty space where the head of her household had just berated her for no rational reason at all. "And who in the name of Çalaht's knotted apron strings is supposed to take your place?

❧

LADY SENESCHAL LEFT THE FIPPLEDIP ROOM AND EMERGED INTO the Salon de Champions feeling a jangle of emotions. Anger and resentment were still there, as fear warred with elation, relief with sadness, nervousness with resolution.

She hadn't meant to quit.

But quit, she had.

Sweet succoring Çalaht, she had walked away from the Flibbertyqueen.

Lady Seneschal Älphonsinä Füüürchtbarkeit Póöòmáäàdéëè was now Lady Seneschal Älphonsinä Füüürchtbarkeit Póöòmáäàdéëè (Retired), and by Çalaht's stretched thumbs, that sure felt good.

❦ 48 ❦

SURE, WHATEVER

L ate that afternoon, First Advisor Bënnïë-Änn Thëjëts found Eloise by herself in the Training Hall. She was working on a series of Balancing Way movements that Sylvia Cloisterfeld called the Baker's Dozen Brief Form, thirteen connected postures that her mother's champion had taught Eloise and Lorch once they had a solid grasp of the foundational steps. She had gone from Strangling the Bombard to Panda Tumbles in the Avalanche, and was just flowing into Axe Splits the Mind Wide Open, when First Advisor's knock on the doorway interrupted. Eloise froze with one leg poised in the air, careful to breathe and keep her balance. "Yes?"

"We've received a response from Queen Aglandau, Your Highness."

"Oh! Good. When?"

"The diplomatic pouch arrived just now. A bandicoot."

"Queen Aglandau employs a bandicoot to carry sensitive correspondence?" Eloise stopped. "Sorry, I shouldn't say that. Their reputation as marauding ruffians is, on the whole, undeserved."

"Yes, even if there's historical precedent for the idea. I admit, I was surprised as well. Perhaps that reputation is the reason Queen

Aglandau uses one." First Advisor raised a single shoulder. "We'll probably never know. Her ways can be strange."

"I'm sure they're saying that about me. 'Oh, that Flibbertyqueen. She's a weird one, for sure.' Certainly, that's what the gossip heralds would have everyone believe."

"I don't know if that's strictly accurate."

"Which also means it's not strictly inaccurate. That's OK." Eloise relaxed out of Axe Splits the Mind Wide Open, lowering her foot to the ground and coming to a normal standing position. "What did our good friend, Queen Aggie, say?"

"'Good friend?'"

"I'm trying to avoid 'nemesis' and 'enemy' if I can."

"I understand. The short version is, she said, and I quote, 'Sure, whatever. Let's parlay.' The longer version is she said 'Sure, whatever. Let's parlay,' and attached a litany of conditions. May I suggest that we go to the Queen's Study and work through her letter?"

"Let's make it the Fippledip Room and get the others."

"Yes, Your Highness."

"And perhaps organize the Privy Council for later. We'll need to bring them into this."

"Agreed."

"I'll meet you there in twenty minutes."

First Advisor headed for the door, then turned back. "Is it true that Lady Seneschal turned in her apron in a fit of pique?"

"Yes."

"That's going to be a problem, isn't it."

"Almost certainly."

"You'll need to appoint a replacement as soon as possible. Otherwise, there'll be chaos."

"I think there already is. But, yes. Is there a clear second in command in the household?"

"No. Lady Seneschal held tight the reins."

"A mistake, in retrospect."

"Yes."

❧ 49 ❧

LUDICROUS DEMANDS

"These demands are completely ludicrous," snapped Eloise. She jabbed her finger at the pages of hemp parchment laid out before her. "That. And that. And that. And that. And that. What's she playing at? Does she want to talk at all? Or does she just want to put up ridiculous obstacles?"

The room held what Eloise now thought of as her Fippledippers— Jerome, Lorch, First Advisor Thëjëts, Tiberius de Sphenodon, and Sylvia Cloisterfeld. It smelled of reasonably tempting cinnamon rolls and haggleberry tea, as RoyLee had brought in refreshments. But the food sat untouched as the group reviewed the message from Queen Aglandau.

"Your Highness," said First Advisor. "This entire communication is about power dynamics as much as anything else. That, and games-manship."

"Power dynamics? Gamesmanship?" Eloise held up one of the pages and read. "'The Western Lands representative will remain at least six full lengths away from the Eastern Lands queen at all times.' What am I supposed to do? Yell at her from across the room? Or, 'The Western Lands representative will provide her own food and beverage, and will neither offer such to the Eastern Lands queen nor ask to eat any of the comestibles the Eastern Lands queen has had provided for herself.' Like she'd have anything other than olives."

"Queen Eloise," said Jerome, "that's an expression of prejudice. You're going to have to not do that kind of thing. Not even jokingly."

"Fine. Fine, fine, fine. But look at the way she says 'representative.' And the way she says, 'Sure, whatever.' It's dismissive. It's insulting."

"It's deliberate," said Sylvia Cloisterfeld. "She's playing to your insecurities. She is trying to rattle you."

"And it appears to be working, if I may speak that plainly." Tiberius de Sphenodon lifted his chin toward the parchment. "That is a tactic. What you need to do is ascertain the strategy behind it."

"What's the strategy, then?"

"Disturb the equilibrium of your opponent," said Cloisterfeld. "Identify their weaknesses, then find opportunities to exploit them. Look for ways to use your opponent's momentum and vulnerabilities against them."

"That's a very Balancing Way kind of thing to say," said Lorch.

"As in Balancing Way, so in life."

"My teacher used to say that often."

"Rightly so. It is core to the teaching."

"Can we please focus on the message?" said Eloise. "What do I do?"

First Advisor raised a hand. "Let's start with the fundamental question: do you still want to parlay with Queen Aglandau?"

Eloise hunched her shoulders, then let them down. "I guess. Yes."

"Then let's go through the stipulations she's trying to put in place, and see what's acceptable and what's not. Is there anything in there you can't live with?"

ANDREW EINSPRUCH

Eloise returned her attention to the handwritten pages. "Why should she insist we meet in Flachberg?"

"That makes sense at several levels, even if some of them are not agreeable," said First Advisor Thëjëts. "For one, it's a border community."

"It's *my* border community."

"I dare say Queen Aglandau would say something about possession being four-fifths of the whole scone, and that would especially apply now that the Adequate Wall of the Realms has been moved to encompass the canton."

"So choosing Flachberg lets her rub my nose in her theft?"

"Yes. Like I said, it's power dynamics and gamesmanship. Another reason it's a logical choice is that it falls more or less halfway between Brague and Grand Azeitona, where Queen Aggie's castle is. So it gives the appearance of fairness without actually being fair. Moving on to the next item—"

Eloise rapped her knuckles on the table, interrupting. Five sharp, irritable *thocks!* "You know what? Just say yes. Just send a reply that says, 'Good-o then,' or something that tonally matches her 'Sure, whatever.'"

"Are you sure, Your Highness?"

"No. I'm not sure at all. But what am I supposed to do? Haggle about all the petty nonsense she's demanding? That would lower me to her level. So, let's just say yes."

"You don't think that will come across as too meek?" asked Jerome.

"I'm not sure I care. But tell you what. We'll send her a reply that says I'll be there and I'll meet her conditions, but we can include some annoying demands of our own to show we can be just as petty."

First Advisor picked up her quill and found a scrap of hemp parchment. "Like what?"

312

"Does it matter?" Eloise could feel her irritation at Queen Aggie lodged in her craw and itching like a jester's joke powder in her foundation garments. "How the tent where we meet must be the exact shade of blue found on a cassowary's face. And inside, there can be no green whatsoever."

"They always wear green."

"Fine. No non-clothing green. That should be suitably annoying. You know what else? I don't want to go into an illegally occupied land. So, how about we demand that the parlay tent where we meet be on top of the Adequate Wall of the Realms and not in Flachberg itself? That should put a wrench in their plans, at least a little. Plus, it looks less like caving and more like making a protest."

"I don't mind that option from a security standpoint," said Sylvia. "We're bringing soldiers. They're bringing soldiers. It strikes me that there's too much opportunity for something that starts with 'Oops' and ends with the letting of blood. To have the two queens out of the way up on top of the Adequate Wall, and to have our people on one side and theirs on the other, would seem to decrease the likelihood of an accidental engagement of force."

"Let's include the top of the wall demand in my response."

First Advisor made a note and said, "Anything else?"

"I don't think so. Let's start getting ready to take the journey. We'll need to leave in a week, and there's a lot to figure out between now and then, not the least of which is who should be in the traveling party. I assume everyone here is willing to come?"

They all nodded.

"Good. Then the six of us, plus a battalion or two of our closest friends, will get to see a little of Flachberg. Let's adjourn."

50

FACE SCRUNCHING

As the others left, First Advisor came over to Eloise. "A private word, if I may, Your Highness."

Eloise's eyes narrowed. "This isn't one of those 'We need to talk' things, is it?"

"Actually, it is, somewhat."

"Is this a sit down 'We need to talk' or a quick, standing 'We need to talk?'"

First Advisor gestured to Eloise's chair. "The former."

Eloise sighed and sat. "What have I done wrong now?" Her tone hardly hid the weariness she felt.

"My first concern is with the Privy Council."

"What's wrong with that lot?"

"That, right there. What you just said."

"'What's wrong?'"

"No, 'That lot.' The Privy Council is supposed to be your most intimate advisors, your closest confidants at Court. Several of them have expressed that they're feeling out of the loop."

"I talk to them several times a week. Or, more accurately, they talk to me. Or at me. Those meetings are not my favorites. I always feel like I'm being schooled or scolded. It's like having my parents second guessing me all the time, but without the tense dinners and occasional family outings."

"May I speak directly, Queen Eloise?"

Eloise moved her flat, open palm in a you're-probably-going-to-anyway-so-go-ahead gesture.

"This is one of those 'Every queen finds her own way' matters," said Thëjëts. "Each queen has certain qualities and activities that she has to conduct in a way that suits her."

"My father said something similar, but what do you have in mind?"

"Well, for example, a queen must decide how she wants to apply the queen's justice—firmly or leniently, with an open heart or a closed fist. Both approaches can work, and sometimes one or the other is more appropriate, but each queen must find a path that fits her temperament and goals. Another example is how, and how often, she wants to receive supplicants. Frequently? Patiently? Aloofly? Tersely? Rushedly? Daily? Weekly? Monthly? Annually? Again, there's no one right approach. It's whatever suits you and the needs you face when subjects come before you."

"OK. And?"

First Advisor shifted in her chair and smoothed down her robe over her massive thighs. "So it is with your Privy Council. How you deal with them is something that has to suit you, your needs, and your personality. If you don't make it clear to them what you want, how you want it, and when you want it, then they can't serve you."

"I may not *want* them to serve me."

"Well, having a Privy Council is optional. You could send them all home and make your decisions unimpeded by expertise or information."

"Ouch."

"Sorry, I don't mean to be so snippy. But I feel your current approach is not serving your best interests. You need people on your Privy Council who will challenge you, but who also contribute to your best understanding in a free and fair way. You want them to advise you, guide you, help with your understanding and sharpen your arguments, support you, but also bring their expertise to the discussion. But more than anything, you need them to be trusted counsel."

"And if I don't trust them?"

"Then you need to at least give them the opportunity to build that trust. Or you need to change the composition of your Privy Council without undermining its purpose or compromising what it can offer you."

Eloise closed her eyes and took a deep breath. It was true. She'd been avoiding her Privy Council. Keeping her eyes closed, she said, "So, I get to choose who's on my Privy Council?"

"Yes."

"Is it limited to the roles represented by the current occupants of those seats?"

"Not necessarily. Its number and make-up vary across the decades. It's a slow evolution, but it does alter over time."

"Right." Eloise opened her eyes again. "Thank you for raising the matter. I'll address it when I meet with them later today. You said there were two matters. What was the second?"

"It's the gossip heralds."

Eloise scrunched her face, a sip-of-bitter-tea kind of look. "Didn't you tell me to ignore them?"

"Yes, I did. And I still do. Mostly."

"Mostly? How does one mostly ignore them? In what circumstances does one not ignore them?"

"When they are dragging public perception dangerously away from your favor, and it is a matter that one actually cares about."

"And what matter is that?"

"The realm's relationship with the Eastern Lands and Queen Aglandau, not to mention the loss of Flachberg."

Eloise scrunched her face again, this time more of a bite-into-a-lemon expression. "What is being said?"

"You're being accused of being soft on inter-realm relations. That you let Flachberg go with, and I quote, 'Nary a peep,' and that your rumored effort to parlay with the Eastie Queen reinforces that perception of weakness. You know you're being referred to as the 'Flibbertyqueen?'"

"I've heard."

"It's a nickname that implies weakness and empty-headedness—"

"I'm aware. No need to dwell."

"Well, its use is spreading."

"Who is spreading it?"

"Do you know the name Helda de Anatidae?"

"Headlong Helda? Really?"

"Yes. She is being particularly... Well, let's say disagreeable."

"She was always so favorable toward my mother. Others at Court took some metaphorical crossbow bolts in the posterior from her, but she rarely had a harsh word for the late queen. My mother seemed to hold a warm spot in the old goose's heart. Why would she turn on me? What did I ever do to her? I've barely warmed the cushion on the throne. It's illogical at best."

"It is a mistake to assume logic, rationality, good will, or good faith. The gossip heralds in general, and Headlong Helda in particular, thrive on the scurrilous and sensational, whether what they say is true or not. The graylag, in particular, has a beak for weakness, and if she smells it, she pecks away at it until it resolves in a spectacular wound or a truth that can be either embraced or explained away with a flap of the wing. Worse is her commenters section. There's not a lick of discernment in any of them."

"Tremendous." Eloise spread her left hand across her face so her thumb was on her left temple and her pinky on the right one. She rested her forehead in her palm and massaged her temples with the two fingers. Through her hand, she said, "So what am I supposed to do?"

First Advisor drummed her fingers on the table, then she rapped it with her knuckles, emphasizing her words. "I." *Thock!* "Have." *Thock!* "No." *Thock!* "Flopping." *Thock!* "Idea." *Thock!*

"That's not an answer I've ever heard from you."

"It's not an answer I'm proud to give. But here's the problem. If you ignore what's being said, then whatever messaging is out there spreads on its own terms. If you engage with a gossip herald, then you have the opportunity to try to shape the messaging. Which might be advantageous, but could also be a disaster. There's no guarantee that the resulting heraldic declamations will be to your liking."

"So I'm damned if I'm a biscuit and damned if I'm a scone."

"Yes."

"Right." Eloise continued massaging out the tension in her temples. "So my options are to engage or not engage. Neither particularly appeals, nor is, for that matter, safe."

"Yes, Your Highness. And no, Your Highness."

Eloise sat up and put her hands in her lap. "If my mother could manage a relationship with the gossip heralds, and with Headlong Helda in particular, then I should be able to do so as well. I'll invite her to morning tea. Give her some Court hospitality. Maybe give her something exclusive, if insubstantial. An unexpected tidbit that she can feed to her audience."

"Are you sure any of that's wise?"

"Not at all. But if the perception of me out there is getting as bad as what you're saying, then I may as well confront it head-on. How hard can it be to flatter, cajole, or at least build some sort of rapport with her? I should be able to come out at least a little ahead."

"I flopping hope so. Because I'm at a loss on this particular matter."

"Arrange for Headlong Helda to come here. Maybe the grandeur of the castle will impress."

"I'll do that, although you shouldn't rely on the castle. Before she was a gossip herald, she was a lady-in-waiting. It's possible she knows more about certain aspects of the castle and Court than you or I do."

"Really? She was a lady-in-waiting? To my mother?"

"Your grandmother. Toward the end. Even though it has been a while, I suspect that she draws on contacts she fostered way back then, although I can't say that from first-hand observation. So don't expect her to be impressed."

"Is it possible to find someone who can teach me how to handle someone like Headlong Helda? There must be a trick to it. Or, at least, I hope so. I can't be the Flibbertyqueen in the eyes of Court and the realm and hope to ever get anything done."

"I'll see what I can figure out. I would have asked Lady Seneschal, but she's gone."

"Yes, she is."

"And you've not appointed the next one yet, which, by the way, you really need to do. The household can coast on momentum for a little while, but not much longer."

Eloise shook her head slowly. "Çalaht dribbling dolmades, I have no idea what to do."

"Find someone capable, promote them, and empower them. Just don't expect them to be perfect from the get-go."

"Ugh. Ugh, ugh, ugh. I guess I'll turn attention to that as well. Like I need one more thing to think about."

"And I'll organize the devil of gossip heralds to darken your door."

"When you put it that way, how can I resist?"

51

RESHUFFLING

That afternoon, Eloise arrived at the Privy early, and watched as her counsellors arrived one by one. Seer Maybelle was first, going in with a smile and a dreamy look, like she'd just gotten back from communing with the Unseen, which undoubtedly she had. First Advisor arrived with Exchequer of the Realm Borborygmus, sharing a laugh at something in which the only word Eloise heard was "flopping." They were trailed by Niville Numptorius, who looked like he wasn't sure if he was allowed to laugh along with the others or not.

Riri Gintsshprik, Supreme Magistrate, Rölf de Phobaeticus, the Speaker for the Land, and Court Nominee Xertz Yarborough showed up together. De Phobaeticus, the stick insect, rode on Gintsshprik's work satchel, which overflowed with scrolls. Similarly, Yarborough carried a number of thick scrolls in his arm, which he clamped to his side as the three of them spoke in confidential whispers. So far, none of them had contributed anything of value to the Privy Council meetings. It would surprise Eloise if that changed with this one.

Last was the Venerable Prelate Herself, who had a similar look to Seer Maybelle's, like she'd been hard at prayer in a devotional house and had only just roused herself. She sat, and then wafted back into apparent somnolence.

The rest took their seats, leaving the one formerly occupied by Brigadier General de Odobenus empty.

"We're here. Let's get started." She looked around the table and her eyes landed on the tapir. The Venerable Prelate Herself might be old and, well, venerable, but she didn't seem to be making much of a dent here with her presence. Perhaps that could change. "I'd like to ask the Prelate to lead us in a benediction."

The old tapir opened her eyes and blinked in surprise. "Really?"

"Yes, Your Venerableness. Really."

"But..." The prelate's prehensile snout drooped. "But you're not a believer. I mean, I'm happy to give a benediction, but I've known you since you were in your swaddles. You've never shown the least sign of true Çalahtist leanings."

"And yet, here we are."

"I guess. I mean, of course."

"I *am* the head of the faith for the queendom."

"Of course you are, Your Highness. I'm just surprised, that's all."

"Your Venerableness, there are serious matters afoot, and I wouldn't mind if Çalaht was, if not looking upon us with favor, at least paying attention so we can have our side heard from where She sits. So, if you could say a few words in Her direction, that'd be great."

More blinking from the tapir. Then she nodded, looked downward, and put her left foreleg's hooved toes flat against her right foreleg's hooved toes and held them prayerfully in front of her heart. Everyone around the table bowed their heads as she said, "Oh, Divine One, we beseech you. Lift your elongated thumbs (which were dislocated, not stretched, as the heretics say, in their elongation) from your lap and wave them in our general direction as a blessing. You, who suffered in your childhood the hanging-from-a-doorknob-wearing-jester-shoes tribulation, smile your gap-toothed smile upon us, so that we may receive your beneficence. We ask that someday, you may welcome us to stand at your side, but while we are in this world, let us behave in such a way as to prove worthy to do so. In Your name, we say, so be it."

"So be it," echoed everyone.

"Thank you, Prelate," said Eloise. "Lovely and inspiring, as always." She looked around the table again. "Now, would anyone like to raise any matters before I dive in?"

No one said anything.

"Really? No one?"

The counsellors looked at each other, faces blank.

"No one has a concern they'd like to express to me before we take on matters at hand?" Ten seconds passed. "Come on. First Advisor has led me to understand that there have been concerns expressed outside these walls. Let them be expressed within them."

Another pause.

To Eloise's surprise, it was Xertz Yarborough who spoke. As always, he was dressed like he was going to a masquerade costumed like a jester's idea of how a courtier dressed, an outfit so gaudy it was a parody of the thing he actually was. "If I may speak, Your Highness," he sniveled. At Eloise's nodded assent, he stood and continued. "It was my honor and pleasure to serve the late queen by representing matters of Court on this council. It is my honor and pleasure to have been asked by yourself to continue doing so."

"And I'm grateful you're willing to."

"Be that as it may, one rather gets the sense that one's advice is not welcomed."

"Not welcomed? That's how you'd characterize my responses?"

"Look at what happened to Brigadier General Odobenus. He disagreed with you and now he no longer sits among us."

Eloise's jaw tightened. "It's not that he disagreed with me. It's that when faced with a potential additional perspective on military matters that was not his, he could not countenance it."

"Potato, po-tah-to, Your Highness. The simple fact was that Her Highness was not willing to put faith in his counsel."

"Not exclusively, no."

"And what of the advice that the rest of us provide?" It was Supreme Magistrate Riri Gintsshprik who'd spoken, giving Yarborough her support. The white-haired woman's wrinkled face was set and tense.

Eloise suppressed the urge to say, "What advice? You've barely spoken three words before now." Instead, she said, "So long as you don't feel like you have a monopoly on the truth, I value it, especially when it comes to me in a tone that doesn't make me feel like I've been caught passing notes during my Deportment and Comportment lessons."

"Monopoly on the truth?" This time it was Rölf de Phobaeticus, Speaker for the Land and That Which Grows On It None. The stick insect raised himself on his back legs and crossed his barely visible forelegs in front of him protectively. "None of us ever claimed to have a monopoly on the truth. Surely we've proven ourselves open to the input of others."

"The Brigadier General wasn't," said Eloise.

"The Brigadier General wasn't open to the counsel of a person not known to him who was making claims that, even in retrospect, seemed far-fetched at first look." The insect's voice was brittle and charged.

"More to the point," said Gintsshprik, "I'm not... We're not Brigadier General de Odobenus."

"So you're fine with incorporating the counsel of others."

"I think we have shown that, Your Highness," said Yarborough.

"Good. I'm pleased to hear it. With that in mind, Court Nominee Yarborough, could you please go to the Privy door and open it?"

The fop blinked. "Pardon me, Your Highness?"

"I asked if you'd please go open the door."

Yarborough glanced at the others, not sure what this was all about. Gintsshprik and then de Phobaeticus each gave a small nod. Permission from his co-malcontents granted, he said, "Um, yes, Your Highness," walked to the door, and opened it.

"Come in!" Eloise called.

In walked the rest of the Fippledippers—Jerome, Lorch, Tiberius de Sphenodon and Sylvia Cloisterfeld. Their manner was confident, but not swaggering. Lorch and Sylvia carried two chairs each, which they brought to the table.

"Come on, everyone," Eloise said. "Budge over."

The Privy Counsellors budged, making room.

Eloise watched to see how everyone reacted. Yarborough, Gintsshprik, and de Phobaeticus each looked like someone had blown their nose on a croissant and then put it back on the breakfast tray. Seer Maybelle smiled, like she was seeing something she'd expected finally happening. First Advisor also smiled, though hers was a tight one that conveyed, "I see what you're doing, and I get it, but you could have perhaps told me beforehand."

And the Venerable Prelate Herself? Asleep. Oh, well. At least she'd managed a prayer.

"Master Sergeant, could you please sit here?" She pointed to the brigadier general's empty chair.

Yarborough, Gintsshprik, and de Phobaeticus stiffened, but no one said anything.

As the tuatara moved to replace the absent counsellor, Eloise said, "Please welcome the newest members of the Privy Council. You already know Former Champion Cloisterfeld from when she served my mother, and we just discussed Master Sergeant de Sphenodon. I assume you were there for my champion's naming, but in case I'm mistaken, this is Champion Lorch Lacksneck. Finally, we're also joined by Jerome Abernatheen de Chipmunk, Assistant Seer to the Court Seer and my long-time friend and confidant. Let's sit."

"This is—" spluttered the stick insect.

"Highly unusual, yes." It was First Advisor Thëjëts who interrupted. "But not unprecedented. And, to be honest, I think necessary."

"Necessary?" scoffed Supreme Magistrate Gintsshprik.

"Yes, necessary, Riri. This is on us. All of us who've been serving the young queen. We've not served her well. We need to do better."

"It's on us, you say?" Yarborough stood up and pointed at Eloise. "She's the one who's assembled a council behind our backs. She's the one who mistrusted and questioned the advice she's received in the Privy. And now she's the one who's stacking it with her feckless cronies. Look at who she's brought in. A failed champion who never should have been champion in the first place. A lug of a current champion. A has-been or never-was—I'm not sure which category the tuatara falls into. The only one of them with any quality is Cloisterfeld, and Çalaht can only guess why she'd denigrate her reputation by coming back for another round of service. I—"

Eloise stood.

The room went quiet as everyone else stood as well.

Yarborough swallowed whatever else he was going to say, but his finger remained pointed at her. Slowly, he lowered it, the realization that he'd gone too far dawning as he did.

"Court Nominee Yarborough."

"Yes, Queen Eloise."

"Answer this. If you were me and you'd just witnessed you saying to me what you just said, what would you do?"

"I... I'd..."

Eloise stepped toward him once, twice. "Be truthful now. What would you do if our roles were reversed?"

Yarborough stepped backward, keeping his distance. "I apologize, Queen Eloise. I was angry. I got caught up in the heat of the moment. Please, forgive me."

"You didn't answer my question." She walked slowly toward him.

"I'd rather not." He moved back, maintaining the distance between them.

"Stand still. Now."

Yarborough froze, and Eloise closed the gap. The dandy stood a head and a half taller than her and was twice her weight, but he trembled as she neared, knowing what was possible at her command. She stopped three steps away. "Answer my question. What would you do?"

"I'd punish you. I'd make you..." He gulped and his eyes watered. "I wouldn't kill you," he squeaked. "Maybe put you in the stocks in the market. Leave you there for children to throw vegetables at."

"Court Nominee Yarborough, I don't think you're being honest. It sounds to me like you're negotiating down what qualifies as suitable punishment. Let me ask a different question. What would my mother have done?"

"D-dungeon."

"Maybe. But don't you think she would have been more likely to ask you which of your fingers you wanted to forfeit?"

"She might have."

"Might have."

"Yes. I've seen... Sorry—I saw her do that on more than one occasion."

"On those occasions, did it seem an appropriate response to whatever had preceded it?"

The fop looked like he was close to wetting himself. "The late queen seemed to think so."

"Did you?"

"At the time, yes. Now, not so much."

"Did she confiscate their lands? Strip them of their titles and privileges?"

"Not every time."

"But sometimes."

"Yes."

"Right." Eloise turned her back on him and walked back to her chair. "Can we agree that I am not my mother?"

"Yes, Your—" His voice cracked and pitched a full octave higher than normal. He cleared his throat and tried again. "Yes, Your Highness."

"Would you say that what you said in anger reflects your true feelings?"

"I don't—"

"Please, Court Nominee Yarborough. The truth. Quickly now."

"Yes. It's how I felt." He looked down at his slippered feet. "Feel."

"So it is fair to say that you don't feel you can effectively advise me, because you don't have confidence in me as your queen."

"It's not that—"

"Similarly, can you accept that I've lost confidence in your counsel?"

"I'm sure that—"

"Yes or no. Can you continue to serve as court nominee and provide fair and open advice, given how you feel about me and my reign?"

"No. No, I can't."

Eloise slowly shook her head and sat back down. "I'm sorry to hear that. I was hoping you'd say yes, and that we might find a way to settle our differences. But I'm fine either way. You may leave. Thank you for your service to my mother, and to me."

"That's it?" He looked up from his feet, confusion mixed with a note of hope. "No dungeon? No lost digits? No stocks? Just 'thank you and goodbye?'"

"I won't even confiscate your lands or strip you of your title. Obviously, Court will have to pick a new nominee, but you can go. In fact, I wish you would. We have a lot to do today."

"Yes, Your Highness. Thank you." He moved to the table to gather his scrolls.

"Leave those. Just go."

He nodded, turned, and left.

As soon as Yarborough was out the door, Eloise scanned the table. "Anyone else?"

Supreme Magistrate Gintsshprik swept her white hair back and heaved herself from her chair. "I think I'm in a similar position."

"I'm sorry to hear that." And Eloise found that she meant it.

"I'll nominate a list of possible replacements from the ranks of the Magistrates Guild. Good luck, Queen Eloise." She picked up her work satchel, looked at Eloise, then quietly removed all the scrolls and documents. She left them in an orderly pile on the table, slung the empty satchel over her shoulder, bowed one last time to her queen, and was gone.

"Is that everyone?" She looked at each person at the table, one at a time. Seer Maybelle still had on her knowing smile. The Venerable Prelate Herself was wide awake, but placid, looking like she had no intention of going anywhere. First Advisor was nodding like she was impatient to get on with things. "Speaker de Phobaeticus?"

The stick insect made a movement, which Eloise thought could have been a shrug or a bow, she wasn't quite sure. "No, I'm good. If you'll have me, I'd like to stay."

"Please do." Eloise drew a deep breath. "Now that all the reshuffling is out of the way, let's bring everyone up to speed on the plans for the parlay."

❧ 52 ❧

HUSH COIN

A day later, First Advisor knocked on the door of the Queen's Study.

Eloise looked up from the scroll she was reading, which detailed some of the preparations being put in place to prepare for their travel to Flachberg. "Yes?"

"I have someone to see you, Your Highness. Shall I send her in?"

Eloise moved to the comfy chair near the fire and sat up straight in it, knees together and angled to the side, a queenlike pose she'd seen her mother strike ten thousand times. "Ready."

First Advisor held open the door for the visitor—an elegant tiger quoll who strode gracefully into the room wearing deep aubergine robes and a self-assured expression. She walked upright on her back legs, revealing the reddish-brown pelage and white spots typical of her species on her forelegs, sides, and tail. Her guild cap sat daintily on the back of her head, pinned in place. The tiger quoll reached the correct distance from Eloise's chair and bowed precisely as Protocol specified. "I am Almandine de Dasyuridae, Master of the Etiquette and

Propriety Promulgators Guild. How may I be of assistance, Your Highness?"

"Pleased to meet you, Guild Master de Dasyuridae. But you said you are Master of the Etiquette and Propriety Promulgators Guild?"

"Yes, Your Highness."

"Then I'm confused."

"I don't understand."

"I don't need help with etiquette or propriety." Eloise dropped her head, resigned. "First Advisor was supposed to find me someone to help me learn to deal with... With certain people."

"As the master of the E&PPG, I know a thing or two about dealing with people and trying to get along with them. Who is or are the 'certain people?'"

"Gossip heralds. And specifically, Headlong Helda—sorry, I mean, Helda de Anatidae."

The quoll's whiskers twitched. "I see, I see. Well, that makes sense, then."

"It does?"

"Absolutely. First Advisor passed word to my guild that the queen needed my assistance. Not my guild's help, but mine, personally. The note we received didn't go into detail, so my guess is that she was trying to obfuscate your requirements. Queen Eloise, I'm not here as head of the Etiquette and Propriety Promulgators Guild. I'm here because I have a certain expertise that I gained from my previous profession."

"What profession was that?"

"I was a gossip herald. And a pretty good one at that, if I may say so."

"Oh. I see." Eloise nodded at the chair opposite her. "Please sit. I have a feeling this might take a while."

"Thank you, Your Highness. And you're right. We might be here a while."

The tiger quoll sat, smoothed down her robe, and said, "Can I start by asking you a question?"

"Yes. Of course."

"What business would you say a gossip herald is in?"

"Business?"

"A baker is in the business of making and selling baked goods. A magistrate is in the business of applying the queen's laws. What is the gossip herald's business?"

"Conveying information. Spreading news of the realm."

"That's generous of you," said de Dasyuridae. "And that's what they want you to think. They want you to believe they're like second-tier bards, spreading core truths, deep wisdom, and current events."

"But they don't."

"No, Your Highness. They don't. Gossip heralds are in the entertainment business, not the fact business. If they say something truthful, it is happenstance. Our bards, certainly the ones blessed to be part of the Bard's Guild, use stories and songs to tell histories, spread sage insight, convey news of the realms, and, if they're good, sprinkle in a little moral learning. Gossip heralds try to be just as entertaining, but what they spread is whatever it takes to grab listeners' attention and keep it for as long as possible. May I ask, are you familiar with this sound?" The tiger quoll did something with her cheek, teeth and tongue that made a distinctive *click!*

"I mean, I've made a similar sound before." Eloise produced a *click!* that mirrored the quoll's. "But I can't say it has any significant meaning for me."

"When listeners like something a gossip herald says, they make that specific sound." She did it again. *Click! Click-click-click!* "More than anything else, hearing that clicking is what drives the typical gossip herald. To them, '*click!*' is the sound of approval, of acceptance, of success."

"I didn't know that," said Eloise. "So the gossip heralds are in it for the clicks."

"Exactly. The more clicks, the better. It's why their pronouncements tend toward the lurid, the hurtful, and the downright atrocious. Because that's what gets the most clicks. If someone else is getting more clicks, they have to do what they can to draw back the attention so they're the ones who get them. It's a ruthless vocation, a click economy that's in a pitched battle for eyeballs and ears. And the gossip heralds get addicted to the clicks. I know I did. I lived for them. The need for clicks dominated my every waking moment."

"I had no idea. I just thought they were simple gossips." Eloise resisted the urge to do her wrist stretches, something she'd gotten in the habit of doing when she was thinking, but avoided doing in public. The small twinges of pain and the relief she felt when she let go of the stretch somehow relaxed her. "So, what do I do?"

"Suffer in silence."

"Really?"

"Really. Giving them a reaction or providing fodder for their stories is like feeding a monster suffering from tapeworm infestation. The monster is never sated, is always looking for the next morsel, and is just as likely to eat you as the food you offer. I wouldn't go anywhere near them."

"Oh." Eloise pouted. "I, uh... I—"

"You've invited her to the castle?"

"How'd you guess?"

"Because that's what they all do. It's what your mother did—I was among those who took tea with her. The targets of gossip think they can influence the heralds to be nicer or fairer or at least a bit supportive or understanding. They think they're the clever one who can sway the gossip herald."

"Well, it seems to have worked out for my mother."

"No, not at all."

"But the gossip heralds were more or less nice to her. I don't remember Headlong Helda ever having a bad word for her."

"And why do you suppose that is?"

"Because my mother *was* the clever one, the one who could sway and influence." Even as Eloise said it, she knew it was wrong.

Almandine de Dasyuridae shook her head. "Have you seen how Helda dresses?"

"No. Maybe once from a distance. What does that have to do with anything?"

"She has very expensive tastes. Gold on her neck and gems on her feet. Now, how do you think one whose job it is to purvey scurrilous tales can afford gold and precious jewels? I don't care how good a gossip herald you are, you don't make that much coin off pedestrian titillation."

Eloise's mouth dropped open. "You're suggesting my mother paid her off? No way."

"Yes, way."

"I don't believe it."

"Believe it."

"Helda could have other means of wealth. She could have inherited or gotten it by marriage or by selling contraband. Maybe she's good with real estate or facilitates illegal adoptions. It could be anything."

"It's none of those."

"How can you be so sure?"

"Because I, too, received coin from your mother in return for favorable coverage. Or neutral at worst."

Eloise tilted forward, her mouth gaping even wider. "What?"

The tiger quoll lifted her shoulders in a what-can-I-say gesture. "Striking that deal with the late queen was the best thing I ever did. It let me get out of debt, break my addiction to the clicks, and change professions. I was able to apprentice under a renowned etiquette and propriety promulgator, and eventually join the guild."

"Hush coin."

"Yes, hush coin."

"How much?"

"Enough to make me hush."

Eloise picked a bit of non-existent fluff from the arm of her chair. "This is unfathomable. My mother paid bribes to keep the gossip heralds off her case." She thought a few moments. "Should I cancel my invitation to Headlong Helda?"

"I don't think you can."

"Will she be expecting me to pay hush coin?"

"She might consider that a reasonable outcome, but she won't assume it. One can't. She'll come. She'll scope you out. She'll see if she can spin a story or three from her visit."

"But if all we do is talk about the weather or the like, there won't be anything for her to say."

De Dasyuridae chuckled. "That won't matter. She can make gossip out of the littlest bit of nothing. The best gossip heralds—and Helda de Anatidae is one of the best—take a tiny truth and then glom onto it falsehoods that might be true, or that people think *ought* to be true."

"I'm not sure I follow what you mean."

The quoll thought a few moments. "Let's take something like a rumor that Your Highness refuses to eat off anything that isn't a solid gold plate."

Eloise wrinkled her nose. "Do people really think that?"

"No, I'm making that up. The tiny truth is that you eat, and there's the reality that, almost certainly, there are solid gold dishes here in the castle. To add the falsehood that you will only eat from gold plates and bowls is a small step. And if people are inclined to think ill of you, which, sadly, many of them are, then attributing to you a diffidence and snottiness that would lead you to only eat from gold fits the 'that ought to be right' part of their world view."

"That's terrible."

"That's people. The gossip heralds just give voice to that inclination. Plus, there's another aspect to this. There's a reason the gossip heralds talk about the royals and nobles, the merchants and the rich, rather than the beggars and the night soil collectors. It's relative position in society."

"Class."

"Class or caste. The pugilists use the term 'punching up.' It's about going after someone who is stronger or more capable. Higher status, or higher class. That's what the gossip heralds do. They punch up, because those are the interesting people. Those are the privileged, the ones everyone else wants to be—or thinks they do. They might not, if they spent a few seconds really considering it, but the gut reaction is 'I want what they have.'"

"Jealousy."

"Maybe sometimes. But it's also aspiration."

"Aspiration? How can anyone aspire to becoming nobility? It happens so rarely other than by birth, and for so few people. Not exactly fair, but fairness doesn't come into it."

"And yet, they do aspire to such a change. Or they yearn for better circumstances, or a prettier or more handsome spouse, or more coin in their purse, or whatever it is they think is lacking in their lives, mirage though that missing piece may be. I've always thought that if you gathered everyone in a room and told them they could pile their troubles on a table in the back and then secretly choose to swap theirs with someone else's, most people would take their own problems back home with them."

"You think so?"

"I do, yes. But back to the issue at hand. The gossip heralds go after those of higher status strategically, too. If the targets of their gossip try to hit back, then they are, by definition, punching down, not up. That's not a good look. It appears, as you said, unfair. And that hesitation, that disinclination to fight back, provides a practical protection for the gossip herald."

"Interesting." Eloise found another minuscule fleck of schmutz on the chair's arm. This time, she rubbed it into the fabric. "Tell me, do you have any recommendations?"

"Yes, I do. First, tell the truth. Second, don't embellish. Third, when she asks an obnoxious question, don't get angry. Instead, say, 'Well, I'm not sure I can say much about that, but what I can tell you is...' And then you say whatever point you want to make."

"Does that actually work?"

"Not always," said the tiger quoll. "But often enough. Fourth, remember that a little flattery is pleasing, but a lot of flattery is odious. Fifth, don't assume she is smarter or dumber than you. Talk to her, person to person, but keep your guard and give away as little as possible."

"Do you recommend that I open the royal purse and cough up some hush coin?"

"I can't possibly answer that for you."

"I know it's my decision, but you might have advice?"

De Dasyuridae shook her head. "I don't know how important these things are to you. I don't know how full your counting house is. I don't know what your tolerance is for having people say unpleasant things about you. There have been queens who couldn't give a tail flick about gossip, while others took even the lightest criticism as the gravest insult and agonized over it for days. Finally, I don't know if you're trying to be strategic in your efforts to influence the gossip heralds or if the project is an extension of your vanity. I suspect the former, but you need to guard against the latter. With due respect, the late queen did a lot that was good, but I suspect the hush coin she paid had much more to do with her ego than anything else."

Eloise wondered if this was true. It was shocking enough to think her mother had paid the gossip heralds, but to do so for vanity's sake didn't quite fit the way she saw her. To Eloise, she'd always seemed a tough, hard-willed woman who ruled firmly and brooked no lip. That's certainly how it had felt sitting around the dinner table. Had her sense of self-worth been so delicate that she needed to control what was said about her? It just didn't match up.

Finally, Eloise said, "I don't think I'm being vain. There are things that are underway that require careful allocation of the queendom's coin."

"I understand. Is there anything else you'd like to know?"

"Maybe something about Helda herself—personal details that might be worth knowing beforehand? Her tea preferences? Pet peeves? Personality quirks or verbal tics that I should be aware of?"

"We were competitors, not friends. Fierce competitors."

Eloise smiled. "Master Almandine de Dasyuridae, you were a gossip herald. Surely you know some gossip."

The tiger quoll lifted one shoulder and a matching eyebrow. "It's possible I might have heard a thing or two."

The queen and the quoll spoke for a full half hour longer. Eloise gleaned what she could, even jotting a few notes on a spare scrap of hemp parchment.

When they finished, Eloise stood and walked the guild master to the study door. "Thank you so very much. You've been incredibly generous with your time and knowledge."

"I'm glad to be of service, Your Highness. If you have any other questions, you'll let me know?"

"I will. And I'll think about what you've said with regard to Headlong Helda. There must be something I can do that doesn't involve outright paying her off. I really don't think I can do that."

"If you did, you wouldn't be the first. Or the second. Or the third."

"Noted."

53
CHEESECAKE

As the horological cuckoo called the top of the hour, Herald Harold Hairauld stepped into the Salle à Manger, cleared his throat, and proclaimed, "Presenting Mistress Helda de Anatidae, Your Highness."

Eloise swallowed.

Showtime.

She'd chosen the Salle à Manger as it was one of the more pleasant rooms for eating, despite being lined with unappetizing tapestries depicting some of the more unsavory moments in Çalaht's early life. There was the lancing of the holy carbuncles and the binding of the seeping sores. Fortunately, the elongation of Her Holy Thumbs was not represented. Otherwise, Eloise didn't think she could actually eat in there.

Also, the Salle à Manger wasn't so overwhelmingly large as the Throne Room, and had a friendlier, less formal feeling compared to the Receiving Room. She'd decided against inviting Helda into the Queen's Study (too personal) or the Salon de la Famille (too private a part of the castle). She'd also rejected the Salon de Gustation, as that's where her family had shared many a meal together. Several of these in the later years had been tense, unpleasant affairs, and she didn't want to stew in troublesome memories while she was trying to match wits with Helda. Similarly, she'd decided against the table and chairs in the Square Root Garden, as she wanted to keep it preserved to the memory of her last serious conversation with her father (at least for now). Plus, it was still too wintry to be comfortable outside.

So the Salle à Manger it was.

Eloise felt a fluttering in her stomach. *Get a grip*, she said to herself. *You are queen. She's a gossip herald. You've had some training now. Just deal with it.*

Eloise swallowed back her nervousness, straightened her back, clasped her hands in her lap, and breathed in a slow, calming breath. "Please, Herald Hairauld, let her in."

The herald nodded, stepped aside, bowed to someone out of sight, and waved to indicate the doorway.

Helda de Anatidae strutted into the room, head high, gray wings and white body salon-primped to a high sheen, with subtle plumage extensions fluffing out her tail feathers. A fine mesh of snug-fitting gold links sheathed her neck from chin to breast. The claws at the end of her webbed feet had tiny sapphires pasted on the tops and bottoms, which caught the eye, set off the gray in her feathers, and made her feet clack more than expected as she waddled across the parquetry floor. She approached Eloise's chair, stopped a little closer than the distance stipulated by Protocol, dipped her orange bill, and gave a graceful bow with her long neck. "Your Highness."

There she was, Headlong Helda, in all her glorious gooseness.

"Mistress de Anatidae. I'm so glad you could make it. It's nice to meet you. I've heard so much about you."

"And I you, of course. The whole queendom has. May I say, thank you for the invitation. I was surprised and pleased to receive it. It's been a while since I've been in Castle Brague."

"You shared tea with my mother, I believe."

"I had that honor, yes. Lovely woman. A once-in-a-century queen. Sorely missed. They sure broke the proverbial mold when they made her."

"Yes, that they did." Eloise wasn't sure if she should take offense at that or not. She decided to let it slide and gestured to the chair opposite her. "Please, sit. Afternoon tea will be here shortly."

"Thank you, Your Highness. That would be lovely." The goose was too short to reach the chair directly and it would have been uncouth to fly up onto the seat. Instead, she took advantage of a small ramp that had been placed next to it, waddling up to the cushion that boosted her to table height. She tucked her wings to her side and settled down with a nod of approval.

Eloise looked over to an internal doorway and waved. Läääcy de Aardvark, on cue, wheeled in a tea trolley holding a sterling silver tea service, each piece decorated with a cartouche featuring the Gumball coat of arms, but so festooned with curlicues, embossed leaves, rococo repousse floral scrolls, and general gaudiness that even Lurid Eddie the carriage maker would have thought, "Nah, that's a bit much." She stopped next to the table and dipped a curtsy to Eloise and then to Helda. "Good afternoon, ma'am, ma'am. May I offer you some afternoon tea?"

"Thank you, Läääcy. I'll have my usual."

"Yes, Your Highness." She turned to Helda. "Tea, ma'am?" Läääcy pointed to the different pots. "Her Highness is having haggleberry tea. It's a particularly high-quality batch imported directly from The South a couple of years ago at the late queen's request. This special blend was irrigated off-season using waters from the River Thurmond to supplement lighter-than normal rains, resulting in an unusual oaky bass note, and harvested with a blade to avoid the bruising that happens when they're plucked by hand." It was very similar to a speech Jerome had once given Eloise, and she'd had him coach Läääcy in this erudite description.

The aardvark went on. "But in case that's not to your taste today, I have two others. One is a maple leaf tea, which is a black tea that's particularly sweet. The other is a blue tea."

The goose tilted her head. "Blue tea?"

"Yes, ma'am. It's quite literally blue. It's made from lemongrass and dried butterfly pea flowers, which give it the blue color, as well as a floral taste."

"How very interesting."

"Chef allowed me to sample some, and 'interesting' is a reasonable way to describe it." Läääcy smiled. "If you're interested in the blue tea, you might like to try adding a squeeze of lemon, which turns it purple. Or sprinkle in some of the hibiscus leaves in that dish, which turns it a rather glorious shade of red."

"Well, now you have my curiosity up. How could I not have the blue tea?"

"Yes, ma'am."

The aardvark poured their tea, placed a dish of hibiscus leaves and a dish of lemon wedges next to Helda's cup, then removed a silver lid that hid a tray of pastries. "Chef spent the morning making these. There's a cheesecake featuring white chocolate and macadamia nuts, which are complemented by white chocolate truffles. There's also a lemon bar made with an oat and almond crust topped by a curd that's mainly cashew cream and coconut cream and, of course, lemon. Finally, there's an apple and carrot dessert muffin that, if I may say so, made me weep, it was so good."

"Goodness," said Helda. "It all sounds so intriguing."

"Perhaps I could serve you some of each, to let you decide what you might like more of."

The goose honked a suppressed chuckle. "Sold. Absolutely sold."

"Sold to me, as well, Läääcy," said Eloise. "I'd love a sample of each."

The goose and the queen watched the aardvark delicately prepare two dessert plates with generous serves of the four desserts. She placed one by Eloise, then discreetly cut the ones on Helda's plate into bite-sized pieces, since she wouldn't be able to use a fork or knife. Läääcy put the plate near the goose, curtsied, and moved the trolley to the side of the room, where she stood on her hind legs, ready to jump in at any moment.

"Simply delightful," said the gossip herald.

Eloise was pleased that Guild Master Almandine de Dasyuridae's suggestion of making the afternoon tea a show of fine eating was going over so well. She only hoped that the quality of new Chef's cooking didn't bring the tone of the afternoon tea to its knees. At least she could rely on it being passable. She picked up her haggleberry tea, blew across the lid, and sipped. Perfectly reasonable. Thank goodness for small mercies.

"Your Highness, I can't really blow on my tea. Would you mind terribly if, while it cooled, I had a look at the tapestries? I have an affinity for Çalahtist representational art, and I didn't have a chance to have much of a gander at them when I was last here."

A gander at them? Was that supposed to be some sort of goose joke? Eloise kept her face neutral and said, "Be my guest."

"Thank you." Helda descended the ramp and headed for the carbuncle tapestry, the largest and gaudiest of them. She got closer to it than Eloise would have expected, tilted her head, closed her left eye, and scrutinized it with her right. She seemed less interested in the overall image, and more in the individual strands of the weaving. "You know this is a Lombardi."

"A who?"

"Vajiokarra de Lombardi, the tapestrist." She used her head to indicate all the wall hangings. "These were commissioned directly by Gwendolyn the Irritable herself."

"I had no idea they were that old. They've always sort of just been here. And I didn't know Queen Gwendolyn commissioned artworks."

"'Commissioned' is perhaps a generous term for it."

"What word would be better?"

"Compelled. Forced. Coerced. Apparently, Lombardi wasn't a fan of her rule and had the temerity to express that once in her presence. She had him locked in a room and demanded that he create something of beauty that was worthy of undoing the ugliness he'd perpetrated against her." The goose moved to a different spot of the tapestry and peered closely at it. "Legend has it that it was literally dyed with some of his blood, although I'm not seeing any."

"That's... That's macabre."

"That it is. Especially since apparently he died in that room lying across..." The goose looked around and pointed at a tapestry on the far wall. "Lying across that tapestry there, which he'd only just finished."

"That's just awful. How do you know this stuff?"

The goose looked at Eloise. "It's my job to know things. Detailed things. Things that other people don't know. Things that people don't *want* others to know."

"Of course." Was that supposed to be a threat, or was it just a statement of fact? Either way, Eloise found it unsettling.

Helda strolled to a second tapestry, then a third, and a fourth. Eloise was happy to let her burn up their time together in silence.

Finally, Helda nodded, seemingly satisfied, and returned to her seat. "Thank you, Your Highness. I appreciate the indulgence."

"No worries."

The goose drank some of her tea, a surprisingly delicate act that involved poking her beak into the cup and making little biting slurps. A third of a cup later, she lifted her head and gently dabbed her chin on the napkin. "So, Your Highness."

"Yes?"

"Now that we've had some small talk, shall we get down to it? Why am I here?"

Eloise had planned for a lot of possibilities, but not such a direct line of enquiry. "What makes you think I have an ulterior motive?"

"Oh, please, Your Highness." The goose furrowed her brow, which Eloise didn't know geese could do. "I'm a gossip herald. And I'm here. Ulterior motives surround me like flies at the Festival of Stenches."

"Right." Eloise paused. "There's a Festival of Stenches?"

"Officially, it's called the Carnival of the Odoriferous, but most people call it the Festival of Stenches or the Rites of the Reeks."

"That's not an event I'm familiar with."

"Like I say, it's my job to know things, like who enjoys attending such occasions."

Eloise wasn't ready to make her pitch, so she stalled by taking a forkful of white chocolate and macadamia nut cheesecake.

A combination of unexpected flavors exploded in her mouth, a riot of tastes that combined in an interesting and provocative way. It was so good and so unexpected, having come from the kitchen of the new Chef, that Eloise was literally stopped in her tracks, reduced to merely chewing, savoring, and swallowing. "Holy Çalaht slurping sweetened succotash."

"What?"

Eloise couldn't help herself. "This. Is. Amazing." She pointed her fork at the cheesecake. "This is the most incredible thing I've tasted in months and months."

The goose nibbled one of the morsels on her plate. "I mean, yes, it's good," said the goose. "Very good, if we're being honest—"

Eloise waved Helda down. "No, no. You don't get it. Ever since the old Chef... uh... passed on to stand with Çalaht, her son has stepped into her role as Chef."

"I know that, of course."

"This cheesecake is far and above the best thing to come out of his kitchens." Forgetting Helda for the moment, Eloise turned in her seat. "Läääcy, can you ask Chef to come in here?"

"Yes, ma'am."

The aardvark ducked through the side door, and Eloise returned to the cheesecake. Two raucous mouthfuls later, a thin man dressed in chef's whites and cap followed Läääcy into the room. He couldn't have been more than five years older than Eloise, and he was so thin he looked like he hadn't eaten in months. His face was half-hidden behind an incongruously bushy mustache and bushier eyebrows, and his neck revealed an Adam's apple that protruded like a corn muffin swallowed whole. He clasped his cap in front of his navel and bowed far too low, his eyes darting around like he was expecting to be skewered, scolded, or scorched. When Eloise waved him forward, he didn't budge until Läääcy shoved him, stumbling toward his queen.

"Chef..." Eloise stopped. "You know, I don't think I know your name. For that matter, I don't think I knew your mother's name. I always just thought of her as 'Chef.'" Realizing that Helda was listening, she added, "I apologize for that."

"It's Quockerwodger, ma'am. Virgilio Quockerwodger." His voice whispered forth like a wisp of dandelion fluff. Eloise couldn't imagine someone so soft-spoken commanding a kitchen with any authority. "My mother, may she stand with Çalaht, was Virginius Quockerwodger." He gulped a few times, his corn muffin Adam's apple bobbing like it was trying to escape. "Is... Is there a problem?" He swallowed the last word like a broken promise.

"No, no, no." Eloise waggled her fork for emphasis. "Not at all. I wanted to compliment you on the cheesecake. It's dazzling. Really excellent."

More swallowing, now with added blinking. Then, without warning, tears fell from his eyes. "Thank you, Your Highness. I can't tell you how much that means to me. The recipe..." He dabbed one eye, then the next, with the cuff of his tunic sleeve. "The recipe was my mother's. The morning that she took her own... That she chose to leave this piteous and sinful mortal realm, she handed me a box, telling me not to open it until that night. I set it in a safe place and forgot all about it in the... the aftermath of her demise. Grief has shadowed my every step since that day, and I couldn't bring myself to open up her final gift to me."

Eloise could relate. She'd avoided opening her mother's final letter for much too long.

"And then last night, I was in a particularly bad way. I'm sure I don't need to tell you that my efforts in the royal kitchens have been lacking inspiration, missing a certain something that my mother always brought to her work. If I may be so honest, I know what Your Highness has thought of my cooking."

Eloise had the good grace to look chagrined, but also the respect to not contradict him.

"I'm not my mother. I'll probably never be as good as my mother. But I was feeling down and I want to do better. As I lit a candle to her memory, my eyes fell on the box. For the first time, I opened it." New Chef fell silent, lost in a sudden wash of memory, his swallowed corn muffin bobbing.

"And?" It was Headlong Helda. Her voice was gentle, but subtly commanding. "What was in the box?"

The young man blinked back to the present moment and looked at the goose as if he'd only then realized there was someone else in the room.

"Recipes." He said the word like he'd been blessed with prophecies from Çalaht herself. "It was a set of scrolls and pieces of hemp parchment. The scrolls were wrapped together, one nesting inside the next. The parchment was in a folio and ranged from ripped scraps to carefully preserved whole pages. There were dozens and dozens of them, each in my mother's handwriting. Each a revelation, a promise, a mystery to explore." He looked at Eloise. "As I explored the scrolls and pages, it was like I was peering into my mother's soul. I've never felt closer to her than then."

"That's lovely," said Eloise. "What a gift, after so much heartache."

"Yes, that's exactly what it was." His corn muffin bobbed a couple more times, and he continued. "Today, I wanted to honor her—and you, Your Highness—by bringing one of those creations into being. Making that cheesecake, which I'm so pleased you enjoyed, was like an invocation of her spirit."

"Well, it worked. It is as good as anything that ever came out of her kitchen."

Quockerwodger's eyes went wide. "Really?"

"Really. The cake was divine. Apparently, quite literally." Eloise put her palms together and bowed to him. "Thank you, Chef Quockerwodger. It's an honor to have tasted it."

"Thank you, ma'am." He bowed his way backwards through the doorway—eyes blinking and corn muffin bouncing—and disappeared back to the kitchen.

Eloise smiled and took another forkful of the cheesecake. "So good," she muttered to herself. "What a delightful surprise."

Loosened up by the cheesecake and the unexpectedly emotional encounter with the new Chef, Eloise had another sip of her haggle-berry tea, then fixed her gaze on Headlong Helda. "Look, Mistress de Anatidae. I was going to try to gain your favor."

The goose fixed her with a wary eye. "Oh?"

"Yes. I was going to see if maybe you could stop calling me the 'Flib-bertyqueen.' Or see if I could convince you of the worthiness of my endeavor to avoid all-out war with the Eastern Lands, or to at least see my efforts to parlay with her as diplomacy, and not appeasement. I was all prepared to appeal to your vanity or love for your queendom or, I don't know, your sense of decency. Anything, save opening up the Court purse and paying hush coin like my mother."

The goose looked surprised. "I never—"

Eloise stopped her with a gesture of her fork. "Whatever you're about to say, don't bother. I have a different idea."

"Oh? What's that?"

"Come with us to the parlay. I'll give you access to our goings on. Not unrestrained access—obviously, I can't bring you into the tent with me and Her Majesty, Queen Aglandau, and there may be other limits. But be part of the traveling party. You'll have proximity like no gossip herald ever before you, and in what are certainly going to be interesting times. You'll be able to see firsthand what's going on. You'll be able to gossip with a verisimilitude that will be second to none."

"Why?"

"Why what?"

"Why would you make that available to me?"

Eloise allowed herself a half-shrug. "A few reasons. First, you're going to be talking about it whether you're there or not, so I may as well do something to help you be accurate. Second, there will be a scribe and at least a couple of official heralds included in the group, so as an experiment, I'd like to see what it's like to have a gossip herald there as well, since your perspective is so different. You'll have to pay your own way and feed and accommodate yourself. This isn't a junket. But, like I said, I'll make sure you get more access than you otherwise would have had. Plus..." She trailed off.

"Plus, you're hoping that if I get to know you and those around you better, I won't be so flippant and derisive."

"I would have said I was hoping you might find greater empathy, but I'd settle for less flippant."

"I can't guarantee that will happen, Your Highness. I have a particular approach to what I do. I can't assure you that what I end up with will please you. I have my audience to think about. I have my clicks to try to get. There are expectations that I cannot stray too far from."

"Well, if it balances the equation at all, I can't guarantee your safety or your comfort. I can't promise that those around me will open up to you. But we can try. Do you accept my offer?"

The goose nodded. "Yes, Queen Eloise. I do. And, if I may say so, it's a much more intriguing offer than straight-up hush coin."

"Then we have an agreement. And allow me to say that hush coin was never going to happen."

"I suspected as much." The sides of Helda's beak curled upward a tad, which Eloise suspected was as close as she got to a smile. "You can't fault a girl for trying."

"Shall we celebrate with a bit more cheesecake?"

"Yes, Your Highness. That would be lovely."

❧ 54 ❧

NEW OFFICE

I t was late, and Eloise was exhausted from the long day, but there was one more task she had to tick off her To Do list. She wasn't sure she was about to do the right thing, but she had to do *some-thing*, and this seemed like as good a possibility as any, especially since Odmilla had seconded her idea.

She made her way down to the now-deserted kitchens and found the office that, until a few days before, had been the home base of Lady Seneschal Älphonsinä Füüürchtbarkeit Póöòmáäàdéëè. The running of the castle hadn't fallen apart yet, but Eloise knew that was simple momentum. Any bump in the usual way things were done would be like shoving a tree branch into the spokes of one of Lurid Eddie's carriages—it would make for a spectacular crash.

Shining her oil lamp around the room, she saw it was stacked, as she had thought it would be, with ledgers, bound volumes, and scraps of parchment with notes. In the middle of the desk, discarded like an orphaned duckling, was the scroll Lady Seneschal always carried with her, the one she was forever checking and which she was not above tapping someone on the noggin with to make her point. What was missing from the room was any personal touch. No framed drawings, no knickknacks, no potpourri, no doodads, no treasured souvenirs—nothing. Póöòmáäàdéëè had cleaned away any trace of her presence, and all that was left was the memory of her stern demeanor, her even sterner black outfits, and the regimented way she ran things so successfully for so many years.

A small voice came from the far end of the empty kitchen. "Hello?"

"Over here, Läääcy," said Eloise. "In the office."

Läääcy de Aardvark made her way on silent feet to where Eloise stood. "You wanted to see me, ma'am."

"Yes. Thank you for coming."

"Can I light the lamps for you?"

"That would be great."

The aardvark took a taper from her pocket, lit it using the flame on Eloise's lamp, and transferred the flame to the candles and lamps in the room. "I was very sorry that Lady Seneschal left us."

"Yes. Me, too."

"She was a hard taskmaster, but she was fair. And she gave me an opportunity when she didn't have to."

Eloise chose not to mention that she was the one who had instructed Póöòmáäàdéëè to find a role for Läääcy.

The aardvark continued. "At first, she scared me. No, 'scared' is too mild a word. I was petrified, witless, and tongue-tied if she so much as looked at me. And then I realized two things."

"What were they?"

"I don't mean to speak ill of her when she's not here to defend herself, but she had what my mother used to call 'an unfortunate manner.' Lady Seneschal didn't mean to be abrasive and domineering, so much as that was just her way. If one could accept that, then one could avoid taking offense and get along with her much better."

"That's very perceptive, Läääcy. And an elegant way of putting it. I wish I'd had that perspective when I was dealing with her. To be honest, she scared me, too."

"You? Really?"

"Absolutely. She'd been telling me what to do since Johanna and I could first walk. It was hard for me to treat her as anything approaching an equal, much less as her superior once I was crown-plonked. I found that very hard, although I was getting used to it when she quit."

"I didn't know that."

"What was the second thing you realized?"

"That she was very good at what she did, and above all else, she wanted everyone who worked for her to be good at what they did. Not just good, but excellent. I came to understand that what other people took as her being unkind was her conveying that she expected a superior performance from you, and she wasn't shy about telling you if you weren't meeting that standard. Again, once I understood that, I was able to get by much better."

"Another very astute observation."

"Thank you, Your Highness. Can I put on a kettle for some tea for you? The fire in the stove is banked down for the night, but it wouldn't take much to get it going again."

"No, thank you. That's not why I wanted to talk to you."

"Yes ma'am."

Eloise looked around. There was a chair and a stool. "Let's sit."

"So it's bad news, ma'am?"

"Why would you say that?"

"Folks like me—"

"You mean aardvarks?"

"No, I mean staff—the kitchen wenches and servers and ladies-in-waiting and the like. Folks like me don't spend much time sitting down. Our role is to keep moving, keep doing our jobs, or maybe stand at the side at the ready. When someone asks us to sit down, it's usually bad news."

"I didn't know that. I'm sorry."

"It's the way it is, ma'am. It's different for you. I've noticed that a lot of what you do involves sitting. You sit on the throne. You sit in your meetings. You sit when you eat. You sit in the Receiving Room. You stand and say a few words when needed, but after that, you sit down again so that everyone else can. In fact, it's an inconvenience for others if you do stand, since they have to stand up with you. So sitting for you is an important part of your day."

"I've never thought about it that way, but you're right. I guess that's one of the reasons I make sure I do my exercise runs or, more recently, work with Former Champion Cloisterfeld in the training room. It counteracts the sitting." Eloise looked again at the chair and stool. "We don't need to sit."

"Whatever pleases you, Your Highness."

Eloise considered the aardvark and tried to remember the first time she'd become aware of her. It was around the time that she and Johanna were just shy of their fourteenth birthdays, before their Thorning Ceremony. There was an incident with quince jam that Eloise was still embarrassed to remember, and a miscommunication where Läääcy thought she was going to have her lips sewn shut. It had taken a while to get past that, but they had, and now Eloise was as fond of the aardvark as anyone in the castle or Court. "Can I ask you a somewhat personal question?"

"Of course, ma'am."

"Have you gotten your letters yet? When we first met, I remember that you could recognize your name, but not read. Is that still the case?"

"No, ma'am, I read really well now. And write. I was able to get some of the other staff to teach me and I..." She trailed off.

"And what?"

"I'm embarrassed."

Eloise elbowed her gently. "Go ahead."

"Well, ma'am, I saw a scroll in your chambers, one that you brought from the Queen's Study. *The Most Torrid Trials and Tribulations of Goodwoman Mountebank*. I could tell it wasn't official or anything, so I snuck a look at the beginning of it one day when you weren't there, and I couldn't stop reading it."

"You like romance scrolls?"

"Yes, Your Highness. Apparently, I do."

Eloise guessed if she could have seen below the aardvark's fur, her cheeks would be pink. "That one was one of my mother's. I took it with me to my chamber one night, thinking it might help distract me so I could get to sleep quicker, but fell asleep before I could crack it open. It's been there ever since."

"Goodwoman Mountebank is so wonderful. She's epic. And resourceful. And saucy. It's such a compelling story that I practiced my reading to get better so I could understand what it was saying. But I looked at it without permission. I'm sorry."

Eloise waved it off. "It's not a problem. There are others, including others that feature Goodwoman Mountebank. I'm happy for you to read them all."

The aardvark's eyes went wide. "Really? That's most kind of you, ma'am."

"I don't know how kind you'll think I am when I've asked you what I'm about to ask you."

"Oh?"

"I'm glad you have your letters. Läääcy, I need you to do something for me. I need you to be the next Lady Seneschal."

The aardvark squeaked, then covered her mouth with her forepaws. "No, no. Not me. Please, no, Your Highness."

"Why not?"

The aardvark sat on the cobblestone floor, half-stunned. "It should be one of your ladies-in-waiting, or someone with more experience than me. Odmilla or someone. I... I... I don't know where I'd even start with it. I certainly couldn't be mean and strict the way Lady Seneschal was. The thought of it makes me want to faint."

Eloise reached for Läääcy's paw and took it in her hand. She lowered herself so she could look the aardvark directly in the eye. "Läääcy, I need you to do this for me."

"What about Odmilla, like I said?"

"We discussed it. Except for a short period, she's been a handmaid most of her life in service. She doesn't have the breadth of experience that you do, nor the contact with other members of staff. It's not a good fit for what needs to be done."

Läääcy shook her head. "This is a bad idea. A very bad idea."

"I don't think so." Eloise gave the paw a little squeeze. "Hear me out, at least. First, you understand the staff and you get along with them. Second, you understand what needs to be done around the castle. You've been part of that for half a decade at least. You're empathetic, capable, and hardworking. It's a role that requires a head for getting things done and motivating others to do the same. I think you have that in you."

"You really think that?"

"I do. And there's another thing. I like you and I trust you. You don't make me feel like I'm six years old when I'm around you. Lady Seneschal Póöòmáäàdéëè had a good relationship with my mother, and

I think that was one of the keys to her success. We get along well, don't we, Läääcy?"

"I like to think so, ma'am, yes."

"And you don't have to do things the way Lady Seneschal Póòòmáäàdéëè did. You don't need to be mean or whack people on the head with a scroll or wear severe black dresses all the time. You can do things your way. Make improvements where you can. Keep what used to work and still does. Will you at least consider giving it a try?"

The aardvark was shaking, she was so nervous. She put her free paw to her forehead and said, "This is all so sudden. I had no idea that's why you wanted to talk to me. I... I still don't know what to say."

"Say 'yes' maybe?"

"Give me a moment, Your Highness."

Läääcy looked at the floor and Eloise could practically hear her thinking things through. A solid minute later, she looked back up. "You really don't want someone else to do it?"

"No. You're my choice, if you'll do it."

Läääcy gave a very aardvarkian curtsy. "Thank you, Queen Eloise. I will serve you to the best of my ability."

"Excellent. Really good." Eloise gestured to the room around them. "Welcome to your new office."

55

THERE ARE APPLICATIONS

A thousand cuts with the practice sword.

A thousand cuts with the staff.

One hundred cycles of the celestial lotus.

Fifty rounds of the thirteen connected postures of the Baker's Dozen Brief Form.

All performed in silent unison by Eloise and Lorch, following Sylvia Cloisterfeld's lead.

It was the morning they were supposed to leave for Flachberg, but by unspoken agreement, they met as they had been every day in the Training Hall.

Show up. Do the work. Try to improve. Repeat.

And she *had* improved. The 2,800 cuts felt like a joy, not a chore, and doing them scratched Eloise's itch to count things.

In the past two weeks, Cloisterfeld had introduced sparring—empty handed, weapon against weapon, weapon against empty hands. Eloise was not very good at it and had any number of bruises to prove it. But even so, she was learning to take a fall, figuring out how to avoid being hit, and coming to understand that getting clunked wasn't always the worst thing in the world.

At the top of the hour, Sylvia said, "We need to call it a morning. We'll be leaving just after everyone breaks fast, and, Queen Eloise, you need to dress and prepare."

Eloise nodded. "Yes, Master Cloisterfeld."

They bowed to each other and put the wooden swords back on the rack.

"If we have time as we travel, we may be able to train," said Sylvia. "Perhaps we can even invite some of the soldiers to join us. I've been working with them as well."

"I'll make sure we have practice swords and staves brought with us," said Lorch.

"I'd like that," said Eloise.

"Good." Sylvia hesitated, like she wasn't sure she should say whatever she was thinking.

"Yes, Master Cloisterfeld? Is there something you want to say?"

"Yes. Yes, there is. I've hinted at something in these sessions, but I'd like to make it explicit. Do you have a few minutes?"

"Of course."

Cloisterfeld sat down on the mat, folding her legs under her thighs and resting her backside on her heels. Lorch and Eloise did the same across from her.

"We train in here in a very specific way. We learn movements in deliberate, sometimes exaggerated ways, training our bodies and minds to habituate to the movements so that when we need to apply them, they'll have become second nature. I hope that the application of the Balancing Way has become apparent, if not obvious, to you."

Eloise nodded and waited for her to continue.

"But there are applications of the Balancing Way that are less obvious, but no less important. For example, you're training to recognize an attack, not just from the presence of a sword or knife coming at you, but from other factors, like the set of a body, the expression on a face, or the sense you get of their intention. Also, attacks aren't just physical. They can come in many forms—emotional, mental, verbal, or psychic. Your options for a response to these draws on what you learn within these walls. Do you choose to move out of the way? Do you move toward them and inside, absorb their energy, and redirect it to your advantage? Do you run away as fast as you can, remembering that often, the best fight is the one you don't have? We practice all of these things, and as we work together, you're developing the discernment to read people, understand situations, and apply a deliberate choice from a range of responses. Does this make sense?"

"I think so," said Eloise. "Or, I get it in theory, at least. I'm not sure I have it in practice."

"It takes a lifetime to master the Balancing Way. The founder reached a ripe old age, and allegedly, on his deathbed, he's supposed to have said, 'I think I may have figured it out.'" Cloisterfeld's mouth curled into a tight grin. "Whether that's apocryphal or not, I like what it represents—a lifetime's devotion to approaching perfection while accepting you may never get there. You've both only started on this path. Yes, even you, Lorch. But the key is that you've started. And these first few steps down the path have shown you keen to learn. Adding that to the situation you're riding into in Flachberg, I wanted to make sure you had an awareness of the greater applications of the Balancing Way."

"Thank you. Is there anything else?"

"Like I said, there's a lifetime's worth. Over time, you learn to accept people for who they are. To be successful with the Balancing Way, you can't wish that the person you're dealing with was different. You have to embrace them, and the situation between you, as they are. That's the only way you can respond with grace and appropriateness. Further, we learn to respond instead of reacting."

"Is there a difference?" asked Lorch.

"Definitely. Reactions are hot. They are instantaneous and soaked in one's biases, prejudices, and beliefs. They ignore the long-term in favor of knee-jerk defensive acts. Maybe a reaction will be the right one, and maybe it won't. Responses are slower, cooler. They're more informed, more deliberate. They consider not just you, but those around you. In my experience, responses are usually easier to live with than reactions. They can also hurt less."

"It seems to me that reactions and responses can look awfully similar," said Eloise.

Cloisterfeld nodded. "True. But even if they look the same, they feel different. If you can, choose to respond."

"Right. I'm going to have to think that one through, but I see where you're going with it. Anything else you want to add to my mental hopper?"

"Sure. My teacher had lots of short sayings that I'm still working through. 'Small changes make big changes.' 'Those who thrive seek balance in all things.' 'Face a storm with a calm heart and an objective mind.' 'Big pictures are better than small pictures, but even big pictures need mindful attention to detail.' 'Have courage.' 'Take charge.' 'Kindness engenders kindness.' 'Be wary of people with no vowels in their names.'"

"Wow. I think my head's full now."

"Good. Write them down when you have a moment, and every now and then, pull one out and mull it over."

"I will," said Eloise. "Thank you."

"One last one."

"Yes?"

"Don't let the batards get you down."

"Batards? Like a small baguette? Don't you mean bastards?"

"Sometimes." Cloisterfeld kept her face neutral, but there might have been a small twinkle in her eye. "But not always."

Eloise furrowed her brow. She'd really have to think that one through. "Yes, Master Cloisterfeld."

❧ 56 ❧

NOT AN OMEN

"It's not an omen," said Jerome, looking at the darkening clouds.

"You can't know that." Eloise, Jerome, and Lorch stood outside the castle watching the traveling party assemble and the weather turn unpleasant. "If it buckets the entire time we're on the road, it'll sure feel like an omen."

"Am I not the Assistant Seer to the Court Seer?"

"Yes, you are."

"So, I say it's not an omen."

"Just because you say it isn't doesn't mean that it isn't."

"Queen Eloise, do you *want* it to be an omen?"

"Not at all."

"Then I hereby declare it non-omenish. I have spoken. It is so."

Eloise arched an eyebrow at him. "Is that how it works?"

"Yeah. Today."

"Fine."

Lorch interrupted. "Queen Eloise, Hector de Pferd and the Nameless One have arrived."

"Oh, good."

"Wow, look at Hector shine, even in this light," said the chipmunk. "I'm going to have to ask him what shampoo he uses."

"Me, too."

The two horses approached. "Blessings of the day, Queen Eloise," said Hector. The Nameless One, silent as ever, nodded agreement.

"Blessings of the day to you both."

"How do you feel?"

"Actually, more nervous than I care to admit. This whole parlay thing could go wrong in about a numptigazillion ways."

The Nameless One snorted, stamped the ground a few times, and waggled his head.

"Good point," said Lorch.

"What'd he say?"

"He said that it's also possible the parlay will go well, and that you should allow for that possibility as well."

"Tell that to the nerves in my stomach." She laid a friendly hand on Hector and then the Nameless One. "Thank you both for agreeing to let us ride you again. I couldn't stand the idea of being cooped up in a carriage the whole way."

"My pleasure," said Hector. "To tell the truth, things have been a little dull since we got back. This makes a nice change. Plus, it'll be good to have the five of us together again for the days and weeks this will take, even if we're just five of five hundred."

"The five hundred soldiers couldn't be helped," said Lorch. "Our queen is queen now. The logistics around her safety alone are astronomically more complicated than on our last journey."

"I know, I know. We'll make the most of it. Of course, there's no way it was going to be the same. Like my father always says: you can never eat from the same paddock twice."

"Ooh, I like that one, Hectorino," said Jerome. "Very deep."

Everyone stopped and looked at the chipmunk. His whiskers drooped. "What?"

"What happened last time you pestered Hector with nicknames?" asked Eloise.

"Ah. Right." Jerome bowed one of his overly hand-wavy bows. "My apologies Formerly Equine Designate de Pferd. I shall refrain from the whole nickname thing."

"And I, Assistant Seer to the Court Seer Abernatheen de Chipmunk, will avoid tossing you into nearby bowls of grapefruit punch."

"Deal."

"Deal."

A chill wind picked up and Eloise hunched her travel cloak more closely around her shoulders. Seamstress Linttrap had offered to make her a new one, since the old one had emerged from her journey looking battered, filthy, and weather-bleached, several shades lighter than it had been when they departed. But Eloise loved it like a lucky charm and had insisted that the familiar cloak with the many hidden pockets be restored, not replaced. Seamstress Linttrap, a clever, dexterous echidna with a short temper and a grand talent with a needle and thread, had worked another sewing miracle, and the dark indigo cape looked almost new. She'd also packed a couple of spares in the trunk of clothes that she'd insisted Eloise take with her.

Rightly so. She couldn't very well meet Queen Aglandau looking travel-stained and disheveled.

Eloise looked around. "It really does feel odd traveling like this. We were so light and nimble before. I didn't necessarily think that then, especially when we had a cart and Turpy with us. But this is something else. It seems like an awfully big inconvenience to a lot of people."

"I've spoken with the soldiers. They're actually happy to be doing this," said Lorch. "It gets them away from the obstacle course and lets them put into practice some of what they've learned from Tiberius and Sylvia."

"Speaking of whom..." Jerome lifted his chin to point out Tiberius de Sphenodon, headed their way.

The tuatara stopped in front of Eloise and bowed. "Queen Eloise."

"Master Sergeant. Blessings of the day."

"Blessings of the day, Your Highness, although the day feels like it has already been going on a year. I believe we are all assembled and ready for you to say a few words."

"You want me to speak? I didn't know."

"It's traditional. Or at least it was when I was a grunt. The queen always sent us off with a few words."

"No problem. Where would you like me to be?"

"I was thinking from atop one of the wagons. I'd position you in the middle of things, so you're more likely to be heard."

They picked their way into the restless throng until they reached a supply wagon being drawn by a sullen-looking, grey-coated donkey who Eloise recognized from her trip to Festering Resentment and the failed blessing of the paddock. "Abelardo de Burro. Nice to see you."

"Blessings of the day, Queen Eloise."

A muffled voice came from underneath a pile of sacks of corn grits. "Abelardo. Abelardo! I don't think I packed my fluffy night coat with the matching slippers. Do you think we have time to run back to the house and get them? I don't think I can live without them." It was Nörbert de Lupus, the longhair apple head Chihuahua who'd organized the activities at Festering Resentment. "Think anyone will notice if we dash off for a few minutes?"

"I think the queen might," said Abelardo.

"The queen? Why would the queen care? She has much more important things to worry about than my fluffy night coat and matching slippers."

"Because she's standing right here and about to step up onto our wagon."

There was a long, awkward pause, followed by the clearing of a Chihuahua throat and what must have been a bow that accidentally involved clunking his head on a sack of corn grits. "Your Highness," squeaked the muffled voice. "It's an honor to have you with us and our small, humble wagon."

"Blessings of the day, Master de Lupus."

"Blessings of the day, Your Highness."

"You're obviously coming with us to Flachberg."

"Yes, ma'am. Abelardo de Burro and I have been organizing a lot of the logistics. Plus, I've been putting together various entertainments, which I think will keep the soldiers occupied, weather permitting."

"Ah, the weather. It's ominous. I'm hoping it isn't an omen."

"Yes, ma'am. It is threatening. I also hope it isn't an omen."

"It's not an omen," insisted Jerome. "How many times do I have to say it?"

"Your Highness, if we can proceed?" said Tiberius de Sphenodon. "With this many people, we really do need to get underway. It'll take some time just to clear the gates."

"Yes, Master Sergeant." Eloise found the step up to the wagon and climbed into it, almost stepping on the Chihuahua, who had to scramble out of the way. "Oh, sorry. Didn't see where you were there."

"Not to worry, Queen Eloise. If I'd remembered my fluffy night coat and matching slippers, I wouldn't have been down there in the first place."

"Right. Again, sorry." Eloise faced the crowd and got a good look at those making the trip with her. It was a huge operation. In addition to the two hundred soldiers, there were half again as many support staff. Eloise had baulked at the size of the group, but just as she couldn't show up to the parlay in tatters, she couldn't arrive without an entourage that, by its very mass, announced, "Yo! Queen present!" She'd relented, and was now looking at the result. It was at least as big as any group her mother had ever traveled with, which she guessed was the point. She began with the traditional opening words: "My friends."

No one responded. Obviously, they hadn't heard her over the cacophony of chatter and preparations. She tried again, a little louder. "My friends."

Again, nothing.

Tiberius de Sphenodon put his injured claw hand into his mouth and produced an ear-splitting whistle. Hundreds of heads turned her way. "Attend the queen!" he bellowed.

As one, the mass stood up, the soldiers snapping to attention.

"My friends," she began again.

"Our queen," responded the crowd.

That was more like it.

"Please be at rest."

As one, the soldiers came to parade rest, legs apart and hands clasped behind their backs, eyes locked forward. Most of the supporters found somewhere to sit, assuming this would take a while.

Eloise liked what she was seeing in front of her. The soldiers didn't look as schmick as they had that first day on the parade ground, but there was a hardness, a discipline, a seriousness to them that hadn't been there before. She doubted they were battle ready, but at least they didn't look like dandies and show ponies.

"Just a few words before we depart—" A flash of lightning struck overhead, with the boom of thunder not more than two heartbeats later. "Depart." A gust of wind picked up, forcing Eloise to raise her voice even more. "This journey to Flachberg has a single purpose—to meet with the Queen of the Eastern Lands and try to negotiate a way for our enduring peace to continue. I thank you for being part—" *Flash! Crack!* "For being part of this historic endeavor."

At that very moment, the heavens opened up, dousing everyone with a fierce late-winter hail squall. As the cooks, attendants, and Court hangers-on dove for cover, the soldiers stayed where they were, getting pelted by pea-sized ice chunks.

"Boring travels to you," shouted Eloise, hoping everyone could still hear her.

"Boring travels to you," repeated the half dozen soldiers nearest to her.

"Let's get going." She raised her fist in the air. "To Flachberg!"

"To Flachberg."

The gates opened and Tiberius de Sphenodon, riding in front of Sylvia Cloisterfeld on a beautiful blue roan appaloosa, led the march forward. Eloise found Hector, mounted, and settled Jerome in front of her, tucked into her travel cape.

"Maybe it *is* an omen," muttered the chipmunk.

"Stop it," said Eloise. "It's not an omen."

❧ 57 ❧

LINGERING

The miserable weather harangued them all the way to the First Night Inn (Formerly the First Knight Inn), which was normally a reliable, if somewhat long, day's ride from Brague, but with rain and intermittent hail pummeling the entourage to a slow walk, they arrived much closer to midnight than they had hoped.

"Do you think they'll have any of the fermented morel and fenugreek soup left?" yelled Jerome. "I'm much too chilled for the cold broccoli and three bean soup."

"Çalaht sledging slack-jawed sleepwalkers, they'd better have something hot to eat," shouted Eloise back at him. "I can't have the warm mulled cherry cider on its own."

"You are the queen. They'll have something for you. And if they don't when we get there, they will about two minutes later."

"I sure hope you're right. Do you think we'll have missed all the gossip?"

"No. You *are* the gossip. By definition, it'll start up the second you step into the courtyard," said Jerome. "Hey, didn't you say you invited Headlong Helda on this little jaunt to the east? I didn't see her at Castle Brague this morning."

"You're right. I didn't see her, either. Maybe the weather scared her off."

"Pray that it's so."

But it wasn't so. Eloise sloshed into the reception area of the First Night Inn (formerly the First Knight Inn), with Lorch just behind her. The first thing she heard was Helda's squawking laugh coming from the dining room, followed by clicking noises.

Ugh, thought Eloise. *I'm in no mood to be on show. I just want to eat and go to bed.*

"G'midnight, g'midnight, g'midnight, Your Highness," said a celery-stick of a woman with eyes like a tawny frogmouth and hair crimped and twisted into a beehive hairdo the size of an overgrown pineapple. She slipped into reception from a back room and clasped her hands together at her cheek. "Welcome back to the First Night Inn (formerly the First Knight Inn). I'm Halcyon Spleenfluke."

"Of course. Mistress Spleenfluke. Once again, I find I must apologize for a late arrival. So nice to see you again, and sorry to drip on your carpets."

"I was a little worried you might not make it tonight. That weather really is something," said Spleenfluke. "It's almost like it's an omen."

"It's not an omen," spluttered Jerome, coming into the room. "It's just rain. And some hail. And a smattering of lightning that was much too close for comfort. And thunder that made my teeth rattle. And what seemed like ghosts clawing at me in the fog that appeared between rain squalls. So, please, not an omen at all."

"Oh, I remember your little friend," said Spleenfluke. "He's so cute in a nervous kind of way."

"My then-champion, you mean?" said Eloise.

"Sure, sure, sure. He and your other companion there argued over who was going to sleep outside your door. I think the big fellow won. Perhaps not surprisingly."

"This is Lorch Lacksneck of Lower Glenth. He's my champion now. Jerome Abernatheen de Chipmunk is actually my former champion. Now he serves as Assistant Court Seer to the Court Seer." At the innkeeper's raised eyebrows, she added, "It's a very important role."

"Oh. I see." Spleenfluke frowned. "What exactly does an Assistant Court Seer to the Court Seer do? I've never heard of one before."

"Uh..." Eloise looked at Jerome. "Assistant Court Seer to the Court Seer Abernatheen de Chipmunk, you want to field that one?"

The chipmunk's whiskers twitched, but Jerome kept his cool. He stepped forward, drew himself up to his full height, and spoke like he stood before a magistrate. "It is my full and sole responsibility to take on any and all types of assisting that the Court Seer may require. This includes, but is not limited to, abetting, aiding, backing up, providing general help, providing of targeted, specialized, or specific help, the rendering of favors small and large, the fronting of bail (although there's not much call for that), the lending of a hand, the giving of a lift, the whispering of encouraging words, and, when and as it is required, the acting as a second." He launched into one of his rococo, hand-wave-filled bows and added, "At your service."

"I see," said Spleenfluke. "It does, indeed, sound important."

There was a scratching at the front door and a frustrated whimper. The innkeeper cracked it open, and in bustled Nörbert de Lupus dripping rain from his coat. The Chihuahua rushed to stand next to Eloise. "My dear Halcyon, g'midnight to you. I'm hoping you saved the Queen's Suite for the queen? Please tell me you didn't let it go to someone else."

"Of course, my wee Nörby. When you say you're going to arrive, I trust you're going to arrive." Spleenfluke winked at Eloise. "Besides, it was paid for already."

"Thank Çalaht for small acts of grace." The Chihuahua turned to Eloise. "I shall have your things brought up?"

"Thank you, Nörbert."

"The fireplace is laid," said Spleenfluke. "I'll have it lit and organize a hot bath for you."

"That would be lovely. I pity anyone who stands between me and that hot bath." She turned to Lorch and Jerome. "Are you two going to argue about who sleeps outside my door tonight?"

"It will be me, Queen Eloise," said Lorch. "But I'm less worried this time, given there are 500 soldiers in and around the inn. Watch will be set and kept in every direction. I suspect you're almost safer here than in Brague."

Another honking laugh emanated from the open door of the dining room, followed by an enthusiastic patter of clicks.

"Headlong Helda must be working hard tonight," said Jerome.

"I might just try to sneak past and get to my room—"

"Theeeeeeere she is," blared Helda, appearing in the doorway. "Your Highness. G'midnight to you. You made it." Her words slurred ever so slightly. Eloise suspected more than a little liquid consolation had been consumed.

"Yes, Mistress de Anatidae. G'midnight to you as well."

"I was just chatting with a handful of your more influential subjects, and I'd love to introduce you to them," she gushed. "They were all such fans of your late mother, and I'm sure would be very grateful to be able to express their condolences."

It was the last thing Eloise felt like doing. Who knew what kind of liquid consolation-soused friends Helda had? Then again, she did need to get to know her subjects. Plus, she'd promised Helda access.

Ugh. Just ugh.

Jerome stepped forward. "Her Highness has had a long and arduous journey today and—"

"That's OK, Jerome. I'm happy to take a few minutes to meet Mistress de Anatidae's friends. But I'm wet, cold, and tired, so you'll understand if I don't linger."

"Not a problem." She waved a wing and bubbled, "Follow me, follow me."

But Eloise did end up lingering. And it was obvious that would happen as soon as she breached the doorway. "There must be three score people here," she whispered to the goose.

"Three score and fourteen," said the goose. "A girl's gotta make a living."

"You're doing your..." Eloise wasn't sure what to call it. "Your gossip herald thing?"

"I call it, get this, 'reporting.'"

"I heard the clicks. I didn't put it together."

"You did say I needed to pay my own way. This is me not being a burden on the crown's purse."

Just on her time, thought Eloise, but she put on a smile and walked into the room.

Helda put on her best herald's voice and honked out, "Please be upstanding for Her Majesty, Queen Eloise Hydra Gumball III."

There were murmurs of excitement mixed with clicks of approval as dessert forks clattered to plates, chairs scraped, and 74 people from a variety of species stood in a way that would have made whoever it was who wrote the *Livre de Protocol* proud.

"G'just-past-midnight to you all," said Eloise.

"G'just-past-midnight, Your Highness," chorused the room.

Eloise was gratified that the response was so warm, although there were enough red noses in the crowd (and none of them mandrills) to testify that Headlong Helda wasn't the only one enjoying the flush of liquid consolation.

"I'm pleased to meet you all." Eloise spotted a fireplace and couldn't resist moving over to it, grateful for the heat. "Apologies for the state of my dress, but we've just arrived, and when Mistress de Anatidae suggested I say hello, I couldn't resist. I hope none of you had to battle your way here through that weather."

"You didn't ride in a carriage, Your Highness?" asked the goose. "Why ever not?"

"I thought it might be nice to ride. And it was. Sort of. No, not sort of. Definitely, it was, despite the weather."

"Well, we're all glad you made it," said Helda. "Aren't we?"

The room erupted in a patter of clicks.

Helda flapped up on a chair near where Eloise stood. "OK, everyone, queue up here so we can do the formal one-at-a-time introductions."

"Oh, I don't think that's necessary," said Eloise.

"Protocol would insist," countered Helda. "And we wouldn't want to cross Protocol, now, would we?"

Eloise wanted to say, *Protocol didn't just ride all day through the most miserable weather and arrive soaked and chilled.* But she didn't. "Of course not." She put on a smile she hoped came across as authentic, and with forced joviality, said, "Let the introductions proceed."

Ninety-seven minutes (not that she was counting), fifty-one humans, a pod of eight leaf-tailed gecko, three pairs of marmots, two black-tailed cockatoos, an herb monger named Basil and his wife Verbena, an astronomer, an astrologer, a mink, a skink, a skunk and a monk later, she'd met everyone. They'd all bowed or curtsied, offered their condolences on her mother's passing, engaged in as much small talk as they could get away with, and then disappeared back into the room. Eloise, in return, had nodded, said thank you, engaged in as little small talk as she could get away with, said, "Thank you for your time and support," then turned her attention to the next in line.

All that being nice was exhausting at the end of an already draining day. For her part, Helda seemed thrilled. She introduced everyone by name, each of them a "close personal friend" or "a person of some importance to the queendom." It left Eloise wondering if this was a particularly elite group (always possible at the First Night Inn (Formerly the First Knight Inn)) or if Helda was just so good at what she did that she connected with everyone she met that closely.

The last person greeted, Eloise said, "Thank you for your time everyone. Now, I'm pretty sure there's a bath with my name on it. G'middle-of-the-blinking-night to you all."

"G'middle-of-the-blinking-night, Your Highness."

Eloise hoped the thing about the bath was still true.

58

AMBIT CLAIMS AND NUBBIN HEADS

T he late night was not matched by a late start. A dawn knock on Eloise's door broke through a dream involving blocks of tofu that needed slicing and a parade ground full of butter-flies. Her first thought was that she should inflict it on Jerome, just to get back at him for always wanting to tell her about his dreams.

"Blessings of the day, Queen Eloise," said Lorch through the door. "We're supposed to leave in 45 minutes. Would you like to break fast in there, or would you prefer to come to the dining room?"

"Blessings of the day, Lorch," said Eloise through the pillow covering her face. She squinted her eyes shut and lifted it. "I'll break fast in here, thanks."

"Yes, Your Highness. Would you like me to see if the inn has someone to act as a handmaid?"

"That won't be necessary. I'll dress myself. Apparently, one has been organized for me in Flachberg. I'll manage until then."

Listen to me, she thought. *Like not having a handmaid is such a huge burden to bear.*

She was up, dressed, brushed, and breakfasted faster than on any day since she'd been crown-plonked. She bade Mistress Spleenfluke goodbye and, with three minutes to spare, was astride Hector and moving with the mass of people back onto the road, doing her best to ignore Jerome's grousing.

"It was there, waiting for me on the serving platter," said the chipmunk. "I turn my back for like a second, and it's gone and El Lorcho here is chewing away."

"Did you, in any way, express that you wanted the last donut?" said Lorch.

"It was implied. I hadn't had any of the breakfast donuts yet. That donut had my name on it."

"I'm pretty sure that the 'possession is nine-tenths of the queen's justice' rule holds here." Lorch suppressed a belch. "I'm happy to give it back to you."

"Ew." Jerome wrinkled his nose. "That's just gross."

Eloise tuned them out.

Mercifully, the rain and hail had eased overnight, and they made good time to the junction with the Queen's Roadway. Instead of taking it toward The South, the way Eloise had when she was trying to track down Johanna, they went in the opposite direction, which would eventually lead them to the Queen's Roadway East, and onwards toward Flachberg and the Eastern Lands. All going to plan, they'd be there within a week, plus or minus, with a day or two to spare before the parlay was supposed to take place.

It turned out that Eloise wasn't the only one to choose to ride on a horse instead of in a carriage. First Advisor Bënnïë-Änn Thëjëts trotted up on a guard horse, who, like the Nameless One, was wearing a particular sash around his neck, and who was also, presumably, nameless. Eloise noted that she rode using a saddle, which brought back a rush of memories about how embarrassed she'd been when Lorch, Hector, and Jerome had insisted that she use one at the start of their

journey. It had been the right choice, of course, and she'd been immediately grateful for it until she no longer needed the security it
provided. It surprised her that her First Advisor used one, as surely she
must have spent many hours on a horse's back in her previous role of
Other Places Advocate.

"Blessings of the day, Your Highness," said Thëjëts.

"Blessings of the day, First Advisor." She nodded at the horse. "And to
you."

The mute horse nodded back.

"I was hoping I could discuss a thing or two as we go," said First
Advisor.

"Certainly. Is it confidential? Do we need to sequester ourselves, somehow? If you need Jerome, Hector, Lorch and the Nameless One to not
hear, we could—"

"No, no, no. Nothing like that. I wanted to discuss some of the things
you might face when you meet with Queen Aglandau. There's nothing
secret about that. Plus, I need to help you get clarity around what kind
of outcome you'd like from the parlay."

"Right. Good idea. I've been pretty focused on getting to Flachberg.
The being there and the part where we have the actual parlay haven't
gotten as much attention."

"Exactly. So I thought we might cover some negotiating tactics. There
are strategies that one should be familiar with and be ready to
counter."

Jerome peeked out from Eloise's travel cloak, and his ears twitched
forward. Hector did the same, turning his face to keep one eye on the
road and one eye on Thëjëts. Even Lorch tilted his head so he could
hear better.

First Advisor continued. "For example, do you know what an ambit
claim is, Your Highness?"

"No, sorry, I don't."

"It's where one party demands something so completely outrageous that it's just off the scale. It's like making an offer or demand, but way, way, way over the line, outside the bounds of reality or what you might get."

Jerome piped in. "What's the point if both sides know it's outrageous?"

Thëjëts glanced at the others. "Anyone?"

"It's so you can give ground," said Lorch. "When you walk what you're willing to accept back from the ambit claim, you're making a concession, but in practice, are ceding nothing."

"Exactly," said First Advisor. "It would not surprise me if Aglandau tries to pull something like that. Don't be flummoxed if she tries it on, and don't let her get away with it if she does."

"How?" said Eloise. "How do you counter an ambit claim?"

First Advisor looked around at her audience. "Anyone?"

"It seems to me you would have a few choices," said Hector. "You can put forward an equally absurd counter offer that goes in the opposite direction. Or you could just laugh at it. That's always off-putting."

"I could simply ignore it," said Eloise. "I could simply pretend she didn't say anything worth commenting on."

Jerome waved his paw in the air like an over-eager student. "You could ridicule it. Really tear it down. Or you could *pretend* to consider it, then pick holes in it from one end of the ambit claim to the other."

First Advisor nodded. "There are, obviously, lots of options."

"Which should I use?"

"You'll have to feel that one out," said Thëjëts. "But I trust that you'll know which to choose in the moment, Your Highness. Or you might come up with something different altogether."

"Çalaht knows, I hope so." They rode in silence while Eloise pondered how an ambit claim might work and how she might defend against one. "I guess I could be the one to make the ambit claim."

First Advisor nodded. "True. You could. Let's play that out. What might our queen's ambit claim be?"

"Donuts every morning," said Jerome, giving Lorch a side-eye.

Lorch made a noise in his throat. "I really am sorry about the donut thing. If I'd known that you—"

Eloise cut across them. "I could demand that she and her soldiers immediately leave Flachberg and restore the Adequate Wall of the Realms to where it was before her invasion."

First Advisor adjusted her seat in her saddle. "That's not really an ambit claim. That's more like what you actually want to achieve at the end of the process."

"Leave Flachberg, restore the Adequate Wall, and donuts every morning," said Jerome.

Lorch groaned softly, but held his tongue.

Hector spoke up. "How about leave Flachberg, retreat to a distance equal to that which was taken, rebuild the Adequate Wall in such a place as to double the size of Flachberg, and pay reparations for losses incurred to the families of those who died or were displaced?" Jerome cleared his throat. Hector looked at him, twitched an ear, then added, "Plus, provide fresh donuts every morning."

"Hah!" exclaimed Jerome, throwing his paws in the air in victory.

"Yes," said First Advisor. "Something that's more in that direction. A demand that would basically be offensive for her to contemplate."

"I think I understand," said Eloise. "Is there anything else you want me to know before I get in there with Queen Aggie?"

"Lots. An infinite amount. I'd love for you to know everything I know."

"You'll have to keep it to highlights, I guess. We have days, not decades."

Thëjëts shifted in her saddle again, looking sore of fundament, no longer used to making long journeys. "Well, let's see. There's the My Hands Are Tied tactic, where the other person tries to say they don't have much room to negotiate. You hear used dray salespeople use this one all the time. My experience is that usually if someone says their hands are tied, they mean they want their hands to be tied so they don't have to negotiate with you. If you're haggling for a used dray, the thing to do is ask to speak with their manager, who presumably has more authority to make decisions. But in the case of your parlay, Queen Aglandau can hardly be skipped over for a higher level. So if she tries to pull a My Hands Are Tied thing on you, just say something like, 'I thought you were queen,' and try to get her to own her authority, rather than deny it."

"I see."

"Then there's 'Good night watch, bad night watch.'"

"That one I've heard of," said Jerome. "You're talking to two people, and while one acts friendly, the other treats you like a total nubbin head."

"Yes," said Thëjëts. "It's popular in certain entertainment scrolls. But this one won't apply to the parlay, because you're not dealing with two people who can trade off on each other."

"Unless Queen Aggie uses two different personalities." Jerome raised a paw to stage-whisper at Eloise, "If the nubbin head personality offers you a donut, don't take it."

She rolled her eyes at him.

First Advisor continued. "That brings us to another one you've probably heard of—Hold It or Drop It. It's essentially saying that the offer is non-negotiable, that its terms can't be changed. You either hold it or drop it."

"Is that likely to bespeak reality?" asked Lorch. "Would terms genuinely be non-negotiable in the circumstance of a parlay?"

Thëjëts shook her head slowly. "I'd say that's unlikely. If both the queens genuinely want to negotiate, they'll negotiate. I think of Hold It or Drop It as a sign of obstinance. Or disinterest in continuing proceedings."

"Got it," said Eloise. "So what do I do if she does that?"

"Start by ignoring it and turn your attention to what's inside the offer she's made. If appropriate, make a counter-offer. She'll either bite, or she won't. Ultimately, they all come down to some version of that—she'll bite or she won't." First Advisor wrapped her cape around herself. "So, what other tactics are there? There's Slagging, where you deliberately insult your opponent to try to throw them off balance or ruffle their feathers. There's Bidding Against Yourself."

"How would that work?" asked Hector.

"You make an offer. Then the other person tries to get you to make some sort of concession before they make any kind of counter-offer. If you do, you're essentially, like it says, bidding against yourself without the other person needing to move their position."

"That doesn't seem very smart," said Jerome.

"It's not," agreed First Advisor.

Bënnië-Änn Thëjëts continued describing hard tactics for negotiating. There was Insult Jester, where the person belittles your position or offer. There was the Fake Punch, where the person makes demand after demand, trying to get the other person to flinch—that is, to eventually concede because they've hit their breaking point. There was Faking It, where you just try to bluff the other person, and there was Baking the Soufflé, where you puffed up your position with lies and exaggeration.

The list of tactics seemed to go on forever.

Eventually, First Advisor finished. Eloise allowed a full strong length to pass, lost in her thoughts about the different negotiating tactics she had described. They danced around in her head, bumping into each other. The different names helped her remember what they were, but after a while, the jostling of ideas mixed with the butterflies in her stomach (a metaphor butterflies complained about whenever they had the chance) and left her feeling queasy.

First Advisor must have seen her face. "Is there a problem, Your Highness?"

Eloise nodded. "I'm scared."

"Of what?"

She shook her head with a dim laugh. "Take your pick. That I'll negotiate badly. That I'll fall on my face. That Queen Aglandau will pull something that I'm completely unprepared for. That she'll disrespect me or treat me like a child or think I'm like my mother, or think I'm nothing like my mother, or that she'll have assassins storm the parlay tent and shoot crossbow bolts into me so I end up looking like a rather dead echidna, or that she'll ridicule me, or... Shall I keep going?"

"No, Your Highness. I get the picture." First Advisor leaned on the pommel of her saddle. "Let me tell you a secret."

"I'm open to learning a secret."

"Maybe you already know it. So, I'll ask instead. Do you know what's the most powerful thing you have up your sleeve?"

Eloise shook her head. "No. I have no idea. None at all. Should I try to hide a crossbow in there? Or maybe a big knife?"

"Your biggest weapon in a negotiation is the ability to quit that negotiation. If you can come at the discussion from a position of low need, and if you can be willing to stand up and walk away, you'll be in a better position when you're in that tent negotiating. But if you have high need and you feel like you absolutely have to come to some sort of deal, then you abso-flopping-lutely will end up getting stuffed, stiffed, or stifled."

"Good to know. Low need: walk away. High need: get stuffed," said Eloise. "Got it."

First Advisor let another few moments go by. "There's one other point to consider," she said.

"That I shouldn't be bothering to do this at all?" mumbled Eloise. "That we should all just turn around and head home?"

"No, but you're sort of in the right direction with that."

"Oh?"

"It's at the opposite end of 'you can always walk away.' It's that, if you want to avoid all the tactics that we've been discussing, you have to commit to not doing them yourself."

Eloise wrinkled her nose. "What? I just leave everything from ambit claims to slagging her off to Hold It or Drop It at the tent flap and just gavotte in wearing a smile?"

"Exactly."

"Then why have we just spent half the morning discussing them?"

"Because you need to discern them. And because you need to get a sense of how they feel. Let me ask, how did thinking about them make you feel?"

"Like I wanted to hit something. Or toss my biscuits."

"That's right. All of those things cause the other person to get their back up. They are perfect if you want to create a nasty circle of demands and threats. If your goal is to foster locked-in positions, mistrust, and a result that is worse for all involved, then you should use as many of the tactics as you can. But if you want to end up with something that you and Queen Aglandau can both live with, then you need to avoid them, and if she tries to use them, you must try not to buy into it."

"Makes sense," said Eloise. "I'll try to keep that in mind."

A few more minutes of quiet passed while she thought over everything.

Jerome broke the silence. "Did you break fast on biscuits?" asked Jerome. "We didn't get biscuits. We had donuts. And I didn't get one. Did I mention that?"

59

PYTHON INDIGESTION

"By Çalaht's green, gangrenous toes, that's a sight for sore eyes," said Jerome, squeegeeing rainwater from the fur on his face. They'd just crested a rise and the tabletop mountain that gave Flachberg its name had finally come into view. "I thought we'd never get here."

At Lorch's insistence, Eloise's group had stayed in the middle of the mass of soldiers, for security purposes, so their pace had been at the mercy of those in front of them. It had been frustratingly slow, and Eloise knew that, on their own, they'd have made the journey at least a third faster, if not in half the time. But this time, it wasn't about speed. It was about making a statement with their (and "their" meant "her") presence. That, and arriving safely.

It took another full day before they reached the Adequate Wall of the Realms and the gateway to the town of Flachberg itself. Eloise considered it as she approached, and had a different reaction than the last time she'd seen it.

She didn't consider the Adequate Wall of the Realms' lack of grandeur and think, "Meh." She didn't imagine what it might have been had the bean counters not taken over the project. She couldn't be bothered to picture it taller, wider, better painted, and dotted with more towers. Her mind didn't go to visualizing it with much more ornamentation—curlicues and statues and arches and inscriptions—as well as more gates, and more soldiers spending their days and nights working those gates. She spent no time guessing where booby traps might have been laid, where cauldrons of boiling oil might have been poised, as well as all the family-friendly elements, like picnic tables, food mongers, grassy knolls with open spaces on top, and spots for the kids to run around and play.

Instead, she got irked. Then annoyed. Then she became angry. And finally, she reached quietly, seethingly furious.

The wall, having been moved, was a visible, tangible symbol of what Aggie had done. She'd had the whole bloody wall moved from one side of Flachberg to the other. Seeing it provoked a rage that Eloise had to work hard to keep bottled inside. Really, who would do that kind of thing? It wasn't enough to just take the territory, Queen Aggie had to show off by moving the Adequate Wall itself.

What a jester.

Really.

And it's not like the Eastie queen had made any improvements to the wall while she was at it. She could have. She might have had them whack in a food stall area or touched up the paint a little. But no, she just moved it from A to B and left it the same adequate thing it had been before.

What an unimaginative jester.

Eloise was coming to realize just how splenetic the whole situation made her feel—not just the parlay itself, but the incursion that had made it necessary in the first place. And as she sat stewing, she asked herself for the thousandth time what kind of outcome she could expect from it. What would be a good result? What would be a likely result? What could she hope to achieve that might leave her and her realm not feeling aggrieved and damaged?

Did she really expect Aglandau to say, "Oh, never mind. I'll just put everything back the way it was. Just kidding."

Of course not.

What was much more likely was that the Eastie Queen would do what First Advisor had said: take another bite, and then another. She imagined Queen Aglandau as a snake slowly trying to swallow the Western Lands and All That Really Matters whole. Maybe that's why she put so much trust in that three-eyed trade negotiator, Bosana de Coluber. Just thinking of him gave Eloise a shiver.

Which meant somehow, from the weakened position she was in, she had to figure out a way to give Queen Aggie the Snake indigestion. Make her decide that swallowing wasn't the thing to do.

But how?

Eloise came to the same conclusion she had every other time she'd considered the situation: she had absolutely no idea.

Hence the anger, which did little to hide the nerves that roiled her stomach.

60

ERNESTINA DE SETONIX

T here were no inns or amenities outside the Adequate Wall at Flachberg, like one would normally expect. Wall gateways were normally a hive of commerce catering to travelers, and, more specifically, to those being processed by the guards at the border. But when Queen Aggie had the wall moved, its associated infrastructure was left behind, at least for now. Instead of inns, cafes, and boutiques, all that awaited the arriving journeyer was a scattering of food carts that specialized in tea, sweets sold from doily-covered wooden trays, large covered pots of what was referred to as "soup," but which featured a swirl of grease that attested to dubious origins, a cartoonist who drew exaggerated portraits that made everyone look exceedingly road weary, and an opportunistic retired bureaucrat who poked his nose in any time he thought he could intercede on behalf of people who had some sort of trouble crossing through the gate in return for a few coins, a few of which he passed on to the guards.

The Queen's Roadway was backed up with the traffic of carts, carriages, those who'd agreed to provide transportation, including horses, donkeys, camels, thirteen cows in a procession, and a particularly elderly yak carrying an even older mallard, as well as people of all species tromping their way forward (mostly) on two, four, six, or eight legs toward the opening at the wall.

"Are we going through?" asked Jerome.

"No, I don't think so," said Eloise. "I left those details to First Advisor. But surely there are too many of us. It'd take forever to go through all the travel documents."

"I think we're over there," said Lorch, indicating a cluster of tents and marquees in Gumball-blue that were one hundred lengths this side of the gate, and about the same off the main road, in a paddock. "You see how our soldiers are heading for them? One of those will be yours, I'm sure."

"Thank Çalaht," mumbled Jerome. "My tailbone's not used to riding like this anymore."

They arrived at the tents and found a quokka wearing blue ambassador's robes and a matching mortar board perched on the back of her head. She was built like a somewhat stumpy kangaroo, but was the size of a cat. The coarse, grizzled brown fur on her back and tail faded to a buff color underneath and at her neck, and it looked like she'd slicked it down with some sort of pomade, as it had a sheen in the wan winter light.

First Advisor Thëjëts leapt off her horse and scooped the quokka into a foot-dangling hug. "Ernie! You ol' misery guts. It's flopping fan-flopping-tastic to flopping see you."

The quokka's reply was inaudibly muffled by having her snout shoved into Thëjëts' chest.

"I flopping missed you, too, you malcontent ol' flop-tailed sourpuss," said First Advisor, hugging her tighter.

Another inaudible remark.

"Why, yes, that is the queen, you grouchy ol' bellyacher."

Muffled comment accompanied by foot movements.

"I suppose you're right, you carping ol' curmudgeon." First Advisor set the quokka back on the ground. "Allow me to present Ernestina de Setonix, your ambassador to the Eastern Lands, my long-time bosom friend and notorious wet blanket."

The quokka bowed into a perfect curtsy. "An honor to meet you, Your Highness. And an honor to serve."

"Thank you, Ambassador de Setonix," said Eloise. "I appreciate your setting this all up for us."

"A pleasure, Your Highness. Also, I suggest you distrust Bënnïë-Änn's characterization of my demeanor. It was a joke to call me a killjoy back when we were at the Studium Gymnasium of the Western Lands and All That Really Matters, as I was disinclined to accompany her on her nightly bouts of imbibing liquid consolation. I preferred to make myself familiar with the inside of the Gymnasium's bibliotheca and scrollarium, where there were far more words to be read." She looked at Thëjëts. "Did you actually manage to find the building in your years there?"

"No, I can't say I did," said First Advisor. "But you were there enough for the both of us. Given you were outstanding, and I was an inebriated flopping mess, on average, we were pretty average."

"I'm not sure that's how math works," said de Setonix, smiling.

"No? Good to know."

"Anyway, Your Highness..." The quokka swept a foreleg toward the tents. "I hope you'll find the accommodation satisfactory, Your Highness. Establishing an encampment outside the wall provided a number of advantages, both practical and symbolic. For one, we can billet your entire entourage without scattering them throughout Flachberg. For another, it lets us remain on what's clearly your land, and not the disputed territory. The security is simpler, since we can establish a guarded perimeter. And we still have easy proximity to the location of the parlay itself."

"Where will that be?"

"We've agreed to a large marquee on top of the Adequate Wall itself. It is wide enough, and while the border is disputed, you won't be required to actually set foot in the contentious territory."

"Right. That all makes sense," Eloise said. "Thank you for your part in arranging everything. It's obvious that a lot of thought and care has gone into the preparations."

"I'll mention that all the soldiers will be provided for, both with things they've brought and locally sourced materials and food. Likewise, your close advisors and companions. Between now and tomorrow morning, when your parlay starts, you should be able to focus solely on preparing for Queen Aglandau. If you'd like to settle in, I can have a bath prepared in your tent, and there's food. Once you've recovered, we can have the briefing I've prepared, if you'd like."

"A bath, meal, and briefing sound great."

De Setonix curtsied. "Follow me, if you will, and I'll show you to your tent."

❧ 61 ❧

PAVILION

To call the structure that had been prepared for her a tent was like calling a cyclone a wee bit of wind with a smattering of rain. It was more of a huge pavilion, with a peaked top and crenelated decorations in Gumball-blue and white. Much more than one person could ever possibly need. Uniformed guards had been deployed at six-length intervals, surrounding and protecting it. As Eloise approached, the two at the entry snapped to attention and saluted.

She stopped and acknowledged their salute with a raised index and middle finger, a gesture she'd seen her mother use often, but which she hadn't adopted until that moment.

Ernestina de Setonix slipped in between the two guards. "Welcome to your temporary home here in Flachberg. I hope you find it comfortable." The quokka nodded to the guards, who opened the heavy canvas entry flaps.

Eloise stepped through, followed by Lorch, Jerome, First Advisor, and the ambassador.

"Wow," said Jerome. "This is something."

"Yes," said Eloise. "It is."

Inside, the space was heated by braziers, lit with oil lamps and soy candles, and smelled like it had been cleaned recently with some sort of citrus wash. A leveled off, temporary wooden floor had been laid over the grass, and the furniture looked as solid and comfortable as anything one would see at Castle de Brague.

What caught Eloise's eye more than anything else were the tapestries that lined the walls. She walked from one to the next, trying to figure out what they depicted. Then it dawned on her. "They're histories," she said to de Setonix. "Scenes from the Gumball history."

"Yes, Your Highness. That's correct. We had them shipped from Brague. I was hoping they would make you feel at home."

Eloise wrinkled her nose. "Does this one show Queen Aubrey the Parasitic?"

"Yes, Your Highness."

"Having her gall stones removed?"

"Yes, ma'am."

"It's very realistic."

"I'd agree, Your Highness. A true testament to the artist's skill and accomplishments."

"And this one." Eloise waved vaguely at the next one along. "I'm guessing this is my mother?"

"Your grandmother, ma'am."

"Right. And what, exactly, is she doing?"

"Yelling at your grandfather, if historical notes are to be trusted."

"He's not actually in this tapestry, is he?"

"No, Your Highness. I believe she's driven him away in this particular scene."

"And that's a throwing knife in her hand? I don't think she ever threw a knife at him."

First Advisor joined them. "Opinions differ on that, Your Highness. The record is pretty clear that she never hit him with a thrown knife, but there's contemporary, anecdotal evidence that on at least one occasion, she tried."

"Really? I didn't know that."

"We can't be certain, of course, but yes."

"Wow. Just wow."

"Funny you should say that," said First Advisor. "Because apparently that's exactly what One's Grand Mistake is alleged to have said when he felt the knife whizzing past his ear."

"Any others that I should particularly see?" asked Eloise.

"If you'll come with me around the corner," said the quokka. "There's a rather special piece I was able to source."

The tapestry was massive, easily three times the size of the alleged knife-throwing one of her grandmother. Around the edges, armies of soldiers stood poised for battle. In the center, an armored queen, brandishing a sword that was longer than she was tall, prepared to step into a tent. Black, curly hair caught the late afternoon sun, and her expression looked grimly determined. But what was really striking were the eyes. Even rendered in woolen yarn, Eloise could see that the eyes were exactly what she saw when she looked into a mirror.

Creepy.

"Can you tell who it is?" asked de Setonix.

"From the sword, full battle gear, the armies, and the tent, I'd guess this was supposed to be Queen Gwendolyn the Irritable heading into her parlay with King Brüüütus."

"That's correct. The tapestry dates from about a decade after that event two centuries ago."

"The artist didn't exactly capture that she'd end up in the family way maybe two days later."

"Yes, that's true. It's a Before image, not an After."

Eloise hated it, but the quokka seemed so proud, so she searched for something neutral to say. "Well, that's quite a tapestry. If ever I wanted a tapestry like that, it would be just like that one."

The quokka beamed. "I'm so glad." She curtsied. "Now, if Your Highness will do me the kindness of following, I'll point out that your quarters are divided into rooms that can be closed off for privacy or opened up for receiving groups. There's a dining area, a small office, a medium office, and a large office. Your private space is through here." She led them toward a narrowed-off passageway. At a small gesture from Lorch, Eloise let her champion go first to make sure there were no security vulnerabilities.

They reached an inner chamber right in the middle of the structure, with wooden walls delineating the space. A massive oak pillar stretched through a hole in the wooden floor to the peak in the roof. There was a canopied bed to one side, a wash stand, several tables, a desk, and a pair of chairs set near a roaring brazier. From behind a screened-off alcove, Eloise heard the sound of water being poured into a bath. Her trunks were already placed to the side, and a handmaid she didn't recognize was preparing to hang up their contents.

"Not exactly like sleeping in a cave in the middle of the Central Ranges," whispered Jerome.

"No," said Eloise. "More like the Legs Not Arms in For The Love of Çalaht Cut It Out You Two."

"That was so posh. Hey, as queen, you're probably almost wealthy enough to stay there now."

"Almost, yes." She turned to her companions. "Give me a couple of hours to clean up and nap. We can do the briefing over dinner."

"Yes, Your Highness," said First Advisor. The others nodded and followed the quokka out of the inner chamber.

62

A'QUIVER

"Is it just us for the briefing?" asked Eloise when she found First Advisor and Ambassador de Setonix sitting at a table covered in scrolls, maps, and a couple of bound volumes.

"Yes, Your Highness," said Thëjëts.

"Is there any reason not to include the rest of my Fippledip Council?"

"Your Fippledip Council?" asked the quokka.

"Sorry. It's a sort of informal privy council. They're all here." Eloise looked at First Advisor. "Would it take long to gather the others? I'd like them to hear this. They might have insights."

"I'll get them."

A quarter hour later, Lorch, Jerome, Sylvia Cloisterfeld, and Tiberius de Sphenodon had joined them around the busy table, and Eloise asked Ambassador de Setonix to begin.

"Let's start with—"

A guard appeared, interrupting. "I'm sorry, Your Highness, but—"

"Excuse me? Hello?" The voice honked from somewhere behind the guard. "Is anyone there?"

"It's Headlong Helda," whispered Eloise. She closed her eyes and rubbed her temples. "I promised her access. I guess she's here to claim it."

"What?" Jerome's tail fluffed. "Now? At your private briefing?"

"Unparalleled access. It's what I offered her." She waved at the guard, resigned. "Let her in."

The goose strode through a flap, her eyes bright with anticipation. "It is a great and glorious day, is it not? A fine day for a parlay prep. Where would you like me? Oh, this will do." Without waiting for a reply, she flapped her wing twice, lifted up, and landed on Jerome's chair. "Oh, sorry. Didn't see you there. Mind if I join you?"

"I... Wh— No f—" spluttered Jerome.

"Thanks, Jerome," said Eloise as the goose, ignoring him, settled in like she was ready to nest.

"Just pretend I'm not here," she trilled.

Like that was possible.

There was an awkward silence around the table.

Eloise cleared her throat. "Go ahead, Ambassador de Setonix. You were saying we should start with what?"

"I was going to suggest that we start with the queendom as a whole. There is a discernible amount of grumbling going on amongst her people. The price of olives is skyrocketing due to significantly lower yields, as a result of the blight that has damaged numerous orchards. With olives being so central, not just to the Eastern Lands economy, but to the Eastern Lands self-identity, this is an unprecedented problem for Queen Aglandau."

"How is she handling it?" asked Eloise.

"She has tried to control the price paid for olives, somehow. But all that has done is create a thriving black market."

"I see."

"She has also ginned up controversy around workers from other realms. She has said publicly that they are coming into the Eastern Lands and taking away opportunities from 'true' Easties. The reality is, of course, that the Eastern Lands olive growers have long relied on temporary help from outside the queendom to get through the very busy harvest time. What's changed is the nature of the current harvest."

"That doesn't seem very fair."

"She's queen, Your Highness," said First Advisor. "Fairness doesn't really enter into the discussion."

Eloise shrugged. "I guess."

"Next, let's consider how Queen Aglandau is in her person," said the quokka. "This has been tightly guarded, but from what I can gather, her health has not been great recently. Exactly what's going on is unclear, but a procession of healers has come and gone from the queen's rooms, each looking dour and pensive."

"Do we know for sure they're seeing her and not someone else?" asked First Advisor. "It could be subterfuge, a head fake for anyone (like us) who might be watching."

"That's always possible. But if the gossip of numerous serving wenches and lackeys can be trusted, then yes, we can be reasonably certain. But the malady is never described directly. It's always vague. They refer to 'the queen's mild distress' or 'Queen Aglandau's distraction.' But she's lost weight. I've seen that myself. It's visible in her face and arms. And there's a sallowness to her complexion that's visible despite the olive tint to her skin and copious make-up."

"Does she lack vigor?"

"Not if her public schedule is to be believed. And not for her age."

"How old is she?" asked Eloise.

"She was seventeen years your mother's senior. So, not young, but far from ancient."

"OK, there are possible health issues," said Eloise. "What else—"

"If I may?" It was Headlong Helda.

"Aren't you just supposed to observe?" sniped Jerome.

The goose gave him a look that would have wilted a satsuma.

"You have something to add?" said Eloise.

"My sources tell me it is an ailment of her humor. Specifically, the yellow bile."

"Well, that would make sense," said Sylvia Cloisterfeld.

They all looked from her to the goose and back.

"How so?" asked Lorch.

Cloisterfeld lifted a shoulder. "Those with yellow bile are known to be daring, but also bitter and short-tempered. That sounds like Queen Aglandau."

"I've heard the yellow bile described in terms of a choleric nature," said Helda. "Those afflicted are known to be ambitious, decisive, and aggressive, and as Champion Cloisterfeld said, short-tempered. Also, they appear greenish and have yellow-tinged skin."

"That would match the descriptions I've heard of her complexion at the moment," said de Setonix. "Though I haven't seen it myself."

"My mother speaks of yellow bile as being ruled by the gallbladder," said Jerome. "Maybe she has gallstones or an inflammation there. Are there agues that afflict the gallbladder?"

"I'm sure there are. But I don't know that we need that level of detail." Eloise drummed her fingers, thinking. "For that matter, we don't know if it's gallbladder or not, yellow bile or not, or even her illness or not. But if she arrives looking peaky, then I'll know there might be something to the gossip of the serving wenches. What else?"

"It's fair to say her emotional state has been more agitated than normal. Queen Aglandau has always been a cool customer who tolerates zero nonsense. She was known for being unflappable, if harsh. But recently there's an edginess to her. I heard one courtier say that she displays the patience of a farrier's rasp on balsa."

"Flappability. Check," said Eloise. "Next? Anything that might clue me in about what she'll want to discuss at the parlay?"

"Nothing has leaked from the castle about that, unfortunately." The quokka's tail twitched, reminding Eloise of the way Jerome's tail betrayed his feelings. "That could mean that security is tight and that Queen Aglandau's deliberations are being held closely. Or..." De Setonix trailed off.

"Or what?"

The quokka swallowed. "Or it could mean that the meeting is of little consequence to her, and she's just not giving it much thought."

"How likely is that?"

"Likely. Very likely."

Eloise narrowed her eyes. "Why do you think that?"

"Because in some matters, the Eastern Lands queen wears her feelings on her sleeve. One of those matters is her contempt for the Western Lands and All That Really Matters. She shared the late King Doncaster's disdain for the 'and All That Really Matters' part of the realm's name. If she was gearing up for a big confrontation or was feeling riled in anticipation of your parlay, the castle would be all a'quiver with it."

"There's no a'quivering?"

"Not a jiggle, not a wiggle, not a waggle. It's like it's not even on the agenda."

"Is she planning on coming?"

"I believe so, Your Highness, but we won't know for sure until tomorrow morning, when we'll see if she shows up or not. I suspect she will, but I can't guarantee it."

"It would be a jester move if she didn't bother to come, given we've come all this way," muttered Jerome.

"True," said de Setonix. "But it wouldn't be the first jester move she ever pulled."

"I suppose not." Eloise looked around at them all. "Anyone else? Anyone have anything to add?"

"I do," said First Advisor.

"OK."

"I think it's important to keep in mind that Queen Aglandau is, at some level, just like you. She has feelings, hopes, and dreams. She has preferences and quirks. She's a person, not a monster."

"Not a monster," repeated Eloise. "Got it."

63

LIGHTNING AND TEA

T hunder roiled across the land, and lightning streaked white annoyance across the pre-dawn sky. The night was marked by an unforgiving, slashing rain, which had soaked through anyone unfortunate to have been out in it.

Inside the pavilion, Eloise's canopied bed had been comfortable enough, and she'd made a point of getting into it at a reasonable hour. She'd been exhausted and had fallen asleep instantly.

Then deep in the night, there was a pop of lightning and an immediate crack of thunder so loud and so close, it was like it had originated inside the pavilion. Eloise was jarred from her sleep and startled into full wakefulness.

And there she remained, despite her exhaustion and the need for a solid night's sleep before the parlay with Queen Aggie. Lying in bed, eyes wide, her head swirled with thoughts that spun out possible futures, then circled back to rehash regrets from the past. Her mother's parlay with Aglandau hadn't exactly been a disaster, but something had to have happened—something that both maintained peace between the realms, but also left her queendom singularly unprepared for anything that didn't look like peace. Eloise didn't relish the prospect of trying to lead her realm into war, even a defensive one, and was certain down to the marrow that she was ill-equipped to do so. Plus, wars had always seemed so utterly stupid. So pointless. So bound up in power games and land grabs and bloodshed—none of which were her cup of haggleberry tea. That wasn't the kind of queen she wanted to be. It wasn't the way she wanted to run her realm. It wasn't how she wanted to spend the queen's purse. Such a waste of time and coin.

And yet…

And yet, here she was. She hadn't sought it out, but the aggression had come to her. Like it or not, somehow she had to deal with it.

With a humph, she sat up and reached for her night robe and eased her toes into her slippers. Standing, Eloise took to pacing from one side of her chamber to the other. Anxiety mounting, she tried to combat the feeling by concentrating on her footsteps.

It didn't help, and she worried that, under the stress, she was regressing.

She found her traveling coat and searched for the hidden pocket that held Odmilla's prayer beads. The beads had been well-worn even before her handmaid had given them to her, and over the months, Eloise's fingers had grown acquainted with the intricately carved spheres made of various woods and in differing sizes, grouped into the traditionally spaced sets of 1, 1, 2, 3, 5, 8, 13, 21, 34, and, unusually for a set of prayer beads, 55. They were smooth like stones kissed for centuries by the waters of the River Thurmond as it spilled into the Gööödeling Sea. Each bead was unique in its own way and a pleasure to touch.

Eloise didn't use them for religious purposes. She used them for counting. They'd been given to her as a way to occupy herself when what she called her habits—the quirks and internal needs that had dominated her life—had been itching at her. Most days, only the echoes of those quirks and needs ghosted her. Using the beads was more habit than anything else.

She pulled them out, wrapped them around her right wrist, raised them to her lips for a kiss (not something she'd ever done before), and began moving them through her fingers, trying to transfer the counting of her habits from her mind to her hand.

But that left her mind free to do what? Continue worrying? She directed her attention to the muted lightning bolts that shone through the canvas roof and tried to determine if the subsequent thunder rumbles were getting closer together or further apart. She noticed there was a difference in the way her blurred eyed perceived the flashes, but it was a vague distinction that she had trouble putting a name to. Similarly, the buzzing ear sought some kind of different meaning in the booms than her not-affected ear.

Or maybe it was the middle of the night, and her mind was wandering, and she was sensing something that just wasn't really there.

"Prin— Sorry, Queen Eloise?" Lorch's voice came from outside the chamber's entry flap. "I can't believe I'm still making that mistake. Apologies. Are you OK? Do you need anything?"

"Peace of mind? A sense of surety? A lepidopterist to help me tame the butterflies in my stomach?"

"I don't know if I can help with any of those. But perhaps I can bring you a cup of tea?"

Eloise smiled. "That would be lovely. Will you join me? I think I could use the company."

"Yes, Your Highness."

Sooner than she thought possible, Lorch was back at the divider. "May I come in?"

She re-cinched her robe, made sure there was no sleep in her eyes, and said, "I'm decent. Come on in."

"Hey, Queen Eloise," said Jerome, entering in front of Lorch. He lugged a basket covered with a napkin, out of which wafted the smell of fresh baking. "I was awake. Hope you don't mind."

"Not at all." Eloise sniffed the air and caught hints of cinnamon, ginger, and lemon. "Where did you find fresh baking?"

The chipmunk waved vaguely in the direction of the pavilion wall. "Lots of soldiers. They gotta eat. It's a bit like the castle. There's almost always someone doing something in the kitchen." He held up the basket and waggled it. "Muffins. Fresh from a camp oven."

"Amazing."

Lorch set the tea set on a table, brought over a third chair, and found a pair of throw pillows that would sit Jerome at table height. "Shall I pour, Your Highness? It's haggleberry."

Eloise slid into her seat. "Yes, please."

The three friends drank tea and nibbled muffins in silence. Jerome even managed to not comment on how flawed the haggleberry tea was, although Eloise could read the desire to do so in the twitch of his whiskers. So Eloise said it for him. "It's a bit bitter, and there's the hint of chalkiness, which means the brewing temperature was at least ten degrees too high."

"Plus, it's been steeping too long," said Lorch. "Otherwise there'd be more emphasis on the fruity highlights."

"It really is hard to get a good cup of haggleberry tea," said Eloise.

"Very true, Your Highness."

Jerome looked from Eloise to Lorch and back. "First, you're right about the temperature and the length of steeping. Second, you didn't mention the bruising that leaps out in the flavor because some nong harvested them by plucking instead of using a blade like a civilized person. Third, I suspect the two of you are mocking me."

"No at all," said Lorch. "Just paying attention. Have been for a while."

Eloise lifted her cup in Lorch's direction. "What he said."

"You know what?" said Lorch.

Jerome's whiskers twitched, unsure if he was being made the fool. "What?"

"I've never appreciated tea like this before. It's been... It's been a revelation."

Eloise gestured her cup in his direction again. "What he said."

"Well." His whiskers perked up again. "Well, thank you. I'm glad it's made a difference." Jerome blew across the rim of his mug and sipped. "It's passable. I've certainly had worse."

The others nodded.

"Your Highness?" Lorch looked unsure about what he was going to say.

"Yes?"

"Do you want to talk about it?"

"About what?"

"About tomorrow. Well, about today, given the hour."

Eloise arched one eyebrow. "Do I want to talk about the entire future of my queendom hinging on my ability to reach some sort of accord with a woman I've never met and who I'm pretty sure my mother hated, who's already bitten off a chunk of my land, whose ambassador and trade negotiator tried to have me killed before absconding without a trace, who may or may not be mercurial, may or may not be controlling, may or may not be a manipulator of the highest order, but whose parlay with me will likely determine if I'm forgotten by the history scrolls or remembered with the same fondness as Queen Albertina, that Incompetent Bungler, the only queen in the Salon des Champions with a 'that' instead of a 'the' between her name and her honorific?"

Lorch grimaced. "Something like that, yes, Your Highness."

"No," said Eloise. "I don't think I do."

"Yes, ma'am. Very good."

They drank their tea in silence and shared the remaining muffins around, letting a fraction of the night pass without Eloise dwelling overtly on the next day's uncertainty, even if it hung like a bad tapestry in the back of her mind. It was nice just to be there with the two of them and to feel something slightly akin to normal, whatever that was.

By the time Eloise slipped back under her covers, she'd relaxed enough to just listen to the rain and let slumber claim her, putting the squabbling of lightning bolts and thunder strikes out of her mind, along with an impending meeting that carried the weight of her entire future.

❧ 64 ❧

THE "THE"

A t first light, Ernestina de Setonix appeared with a breakfast tray and a cheery, "Blessings of the day, Queen Eloise."

Eloise blinked open her eyes and croaked, "Blessings of the day, Ambassador." She saw her breath in the air as she spoke. The temperature must have dropped dramatically. She sat up and saw that a brazier had been placed near her seat at the table so she'd be comfortable while she broke fast. Another warmed the spot near a full-length mirror.

"With your permission, I'll act as your handmaid this morning. I can help you prepare for the big day, answer any last-minute questions, and do your hair and get you dressed."

"That will be fine. Thank you." Eloise sat up, reflexively touched the box with the Star of Whatever to make sure it was still there, pinched the corners of her eyes to wipe away any sleep, and slid from the blankets.

Ninety minutes later, a distant horological cuckoo called the top of the hour as Eloise gave herself one last look in the mirror. She wore a simple band as a crown, an elegant, if practical, gown of indigo that covered the box with the Star of Whatever, which was, as always, on her hip. She also wore her beloved travel cape because it was familiar, made her feel comfortable, hid the Star, and its pockets held all kinds of hidden secrets. Her white hair was still nowhere close to being long enough to braid, and she'd declined Ernestina's offer to adorn it with beads, flowers, or ribbons. The quokka had washed it, combed through it, and misted it with an oil that she said would "bring out your curl," which Eloise wasn't sure was a good thing but had assented to none-theless. Looking in the mirror, it looked pretty much like it always did, if a tad oily. "So, do I look OK?"

De Setonix smiled and thumped her tail a little. "You look beautiful."

That was not a word Eloise ever associated with herself, and she couldn't objectively see it in the mirror. She knew she wasn't hideous, but Eloise had always thought of Johanna as the prettier twin. "That's kind of you. Probably more to the point, do I look like a queen?"

"That you do, Your Highness. But that's not from the hair or the clothes or anything. You carry yourself like a queen."

"I do?"

"Yes, ma'am, you do. And it's different from what I experienced of the late queen. Your mother, may she stand with Çalaht, had a..." She trailed off. "I don't want to give offense."

"No, no." Eloise nodded encouragement. "I knew my mother pretty well. I doubt anyone can say anything that will come as a surprise."

"The late queen had a sternness to her. A coldness. Her way of rule was to control, and, where control was difficult, to intimidate. I can't imagine the late queen deigning in this situation to let me, someone she'd only known a few hours, do her hair."

"Sounds like my mother. And you're right about the hair thing. She was particular about being touched. Didn't like it much. And she was espe-cially thingy about her hair being touched. Her hair and her neck."

"I didn't know that about her."

"Not many people did. But you're right that it affected the way she interacted with others—my sister and me included."

"I've only just met you, but from what I've seen and from what people have said, you're more... I'm not sure the exact word. Approachable, maybe? Warmer? You seem to take into account the feelings of those around you. You say thank you to those who serve. My impression is that you don't take your position as queen for granted, but you do take it seriously."

The quokka seemed like one who'd be skilled at flattery, but Eloise didn't think she was blowing smoke at her. "Thank you. That's kind. But surely all queens take their duty seriously."

"Have you heard of Queen Aglet Wabbit Gumball?"

"Maybe?" Eloise narrowed her brow. "If so, it's only vaguely."

"She's not one of the queens one comes across during lessons. She's more the run-into-her-portrait-in-a-gallery-somewhere-and-wonder-why-you've-never-heard-of-her kind of queen. There are others like that. Queen Blather Quelle Gumball and Queen Yardarm Ignify Gumball spring to mind. They had so little impact that no one bothered to give them a 'the.'"

"A 'the?'"

"A 'the' nickname. Like Queen Gwendolyn the Irritable or Queen Uhhh the Forgetful. There's no record of any Queen Aglet, Quell, or Yardarm the anything in any record I've ever seen. I find that sad."

"That's interesting," said Eloise. "I've often thought about the 'the' nicknames, but I never really considered the queens who don't have one."

"My point is that not all queens took their duties seriously enough to warrant a 'the' descriptor. Mind you, it isn't always seriousness that earns one a nickname. Queen Aubrey the Parasitic springs to mind in that category."

414

"I'll admit that I've sometimes wondered—or worried—what my 'the' might be. Jerome tells me not to think about it."

"He's right. Don't torture yourself with it. That nickname is something history will bestow, or not, years after you've shuffled off to stand with Çalaht. My advice is to do your best, and leave the 'the' to those who come after you."

Eloise nodded. "Solid advice, Ambassador."

The quokka straightened Eloise's gown. "Are you ready to face the parlay with Queen Aglandau?"

"As ready as I'm going to be when trying to wrangle for the future of my queendom."

"Then I think it's time to head to the tent."

Eloise took one last look at herself in the mirror, straightened, and said, "Let's do this."

🕉 65 🕉

THREE

Eloise led Ernestina de Setonix toward the entrance of the pavilion, where Lorch, Jerome, First Advisor, Sylvia Cloister-feld, and Tiberius de Sphenodon waited for her. "Blessings of the day," Eloise said, nodding to each of them.

"Blessings of the day, Your Highness," said First Advisor. "I hear it wasn't the most restful of nights."

"Nerves. But I did at least doze in the end."

"Do you need anything else before your meeting with Queen Aglandau?"

"Other than more and better options, no, I don't think so. Let's get me there."

At First Advisor's nod, a guard moved aside the front flap, and Eloise emerged into a morning lit by a wan, miserable sunlight that barely made itself known through low, threatening clouds. She stopped when she saw what greeted her. Hector and the Nameless One waited for her, both decked out in ceremonial regalia. Beyond them, soldiers in their formal dress uniforms stood at attention, straight-faced and eyes forward, lined up three-deep on either side of the doorway. They formed a corridor that stretched from her tent to the Adequate Wall of the Realms.

"Wow," said Jerome. "That's impressive."

Eloise hadn't expected anything like this at all and was surprised at how humbled and proud she felt. She turned to Tiberius de Sphenodon. "Is this your doing?"

The tuatara shook his head, but there was a glint in his eye. "No, Your Highness. They've done this for you on their own."

"I see. Well, Jerome's right. It's impressive."

Eloise stepped forward into the space the two columns of soldiers created, followed by her Fippledip Council. Unlike that first day on the parade ground with Brigadier General de Odobenus, when she hadn't known any of them, she now recognized most of them from her time battling the obstacle course, and knew more than she expected by name (or at least by nickname). She mounted Hector's back and Lorch got up on the Nameless One. As they moved forward, Eloise nodded acknowledgement to the shining faces and spotless uniforms. A few nodded back, although most remained at rigid attention, eyes unwavering. Striding through them gave Eloise the sense that she wasn't in this queen thing all by herself. Also, it made her feel like she wanted to get a good outcome from the parlay, not for herself, but for them, her soldiers, as well as the rest of the people in her queendom.

Three-quarters of the way down, she passed Squat and Lanky, who both grinned at her. "Good luck, Your Highness," whispered Squat.

"Thanks," she said as she rode past.

Behind her now, Lanky broke discipline and shouted, "Honor to the queen!"

"Honor to the queen!" called Squat in response.

"Honor to the queen!" cried Lanky again.

More soldiers joined in with the reply, as did Jerome. "Honor to the queen! Honor to the queen!"

Soon everyone was joining in, cheer after cheer, until it washed up and down the parallel lines of soldiers like waves on the Gööödeling Sea.

Eloise felt herself moved—not to tears or chagrin, the way she might once have been. Instead, she felt her resolve strengthen, and she held herself taller on Hector's back. Just as she reached the end of their corridor at the Adequate Wall, a powdery snow began falling. Snow, at this time of year. Eloise tried not to think of it as an omen, but of course, that meant she immediately did.

She turned and looked back over the columns of soldiers and raised both arms above her head.

A raucous cheer replaced the more formal call and response, then formed into a chant of, "Go, Three, go! Go, Three, go! Go, Three, go!"

It was the first time she'd heard herself referred to by that name. Her grandmother, the first Eloise Hydra Gumball, had been "One," and the nickname, even today, was hissed in disdain. Her mother, Eloise Hydra Gumball II, had been called "Two," always spoken with affection and respect. For the first time, she was Three, and for now at least, it was said with full-hearted support. She hadn't ever felt this accepted, not since the disaster of her Crown Plonking. No, it went farther back than that. The doubts had begun with Jerome's Naming Ceremony, when she'd made him her champion. That had been a disaster as well.

What a strange feeling it was to stand there, arms in the air, being cheered. Strange, but nice.

She hoped they would feel the same about her once she emerged from the parlay.

❧ 66 ❧

JESTER MOVE

The Adequate Wall gate guards stepped aside as she crossed under the archway. Above her, a heavy iron gate dangled, having been ratcheted up using a complex chain, pulley, and crank system. The bottom of it looked rusty and spiked, like it was meant to convince you to get you out of the way in a hurry if it was being lowered. It struck Eloise as a terrible occupational health and safety hazard.

Which, presumably, had been the point when the thing had been made all those years ago.

She didn't remember ever seeing gates like that when she crossed through the Adequate Wall. Perhaps it was installed when Queen Aggie rebuilt the entryway. Or maybe Eloise just hadn't looked up like that before. It made her wonder if there was a matching gate on the other side.

Then Eloise realized something odd. When she'd gone through the Adequate Wall into The South, there had been guards, customs officers, and tithe assessors from the Western Lands and All That Really Matters on one side and Southie guards, customs officers, and tithe assessors on the other.

Here, there was no one from the Western Lands at all. Just Easties. None of her people were there conducting the queen's business or seeing to her interests.

That would need fixing.

Somehow.

They rode up to the high-tunneled roadway where the customs officers and tithe assessors for both realms conducted searches and collected coin, where everyone dismounted. They all walked to the halfway point, where to both the left and right, stairwells led up to the open space above the wall. There the parlay tent awaited the two partici- pants. At her nod, Lorch turned right and ascended ahead of her, making sure there were no unpleasantries or ambushes waiting at the top.

"Nothing untoward," he called down. "Come on up."

Eloise turned to First Advisor, Jerome, Sylvia Cloisterfeld, Ernestina de Setonix, and Tiberius de Sphenodon. "I guess this is it. Thank you for all you've done to get me here and get me ready."

"It's a historic moment," said Bënnïë-Änn Thëjëts. "Best of luck to you, and may Çalaht guide your words and decisions."

"We await your return," said the tuatara. "Good luck."

"Thank you, both."

The others wished her luck as well, and Eloise turned, settled herself, and headed upstairs.

The simple stone stairwell was lit by oil lamps and smelled of soldier sweat, picnic lunches, and mold. The handrail was smooth wood, polished from decades of use. There were twenty-two steps leading up to the first landing, then twenty-four more to the second, and then a final set of twenty-six. Eloise noticed that the last ones were much less footworn than those at the bottom, as though more people over the years had started the upward journey than had finished it. She wondered why. Was it that hard? Had they been distracted along the way? Were they playing hide-and-seek, so there was no need to go all the way up?

Focus, she scolded herself. *Mind on the task at hand.*

She emerged onto the top of the wall and took in the snow-dusted view of the village of Flachberg and the canton beyond. She could see in the distance that there was a gap in the buildings and a long, bare stretch of dirt-covered land. Eloise pointed to it. "What's that?"

"I'm guessing that's where this section of the Adequate Wall stood before Queen Aglandau had it moved."

Eloise looked down at the surface where she stood. "These stones look fitted, not mortared. And there's moss on them, like they've been here since Çalaht was in diapers. Goodness, those steps must have been moved and put back in the same order they'd been in before. They seem like they've been here forever."

Lorch nodded. "The effort to move it must have been enormous, and it's been done with incredible care and precision."

Eloise shook her head. "Why do such a thing?"

Lorch shrugged. "To make a statement. She's showing you that she can have this kind of thing done, and implying that if she can pull this off, there are other things she can accomplish. Then, there's the obvious— it would be just as much effort to move the wall back, which means it's much more likely to remain here."

"Ugh. Just ugh." Eloise looked up at Lorch. "I'm not looking forward to this."

"You'll be fine, Queen Eloise. I have every confidence in you."

"Really?"

"Really."

"Why? It feels like I'm in over my head all the time, and that all I've done since my crown was plonked is stumble from one thing to the next."

"I can see why it might feel that way. But let me ask this. Which strikes you as easier, parlaying with Queen Aglandau or surviving a plummet over the edge at Mortimer Falls?"

"The parlay."

"Meeting with the Eastie queen or getting yourself out of the Whacking Great Hole, the hugest whole in the realm?"

"I'll take the meeting."

"You've done difficult things, Your Highness. If you've proven anything to anyone—to yourself most of all—it's that you can do difficult things. Keep that in mind."

"Thank you, Lorch." She reached out and touched his forearm. "I appreciate it."

Then Lorch did a very un-Lorch-like thing—he put his hand on top of hers and gave it a squeeze. "Go get 'em, my queen. Show them what Three can do."

She put her other hand on top of his and squeezed back. "OK. I will."

He gave another gentle squeeze, then let go.

"I'd best get going. Don't want to be late."

"No. That would be rude."

"Indeed. One doesn't want to be rude."

The parlay tent was much smaller than the pavilion she'd spent the night in, but still large enough to span from one side of the top of the Adequate Wall to the other, occluding visibility and creating a barrier. Protocol stated that she was to enter from one side and Queen Aggie would go up the other stairway and come in opposite her. The outside of the tent was navy blue with silver trimming, and the Gumball crest, with its weasel on a bushel of onions and one-eyed otter holding a fire poker, looked reassuring and welcoming. The snow falling on the roof didn't stick, which meant it would be warm inside, thank Çalaht. She wouldn't have to shiver through their parlay.

As Eloise approached the tent, she felt the knot in her stomach tighten. Well, no surprise there. Maybe eating breakfast had been a mistake. Tossing her biscuits in front of a fellow monarch probably wouldn't be the first impression she'd like to make. It made her wonder how far away a slippery elm drink might be.

Focus, El, she thought. *You can do this.* She took a deep breath and touched the box with the Star of Whatever for good luck, and to settle herself.

Ducking inside the flap, Eloise saw she'd arrived first. Good. She could get used to the space before Aggie showed up.

The way it was set up fascinated her. A black line running along the floor divided the space in half. The tent material on her side was navy blue and silver inside, like it was outside, but across the line, it was deep olive-green with kalamata-brown trim. A pair of armchairs faced each other by the left-hand wall, spaced three lengths apart, one on either side of the line. Both chairs had a side table and tea service decorated with their respective royal insignias and a heated brazier for warmth. In the middle, a large, empty table straddled the line with a single chair on either side—hers with navy upholstery and Aglandau's in olive. In a back corner on each side was a table with food. Eloise walked over to hers and saw a variety of pastries, fruits, fruit juices, and tea makings, including a kettle and water urn. The food was standard Western Lands breakfast fare. Ernestina de Setonix had assured her that the food would be prepared and delivered by her own people, so would be safe to eat. A glance across the tent at the Eastie queen's food table revealed a variety of jars and dishes, each containing olives. Nothing else, save a loaf of what looked like olive bread, a branch with leaves (Eloise assumed it came from an olive tree), and a water urn and kettle.

Eloise stood for a while in the middle of her side of the tent, a few paces behind the table, and waited for Queen Aglandau. Somewhere in the distance, the horological cuckoo called the top of the hour.

It's show time, Eloise thought.

She composed her features and waited for the Eastern Lands queen's imminent arrival. Eloise wanted to look deliberately calm, alert, and ready.

Minutes passed.

The distant horological cuckoo called the quarter hour. Still no Aglandau.

It was tiring, standing there looking deliberately calm, alert, and ready.

When the half hour was called, Eloise decided she'd had enough standing, and took her seat at the table. She could look deliberately calm, alert, and ready while sitting.

Another quarter hour went past, and another, taking it to a full hour that the queen was late.

Stuff this. Eloise got up, filled the kettle from the urn and put it on the brazier to heat. She picked out a haggleberry tea that smelled good enough that even Jerome would approve, and put a healthy pinch in the pot (Jerome would have said it was more than she needed), ready for the water once it was boiled. Then she flopped into her armchair to wait some more. She could look deliberately calm, alert, and ready while sipping her tea and nibbling on a breakfast muffin.

This is just rude.

It was getting to her, which, clearly, was the point. Aglandau was trying to rattle her with discourtesy and tardiness. A power play. A way of saying that Eloise wasn't important enough to show up on time for. That her time wasn't worth respecting. That *she* wasn't worth respecting.

Once again, Eloise had to wonder if Aglandau would show up at all.

Once the kettle reached the not-quite-boiling temperature she'd learned from Jerome, Eloise poured the water into the pot, let it steep for 87 heartbeats (another Jerome tip), served herself a cup (which Jerome would have found at least adequate), drank it, and ate a muffin

—a blueberry and apple cinnamon mix that wasn't half bad. Then she had a second cup and another half muffin.

Still no sign of the Eastie queen. She was an hour and a half late, according to the horological cuckoo.

Had she gotten the day wrong? No. Otherwise, the tent wouldn't have been prepared the way it was.

No, it was just a jester move on Aggie's part. Eloise had no choice but to let this move play out. For now, at least.

She rooted around in the pocket of her travel cloak, pulled out a hemp bag, and again spilled out the Çalahtist prayer beads that Odmilla had given her.

She began counting and immediately felt her tension easing. She sat in the chair and slid the loop of beads one to the next across her palm. For something to do, she examined the tent and its contents through her fuzzy eye. Nothing particularly jumped out at her as worth noting. Then she listened with her buzzing ear. Again, nothing to note. As she counted, she practiced shifting her focus from good eye to fuzzy eye, good ear to buzzy ear, allowing her perception to move from one to the other and noticing the subtle and not-so-subtle differences that each provided.

A full two and a quarter hours after their parlay was supposed to start, a noise jostled Eloise's attention. Not a noise. Music. A brass melody. Eloise recognized it—a fanfare called "Oi! Youse All Look Sharp! There's a Big Honcho A'Comin!" It was an old and venerable fanfare that Eloise thought had fallen out of favor because it was so pretentious.

Apparently not.

The tent flap slapped open, letting in a flurry of snow. In stepped a frocked-out herald who stood at attention and declaimed in a voice that was much too loud, "Presenting Her Majesty, Queen Aglandau Gaeta Cerignola Ponentine, Shining Light and Sovereign Voice of the Eastern Lands, Plenipotentiary of Peace, She Who is Beloved by All

Her Peoples and Who Brings Forth the Bountiful Harvest from the Olive Groves."

That struck Eloise as a bit over the top, but whatever.

Should she stand?

No. No standing. If Queen Aggie didn't have the decency to show up on time, then Eloise could skip the part of Protocol that would have had her on her feet. She nestled back into her armchair and sipped what must have been her fifth cup of tea.

The flap opened again and in walked one of the most striking women Eloise had ever seen. Ernestina de Setonix had shown her a couple of portraits of the Eastie queen, but they were several years out of date and did nothing to capture Aglandau's actual presence. The Eastern Lands monarch strode into the tent like an olive-green whirlwind. She was incredibly tall, probably two heads higher than Eloise. She wore her hair out, and despite her years, it was as ebony-black and glossy as Hector's mane. Eloise's own Purple Haze-whitened hair was like a dirt-covered mop in comparison. Aglandau's crown was an ornate, finely wrought, if stylized, olive branch laurel with leaves of silver and stems of gold. Heavy make-up spackled smooth her wrinkles and dark green eyeshadow brought ferrets and raccoons to mind. Instead of a formal gown and cloak, she wore exactly what Acting Other Places Advocate Niville Numptorious had reported, a gussied-up version of the breeks and tunic worn by olive growers, in forest-green with black embroidery that mirrored the pattern of her crown. The only thing that marred the first impression was her teeth. They were a greenish brown, stained in the hues of olives. It was impossible to tell if this was deliberate or the result of eating the things all her life, but either way, it was creepy.

"Fuuuuuuuuuuuuuhg me," she muttered, stamping snow off her boots. "It's fuhgging cold out there."

67

PARLAY

Eloise looked at the Eastie queen from her armchair and didn't say anything, since the comment hadn't been directed at her. She took another sip of her haggleberry tea, set it down on the side table, and stood. "Blessings of the day, Queen Aglandau Ponentine. I trust you are well."

The Eastie queen's head turned, and she locked eyes on Eloise with the intense stare of a crazed cassowary ready to do damage. After a moment that stretched much longer than it needed to, she dipped the smallest of nods. "Blessings of the day."

No acknowledgement of Eloise's title. No mention of her name. No apology for her lateness.

And from four small words, Eloise could hear that Queen Aggie had one of the heaviest Eastern Lands accents she'd ever heard—far stronger than former First Advisor Ligurian's. It gave extra syllables to her words, so "Blessings" became "blay-uh-sangs" and "day" was "day-uh." If a jester had wanted to mock the Eastie accent, it would have sounded like Queen Aggie.

"You don't look all that much like her," said Aglandau. "Obviously, you're not as pretty as she was, but there is a family resemblance. Mainly in the nose, which is unfortunate. You'd have been better off if you'd looked more like your father. By Çalaht's toe fungus, Chafed was a looker back in the day. Fuuuuhg me, for sure."

Eloise was taken aback, but remembered First Advisor saying something about her making deliberately negative comments, like backhanded compliments, which were meant to undermine her confidence. It seemed best just to keep her face neutral, ignore Aggie, and wait for her to say something that warranted a response.

Aglandau swirled off her cloak and hung it over the back of her armchair so the heat from the brazier would dry it. Then she walked to her food table and picked up one of the dishes of olives. She flopped into her armchair and ate a dozen olives, one after the other, without even looking at Eloise. "Didn't have brekkie," she mumbled. As she finished each olive, the queen plucked the pit from her mouth and lined it up with the others on her knee, forming a neat row that headed up her leg.

It was one of the more disgusting things Eloise had ever seen.

And maybe Queen Aglandau was on some kind of stimulant, but apart from a slight yellowish tinge to the backs of her hands, there was little visible to betray any problem with her humors, yellow bile or otherwise. The rest of the yellow bile profile, though—the daring, the bitterness, the short temper, the ambition, the decisiveness, and above all, the aggression—those looked like they were pretty spot-on, or at least still on the table.

Eloise watched as Aglandau finished the entire dish, swept the line of seeds into her hand and slid them into her pocket. "You know, I hated your mother."

More aggression. Perhaps return the favor? "Did you now?" said Eloise. "I wouldn't know. She didn't ever talk about you."

Queen Aggie's eye ticked, and she lifted a nostril like she was testing the smell of the comment. "Humph," she grunted and stood to get another dish of olives. She brought it back to her chair and repeated the eating-then-putting-the-pits-on-her-leg thing. It wasn't any less revolting the second time. Again, she went through the whole dish without comment, like stuffing her face was far more important than anything else that might be going on. When finished, she slipped the seeds into a different pocket, like it was important to keep the two kinds apart.

Aglandau crossed her arms and leaned back in her chair, using a pinky finger to dig something out of a molar. She pulled her hand away from her face just long enough to say, "So, you wanted to parlay, start parlaying. Or are you sulking?"

Another disrespect. Eloise cleared her throat quietly and began with some words she'd had rattling around in her head. She was aiming for something that would set a constructive tone and build an initial rapport. Eloise stood up, drew a breath, and launched in. "Queen Aglandau. It is very kind of you to make the time to meet with me at what I'm sure will come to be seen as a historic milestone in the relationship between our two queendoms. We come together in what I hope will be a spirit of cooperation and good faith, for a parlay that I'm sure we both hope will lead to outcomes that will prove mutually... What?"

The Eastie queen had interrupted with a bored wave of the hand that wasn't exploring in her mouth.

"What what?" said Aglandau, her tone possibly mocking.

"What was..." Eloise imitated the bored wave.

"Fuhg me, child. Blah, blah, blah. Yada yada yada. By Çalaht's herniated disc and gangrenous toes, don't blather. Just..." Aglandau waved again. "Just get to it. Some of us have better things to do."

Child? Blather? Better things to do. That told Eloise pretty much everything she needed to know. "Right." She sat back down, picked up her cup and saucer, and had another sip. Then she set them down, clasped her hands on her lap to make sure they didn't shake, and locked eyes on Aglandau. Her blurry one gave her a sense of something off, but she wasn't sure exactly what, so she ignored it for the moment. After what Eloise hoped was a suitable pause, she said the one word that really had been on her mind. "Why?"

The Eastern Queen lifted a single eyebrow. "Why what?"

"Why do what you did? Our two realms have been in relative peace and harmony for decades. Why fracture that in this way, with these hostilities?"

Aglandau shook her head. "The framing of your question is flawed."

"Oh? And how would you frame it?"

"This way: yes, our queendoms have existed in relative peace. Your mother and I managed that, at least. But the Western Lands has been in possession of certain amounts of our territory for much longer. The question is not why break the peace. The question is, why did we wait so long to take back that which is ours, by right and by history?"

Eloise unclasped her hands and slid her palms along her thighs. "Huh." She crossed her arms across her chest and sank into the armchair. "Is that really how you see it?"

The Eastie queen nodded. Just once, but firmly.

Aglandau stood, decanted water into her own kettle and set it on to boil. She plucked olive leaves from a stem and put them in her pot.

Eloise spoke to the older woman's back. "What did my mother say when you represented that position to her at the parlay the two of you had?"

"It didn't come up."

"Really? That surprises me."

"I may have been a few years older than your mother when she and I met, but I was still new to my crown. Not so new as you are to yours, but still new. Certainly, I was as stupid about things back then as you are now. So, no, I didn't bring it up. I should have, though. Might have saved me some effort."

"So, what *did* the two of you discuss?"

"No, no, no." Aglandau wagged her finger, then plucked out another olive. "If your dearly departed mother didn't see fit to break our confidence, then I won't, either. What happened last time is off limits. Suffice it to say, it was less pleasant than our little chat here so far, but was adequate for the task of establishing that we'd stay out of each other's way."

Eloise looked at her. "Fine. So, what *are* you willing to discuss?"

Aglandau smacked her lips and lined up another olive pit. "You're the one who wanted to parlay. Go ahead. I'm more or less listening."

Eloise had no idea how to proceed. She'd expected some sort of dialog. An exchange of ideas. Offers and counter offers. She wasn't prepared for disinterest, insolence, and dismissiveness. The way this was going, it didn't seem like their talks were destined to go down in the annals of parlay history as anything resembling fruitful. With nothing else for it, she decided to be direct. "I demand an end to the hostilities you've instigated, and I demand a return of Flachberg, both the town and the canton. I'm happy to end up with things as they were before this episode began."

That got her attention.

Queen Aggie set the olive bowl down on the side table, pocketed the pits, and leaned forward in the armchair, coming dangerously close to the line that divided one side from the other. Eloise slid her chair back a little to maintain distance. Fierceness replaced the flippant tone in Aglandau's voice. "Hostilities. That's the word you're using?"

Eloise met her gaze. "You invaded Flachberg. Took land. You had the Çalaht-cursed Adequate Wall moved, for Çalaht's sake. 'Hostilities' seems a perfectly apt word. What would you call it?"

"I would say that I was righting a very old wrong."

"Would you now?"

"Yes, child, I would. It's a wrong that dates back to your Queen Gwendolyn, who, by all historical accounts, was, with due respect to our mole-like mammal subjects, a first-class shrew. Certainly, poor King Brüüütus thought so. Once he finished thinking with his nethers and saw the result of the attentions he visited upon Gwendolyn, he tried to back-pedal. Not the most honorable choice he might have made, but there you go. Instead of taking it like a grown-up or working things out with him, she summoned her armies and attacked him and his realm. I assume you know the rest."

"That's not how I would characterize the story. Queen Gwendolyn was the wronged party in that story. He got her in the family way. Brüüütus then left her in the lurch after promises were made and not kept. Some desire for retribution is understandable."

"Typical Western Lands bias." Aglandau shook her head in disbelief. "You're saying that having half his kingdom wiped when it was engulfed by a deadly purple fog would be considered a proportionate response?"

"No. I wouldn't go that far. It was extreme," said Eloise. "The spell that was cast got out of hand, for sure." This was something Eloise knew better than anyone. "But what does that have to do with your realm? The dispute was between the Half Kingdom and the Western Lands and All That Really Matters."

"The Eastern Lands queen at the time, Queen Arbosana the Badly Done By, tried to intervene and bring some sanity to the situation. Gwendolyn met her efforts with derision and aggression. She sent troops and seized Flachberg as a way of saying, 'Bite me, Arbosana.' When the Adequate Wall of the Realms went up, Flachberg was on the wrong side. From my point of view, all I've done is return this part of the world to its rightful, historic realm."

How reasonable that sounded. Too reasonable. "You'll understand if I don't share that perspective."

"No, but then you've probably been lied to about the history there since you could hold a slate. I'm willing to ignore that particular ignorance."

Eloise suppressed a desire to reach out and whack the old queen. Was she trying to goad her? Did she just have an unfortunate manner? Or was it deliberate, calculated to get a rise out of Eloise?

Aglandau looked around like she needed another olive fix. "Tell you what. I'm prepared to end what you've called 'hostilities.'"

"You are?" Eloise hadn't expected this. "Well, that's good."

"There would be conditions, of course."

Eloise tried not to roll her eyes. "And what would those be?"

"You formally cede Flachberg back to its rightful realm—mine, just to be clear—in addition to the lands within one hundred strong lengths of the Flachberg border."

"Really now."

"You also formally acknowledge the wrongdoings perpetrated by your ancestors on my lands and people, and pay reparations for crimes committed."

"Reparations. I'm supposed to pay for supposed crimes committed two centuries ago. That's a joke, right?"

The Eastern Lands queen looked at her. "No. No joke. Wrongs have been committed. They must be righted. I'm with Queen Gwendolyn on that one."

"Anything else? Am I supposed to make you tea in bed every morning? Maybe give you a shoulder massage whenever you want it? Perhaps you'd like me to sing lullabies to your olive groves."

"No. That's my offer. Take it or leave it."

"Those are ridiculous demands. How about instead—"

"Which part of 'take it or leave it' don't you understand?"

"I'm just trying to suggest—"

Aglandau stood, stepping on, but not crossing, the dividing line. "You. Don't. Fuhgging. Get. It. Do. You."

Eloise stood as well, meeting both her gaze and her tone. "Get. What?"

The Eastern Lands queen jabbed a finger toward her. "You are apparently clueless, absolutely blind clueless, about how things stand."

Eloise jabbed back. "Clueless? I have dead bodies and land stolen. There are a couple of clues right there."

"Open your eyes, child. Have you looked at your soldiers recently? They couldn't fight their way out of a blancmange. Your weapon stores are practically empty and what's there is either dull, forgotten, broken, or rusted. Just like your soldiers. Sure, you've spent a few weeks trying to knock the rust off of them, but it'll take years before you have something that could be considered much of a threat."

"I... That... That's not—"

"There's more. Lots more. Like, who do you think you might turn to? Who will come to your aid?" Aglandau's expression changed from angry to smug. "Did you know that your sister has entered into an alliance with me?"

Eloise forced a laughed. "What? That's ludicrous." It almost sounded genuine. Inside, she wanted to scream, and she felt unwanted reactions flitting across her face, betraying her turmoil. Was this a lie? A negotiating gambit? The truth?

The older woman smiled, her olive-stained teeth adding a tinge of horror to her leer. "You *didn't* know. I thought that might be the case. Yes, your very own sister—and the smarter one, from all appearances—has tied herself to me and my queendom. She's in no position to take your side in any dispute. I made sure of that weeks and weeks ago. And all it cost me was a ridiculously small pile of coin."

"She wouldn't. No way."

"Next time you write her, ask her how she's funding her improvements."

Eloise's head felt like it was going to pop. The old bag had to be lying. Had to be. How could Johanna possibly betray her like this? For a stack of coin? Impossible. Yet her buzzing ear didn't give her the sense of a lie. Her weird eye felt the same. And Aglandau looked so smug and sure of herself. Maybe it was true.

"So think about it. Help from the Half Kingdom is off the board, and Johanna couldn't afford to, even if she wanted to. That addle-brained uncle of yours rode the place into the ground. You could look to The South, maybe. Queen Onomatopoeia is at least marginally competent. Maybe she could help you out, if you can pry her away from her Çalahtist dalliances. I swear, the woman can pray a devotional house minder under a pew. What a fuhgging waste of time. That leaves the Central Ranges. Those horse nimrods may look fierce, and who fuhgging knows, they might even *be* fierce. But they are so insular. They have their noses shoved so far up under each other's tails that they're not going to be much use to you. Besides..." Aglandau waggled her fingers. "No opposable thumbs. They might be able to kick you from here to Çalaht's holy home in the heavens, but they're no match for modern weapons. An arrow or two, and they're gone. And they know it. Why do you think they keep to themselves?"

Eloise swallowed and felt emotions crater in on themselves. If Aglandau was right, she was more isolated than she ever could have dreamed.

"But why?" Eloise sounded weak and pathetic, even to herself. "Just because you could?"

"Isn't that obvious? I needed a distraction." The Eastie queen was gloating now. "My people were all riled up about migrant olive pickers and failing olive orchards. I needed to give them something else to focus on. I couldn't very well attack Her Maj Ono. She knows what she's doing and would have thumped me, or at least made it hard. You, on the other hand, are still wet behind your wee pokey-outy ears. You're barely crown-plonked. So I took advantage of the opportunity. You can hardly blame me for that."

Eloise could, and very much did. But she resisted saying it out loud.

"It was such a ripe olive ready to pluck. I rolled in and snatched Flachberg out from under your very prominent nose."

Eloise sat back down in her armchair, breathing fast and blinking hard to keep tears from spilling. If Eloise's vision of what happened in Flachberg was true, then Aglandau was lying to her face. She hadn't taken advantage of the opportunity. She'd *created* it, sending that three-eyed snake to destabilize and sow chaos. The woman had had her mother killed and there wasn't a flicker of it in her eyes. But other than her vision, there was no proof. What could Eloise say?

The Eastie queen stepped across the black dividing line, invading Eloise's space. She crowded forward, towering over her. "You are truly, singularly unprepared to wear your crown, aren't you?"

"I don't think—"

"No, I can tell you don't."

"I meant, I don't—"

The Eastie queen lifted a hand for silence, like Eloise had seen her mother do a hundred thousand times. There was menace in the movement. "It's clear that there is nothing useful left for me to say, and you obviously have nothing to offer. I knew this would be a waste of time, but I'm disappointed at how profoundly so it has been. Next time we meet—*if* we happen to meet again—there will be much less yammering and much more..." Aglandau stopped, like she was searching for the perfect word. "Much more doing." She leaned forward to whisper in Eloise's ear, her bearing menacing. Her breath reeked of decaying olives and a soul full of malice. "Enjoy my parting gift," she purred.

Eloise's blurry eye flared with the sense of *Danger!* and her ear buzzed like a rabid hacksaw on bone. A cold fear shot through her.

Queen Aglandau Ponentine turned her back and, without a backward glance, left the tent. Outside, Eloise could hear her say, "Proceed."

Eloise jumped from her chair and ran for her own tent flap. Whatever was about to happen was going to be bad.

Very bad.

68

DETACHED AND PANICKED

E loise exploded from the parlay tent onto the snow-covered upper level of the Adequate Wall. She scanned left and right, but nothing looked out of the ordinary.

Lorch rushed forward, face puzzled. "Queen Eloise?"

"Aggie has something planned. Something very not good." She continued looking around, but nothing struck her as amiss. From below, there was a sudden scraping sound, a deep rumble, and the groan of a chain under stress. "What's that?"

Lorch listened, brow furrowed. Then his eyes went wide. "The gate. They're closing the gate. With you on this side."

They sprinted into the stairwell, with Lorch taking the lead, but soon had to slow. The oil lamps that had lit the way when they'd gone up were dowsed and they found themselves descending into complete darkness. Eloise felt for the handrail and tried to remember how many steps there'd been.

"Landing," said Lorch.

Halfway down, Eloise heard shouts coming from below. An argument had broken out. She thought she heard Jerome and Hector yelling, but couldn't make out the words.

"Second landing," said Lorch, hustling ahead of her.

The yelling got louder as the light from below lit the last stretch of steps, and she could hear that the grinding sound of the gate being lowered had slowed but not stopped.

Seven steps from the bottom, she could see the commotion. Half a dozen Eastie guards stood a few lengths away from the stairs, in a semi-circle, blocking the way. Lorch pulled up short and his hand moved to his pommel. Beyond them, two dozen Eastern Lands guards formed a wall, facing off against Hector, the Nameless One, Sylvia Cloisterfeld, and about the same number of Western Lands soldiers, one of whom had Tiberius de Sphenodon on his shoulder looking as angry as she'd ever seen him. They faced off below the nasty-looking gate, which was halfway down and getting lower. Swords had not yet been drawn, and while no one was pummeling anyone yet, it looked like it would be mere seconds before red stained the snow-flecked ground.

She didn't need her blurry eye or buzzy ear to tell her this was as dangerous as it got.

"Stand back! Move back!" bellowed the loudest of the Eastie guards. "We've been ordered to close the border!"

Hector, the Nameless One, and the others stood beneath the gate arguing. Jerome, on Hector's back, chittered with rage. "Not with our queen still in there!"

"Lower the gate!" demanded the loud one.

The team controlling the crank saluted a "Sir! Yes, sir!" and resumed lowering the gate, threatening to impale everyone below it with the rusty, spiky bits at the bottom.

One of the six guards blocking the stairway exit stepped forward. "Queen Eloise, you're to come with us, ma'am."

That wasn't going to happen. "No." The single syllable came out with a calm she didn't actually feel.

"By order of Her Majesty, Queen Aglandau Gaeta Cerignola Ponentine, I hereby formally accuse you of false representation to a monarch and cause you to be detained at Queen Aglandau's direction until—"

"Buzzard Left Splutter 30 Joust Eagle!" yelled Lorch.

What? Why would Lorch yell out a hockey sacking play? Didn't they have better things to do, like escaping with their lives and not getting stabbed or sliced? Plus, Buzzard Left Splutter 30 Joust Eagle was a dumb play, a trick-filled gimmick of a play. You didn't call that one unless you were behind by way too many points, time was running out, all you had left was doing something desperate, and the other team had never seen the play before.

Oh.

"On two!" she called, letting him know she'd understood. Eloise hunched down, in a ready stance. Lorch did the same in front of her. "One! Two!"

Lorch screamed forward toward the right side of the blocking line, while Eloise did the same to the left. In unison, they spun and put their backs to the guards, yelled "Joust!" and ran back to where they started. They repeated this with Lorch going left and Eloise going right, spinning, yelling "Joust!" and returning to the starting spot.

The puzzled looks on the guards' faces were precious.

Eloise and Lorch faced the guards two steps from the bottom, standing side by side with arms spread wide. They began an arm-wavy, choreographed, clapping dance movement and chanted, "Banger hanger slanger slouch! Lather blather marsupial pouch! I'm a croissant, I'm a sledge. I'm gonna crawl right under your hedge." They hopped forward like inebriated wallabies with arms up in front of them and hands bent like short, useless paws, grunting "Hhnnurk, hhnnurk" on each bounce. One length from the guards, they dropped to all fours like they were going to crawl through their legs. The Easties hunkered low, ready to stop them.

"Badger bucket!" cried Lorch. That was Eloise's cue to plant a foot in his laced hands. With a heave, he stood and flung her up and over the guards.

Lorch must have been scared, or maybe his battle instincts had kicked in, because he pitched her higher and farther than anyone had ever thrown her before in a Buzzard Left Splutter 30 Joust Eagle. While Eloise went airborne, drawing their eyes and arms upward, Lorch ran through them like the hockey sacking left flutter that he was. He flattened the two in the middle, and stiff-armed the other four, shoving them out of the way, leaving Eloise plenty of room to vault well clear of them.

Plenty of room, that is, to crash into the back row of guards facing off against Sylvia, Jerome, Hector and the Nameless One. They'd put their biggest soldiers up front, so the one she hit most directly wasn't that much bigger than her. He went down in a thunk of armor and weapons, and Eloise tried to use his momentum to propel herself past him into a roll, but their legs got tangled and she splatted onto the cobblestone, scraping a tear into one of her sleeves. As she scrambled back to her feet, Lorch charged past her, clearing a path through guards that were turning around to see what was happening behind them.

"It's her!" yelled the loud guard. He waved wildly at the crank team. "Drop the gate! Drop it now! Don't let her pass!"

"Sir! Yes, sir!"

She could hear Lorch yelling at the others, "Back! Back! Don't get caught!" There was the sound of latches clacking and catches freeing. Her buzzing ear filled with a moan, like the gate was warning her not to push past it. The gap Lorch had created was filling in behind him with armored bodies and grasping hands, all of which were bent on stopping her. It was like the hockey sacking game from hell.

Eloise's sense of time went wonky. An emotional, panicked part of her mind supplied a surprising string of not-very-queenlike obscenities, which she hoped her mouth wasn't delivering to the world around her, but she couldn't be sure it wasn't. A detached, rational part of her thought, *That moaning in Buzzing Ear is certainly interesting. I wonder what Blurry Eye might have to say about all of this.* She closed her good eye, to which the panicked part of her remarked that she needed both eyes for depth perception, which might be rather handy when facing a pack of armored adversaries and a plummeting gate. She left the panicked part's commentary aside for just a moment and focussed on what Blurry Eye might be seeing. It was a glowing, white looping squiggle. No, not a squiggle, more of a circuitous path, a kind of drawing that wound around the people in front of her in an improbable way. It reminded her of the kind of thing a coach might draw to instruct players on how to conduct a play—if said coach had spent a month on a bender after being granted three wishes by the Preposterous Fairy. She had no idea if Blurry Eye was any kind of hockey sacking expert, but this was a pretty clever approach to the problem at hand, even if it looked like she was more likely to end up knocked onto her rear than to clear the gate.

The whiteness of the path began to tinge with red. The detached part of her thought about the redness, and decided it was more of a scarlet or ruby red than a rose or brick red. Less bright than a cherry red, but it had much more pep than blush red, berry red, or garnet. The panicked part of her screamed, *For the love of Çalaht stop considering hues and follow the path before it turns red with your blood.* The detached part of her thought about that, giving it full consideration. It decided that it agreed with the panicked part's sentiment, even if it had issues with its word choice. It was, indeed, really time to get moving.

Keeping her good eye closed, Eloise strained every muscle as she ran, following the path spelled out by Blurry Eye. She dodged, ducked, spun, and jumped, and to her amazement, it seemed to be working. The Eastie guards seemed to just miss her or be looking right where she wasn't. As she moved, the path got redder (the detached part noting that it headed from jam red to wine red to currant red, but more like a black currant than a red currant, which was a little confusing in its naming, but there you go, at which the panicked part of her screamed, *Stop it stop it stop it!*), like the color was warning her that time was running out.

Which it was.

Blurry Eye's path brought her closer to the closing gate, but with each step, Buzzing Ear's moan became more ominous (from lamentation to cry to wail to howl to keen to—*Stop it stop it stop it!*). The gate was gaining speed. Lorch crossed under it, which was great. Hector, the Nameless One, Sylvia and the others also fell back so they wouldn't get hurt. But she saw fear in their eyes, worry for her that she'd be stuck on the other side. Or worse.

The detached part of her knew that was a distinct possibility, given how fast the gate chain was unspooling. The odds of her getting through without serious head trauma—

The panicked part of her shoved the detached part of her aside with an exasperated groan and took over completely. Eloise ignored all sense of self preservation and rationality, and shot toward the plunging gate like her life depended on getting past it.

Which, of course, it did.

Heartbeats seemed to take hours. The path shortened as she hurtled along it, and it went from the badly named current to a soothing merlot to a nice shade of mahogany. The detached part of her fought back and warned that this was not a smart thing to do. *Look at the angles*, it said. *Look at the speed of descent. You're about to have a rusty gate spike probe the inner workings of your mind.*

Eloise ignored it, leaning into the panicked side's *Gaaaahhhhhhhh!* There was no way she'd let herself be trapped on the Eastie side of the gate. She'd rather get spiked than submit to Queen Aglandau's control.

Step. *This is a terrible idea.* Step. *Gaaaahhhhhhhh!* Step. *Wow, that gate's coming down fast.* Step *Gaaaahhhhhhhh!* Step. *Actually, panicked is right. Gaaaahhhhhhhh!*

ANDREW EINSPRUCH

Should she dive past it? No, that would leave her legs in the way. Better to be pierced through the skull than trapped with skewered, crushed legs.

Eloise ran even harder. Lungs bursting, heart hammering, legs a blur.

She cleared the gate, feeling the rush of air tickling the back of her neck as it went down behind her.

That was close, thought Detached.

Panicked was still back at *Gaaaahhhhhhhh!*

Something grabbed her by the neck, choking her. It was like a giant had grabbed her from behind. Eloise's feet and legs flew out in front of her and she slammed down hard onto her back. Air tried to whoosh through her constricted throat, but it couldn't make it out so instead compressed painfully in her chest. She tried to sit up, but the giant seemed to be holding her in place. Eloise glanced to the side, but couldn't see much more than a forest of horse and human legs. There was a lot of yelling going on, but that had been the case for a while.

She looked up and saw Sylvia Cloisterfeld. Her mother's champion's sword was drawn and arcing down toward her.

The gate hadn't killed her. But Sylvia looked like she was going to do it instead.

Why? She'd known Sylvia her whole life. She *liked* Sylvia. Admired her —her fitness, her knowledge, her skill with weapons. Heck, Eloise even liked her singing. But that Master Cloisterfeld was a murderous, regicidal traitor? That one took her by surprise. It just didn't make sense.

Yet, here it was. As Eloise's eyes darkened from the choking, her sense of betrayal was profound. Deep and painful. Sylvia really must have hated her to let her go through all this, just to take her life now. She must have been Aglandau's backup plan or something. Confusing, but stranger things had happened.

444

She wondered if she'd be invited to stand at Çalaht's side. Would her mother and grandmother be there to welcome her?

She hoped so.

Unable to move and losing consciousness, Eloise braced herself, ready to feel the sword cleave through her forehead.

She heard the swish of air, the sound of metal on cobblestone.

Not metal on skin and bone.

Eloise felt the giant let go of her neck.

Sylvia wasn't a traitor or a murderer. She was a savior. A slayer of giants, apparently.

"Sorry about your cloak, Your Highness," said Sylvia. She grabbed Eloise's arm and helped her to her feet. "The gate caught it. Is your neck alright? That looked nasty."

"Fine," Eloise rasped. "Thank you." Her legs were wobbly, and she had to lean on Sylvia to stay up.

"Thank me later. No time." Cloisterfeld pointed to Lorch. "Get her out of here. We'll cover you. Look!" The gate was being raised again. It wouldn't be long before Eastie guards poured through, trying to capture her.

Lorch nodded. "Apologies, Queen Eloise."

"For what?"

He grabbed her under the arms, lifted, and swung her up. Lorch never touched her. Well, not *never* never. There was the time he had to save her from the soldier's cold. And the time he reset her dislocated shoulder and splinted her wrist. And that moment just before she went into the parlay. But he never did anything so personal as pick her up and swing her around like they were dancing. Plus, it tickled, which seemed completely inappropriate. Still, it was kind of nice in a fleeting way, which Eloise hadn't expected.

Lorch spun once to get momentum, then landed her on a horse's back, right behind Jerome. "Hector, go!"

"Hold on, Your Highness," said the horse. Hector wheeled around and took off, away from the Adequate Wall of the Realms as fast as he could gallop. Within seconds, Lorch and the Nameless One were racing along next to them.

That's when the sky darkened with flying death.

❦ 69 ❧

THWIP!

Eloise hunched forward, threading her fingers into Hector's mane. There was an audible *thwip thwip thwip thwip thwip thwip!* Eloise looked up to see a rain of arrows arcing through the sky. Archers on top of the Adequate Wall had let loose hundreds of them.

Moments later, shrieks of alarm and pain came from the Western Lands encampment. Screams like she'd never heard before, not in such numbers. Those arrows wouldn't have just struck soldiers. They would have hit anyone in their path, whether they held a sword or a spatula.

Eloise didn't think much of Aglandau's parting gift. "We have to go help them," she said.

"El, we have to get you out of here," said Jerome. "Nothing's more important than that. We have to get you to safety."

"Jer, I'm their queen. I can't just ignore what's happening. I won't high-tail it out of here to save my own skin."

"And what do we do when the next arrow volley comes?" The chipmunk turned around to look her in the eye. "Stand there ready to be a pincushion?"

"There will be shields at the encampment. We can grab some and be ready."

"Jerome's right," said Hector, breathing hard at full gallop. "It's risky. Very risky."

"Please. Just do it."

Hector looked at the Nameless One, then swiveled an eye up to look at Lorch. They gave small nods of assent. "Yes, Your Highness," he said. Without breaking stride, the horses swerved toward the cries of distress.

Lorch looked back and forth between the Adequate Wall and where they were headed. "If there is any upside, it's that the arrows have travelled a very long distance."

"So?" said Jerome.

"Many will have fallen short. Those that make it will be more likely to wound and maim than kill."

"That's good, I guess. But it'll be cold consolation to anyone who's been hit."

They arrived to find the camp in chaos. Arrows were everywhere. Some stuck into tents, others had buried themselves into the ground. But many had found unsuspecting targets, and there were signs of blood everywhere.

Eloise jumped off Hector and ran to the first injured person she saw, a woman wearing kitchen-wench garb who stared dumbly at an arrow protruding from her calf.

"Please, Queen Eloise," pleaded Lorch. "You must take some sort of shelter. I can bring the wounded to you, if you insist, but I can't have you exposed."

"Fine." Eloise looked around. "How about under that wagon?"

"Yes, Your Highness. That will be good."

"Jerome, come with me." She patted her shoulder, and he jumped onto it. "Hector, Nameless One, please find something to stand under, and keep watch."

"Yes, Queen Eloise," said Hector.

"Lorch, see if you can find the healers, or at least healing supplies. If people can come to where I am, I'll render what aid I can. Let's get started."

"Yes, my queen."

Eloise and Jerome jogged toward the wagon. "Hang on," she said as they approached it. "This looks familiar."

"Is it the one you stood on to give your speech before we left?"

"I... I think it is," she said. "Is someone crying? Nörbert? Nörbert de Lupus? Is that you? Are you OK?"

The Chihuahua appeared from the other side of the wagon. His eyes were red and wet. From laughing. "Yes, *gasp!* Queen Eloise. How *gasp!* can I be of service?"

"What happened?"

"I was shot in the ass."

"That's not funny!" The voice was Abelardo de Burro's. The donkey emerged from the far side of the cart with an arrow poking out of in his flank. "It hurts!"

"I know, I know. Sorry," said Nörbert. "It's one of those once in a life-time things, though. I have to take advantage of it while I can."

"I don't think you could find a less appropriate time to make that kind of comment." Eloise stepped closer to look at the wound. "Don't take offense, Abelardo. Nörbert's having a stress reaction." She shot the Chihuahua a sharp look. "Aren't you."

"Yes, Your Highness. I'm sure stress is behind this. Stress has reared up. My amusement should be put in arrears. That's fundamental. There butt for the grace of Çalaht go I."

"Nörbert!" brayed Abelardo. "Did I make fun of you when your nose got stuck in the jam pot and we had to go for help? That Blue Heeler healer made fun of you, but I didn't chide you once. Not once."

The Chihuahua had the grace to look abashed.

"Can you please, for the love of Çalaht's emaciated mien and all that is holy, get this thing out of me!"

"Of course, of course, of course," said the dog. "Sorry. I don't mean to be a pain," he tried to repress the next bit, but couldn't, "in the derriere."

Abelardo scowled. "Nörbert de Lupus, do you want to walk back to Brague?"

Lorch returned then with half a dozen people who needed medical aid. "Miraculously, I don't think anyone is dead. Plenty of injuries, but no fatalities. If you ask me, Queen Aglandau wasn't really trying to kill everyone."

"No?" said Jerome, tail swishing. He gestured to the surrounding damage. "What was she trying to do, then?"

"Send a message."

"What message?" asked Eloise.

"I'd say this is the arrow equivalent of a raised middle finger."

Eloise scoffed. "Really?"

"That's what I think, Queen Eloise. If she'd wanted to do real damage, she could have done so in a dozen different ways. Shoot more arrows in that volley, or reload and send a second wave. Or target the soldiers instead of the encampment. Or send a battalion against our two hundred. There are many, many outcomes that could have been much worse. So, yes, I think this is more or less 'up yours.'"

"Her last words to me were 'Enjoy my parting gift.'"

"There you have it. She wasn't serious. This is her 'gift.'"

Jerome snorted. "What an ars—"

Running footsteps. Dozens of them. Hundreds. The sound of fleeing. And from further away, what sounded like more footsteps, but those were more orderly, more regular. Marching.

Eloise turned toward the sound. The running was from her soldiers, returning to the encampment. One of them carried Tiberius de Sphenodon. The soldier had blood on him, but it wasn't clear if it was the soldier's or the tuatara's. "Master Sergeant!" Eloise called.

"Your Highness. You're still here?" He tapped the soldier on the arm. "Put me down here."

She placed him on the ground and saluted Eloise, then the tuatara. "Ma'am. Sir." Then she left for some other errand.

"I came to help the wounded after the arrow attack. What happened? Are you hurt?"

He raised his right foreleg, the damaged one. It was wrapped in bloody cloth. "Nothing fatal, ma'am. I won't be brushing my teeth with this anytime soon. But it's nothing that didn't happen once before, many decades ago. But we need to abandon the encampment and leave."

"Why?"

"It looks like she's sending out a battalion. Possibly a whole regiment or some kind of brigade. It was hard to say from where we were."

"What..." Eloise hesitated to ask, but now was not the time to hide her ignorance. "What's the difference?"

"With respect, now's probably not the time for a discussion of military basics, Queen Eloise. We need to go. We need *you* to go."

"Shouldn't we stand and fight?" asked Eloise. "Protect our turf?"

The old tuatara shook his head. "With respect, ma'am, I don't think we should. We are just two hundred strong. The soldiers have accompanied you, but let's face it, it's a fancy escort. We were enough to protect you in transit from bandicoots and other brigands, but we were never coming here to exert serious force. This was supposed to be an exercise in diplomacy, not a military action."

"But the diplomacy has failed. So it's time for the other."

The tuatara looked sad. "This is not the time or place to make a stand. We don't have the numbers, the tactical advantage, a defensible position, the equipment, the training, or the experience. You're right that if you gave the order to stand and fight, I believe these men and women, no matter their species, would do that for you. But you'd be wasting their blood. Your Highness, this is a time for living to fight another day. Please, Your Highness. Go. We'll cover your retreat, but retreat is the correct choice. This time."

First Advisor Thëjëts and Sylvia Cloisterfeld ran up to them. Her mother's champion favored a leg, but did not have any visible injuries, and First Advisor simply looked livid. "Your Highness," said Thëjëts. "You're still here?"

"What's happening up there?" asked Tiberius de Sphenodon, his head indicating where she'd come from.

"It's weird," said Cloisterfeld. "The Easties are coming out of the gate and there are a lot of them. But they're not moving fast. It's like they don't care if we're there or not. We can stick around and fight or we can go."

"Another message," said Lorch. "Queen Aglandau is not trying to slaughter us. She's saying we don't really matter. She can afford to let us go."

"Champion Lacksneck is right," said First Advisor. "She's communicating about a hundred different things at the moment, but top among them is that she has no respect for you, your rule, or your might." She hung her head. "I really thought the parlay might work. I'm sorry, Your Highness. I shouldn't have counseled you to go ahead."

"It was my choice." Eloise gritted her teeth. "That woman is really starting to get on my nerves. Tiberius has suggested retreat."

"Oh, you should absolutely run for it," said Cloisterfeld. "No point standing here and getting smashed like spuds on their way to a puree. We'll get everyone away and cover your retreat." She gestured around her. "You'll have to give up what's here, but that's just stuff. Stuff like this can be replaced. Master Sergeant is right. You should skedaddle. We all should. We'll be overrun within the hour."

Eloise felt emotions flooding her, pooling in her guts and filling her chest. Rage mixed with embarrassment, despondence with fear. This was really happening. Her parlay had been a disaster. Her defense of her position was nowhere close to adequate. Now she was supposed to tuck her tail and slink back home to come up with some other plan. "I feel such a failure."

Tiberius de Sphenodon reached out and touched her calf.

She looked at her Fippledippers. Devoted, patient, and, above all, supportive. She couldn't risk losing them. Not them or anyone. Not with the way things stood with her realm. Eloise dropped her shoulders, not realizing how far hunched into them she'd been. "Fine. We go. And we come up with a solution that doesn't involve getting rolled over by Eastie soldiers."

They all nodded.

Lorch looked around. "Hector! Nameless One. We're leaving!"

As the horses trotted over, Eloise said, "Thanks for keeping everyone safe. For keeping *me* safe. I look forward to seeing you back in Brague."

"Yes, Your Highness," said the tuatara. "We'll see you there."

Moments later, Hector and the Nameless One galloped at full speed across the landscape. As they ran, so did her thoughts. She replayed the parlay in her head. The waiting for it to start should have told her everything she needed to know without having set eyes on the Eastie queen. Her manner was so smug, so dismissive, and it grew worse in her reliving of it. And an alliance with Johanna? That cut deep. How could her sister have done this? She knew Flachberg had been taken, but she had come to an accord with the Eastern Lands anyway. That betrayal stung as much as anything else.

As she held on to Hector's mane, Jerome in front of her and Lorch and the Nameless One flying along beside her, she realized that First Advisor Thëjëts had been wrong. Very wrong. Queen Aglandau was most definitely a monster. The old olive-sucker was an ill-tempered, duplicitous monster who wanted to eat Eloise's reign and realm. She'd agreed to parlay, then sucker-punched her. There'd never been a hint of good faith in her actions, only a patina of it, the thinnest of veneers.

There was no way she'd let Aglandau take her queendom. No way at all. She'd save her queendom if it killed her.

Even if the odds of that outcome were exceedingly high.

⚜

The series finishes with Eloise trying to work out how to survive the direct threat from the Eastern Lands. It'll take a miracle to keep her throne and her land. **Read The Magic of Last Resort to find out how it all ends.**

⚜

Want to read more about Eloise and Jerome? Six months before the start of *The Purple Haze*, they
played hooky from Court and headed out for a stolen adventure. It goes well. And then it really doesn't. **Claim your copy of The Wombanditos today to find out what happened!**

⚜

And if you're wondering just what exactly happened at their Thorning Ceremony that caused Eloise and Johanna to go from being as close as twins can be to as estranged, then you'll definitely want to check out the standalone prequel novel, *The Thorning Ceremony*. I promise you, you'll never guess what caused the rift.

THANK YOU

Thank you for reading *The Eastie Threat*. Reviews are crucial for helping other readers discover new books to enjoy. If you want to share your love for Eloise, Jerome, and all the gang, please leave a review. I'd really appreciate it!

Recommending my work to others is also a huge help. Feel free to give this book and the whole series a shout-out in your favourite book recommendation group to spread the word.

NEXT IN SERIES

Her attempts at parlaying peace completely failed. With no military and no funds, how can she hold on to her queendom?

If you like characters seriously in over their heads, strange magic, and perfectly crafted prose, then you'll love this royally rich rollick. *Read The Magic of Last Resort today* (and get it using the QR code below).

NEXT IN SERIES

ACKNOWLEDGMENTS

It is always joy to get to say thank you to those who have helped me bring this book to the world.

Tamsin Dean Einspruch, our daughter, has from the word go been my first port of call for ideas, perspective, and thoughts on words. She is my first reader, and has been with this story and the whole series every step of the way. Over and over she has helped me stay headed in the right direction. Thank you, sweetie.

Many, many thanks also to Cheryl Hannah, Olivia Martinez, and Brian Busby for their beta reads. Cheryl has been, for each of these books, the first person outside my family to read the manuscript, and her encouragement always gives me the heart needed to keep going. Olivia brings an always-keen eye to the words, and she and Brian provided very different perspectives to what they read. Valuable and valued input all.

Thank you to my editor, Vanessa Lanaway, and my proofreader, Abigail Nathan. Sharp eyes and red pens, both. Y'all rock. It's that simple.

Thank you to Maria Spada for the wonderful cover.

As always, a massive thank you to my bride, Billie Dean, who reads and gives incredible input on everything I write, who has encouraged me forever, and who believed in my creative soul much, much earlier than I ever did. I love you and I thank you. L^3.

And finally, thank you to you, whoever you are, for picking up this book and having a read. I appreciate it very much, and I'll see you in *The Magic of Last Resort*.

ABOUT THE AUTHOR

Andrew Einspruch is fond of the wordy, the nerdy, and the funny, which means that if you arranged for him to have lunch with Weird Al Yankovic, Tom Lehrer, William Gibson, and any of the Monty Python guys, he'd be your friend forever. Visit his web site for a complete list of his books at andreweinspruch.com.

Andrew is an ex-pat Texan living in Australia, and is the co-founder of the not-for-profit charity the Deep Peace Trust, which fosters deep peace and non-violence for all species. With his wife and daughter, he runs the Trust's farm animal and wild horse sanctuary. (You can see why there's the odd animal or two in his books.)

If pressed, he'll deny he ever coded in COBOL for a bank.

If you haven't done so yet, use the QR code below to claim your copy of the standalone prequel, *The Wombanditos*.

www.ingramcontent.com/pod-product-compliance
Lightning Source LLC
Chambersburg PA
CBHW050104120726
47904CB00004B/1209